SPANKY

Christopher Fowler

S P A N K Y

A *Warner* Book

First published in Great Britain by Warner Books 1994
Reprinted 1994

A CIP catalogue record for this book
is available from the British Library.

ISBN 0 7515 0959 0

Typeset by Solidus (Bristol) Limited
Printed in England by Clays Ltd, St Ives plc

Warner Books
A Division of
Little, Brown and Company (UK)
Brettenham House
Lancaster Place
London WC2E 7EN

WARNER BOOKS

Dedication

Especially for Kath, with much love

Acknowledgements

This novel is both a departure and a new direction for me, for which I thank intrepid guide Nann du Sautoy for leading the way and trusty Sherpa Andrew Wille for his excellent sign-posting, with *en route* map reading by Ann Hebden and that literary equivalent of the RAC, my agent Serafina Clarke. Jim Sturgeon gave helpful directions, and Richard Woolf made the journey easier. I'd also like to thank my international agent Jennifer Luithlen, and publicist Jane Warren. Love to everyone at Soho's megaglamorous movie company The Creative Partnership, especially designer Martin Butterworth for his startling cover concept. The sexier ideas in this tale arose from a wild night out with the Dangerous Girls Club, Rebecca, Di and Jane, who ended the evening being carried down a nightclub fire escape in leopard-skin rabbit ears and handcuffs to which, naturally, we had lost the key. And they say research is the easiest part.

Hell hath no limits nor is circumscrib'd
In one self place, where we are is Hell,
And where Hell is, there must we ever be.
Christopher Marlowe

Hell is part of the human condition.
Kenneth Williams

CHAPTER ONE

Retribution

ALL THIS has happened before, and will happen again.

But this time it happened in London, to the most ordinary of mortals. It happened to a man lost and damned in a tangle of wet North London streets, a man who appeared to be running for his life.

But I wasn't running for my life; I was running for someone else's.

As I ran, I checked my wristwatch and swore aloud. Ten before midnight. I knew there were only minutes left. I glanced back over my shoulder again. No cabs on the roads, not a bus in sight. No driver would stop for me anyway, not looking like this. Nothing for it but to keep going, and try to catch my breath at the next corner.

I missed the green pedestrian light. Dropped my hands to my knees and bent forward, gulping air. An overdressed couple emerged from a restaurant arm in arm and stared in careful disgust before skirting around me. The light changed and I ran on, stitch stinging my side. An empty cab ignored my hoarse shout and veered around my outstretched hand.

With five and a half minutes to go I was still several streets from the address I had memorized. I knew I was going to be late. But late implied running for a train, late for a blind date, late for a business meeting.

Not late for a death.

On past a glaring neon supermarket staffed by sad-looking Asians. An all-night garage, two West Indian Girls trying to buy cigarettes, arguing with the Turkish cashier through a scratched Plexiglas window. Walls plastered with band posters and graffiti. A main road ahead, traffic lights about to change against me, amber and green slashing the wet tarmac. I managed a spurt of speed, dashing to the other side, just missed by a newspaper van. Reached the next turning and looked up.

There in the middle of the road, slowly emerging from a mist of rain, walked a hollow-eyed funeral cortège of thin, bowed figures. I had an impression of top hats and draped bustles, following behind twin horses plumed in black. Snorting and stamping, the percherons were pulling an ornate ebony coffin wagon, clip-clopping on against the creaking wheels, setting their hooves firmly on cobbles as they rounded the corner; an absurdly anachronistic vision.

That was when I threw my arm across my face and shouted out; 'There is nothing there, damn you!' I knew this was a sight no one else could see. When I opened my eyes again, the solemn procession had faded from view. The street was empty.

I ran on.

At last I reached the building, a thirties apartment block rising above a darkened delicatessen. Ran up the steps and pushed through the glass doors at the top. The semi-conscious concierge didn't try to stop me. I shoved my way past him and took the stairs three at a time, hauling myself up by grabbing at the banisters.

The smell of frying bacon lingered in the stairwell, blending with stale boiled cabbage in the halls. The distant sound of sobbing, misery unfurling behind closed doors.

The third floor, end of the corridor.

The overhead lights were out. This was real, not imagined; the ceiling globes had all been smashed. Glass crunched under my track shoes. I slowed to a walk in the thickening darkness, stomach churning, pulse hammering. Already I could see that the jamb of the front door had been shattered. I stood before it, pausing to gather my strength. Then I pushed. The door swung wide at my touch. As I entered, the hallway slowly illuminated itself like a stage set. Another of the bastard's little tricks, I supposed. I stepped further into the apartment.

The brass hall-clock read one minute past midnight. For a moment, hope surged. Was I still in time? Then I noticed that it would never read anything else. A crack ran across its face, conveniently fixing the time of death.

A thin, agonized wail startled me. Could he still be alive? It came from the end of the hall. Beneath the scent of furniture polish, the air held the cuprous tang of fresh blood. I walked forward, checking each of the rooms as I passed. One by one they glowed as bright as theatrical sets and faded as I looked in, just so that I could see everything clearly. Games, even in matters of death, my enemy loved playing games. Now the crying was continuous and low, the sound of a snared animal in constant suffering. I reached the end room and dared myself to look.

The only signs of disturbance were an overturned chair and a single broken cup and saucer, a little spilled tea. The young man was face down on the floor, crawling toward the fireplace. His face was jaundiced with shock, his pale trousers opaque with urine. Several inches from him, a neat oval of blood was soaking into the carpet. Something was protruding from the small of his back at a sharp angle, the handle of an iron poker.

Retribution   3

Judging from the length of the exposed section, the other two thirds was lodged inside his body.

His limbs moved ineffectually, so that he looked like a pinned insect vaguely attempting to free itself. The overhead lights became intense, raised voltage crackling through the filaments.

I stumbled further into the room, appalled by the pathetic efforts of the dying man. I didn't know what to do. As I watched, he looked up at me and spoke.

'Why you, of all people?' he asked, wincing. His teeth squeaked as he ground them together. 'Martyn, you're my friend. Why would you want to hurt me?'

'It wasn't me,' I replied flatly. 'I only just got here.' It sounded absurd. I was standing in a brilliantly lit room, talking to a man with a poker through his gut. It was like being trapped inside someone else's hallucination.

'I saw you, I know it was you. Don't come any closer!'

The fearful figure below me attempted to push away, but the protruding poker handle prevented him from backing against the wall, and then the effort killed him. He said something inaudible, and one eye filled with blood. His shoes drummed against the floor a few times and he was still.

I had never seen a life leave before, but something left right then. His body, living a moment ago, was already a corpse. In the silence that followed, I gently pulled the door closed, providing a little privacy for death.

I reached the ground floor and looked out for the concierge, but he wasn't in his booth. What would I do if he remembered me dashing past? The police would be bound to question him.

No time to worry about it now. As I left the building it began to rain again, and then to pour. I stood before the little row of shops wrapped in glittering strokes of water as tears poured down my face, and indignation rose within me.

If I was going to be turned into a murderer, at least Spanky could have told me.

I looked up into the sky and let the rain splash on my face. That's when I saw him, looming far above the restaurants and shops and pubs and coffee bars, dressed in his immaculate black tuxedo, literally larger than life. He was chuckling to himself, resting his elbows on the flat terraced rooftops as he looked down at the earth. His giant torso seemed shaped by the clouds, like those old drawings of the North Wind taking human form. He shook his head slowly and tapped his watch, as if to rebuke me for even trying to outrun him.

I listened to the crackle of rainwater dropping from broken gutters and looked around at the empty streets, praying that someone would turn into the road and look up. But I knew it would be useless. No one else could see him. No one else would ever see him.

No one but me.

Induction

ALL THIS was before I died in the ambulance, of course. Months ago, in the middle of a terrible, wet August.

Back then I was doing all the usual things a person does. Working, shopping, sleeping, fucking, reading, watching television. If you'd seen the state of my body when they brought it in, lying there crusted with black rinds of blood, you wouldn't think it was the same —

I'm confusing you.

Listen, this is difficult for me, too. I shouldn't have started in the middle like that. I did it to get your attention, because somebody has to believe me. I want to explain events as they happened, but I keep rushing ahead.

Cool down, Martyn.

Calm and clear.

Okay.

My name is Martyn Ross. I'm five feet eleven inches tall, twenty-three years old, and I've recently discovered that there are more reasons to be scared than I had ever thought possible.

Let's go back.

The middle of August.

A Tuesday morning. Traffic sloshing through heavy rain

beyond the plate glass. The yellow special offer banners that had been pasted over the inside windows of the store were sagging with condensation. I was at the rear of the showroom studying the stock book, slowly turning the pages, trying to look busy. As usual, Max came over to see what I was doing. I stared at the catalogue and ignored my boss, wondering if he would ever stop trying to catch me out. The shuffling footsteps ceased and I could see the highly polished toecap of Max's shoe, the left, from the corner of my eye. One of his legs was a little shorter than the other and he walked with an odd scraping gait, but as he never acknowledged his handicap we all pretended we hadn't noticed.

I could feel him glaring at me. I knew that I was expected to account for my time. No problem. I could run rings around Max, whose thoughts were as methodical as his movements.

'Sconces,' I said, looking up. '*Faux*-Edwardian molded ceramic toothbrush sconces.'

'What about them?' Max was thrown, but determined to master the conversation.

'Do we have any?'

'Well, I don't know. What do they look like? What exactly is a sconce?'

'A holder. A bracket. A circle with a stick, like the biological sign for a woman. We're supposed to have two styles in stock, Mr Deakin, *Delaware* and *Rhapsody*, but I can't find either.'

'If a customer has placed an order for them and they're not in the stock book, check the computer and see if they've been correctly requested from Swindon. Don't just stand there, Martyn, go and have a look.'

I slammed the catalogue shut and dropped it on to my desk. The embossed gold logo on the cover was the same as the one emblazoned on the staff pencils, biros and erasers. It graced the front of the store, the pockets of our jackets, and the gaudy ads in the middlebrow colour supplements. **Thanet Luxury Furniture** it read, in elaborate gold calligraphy. I found the middle word superfluous and irritating, like an unwarranted nickname. The store was sandwiched between a dry cleaners and an Indian restaurant. On a hot day the mixed fumes of cleaning fluid and curry were strong enough to induce epilepsy.

I walked off towards the farthest IBM, knowing that Max would not be able to see me through the alcove. I usually passed most of my day this way, shifting from one strategic invisible position to another. The work was mind-numbingly dull but at least it wasn't disgusting, like being a specialist in diseases of the feet or working down the drains. Even I had to draw the line somewhere. The sofas and coffee tables and bathroom sets we sold were flash-trash, expensive vulgarities for rich people with no taste, so the shop was always busy.

On Saturdays it was usually packed, which made suitable hiding places even harder to locate. When it was quiet the hours always crawled by on crutches, the afternoons crepusculating as if designed to accompany Chopin's *Funeral March*. I hated it here. I hated the giant yellow stickers that read *Stylish Bargains*, the two words cancelling each other out. I hated the view from the window, a lime-green turf accountants and a craft centre filled with misshapen pots and brown rugs. Most of all, I hated myself for not being able to find a better job.

At 2.45 p.m. I talked a customer out of buying a *Devonshire* Buffalo-grain leather swivelling armchair. A victory for good taste.

At 4.15 p.m. weird Lottie came up and stood beside me, coughing cartoonishly into her fist to attract my attention. As always I remained hunched over my paperwork, ignoring her.

Finally she squeaked something about going out for coffees and what would I like.

I told her that I would like a glass of Himalayan Yak Tea, but I'd resist it on principle until the Chinese got out of Tibet.

She looked confused. 'I'll get you a *cappuccino*,' she offered. Lottie was tall and freckled, with straight sandy hair that fell around her thin face like a polished wooden frame. Presumably her height bothered her, because she kept her head low all the time, as if ducking through an arch. She spoke defiantly, with the air of someone defending their reputation. And she had a reputation. Rumours abounded about her and Max, who was separated from his wife.

As I watched Lottie slide between the natural-finish dining suites, with a makeshift tray cut from a cardboard box, I wondered how much longer I'd last in my career as furniture sales coordinator. I knew I wasn't dull enough to excel in the position. My heart didn't soar at the sight of a well-plumped chenille sofabed. A firing was imminent. I doubted I'd get much support from my colleagues. They didn't care too much for me, and the feeling was pretty damned mutual.

At 6.00 p.m. came closing time, and blessed release from the grim pedantries of supervisor Max and weird Lottie, from ambitious Darryl and stupid Dokie, who sang off-key while he picked his nose and loaded tables and chairs and sinks into the company vans. After work I caught a bus over the bridge to Vauxhall, where I shared rented accommodation. Vauxhall makes Mexico City look like Beverly Hills. As one of the ugliest, dirtiest, most dangerous London boroughs it is primarily famed for the vindictiveness of its skinheads, the terrorised exhaustion of its remaining elderly residents and the vastness of its fume-choked traffic system.

Reaching home, I locked myself in my room and lay back on

my bed, dreaming of places I would never visit and people I would never meet.

I know how that must sound – like someone with a grudge against the world. I don't mean to give you the wrong impression. Like a zillion other people, I was stuck in my attempt to figure out what to do with my life. I had to keep the job at Thanet even though I hated it, because I wasn't exactly overqualified for any other position of responsibility. I'd failed most of my exams at school, including woodwork, which nobody ever failed. I was still trying to decide what I was good at.

I'd recently applied to take evening classes in business studies, but the courses in my area were full and I couldn't afford to pay for private tuition. I combed the papers for more interesting employment, but every post I applied for seemed to be filled a few nanoseconds before my phonecall.

I spent a lot of time lying on my bed, wondering and worrying about the future. It didn't look too bright.

I felt as if there was a faultline running through me, something that constantly diverted my energy into the wrong moves. I had a damp rented roof over my head, hardly any friends and a lousy job. Twenty-three years old and already my course was set, a narrow-gauge track leading around in a circle.

But on Tuesday night, something happened to break open that track and set it free.

About an hour and a half before it did, I was scuffing my hair with a towel and checking the crotch of my Levis to see if they had dried on the radiator when there was a knock on my bedroom door. It was my flatmate Zack, awkwardly asking about my share of the electricity bill. Zack had the larger bedroom because he paid more rent, or rather his parents did;

he'd made them feel so guilty about not being able to find a job that they posted him a monthly cheque. Zack hated talking about money. He considered such conversation capitalistic and offensive. He'd long ago stopped looking for work because he'd lost faith in the system. Instead Zack believed in conspiracy theories, alien abductions, corn circles, Atlantis, satanic cattle mutilations and anything else that cropped up in his extensive collection of occult magazines. I got the feeling he didn't really like me because I had a job and was therefore 'part of the problem, not the solution', as he put it. But he had to admit that I was a useful source of cash at the end of every month.

'Are you going out tonight, Martyn?'

Zack hovered half in, half out of the doorway, aware that, Dracula-like, he hadn't been invited to cross the threshold.

'I'm trying out a new club,' I said. 'Free ticket.'

'Who from?'

'*From whom*. A friend.' I didn't want to admit that the card had been thrust into my hand outside Burger King on Tottenham Court Road. You could collect hundreds of flyers walking through the West End, tickets for every conceivable kind of clubnight. All tastes were catered for at the end of the twentieth century. 'Why,' I asked, 'do you want to come along?'

'Nah.' Zack's lank black hair fell across his face like a pair of old curtains. 'Debbie's coming over. We're gonna watch a video. You've got a massive spot coming up on your neck. I can give you some stuff for that.'

'No thanks.' I'd seen the mildewy muck Zack kept in brown glass pots in the bathroom. 'I'll leave you a ticket, in case you change your mind about the club.'

Zack studied the ends of his hair, abstracted. 'Thanks, man.'

I had to gently push the door shut to get rid of him. Zack was capable of standing in one place staring at nothing in particular for hours. There was no sense of urgency in his life. Once, some neighbours he'd managed to annoy by requesting they turn down their rap music at 3.00 a.m. smashed his bedroom window with a milk bottle, and I had to organize a glazier because he didn't even pick up the broken glass for three weeks, let alone arrange to have the pane replaced.

I donned the damp jeans and a blue sweatshirt, and checked my appearance in the mirror. I was not unattractive, but then I was not a lot of things; not short, not fat, not shy, not slow-witted. My qualities usually revealed themselves in the negative. I possessed an abundance of one quality, more of a curse – my powerful imagination. At school I had missed entire chunks of history and geography because my attention was fixed elsewhere. Lessons passed in a mist while I drew meticulous depictions of space battles in the back of my exercise book. Being caught and warned a hundred times made no difference.

Teachers gravely warned my parents that I was a dreamer. From the way my father reacted, you'd have thought he'd been told I was dealing heroin. But my brother Joey explained that dreaming was good so long as it had a goal. So one day I sat down and drew up a list of goals, beginning with university and ending with the Nobel prize. I thought that having dreams would make me different from other people, that another set of rules would apply. I wanted to be unique. It took me a while to realize that this was what everyone else wanted too.

In the face of such competition it was a foregone conclusion that I would fail my exams. My father shouted, my mother cried, so I worked harder. Eventually my grades began to improve. Teachers smiled, keep this up Martyn and you'll pass your finals with flying colours. Your dreams will come true.

They would have, too, if Joey hadn't died.

I'm getting ahead of myself. Back to that fateful Tuesday evening. Before I left the flat I made my bed, binned my laundry, phoned my mother, drank some suspicious-smelling milk and ate a *Sell By Date: Yesterday*' frozen lasagne from the otherwise empty fridge. I nodded to Zack, who was sitting cross-legged in front of the TV watching baboons picking meat out of their teeth, and went to the club.

It was still raining when I arrived, and a long queue had formed outside the building. The organizers had obviously given away too many tickets. A sheet of tacked-up orange cloth read blUeTOPIA above a cellar entrance. I joined the tail of the line and shuffled slowly forward, gradually getting soaked. Someone handed me a flyer detailing the week's one-nighters. Tomorrow it was the turn of Club Dread. Saturday was Rubber Bunny. Fetish night. Forget it, I had enough trouble finding a clean shirt. The queue moved on.

My 'free' pass wasn't anything of the kind. The gorilla on the door gave me a smug look as he relieved me of a ten pound note, handing me back two coins and a vodka voucher. At least, I thought, it'll be warm and dry inside. My reflection in the stairway mirror showed a person who appeared to have fallen in a river. My short blonde hair was plastered to my head like a bad wig. My jacket was already starting to steam.

Below, the techno/rave/garage/house/whatever-it's-called-this-month pounding of the dancefloor beckoned. I enjoyed dancing, and usually in the way of things found a partner to move with. It was an impersonal arrangement, me and the girl shuttling past each other like crabs, never making eye contact and parting when the track collapsed, but I liked it well enough. On the matter of sex, let's just say that while I currently had no girlfriend I was certainly no virgin – those negatives again – still, I moved well and women liked me because I was attentive, or perhaps they just sensed that I was a reasonably honest sort. I didn't communicate well with them because I'd never had much practice. My sister and I rarely discussed the things that mattered to us.

I went to the bar and ordered a beer. The girl next to me was trying to get her finger out of a bottle of Evian water.

'Try butter,' I suggested, giving a pleasant smile.

'Try slamming your dick in a door,' she replied, returning her attention to the bottle.

I didn't dance that Tuesday night. I felt uncomfortable in the new club, which smelled of fresh paint over damp patches, and bore no stamp of character. I watched the barmen bickering over till arrangements, the supposedly-VIP guests crushed into a ludicrous roped-off corner, the ill-timed blasts of dry ice that caught unprepared dancers, and wondered why I had come here at all. In its half-hearted attempt to be bizarre and different it was exactly the same as every other club. And I was the same as every other punter, looking for something better to do and somewhere better to be. Think positive, I told myself, lighten up. I looked around, trying to see if I knew anyone.

I recognized two girls on the dancefloor, distantly pleasant types who went everywhere together in complementary sixties-style clothes. Lost in their own world, they would sometimes stop by to speak to me in forgotten TV-catchphrase jargon, most of it coined before they were born. They were friendly because I could do the vocabulary thing with them, but weren't really interested in outsiders. There was a huge Jamaican guy whose drink I had once accidentally spilled, and who glowered menacingly every time I looked over because he thought I was trying to pick up his minuscule girlfriend. And there was Darren.

'Lo, Martyn.' I felt his fingers on my back before I saw him. He peered over my shoulder and stared at me with unfocused eyes, his hands in touchie-feelie mode, a sure sign that he was enjoying the drug of his choice.

'Thought you'd be here. There's nobody else here. They're all somewhere else.'

I wished he was somewhere else. Darren was thin and yellow beneath the lights, and looked like he could do with a hot meal and a bath. He had come down from the north to find work as an electrician, and like so many others had wound up dealing Ecstasy in clubs. He was nice enough in a walking-wounded way, but I had once lent him some money, which meant that every time I ran into him he was forced to perform an elaborate charade about returning it.

'I've been out of town for weeks,' he began, 'managing a band, so I'll have your cash really soon because we're *this* close to a really massive major deal. You should hear them, because they're just incredible.'

'Where are they playing?' I asked, calling his bluff.

'They're not doing live gigs. It's all sampled electronic stuff. They don't relate to an audience.'

'Okay.' Took this on board. Waited a second. 'What are they called?'

'*Arthritis.*'

I couldn't wait. 'Forget the money,' I said wearily.

This was his cue to pantomime outrage. 'No way! I owe you, and I'll pay you back. No bullshit.'

'Look, don't worry about it.'

'You saying I don't pay my way? Is that what you saying?' His voice was high and his face looked inflamed. I didn't want to argue.

'No, just forget about the money.'

'Nobody calls me a liar. Fuck you, Martyn, all right?'

He released his grip and blundered off into the crowd. I decided I was getting too old for all this aggression. Last week I had asked a girl to dance and she had told me to go fuck myself with a cactus. What *was* it with people?

I tilted my watch toward the strobelight but couldn't read the face. I remember feeling more than just uncomfortable; time was dislocated. I was sure that outside, far above us, the winds had changed and the sky was odd. Inside, I stood beyond the dancefloor, trying to decipher the music as it vibrated the rivets in my jeans. I drained my third beer and set the bottle down. Uneasiness was creeping into my bones like frost. I tried to make sense of the sensation, but thinking about it only made it worse.

I realized with horror that I had been absently staring at the Jamaican guy's tiny girlfriend. Her protector suddenly lumbered away from the bar with blood-rage in his eyes, stabbing his finger in my direction. I froze, fearfully rooted to the spot.

'It does feel strange tonight, doesn't it? Like something is about to happen.'

I turned to find a man standing close beside me. It was almost as if he had deliberately interposed himself between us. The Jamaican guy reached him and seemed to lose interest in clouting me. He paused, studied the floor in puzzlement, then wandered away.

Startled, I shifted back slightly and examined my rescuer. The eyes instantly drew my attention, green and iridescent, as beguiling as a cat's. The lower half of the face was in shadow.

'The wind has shifted,' he said. 'Turned with the tide and the pull of the moon. Madness has settled. Anything can happen from this moment on.'

The figure stepped into the light.

One hand was hiked into the pocket of a nineteen-fifties dinner suit with lapels like black mirrors. He was dressed for the wrong era, but somehow it suited his style. Although he had roughly the same height and build as me, the sharp symmetry of his face made him extraordinarily handsome; too perfect, like a retouched photograph. An odd, spicy scent hung about him.

I could think of no way to respond. I occasionally spoke to single women, but never to men. In a place like this they were most likely to be dealers.

'You know what your trouble is, Martyn? You hate your life because you don't know how to control it. You do what you're told. Most people do, of course. One chooses from the selection provided instead of seeking a new selection. That's how everyone stays in line.'

'How do you know my name?' I turned on the stranger a little more aggressively than I had intended. 'Do I know you?'

He shook his head in self-rebuke. 'Sorry, I forgot that can be a little unnerving. I couldn't help noticing the name on your travel card.'

Some explanation. My travel card was in my wallet, and that was in the back pocket of my jeans. After checking that it was still there I examined the smiling face before me, trying to place it. 'Have we met before? Who exactly are you?'

'Exactly? The shortened version of my name is *Spancialosaphus Lacrimosae*. Still a bit of a mouthful, I'm afraid. You can call me Spanky.'

With another luminous smile, he held out his hand. I gingerly shook it. I have that natural suspicion of strangers which tempers the sociability of all city dwellers. Standing beside each other like this, I suddenly noticed how alike we were. True, my companion looked a little older, and his hair glistened in loose black curls, but we had the same mannerisms, the same way of standing. Spanky had something extra, though, an indefinable magnetism that caused a pair of passing girls to pause and glance him over.

'Tell me, Martyn, do you ever feel that you've missed your exit on the highway of life?' he asked, passing me a fresh beer, the exact brand I had been drinking. 'Do you always want an Egg McMuffin just after they've stopped serving breakfast?' Modern phraseology seemed unnatural on his lips. His accent was dated, very British and charming, like an old Ealing film.

I had been about to accept the drink when I stopped and asked myself how I had managed to do it again. Just lately I seemed to attract lunatics, babblers, religious nuts on tubes and buses, in parks and pubs. Why did they always aim for me? How were they best dealt with?

'I don't know what the hell you're talking about,' I replied, looking away at the dancefloor.

'It's okay, I'm not some born-again deadhead looking for converts. Let's not get embarrassed about having a conversation. I'm extremely sensitive to emotional vibrations, and I can sense a feeling of grave dissatisfaction around you.'

'I don't believe in all that new age stuff,' I replied, affronted. 'I think you'd better go and pick on someone else.' I began to move away, but he followed me across the floor.

'Martyn, surely you agree that some things can't be explained by rational scientific thought?'

'No, I don't.'

'You mean you have an explanation for everything?'

I remained silent. If he didn't receive a reply, I figured he might go away.

'Black holes, the mysteries of the body, the infinity of the universe, the popularity of quiz shows? Don't you ever think, when you lie on your bed staring at the ceiling, How did I ever get stuck on such a narrow track? Why don't my dreams make me different from others? *When will I become unique?*'

He was still there, still smiling.

This was too weird. He knew my thoughts.

'That's what happens, Martyn. The life you had planned for yourself suddenly becomes the life you *had* planned. For too many people the future becomes the past without ever being the present.'

I could find no explanation for it.

'So there *is* something you can't explain. Look at me.'

Before I could react, he reached forward and clasped my hands together, bringing them up before my face. As he released his grip, a tingling sensation prickled across my fingers. I slowly unfurled them to find a pale blue flame burning lightly in my palms. Several inches high, it radiated coolness and threw a soft reflected glow on to the sleeves of my jacket.

At the centre of the nacreous light the figure of a woman turned, tiny and translucent, a naked homunculus that span faster and faster on the tips of my fingers, proliferating into two, three, four of the sensual creatures. Gradually they ceased dancing and attended to each other, arms clasping thighs, necks and spines arching as they joined in ecstatic embrace. As they filled my vision, the exposed vulgarity of their sexual appetites was shocking and arousing.

My hands were clapped together, the light was suddenly extinguished and the vision was gone. He looked up at me, his smile glittering in darkness. 'They're just maenads, orgy nymphs. They come and go, so to speak.'

'Look —'

'Spanky, please.'

'How the hell did you do that?' I was amazed. It had to be a trick, some kind of instant hypnotism.

'Work it out, Martyn. You're smart enough.'

Clear thought failed me. The room was hot and stale, and my head was filled with pounding music.

'Tell me, Martyn, do you know what a daemon is?'

'A devil, I guess.'

'You guess incorrectly. A daemon is the link between God and man.'

'And that's what you are?'

'Indeed. We're a very noble breed. Socrates himself had a very superior one, called a δαίμων in the Greek language. In Homer's *Odyssey* the word is interchanged with Θεός, the terminology used to describe a god.'

'You mean you're a muse.' The beer was obviously going to my head, because I found myself being drawn into conversation with him.

'Rather more practical than a muse. But like those insight-bearing creatures, we have a tendency to attach ourselves to one person and operate in a problem-solving capacity, yes.'

'Let me get this right. You're a familiar. A personal daemon?'

'I could be *your* personal daemon – if you require my help.'

'D'you have any idea how completely fucking ridiculous that sounds?'

Spanky gave me a cool, hard look. 'You're the one with the lousy life, chum. Tell me you don't require my services and I'll walk out of here right now.'

That made me angry. 'Well, I don't, okay? Who the hell do you think you are, walking up to a complete stranger and telling him he's having a lousy life?'

He stepped nearer, pointed an accusing finger. 'Martyn, I know all about you. You work in a tenth-rate furniture store and you can't even do that right. Your supervisor is about to fire you and promote your fellow workmate, the little fat chap. Your attitude sucks. Your last girlfriend left because she was sick of not getting any emotional reaction out of you. You can't remember the last time you had fun with someone. If you don't want my help fine, everything's tickety-boo. There are thousands of mortals begging for a break like this, a chance to change their lives and realize their deepest desires. I can take you out into the freezing black universe through an infinity of starlight. I can fill your mind with the sentience of harmonic world order and your body with the mobius-chords of hedonistic fulfilment.'

I looked at him blankly.

'Or you can throw the opportunity away. It will never, ever come again.'

He turned sharply on a highly polished heel, walked off into the throng and was quickly lost from sight.

Even though I hadn't believed a word he'd said, the sudden, sinking sense of loss was so strong that I found myself moving quickly across the floor of the club. I caught up with him near the staircase leading back to the street.

'Wait, how do you know so much about me? This is some kind of scam, isn't it, like timeshare sales, or est or something.'

'Are you asking me or stating a fact? It sounds like you've already decided. You should try to keep an open mind.'

'I *have* an open mind.'

'Just for the record it's not a trick, Martyn. I can look right into you, and I know how to help. I'm attuned to people in need. I can see you're going to take further convincing. Okay, give me an hour of your time.'

'When?'

'Right now, before you have a chance to talk yourself out of it.'

'Why, what do you want to do?'

'Bite you on the neck and drink your blood, what do you think? For heaven's sake, don't you ever make a decision? No wonder you're not considered management material. But with my help, you might be.'

And something snapped. Right then.

What could happen in an hour?

I didn't want to stay at the club. The music was lousy, and drunk secretaries were starting to dance around their bags. What did I have to lose?

'All right,' I agreed against my better judgement, following the shiny black shoe-heels as they retreated up the stairs ahead of me. I wanted to know where he'd got his information, and how he'd done the trick with the flame-women. So I let him lead me from the club.

Can you definitely, absolutely say that you wouldn't have done the same thing?

CHAPTER THREE

Illusionism

WE WERE walking through the wet city streets at twenty-five minutes past midnight, me and my new friend Spanky, arguing about God. It was the kind of argument you should only have with a complete stranger. I know it's boring, but I have to transcribe part of our conversation; it'll help to explain some of the terrible events that occurred later.

I said, 'I thought demons were automatically evil.'

'There are demons and *daemons*,' explained Spanky. 'Angels are often devils, and vice versa. It's a theological minefield. Satan was an angel who fell from God's side, remember. By its very nature, a daemon is far closer to an angel.'

'You would say that, wouldn't you? If you really wanted me to believe this stuff.'

'Your chosen family religion is Church of England, isn't it, Martyn?'

'I suppose so . . .' I agreed, striding to keep pace with him.

'Then how can you know anything? These days the Church of England isn't about religion, it's a real estate business. You should try Catholicism, my friend. As a belief system, it's a lot more demanding. You have to cope with the transubstantiation of the eucharist before you can get anywhere.'

Religion had never been my strong point, and I felt uncomfortable talking about it. Church services seemed available in two strengths: high-exotic, which was eerie and incomprehensible, and user-friendly, which had fanatical pro-lifers banging tambourines. Then there were the blurry bits; people who wouldn't give dying children blood transfusions, and perky Americans who insisted on telling you how happy they were with Jesus. Perhaps this guy was a recruitment officer for the Scientologists.

'If you hadn't dropped out of Religious Education when you were in the fifth form, Martyn, you'd know that far from being malign creatures from the Pit of Hell, most of us are highly spiritual, rational –'

'– Non-human –'

'I didn't say that. All spirits exist in man. Allow me to quote from the works of the Franciscan theologian Lodovico Sinistrari. He defined us thus: *There are in existence on earth rational creatures besides man, endowed like him with a body and soul; they are born and die like him; they are redeemed by Our Lord Jesus Christ, and therefore are capable of being saved or lost. These rational creatures are swayed by the same emotions and passions, jealousies and lusts, as man.* Be careful there; you're about to step in dogshit. Where was I? *They are affected by material substances; therefore they have corporeity. But this corporeity is far more tenuous and subtle than the body of man. It enjoys a certain rarity, permeability, volatility, and power of sublimation. These creatures are able at will to withdraw themselves from sight.* There's a lot more; I won't tire you with it. Mind the bus.'

We crossed the road north, heading for the great spiked iron gates of Regent's Park, where my folks had always brought me as a kid. It was a favourite place, a safe haven. The rain had finally stopped. Spanky's image bounced back from the shining roadway and splintered in a hundred pools. He waved his hands expansively as he talked. 'Feel free to ask me anything you want.'

I thought for a moment, hopping up on the far kerb. 'How old are you?'

'In human terms, twenty-five. To a daemonological way of thinking that would represent a much longer period of time. It works rather like dog years. Let me see.' He removed a small leather pocketbook from his jacket and checked it. 'I have the exact date of my human birth here somewhere.'

'So you were born in human form?' I asked, playing along.

'Let's say *re*born,' he replied. 'It would take me forever to work out how long I've been around as a daemon.' He snapped the pocketbook shut. 'Well, I know that my present body came into the world at some point in the mid-nineteen twenties.'

'That would make you around seventy.'

'I'm wearing rather well, don't you think?'

'I'll tell you what I think. I'm an imbecile for even listening to this crap.'

'Look in my eyes and you'll know it's not crap. See what I've seen.' He turned and thrust his hands in his pockets, staring defiantly at me. I knew it had to be a trick, a fake, that he was probably an out-of-work mesmerist operating some kind of scam, but I turned and looked.

And saw.

I was no longer standing on a darkened city street.

Instead I was surrounded by green and white walls. Paint on stone.

The smell of liniment and disinfectant.

The ward of a military hospital, harshly illuminated with grey tin lamps. Disoriented, I tried to see ahead.

In the distance, a partitioned room was filled with whispering white-coated figures. The lights here had been dimmed. The doctors stepped aside to provide a glimpse of a supine patient, a sleeping man with a handsome, craggy face. He looked very ill, close to death. The top portion of his head was shielded from view by a linen tent. He was barely breathing. The murmuring figures closed back around him, hiding his inert form behind white sheets. I felt the closeness of death, and was mortally afraid. I heard Spanky's voice from far away.

'I was ten years old. My father was a doctor. Sometimes he would take me into the ward at night. On this night he took me to catch the last glimpse of a legend. Lawrence of Arabia, expiring from a fractured skull after a collision on his motorcycle.'

The corridor shimmered and vanished. Shaking with cold, I suddenly found myself back on the street. I looked about. No vestige remained of what I had just seen.

'What the hell do you want with me?' I asked, shocked by the child's vision of the dying hero.

Spanky pouted, momentarily stumped. 'I thought that was obvious,' he said at last. 'Perhaps you don't realize it, but you're looking for someone with the power to change you. You clearly can't do it by yourself.'

I drew back, ready to argue, but before I could say anything Spanky raised a neatly manicured hand. 'If you're going to be offended every two minutes, we won't get anywhere. I need to look at your case factually and objectively. Certain personal failings will have to be acknowledged. It's what they tell alcoholics; admitting the problem is halfway to overcoming it.'

'So now I'm an alcoholic, am I?'

'I'm merely illustrating the point. You're basically a good person, Martyn, but your life has come off the rails. With most people that doesn't happen until they're at least forty.'

He had a damned nerve. My life wasn't so bad. Lots of people were worse off. 'So what's the deal?' I shouted. 'You're going to pitch me a bargain, right? You sort out my life and get to keep my soul, then you damn me to hell for eternity. I'm not prepared to surrender my soul to anyone.'

'Don't flatter yourself, Martyn. I don't suppose you even have a soul. Few people ever do. They're as rare as honourable men. You've been watching too many old movies. Besides, only the devil gets to take souls.'

'And I guess he's a good friend of yours?'

'No, I honestly don't think he exists in corporeal form, any more than God does. They're more of a general sensation, an aura of good and evil, not actual physical entities. We don't work like that. For a start, I'm real. And I'm here to make sure that you get your life back on the right lines. Once it's running the way you want, I'll leave.'

Suppose he's for real, said a tiny voice in the back of my head. *Suppose, against all that's sane and rational, he has the power to do what he says. He could do more than just set things right. He could give you everything you ever wanted.* The thought took hold and grew.

Well, no one would refuse three wishes from a genie.

The park was closed. Spanky slipped his hand through the wrought-iron bars and gently lifted away the lock, swinging the gate open wide. We walked into a gravelled avenue of rain-heavy plane trees, dimly lit by the street lamps outside. I noticed that my new acquaintance threw no shadow.

'No, I'm like Peter Pan in that respect,' he called back.

'I'd prefer it if you wouldn't keep pulling the mindreading trick. It's an invasion of privacy.'

'Sorry, Martyn. Force of habit I'm afraid. I know it must

seem rude. You'll have to learn to shield your thoughts from me a little. I absorb light, but I do cast a reflection. And I have a mirror image, don't I?'

'I don't know.'

'You should. It's you. Surely you see the resemblance between us? I noticed it at once.'

'I suppose there is a bit,' I grudgingly acknowledged.

If Spanky was my mirror image, he was certainly the more colourful half. Everything about him, from the way he moved to the cheerful confidence of his speech, suggested enthusiasm and excitement, an energy that somehow seemed rooted in sexuality. I suddenly wondered whether thinking such a thing made me queer.

'So many insecurities,' Spanky commented on my unspoken question. 'Let me put your mind at rest. In my natural state I am neither male nor female. I chose to appear as a man in this incarnation, and a *damned* handsome one at that, because men's opinions seem to carry more *gravitas*. A shameful state of affairs, but that's how things were when I was born.'

'They're still largely the same,' I said. 'Women have made a bit of headway since then, but not much. They say the top jobs are all held by males.'

'In my day, women controlled society. Men ran business.'

We had reached the fountain at the centre of the park. The June night was cool and pleasant, with the tang of rain still in the trees, but I was growing increasingly uneasy. There was an ozone-scented voltage in the air. The wind felt strange on my skin. The park was empty and full of noise. I think I began to feel once more that I was in the company of a madman.

'I can tell you still don't completely believe, Martyn. Sit down for a minute.'

Spanky passed his hand above one of the green park benches. Raindrops scattered from the painted slats until the seat was bone dry. He brought his left fist before my face and opened it to reveal a lethal-looking shard of green glass. 'You believe that glass will enter flesh because it's sharper, don't you?' He flattened his right palm and pressed the spear-tip of the shard into it, pushing until the glass passed clean through his bones to protrude from the back of his hand. Even though there was no blood, I could barely look.

'But I believe flesh is harder than glass.' He withdrew the shard and slowly pressed his index finger against the flat green pane until it pierced the vitrine and reappeared on the other side. 'So which system is right, science or belief? I want to show you something else about the power of conviction. Let's see now, who shall I call upon?'

He pointed along the neat tree-lined avenue to a gloomy patch in the middle distance. As I watched, a series of figures slowly detached themselves from the darkness and came walking into view. At first I could see nothing clearly. Then they shifted into the halo of lamplight, and I realized that the first of them was an extraordinary-looking, yet oddly familiar woman.

She was dressed in a jewelled white bodice that flared out into a wide-bustled gown of blue brocade, sewn with roses and salamanders about the hem. At its base the dress was more than two yards across. It occupant was of haughty appearance, old and very ugly, with a tall periwig of tight white curls and large briolette earrings. Behind her, two liveried footmen walked bearing an upholstered farthingale chair between them, in case the lady should require a rest.

She noticed us now for the first time, turning her disconcerting gaze upon me as if discovering a marauding pig in her garden. I found myself looking up at a face that seemed barely human, having a narrow chin, rotten brown teeth, a large nose, no eyebrows and no lashes, and skin so pale it required thick powder to prevent translucence.

'Elizabeth the First,' Spanky whispered from the side of his mouth. 'Bow your head. She's a bit cranky. So would you be if your mum had been beheaded when you were three.'

Just then a page ran into our vision. As I had my head inclined, I could only see the lumpy, silk-stockinged ankles of the Queen, and the page's shoes, which sported purple satin rosettes the size of saucers.

'Your Majesty, My Lord Essex requests an audience with you, and awaits without.'

'Then he shall wait, and wait on; for I will not see him ere winter passes.' The voice was the dry, flaking croak of a very old woman, not regal at all, yet there was a timbre to it that commanded full attention.

'She thinks we are her courtiers,' Spanky whispered. 'I can't afford to upset history. She's in one of her snits with Essex. She could sulk for months. Let's get someone else.'

As the Virgin Queen moved slowly past, her gown shifting gently from side to side like a tolling bell, she began to fade from view.

A new voice was heard in the distance, loud and argumentative, with a strong Tennessee accent. I raised my head and looked back, but the royal entourage had already vanished. When I squinted ahead at the avenue, I had another shock.

'I don't care what fuckin' deal you had with him, you can tell Tom I ain't signing it.'

Marching towards us dressed in a black leather suit, boots and wrist-straps, leaking sweat from every pore, was Elvis Aron Presley, and he sounded mighty pissed off. He was looking good, still trim at the waist, although his hair was an unnatural shade of black and had been combed forward over his face. I figured this had to be Presley *circa* 1968, before the real decline set in. Behind him trailed a pair of dark-suited figures, not unlike Elizabeth's nervous footmen.

'But Mr Presley,' pleaded one of them, 'everything's been prepared. The camera crew...'

'I never agreed to no TV appearance,' Presley shouted back, 'you can tell the Colonel that. I've just done a two-hour show, for Chrissakes. Don't I get any damned privacy?'

'No, no, no.' Spanky jumped to his feet and clapped his hands together hard. The figures before us shattered and vanished like particles of glass, dispersing into the night.

'I wanted the other one, the Big Bopper, not him. Forgive me – I wasn't concentrating. They're just illusions, anyway,' he pointed out, 'but not without their uses.' For the first time I saw something in my companion that I understood. Spanky was showing off, waiting for me to compliment him.

'As you say,' I remarked drily, 'they're just illusions. They wouldn't be of much use if you were planning to sort out my life for me.' I wanted him to tell me what he had planned, what I would get out of it. Greed is an underestimated motive.

'Oh, I never said I'd do it for you.' He stuck his hands in his pockets and kicked petulantly at a flower bed. '*If* I decide to take your case, I'd just give you a helping hand. Improve your personality, that sort of thing.'

Spanky's parlour tricks were already a fading memory in my mind. Nothing had really happened. My cynicism quickly returned. 'So your powers aren't that far-reaching after all. How long does the personality-improvement process take?'

His temper suddenly flared. 'Christ, I don't know. It takes as long as it takes. It's not a fucking Spanish course.'

'Would I have to sign a contract? Because I wouldn't sign anything legally binding.'

'No, Martyn, I don't get people to open their veins and sign documents in blood.' He spoke as if dealing with an awkward child. 'I'm not about to give you riches beyond your wildest dreams, then send you off to hell. I am not the Devil. There is no such person, *capice*? Hell doesn't exist. The only souls most people have are on the bottoms of their shoes. What does it take to get the daemonological concept through your thick head?'

A little more than this, I thought. It still felt like I was the victim of a trick, an elaborate ruse for a purpose I couldn't begin to fathom. 'Listen, I don't need your help. I really think you should go and impress someone else.'

Torn between a natural avarice and the fear of being duped, I settled on the latter. There was safety in staying with what you knew. I could handle my own life. Hell, I was young. I was independent. So my career hadn't come together yet. So I had no one to share my problems, no one to fall in love with. So what? At least I wasn't like Zack, who treated his girlfriend like dirt and ran to his parents every time there was a financial crisis. I could recognize my faults and deal with them.

'Fine. I guess I made a mistake, Martyn. I saw you in the club and instantly sensed a bond. Obviously I shouldn't have picked you. You're perfect. You don't need anyone. To think of all the other people I could have chosen instead. Desperate, grateful people. You'll wake up tomorrow, and you'll kick yourself.' He seemed to reach a decision of his own, and suddenly walked off along the avenue, whistling tunelessly. An uncomfortable sensation still nagged at me, that perhaps I really was throwing away the chance of a lifetime, as Spanky had warned. Once again, I found myself setting off after him.

Decisive is another of the things I'm not.

'Give me one honest answer,' I shouted. Spanky slowed his stride, but refused to turn around and face me. 'If I was prepared to let you help me, what do you expect to get in return?'

'Always the same question with humans.' He raised his voice. 'I'd like your comradeship, Martyn James Ross. I thought perhaps we could be friends. I've never confided in anyone, and to tell the truth I'm beginning to wish I had.'

I couldn't leave it there. 'Why me?' I asked. 'Why should I be the one to benefit from your wisdom?'

Spanky shrugged. 'One of those things. It could have happened to anyone. You were in the right place at the right time. Like winning the pools. Or being mugged. You looked lost. You reminded me of me. I felt that you would want me to help you.' He stopped for a moment and looked back. Even from this distance, I could see an angry light in the emerald eyes. 'You're not the only one. This has happened to people throughout history. You're just not aware of it.'

'Then how do I know you're who you say you are? The things you've shown me could be just – special effects.'

'That's what you really think? Well, forget it. Forget I ever spoke to you. Go back to your ghastly furniture store, mortal. Return to your grim little dead-end of a life. And tell no one of our meeting, or there'll be trouble for you.'

He diverted from the path and began to speed up. There was a roar of closing air and he became a sparking streak of light, a comet passing away through the rasping trees. I stood alone in the middle of the park, watching the darkened grassy spot where Spanky had blasted from view, until the rain began to patter on the leaves once more.

CHAPTER FOUR

Confirmation

WHEN I returned to the flat, I found the kitchen on fire. Zack was making toast, but had forgotten to remove the bread from the grill. Dropping the burning steel tray into the sink, I called to my flatmate but received no reply. I discovered him in the lounge, sitting cross-legged on the floor smoking dope. He was watching a heavy metal concert on television with the sound turned off.

'I bloody hate this band.' Zack coughed and held up the joint. 'You want some of this?'

'No, I'm going to have something to eat.' I wearily pulled off my jacket and threw it on to the couch. It had been an unusual evening, to say the least.

'That's a good idea. Have some toast. I'm just doing some.'

'Really? How long has it been on?'

'Fuck.' Zack attempted to climb to his feet, but had to be helped up.

'You're going to burn this place down one day,' I complained. 'Where's Debbie?'

'She went home. We had another row. She wants me to get a job.'

'Why don't you?' I returned to the kitchen and began scraping the toast-tray clean.

'And she still won't consider an abortion. I told her I'm not ready for the commitment of children.' He shambled into the kitchen and leaned against the fridge, watching as I prepared fresh toast. 'I don't think it's right to bring a child into a world that can't even keep its rivers clean. The butterflies are disappearing from our hedgerows, did you know that?'

'When was the last time you saw a hedgerow?'

'You don't have to see something to know that it's there.'

There was no point in arguing. Zack was twenty-eight, hardly too young to consider raising a child, but he was like a child himself; unformed and ill-prepared for responsible living. Debbie, his girlfriend, at least possessed the virtue of knowing what she wanted even if she had no means of achieving it.

I brought toast and tea into the lounge. Most of the furniture belonged to Zack's parents, and reflected the taste of fifty year-old suburbanites. There was one exception; a huge primary-coloured mandala hung on the wall behind the television. Zack had made the Buddhist universe from thick, dusty strands of wool, most of which were now becoming unravelled. The process of repairing it occupied a large proportion of his waking hours.

'By the way,' said Zack, 'part of the ceiling fell in earlier. Debbie cleared it up.' In a corner above the stereo, the spectacularly mildewed patch of damp I had grown used to seeing on the ceiling was now broken by a large hole. The landlord had refused to sort out the problem, saying that Zack had caused it by leaving the attic window open for six months, which he had. The wood had expanded and the window could no longer be closed, causing the rain to soak through the boards to the plaster. A virulent black fungus had started appearing around the room as the wetness spread.

'You let a pregnant woman clear the mess up?'

'She knew where all the stuff was kept. I offered to help.' He was trying to work something through in his head. 'You don't think I pull my weight. You think you're more capable than me, with the job and everything.'

'Listen, you can have my job anytime.'

'And even if I tried my best, how long do you think I'd last?'

I looked at his shaking fingers scissored around the joint and knew he was right. There was nothing holding him up. I crunched through a slice of Marmite-smeared toast and studied the overloaded shelves behind the couch. After a few minutes, I decided to ask him. 'Have you got anything up there on daemons?'

'Demons?'

'No, with an 'a'. Spirit muses. Aristotle had one, or Socrates, I forget which.'

Zack was lying on the floor trying to figure out how to operate the TV remote, something he'd been working on for nearly a year. Now he pulled himself upright. For the first time since we'd agreed to share the flat, I was talking about something he understood.

'Hang on, I was reading an article just last month.' Confidence had returned to his voice. He rose to the shelves and clawed through a stack of magazines. 'They're not always evil, you know. There are all kinds. An incubus is one that comes to earth for the specific purpose of shagging women, a bit like Club 18-30, and a succubus is a demon in female form, a bit like Debbie.' He pulled out a dog-eared periodical and passed it over. 'Take a look at the page I marked. They list the most common kinds.'

I opened the magazine and studied the editor's photograph.

The man in the picture had the same haircut and beard as Zack. They obviously went to the same school of thought. I located the appropriate page and began to read: *Terrestrial daemons include Lares, Fauns, Foliots, Nymphs and Trulli...* I flicked over the page. *Daemons are ethereal animals endowed with acute intelligence, and although they feel the lust that incites them to copulate with women, they cannot do so.* I looked up from the magazine. 'This is all old stuff. Aren't there any recent examples?'

Zack stopped scratching his exposed stomach and thought for a moment. 'All the first-hand reports I've read about them are hundreds of years old, mostly from nuns who got caught shagging stableboys. Doesn't mean they don't exist, though.'

'I know. I was talking to one only this evening.'

Zack's attention redoubled. 'What do you mean?'

I described the events of the night as my flatmate grew increasingly animated. I was forced to recall in exact detail the illusions I'd witnessed in the park, and the offer that had been made to me. If I'd been hoping for a display of healthy scepticism, I'd obviously taken the wrong person into my confidence.

'Did he have horns? He must have had horns, they always do according to my *Encyclopedia of Supernatural Netherworlds*.'

'He looked human. More than human. Superhuman. But no horns.'

'He must have had them somewhere. They're not always on the head, you know. He could have had them on his back, running down the spine. Of course, you have to be careful that you've got a decent one. They can be tricky. Some of them are shapeshifters. They can appear as your heart's desire and fool you into parting with your soul.'

'According to this one I haven't got a soul,' I muttered.

'The trouble with spiritual daemons,' Zack pointed out, sucking down a final lungful from another emaciated joint, 'the trouble with those guys is, you have to take them on trust. All the Greek philosophers trusted theirs, and were rewarded with, like, great insight into the human condition. But these days there's a lot of trash about, some right unscrupulous bastards, out to ensnare unsuspecting humans.'

The hour was late, and I was growing exasperated. 'How do you know?' I asked. 'Have you ever seen a real one?'

'No, but you have, by the sound of it. And I've been reading about them for years.'

'But if they're as common as half these books say they are, there must be hundreds of them wandering about. Doesn't it strike you as strange that no one ever sees the things you're most asked to believe in?'

'No one sees God.'

'You know what I mean. It's like UFOs. Why do they only ever kidnap crazy people?'

'The government just tells us they're crazy to discredit them, everyone knows that.'

I was getting a headache. 'Zack, it's late. I'll see you in the morning.'

'You should have taken his offer,' called Zack as he wandered off to his bedroom. 'You'll never get another chance.'

Perhaps that's a good thing after what I saw tonight, I thought, dropping gratefully into bed. I wasn't thrilled by the idea of an overdosed rock star hanging around giving me advice.

Wednesday dawned to clear skies and warm winds that removed the grey lid from the city, freeing it to the world. Three weeks earlier my bicycle had been stolen from the ground floor hallway, so now I walked across Vauxhall Bridge to work. Still, my buoyant mood lasted right until I reached the entrance of the store, twenty minutes late.

Darryl was already out on the floor selling hard, determined to surpass his monthly quota. His enthusiasm for furniture of all kinds was extreme, but his knowledge of bathroom equipment bordered on the fetishistic. I couldn't tell a three-quarter inch double-ply nylon shower grommet from a banana trifle but Darryl could, and was proud to tell me so.

Darryl was rotund and jolly and stale-smelling. He never seemed to wash his hair, and bounced perkily when he walked, and had a laugh like someone trying to jump-start a Ford Sierra, and was always sniffing the ends of his fingers. He was fond of making remarks like *Rome wasn't built in a day* or *Time and tide wait for no man.* If he saw a black guy walking in the street with a white woman, he would sigh and say *I suppose there's a lid for every teapot.* I longed to beat him to death with a length of shower tubing.

During our mid-morning coffee break, by which time Darryl had served about a hundred customers and I had spoken brusquely to two, Max stopped by and asked for our thoughts on the forthcoming sale. In a rare moment of job enthusiasm I had drawn up some ideas, and showed them now, but Max quickly found fault with them, gleefully squiggling his biro across my proposed banners and stickers.

'You know the trouble with you, Martyn?' he asked, not waiting for an answer. 'You're a dreamer. Look at this wasted space. You could have a big sign there; **SAVE POUNDS!** Something like that.' He tapped his pen on the meticulous drawing, dabbing random ink-marks all over it. 'This won't do at all. It's not practical to our needs. Too clever by half. You have to remember that customers are basically stupid. They won't understand any of this.'

Naturally, Darryl's ideas for the store displays were practical. They just weren't very interesting. I thought the whole point of a sale was to draw attention to the store and create interest. As Max set about implementing his favourite employee's posters, which included the aforementioned **SAVE POUNDS!** (something he'd presumably drawn up just to please Max), I decided to go out for lunch. Alone, naturally. First, though, I got a phonecall from my mother.

'I hope you don't mind me calling the office,' she began. 'At least with your job I know I'm not interrupting anything too important.' She let that sink in and followed it with the Property Prices gambit. 'If only we lived nearer we could see more of you, but property prices being what they are . . .' A sour tone in the voice now. 'Your sister's worse than ever, and as for your father . . .'

The usual exasperations emerged. My mother was supposed to enter hospital for a knee operation, but refused to make the appointment 'until she was ready', something she gave no indication of ever being. When I offered to speak to the doctor for her, she changed the subject. My father clearly needed a hand to do repairs around the house, but wouldn't let me help him. They had taken care of me as a child, but were reluctant to let me do the same for them as an adult, as if it somehow diminished their role as parents. Joyce and Gordon would rather make an awkward scene than let me 'put myself out' for them.

They would have been happy to let my big brother help, I was sure of that. As far as my folks were concerned every conversation led back to Joey, whether they had intended it to or not. Everything had changed when he died.

40   S P A N K Y

As a kid I'd imagined that my brother would always be around to make things right. I did everything he ever told me to do. I would have done anything for him. He was twenty-four when he checked out. The way my father talks, you'd think the angel Gabriel came down and took him away in full view of the housing estate.

The phonecall lasted twenty-two minutes. Seconds longer and I would have slit my throat.

The only bright spot in the day occurred when Sarah Brannigan came by. She worked for one of the companies that supplied Thanet Luxury Furniture with bedroom items. I watched as she sat with Max in his office, crossing her long legs and running an elegant index finger down the catalogue price list. The way she pursed her crimson lips when she accepted an order for *Pompadour* Dralon Boudoir Stools gave me a painful erection. She wore a black suit and glossy black stockings, and had long red hair that tumbled like fire to her shoulders. To me she looked like the physical personification of sin, depravity made flesh. Women like Sarah didn't settle down. They broke men's hearts and walked away laughing. I liked that in a woman. She never noticed me, of course. She noticed Darryl as she left the store, only in a scurrying-past-with-a-shudder-of-revulsion way, but at least she realized that he was alive. Depressed, I closed my order book and collected my jacket, which was still damp after Lottie had managed to knock tea over it.

I knew it was time to get out of here and get a life.

After the deadening reality of another working Wednesday, my conversation with Spanky had taken on an unreal air, as though the meeting itself had been part of his hallucinations. I had no plans for the evening, or the week ahead. Not much money, either. Enough for a movie and a burger.

I caught a bus home, ditched my regulation suit with the stitched Thanet badge, put on jeans and returned to the Prince Charles Cinema in Leicester Square, just in time for the start of the main feature. They were showing a big-budget American thriller. In it, two undercover policemen screamed and hit each other until they became friends, a large building exploded and a girl with no knickers on had her head stuffed into a sack of cocaine.

I left before the end.

I was halfway through a bag of chips when I caught sight of a familiar figure walking past the window of the burger bar. Twice in a lifetime? This was too much of a coincidence to pass up. The daemon was staring straight ahead, and didn't glance in my direction. He was wearing an electric blue Gaultier jacket and a black roll-neck sweater, and looked late for an appointment. Although he was moving along the pavement like just another well-dressed urbanite, something set him so far apart from the crowd that I instinctively knew he was not human. Then I realized. It was as if no one else could see him.

Without thinking twice I left my place at the counter and pushed out of the bar. I just managed to catch up with him before he turned the corner.

'Oh, hello.'

Spanky appeared to have no idea who I was. He squinted distantly, then looked me up and down.

'We met last night, remember? You got Elvis by mistake.' What if it wasn't the same person? I'd look a real dickhead.

'Oh yes, Martyn, isn't it? Look, I'm afraid I'm in rather a hurry.' He glanced at the road ahead, checking the traffic lights. It suddenly seemed very important for me to successfully detain him.

'I just wanted to say –' I began, not knowing what I wanted

to say at all, 'I didn't mean to be rude. Last night. I mean, naturally I was sceptical. You would have been, too, if the situation was reversed.'

'There's really nothing to apologize for.' Spanky smiled vaguely, shifting aside to allow a young woman through.

'I believe you're who you say you are. I really do.'

'Well, I'm pleased for you. I've moved on to someone else now, so everything worked out fine.'

'Oh.'

I watched as the young daemon turned to go. Neon sparks were trapped in the fine raindrops that frosted the shoulders of his jacket, and fell in streaks from his brilliantined hair. He looked as if the night and the city belonged only to him. 'Spanky?'

It was the first time I'd used his name. He paused, about to step off the kerb into the light-scarred road.

'You're supposed to have horns. Is that true?'

He searched the ground, looked up and smiled knowingly. 'They're not horns exactly. Residual spines.'

'You're for real, though.'

'Yes, I'm for real.'

Further along the kerb, a newsvendor began unloading bundles of magazines from the side of a truck. The striplights of the sign at Spanky's back began to flicker out, throwing us both into shadow.

'Listen, Martyn. I'm late already, so if you haven't anything else to ask me, I really have to be going . . .'

'Wait.' I realized that even if he turned out to be a phoney, even if he made me look a complete fool, nothing could be worse than the current on-hold status of my life, a never-ending string of wet Wednesdays that stretched off into the darkness of the years ahead.

C o n f i r m a t i o n   43

The shadowed figure squared off before me, his head cocked to one side, challenging. Suddenly I felt enervated and desperate, as though I was about to miss the last relief train out of a besieged town. If he was teasing me about this, trying to get me to beg him before he walked away . . .

I took a step forward and cleared my throat. 'You said you could change my life. Put it in order. There are others worse off than me.'

'Indeed there are. Let them find their own spiritual guidance. I made my proposal to you, no one else. But the question is academic now. You refused my offer.'

'What if I told you I'd made a mistake?'

The figure slowly shook its head. 'That would be awkward. I'm already working with someone else. I told you, I only make the offer once. But I'm not the only one. There are three others like me, creators of futures, absolvers of pasts. They walk the highways of the world, crystallizing dreams and fulfilling secret desires. One day you might run into one of them –'

'Please, Spanky. I can't wait around for a second chance to come along. I'd spend the whole of my life on the lookout.'

Now that the offer had been rescinded, I wanted it back. I'd been cautious – who wouldn't be? But anything was better than never knowing the truth.

'Are you asking me to help you, Martyn?'

'Yes.'

Silence fell between us. The road ahead was devoid of cars. The streets were empty. For a moment it seemed that the city had ceased to function. Even the stars had halted their rotation above the darkened office blocks. My blood ceased pulsing through my veins. Then the lights changed, cars appeared, the newsvendor tossed another bale of papers onto the pavement with a thud.

'I'll see what I can do. I can't promise anything. This isn't the way it's supposed to work, Martyn.'

My heart began to beat again.

He raised a hand as I walked toward him. Recovering myself, I dug into my pocket for the number of the furniture store. Zack always forgot to write down my messages at the flat. Spanky looked at me as if I was behaving like an idiot. 'I know where you live, Martyn.'

He turned and stepped into the road, and was gone with the passing of another truck. I stood and stared after him. I had never asked anyone for anything since Joey died, and the shock of submitting disturbed me. It felt unmanly somehow. Cowardly. The world was full of people who thought their lives were fine until a mirror was held up to them. Was this how others reacted?

Finally I stopped watching the road ahead and returned to the apartment to pace my bedroom, hypertense with anticipation.

I barely slept that night.

Or the next.

CHAPTER FIVE

Memory

I HAVE to explain something about Joey, and the effect his death had on our family.

First, there's a memory.

Gordon, my father, had always been a great proponent of the Day Out. Every other Sunday we would venture forward from the warmth of our little terraced house to march along storm-swept seafronts or dawdle through the roped-off rooms of country houses.

One such Sunday, when I was seven years old and Joey was nearly eleven, we headed off in the direction of Oxford to join the guided tours around Blenheim Palace. A discrepancy in my mother's map-reading technique resulted in a heated argument, so that by the time we drove through the gates my father wasn't speaking to her. This was a common occurrence, and we three kids were familiar with the drill. For the next hour or so our parents would use us as conversational conduits through which they could address their grievances, taking turns to insult and slight each other.

'Look how you've upset the children,' my mother would say, staring accusingly at her husband. 'Joey's disgusted by your behaviour.'

'They're not upset, Joyce,' Father would reply. 'He's embarrassed by you.'

We weren't upset or embarrassed so much as bored by the whole routine. Joey once told me that he felt like a medium when they did this, having his unvoiced thoughts interpreted as evidence of poor parenting.

On this particular occasion, the row escalated so quickly that my father stormed out in the middle of the tour, and we all had to follow him. Outside, more heated words were exchanged while I looked away, squinting up at the clouds above the water gardens. There was a crack of flesh and I turned around. My mother was holding her face, shocked into silence. Then she burst into tears, and my little sister Laura started grisling in sympathy.

Joey had lately turned into a gangly daddy long-legs of a boy, so that he was now a full head and shoulders above me. He was quick-tempered, and I fully expected him to launch himself at my father.

But he didn't. Instead, he led Joyce to the circular rose garden beyond the palace and sat her on a bench overlooking the lake. As I watched, he took out his penknife and cut off a rose, a Royal William, deep crimson and heavy-scented. He spoke to her quietly, threading it through a buttonhole in her cardigan as he did so. I never found out what he said to her, but she stopped sniffling and walked back to the car without us.

By the time we returned she had completely forgiven my father, who was sitting on the grass with his arm around her waist. Joey had the power to heal them, and they both knew it. They were awed by him, and loved him more than they loved Laura or me. Who could blame them? His death was just about the cruellest trick anyone could have played. Losing him was like breaking the rudder off a ship.

When he was two years old, my brother caught pneumonia and nearly choked to death. The doctors put him in an oxygen tent and pumped him full of drugs that left a weakness in his lungs. Because he had nearly been lost, he became the family favourite. Laura and I weren't neglected, but Joey had a golden aura around him. When he spoke, others listened. It was commonly understood that he'd been spared for a purpose. At some unspecified point in the future, he would make us all proud. I grew up worshipping my brother because he was tougher and smarter than anyone I knew. Oddly enough *I* was the fragile one, the one who caught the colds and had to wear a sweater in the middle of June. Although Joey was almost four years older, we were rarely out of each other's sight. He was my protector.

When the government decided to build another oversized motorway through South London, a compulsory purchase order was issued for our house, and we were forced to move. I had been happy there, and dreaded leaving my friends. Money was tight, so my father selected a small house on an estate in the suburbs, where property prices were lower. The day the removal van arrived I ran away, and my folks had to send Joey to bring me back. Eventually he managed to calm me down with promises of how much fun we'd have in the new place.

The chances of staying out of trouble in Twelvetrees were slim. The estate, built as an idyllic commuter-belt arcadia, had no identity, no class and no amenities. Kids sat smoking low-grade dope in doorways, watching the rain fall, waiting for something to happen. We were often at a loose end. Much of this time our parents were barely visible; Father was obscured by claims and invoices, Mother was lost in the steam of the cooking. Laura, being younger, was usually off playing with girlfriends. So, Joey and I hung out. And he was full of good advice.

If the other kids see you cry, they'll start picking on you. Don't try to climb over the fence, you'll fall through it. Being good at one thing is better than being an all-rounder. Tell the drug kids to leave you alone or they'll have to deal with me.

He told me about the things he could see from the height of his extra years.

You know those big thirties stations at the ends of the underground lines, giant spaceships of concrete and curves? Joey thought they were wild. They made him want to be an architect. That's what he was studying when he died. He chose his path and I copied him each step of the way.

One day he said: *You don't want to be an architect as well. Pick something that's right for you. Our family hasn't amounted to much. If you put your mind to it, you'll be better than any of us.*

When my brother began his apprenticeship in the city we saw a lot less of him, but he usually managed to come home at some point over the week-end, and would always end up taking one of us aside to settle an argument. Even at this late stage, he was the glue that held us together.

I didn't even know he was sick. He looked a little thinner in the face, and came home tired all the time. I heard him coughing behind closed doors. Then he had a tense, muted argument with my father, and they stopped talking. After that, Joey's attitude toward me changed. His patience evaporated easily, and he stopped offering advice. One day he shouted angrily that I would have to learn to make my own decisions. The tablets he took belonged to my mother; she often had trouble sleeping. Late one night, he drank a bottle of Evian and ate the entire prescription of Nitrazepam. He went back to bed and never woke up. I took him tea in the morning, and couldn't wake him. His head was pushed down beneath the sheet, and when I pulled the cover back from his face I saw that his eyes were wide open.

It took me a while to realize what had happened. He'd known that his lungs were collapsing, and had delayed going into hospital. He hadn't wanted me to find out until the last possible minute.

With Joey's death a knot unravelled and we went into freefall, changing as we lost sight of each other.

Laura took to her room. Dad simply stopped speaking. But Joyce went off the deep end. Even though she knew he had been in great pain and suffering from depression, my mother was mortified by the idea that her favourite child had committed suicide. A weird silence settled over us. Soon even friends stayed away from the house.

At the funeral none of us cried except Laura. My parents were in a state of shock. I had expected to be miserable, but was surprised to find myself filled with anger. A few weeks after his funeral, I went back to the cemetery and defaced the headstone, kicking mud at the inscription until it was obliterated.

I knew Joey had tried to protect me from the discovery of an abyss. But he should have told me he was sick. We weren't supposed to have secrets. At least I could have prepared myself.

I want you to understand why my life was a mess, why I couldn't change things alone. I didn't know how to do it without him, and I didn't trust anyone else.

That is, until Spanky came along.

Eligibility

BY FRIDAY evening the whole damned business bothered me more than ever. I sat at my work station verifying order forms for kitchen accessories, but my mind had never been further from the job. All I could think of was the incredible opportunity I had missed. I thought about the planes of life that might exist if I were not too blind to see them. Why should our daily existence be the sum total of all physicality? Why *couldn't* there be other forms beyond our comprehension?

Because this is life, not an episode of *Star Trek*, came the answer.

When I'd exhausted that line of thought, I consoled myself with the idea that Spanky was a lunatic, a fake, and that I'd probably had a lucky escape. And when I could pursue this idea no further, my belief in him began to grow again. I even tried to draw a picture of the daemon, but couldn't capture the strange mixture of mystery and innocence that existed in his face. Still, saint or charlatan, Spanky had made me do something I hadn't done for a long time; think seriously about my future, a world of possibilities to which I had pointlessly blinded myself.

Some men rootlessly roam the planet. Others settle fast and

build. I fitted neither category, too insecure for the one, too restless for the other. And all the time there was the sense that life's real pleasures were passing me by. It would help if I could identify what I was looking for; but how would I know until I experienced it?

At a quarter to six on a wet Friday evening, fifteen minutes before the store was due to close, I sharpened a pencil, tore off a fresh sheet of paper and began to evaluate my life.

After breaking the lead three times I gave up and set the pencil down. The smell of dry cleaning fluid permeated the entire store and made my throat raw. I looked out into the showroom.

A tall black guy who had been standing beside a standard lamp for half an hour, trying to decide whether to buy it, was unscrewing the thing section by section and peering down each length of tubing, as if he'd lost something in there. Max was stumping over to the main doors to turn down the **CLOSED** sign, and Lottie was outside trying to pull the heavy steel trellis across the store entrance. Darryl was furtively talking on the phone to the married woman he dated, one hand cupped around the mouthpiece to prevent anyone from catching the conversation. I think he overestimated our interest in the affair. Dokie was leaning against the rear wall staring off into space with one finger buried inside his nose, weighing his genitals with his free hand. Lottie shrieked as she shut her hand in the trellis. Dokie glanced over at her, then returned his attention to dislodging his nasal blockage.

Martyn Ross, this is your life.

The start of a week-end, and once again I had no plans. It was truly pathetic. There had to be something I could do. Right now there were people out there bungee-jumping, hang-gliding, deep-sea fishing, climbing to the peaks of the Nepalese mountains, drinking that yak milk tea in cafés where the air was so thin they had to use asthma inhalers to keep from passing out.

I thought perhaps I should go to the library and read up on daemonology. Maybe I could discover where the other three Spanci-whatever-they-were hung out. I decided to go first thing in the morning.

Meanwhile, there was the matter of tonight.

Nobody even noticed my departure except Lottie, who anxiously wished me a nice week-end. I left the store and walked along the Strand into the West End, through the courtyard at the rear of the Wyndhams Theatre, looking in the windows of the antiquarian bookshops. I wasn't headed anywhere in particular, and was half-looking for a book which could tell me more about my strange experience when I saw Sarah Brannigan alight from a taxi at the far end of the alley.

I quickly caught her up. I didn't need the help of some supposed supernatural entity to ask a beautiful woman out. I would see what she was doing tomorrow night. I called out to her and she looked up in surprise, but I knew at once that she didn't recognize me. She was wearing a long black gown, the kind of outfit you wore to the opera. Her fiery red hair was tied back with a silver clasp. Her bare shoulders were as smooth as vinyl.

'I'm sorry,' she began, slowly shaking her head, 'I don't . . .'

'Martyn Ross,' I reminded her. 'I'm at Thanet Furniture. We order stock from you. I wondered –'

And as I began to speak, the thought of what the gown meant slowly began to filter through. Even as I asked her for a date, I realized that she was with a very large man right now, and that he was on the other side of the taxi paying the driver. But it was too late, I couldn't stop myself and the words came out just as the man appeared in full evening dress and looked at me with an eyebrow raised in puzzlement, ready to ask her if she was being bothered by a stranger.

She had been half listening to me, and now snapped her head back in the direction of her escort. 'It's someone from work, Roger,' she explained, casually indicating me with a wave as if pointing out a statue or a type of tree.

'We're going to be late, love.' The accent was refined, upper-middle class. He threw a look that almost acknowledged me but not quite, then slipped his arm through hers and towed her away.

'It was nice to see you again, Michael,' she managed before disappearing around the corner in a cloud of Poison.

If I had wanted to prove that I could manage my own affairs, it wasn't a promising start. It took a distinct lack of sophistication not to recognize the signs she had given out. Most people can tell when someone doesn't want to talk to them. I walked on into Covent Garden, determined to steer clear of the Opera House, and ate alone in a noisy American burger restaurant.

I had never felt at such a loose end. Why is it that when you're lonely everyone else seems to be hugging and kissing? I wanted to sit with a girl, just to sit and talk and look at her, but the ones I met at the clubs didn't seem interested, and I knew no others. After the meal I found myself in a pub called the Lamb and Flag, where I decided to sit with a pint of stout.

Several hours later I was still there, thinking but mostly drinking.

The barman called time and the darts team packed up. I morosely hugged my Guinness, determined to be the last to leave.

Outside, a drizzling mist had settled in for the night. It was one of those British summers that you could only tell had arrived because the rain was getting warmer. I stood in the alleyway planning my next move.

'It's an odd alley. If you don't look to the modern roadway showing at the gap between the buildings, you could still be in the nineteenth century.

I thought I heard the sound of a whinnying horse. At first I assumed mounted police were about, checking that people behaved themselves as the pubs closed. Then I saw the stallion, a magnificent creature with a crimped mane and a coat of polished ebony, walking up the middle of the alley as carefully as if stepping over crockery. Spanky was perched high on the animal's withers, dressed in black leather jodhpurs and a crimson cutaway coat with gold buttons. He dismounted as he reached me and cracked his stick across the rump of the horse, so that it glanced back at him with a wild eye before noisily cantering off toward the end of the deserted street.

'That's a dead end,' I said stupidly. 'He won't be able to get out.'

Spanky sighed and scratched the tip of his nose with his stick. 'The horse doesn't exist, Martyn. Do I have to keep explaining?'

'I'm trying to make sense of the things I see.'

'First mistake. You're misreading my visual signals. It's a language, like any other. It's just that I know how to change the meaning of the words.' He clapped me on the shoulder and we began to walk. I realized I was glad to see him. 'I could give you a long, boring scientific explanation, but it's easier if you think of what I do as a form of spiritual hypnosis. You have to learn where to draw the line; I'm real, the horse wasn't.'

'But you were riding it.'

'That's what I made you believe. You must try not to be so *linear*. I'll tell you all about myself one day, but I thought you'd

E l i g i b i l i t y   55 be more interested in why I'm here now.'

'I am.'

'My other case isn't working out. In fact, we've reached a decision to part company. I made her forget that she'd ever met me. I thought it best.'

'A woman? How did you pick her?'

'Oh, she sort of picked me really. *Melanie Palmer*. With a name like that you'd think she'd be a sensible type, wouldn't you? But not at all. She was too neurotic for my taste, too complex. I prefer the simple ones.'

I wondered if I should be offended.

'It means I'm free for a while, so we might as well sort out your problems.'

'You make it sound like a freelance assignment.'

'It is rather. When do you want to start?'

I looked over at this horseless rider, dressed like an Edwardian country gentleman, exhaling pale clouds into the mist. I decided I wouldn't make the same mistake again. 'Why not right now?' I asked.

'Why not indeed?' he replied with a grin. 'Very well, then. Here commenceth the first lesson.'

Sartorientation

`I HOPE you won't think me too shallow if I say that clothes help to make the man. Perhaps we could start by getting your togs sorted out. If I can find you the right look, then we can start on the inner self.'

'What's wrong with my clothes?' I asked, indignant.

Spanky made a face. 'Frankly, I've seen better dressed wounds.'

'But I like what I'm wearing.'

'You're too casual. No one will ever take you seriously dressed like that.'

We had taken a cab to Knightsbridge and were now standing half-way along a deserted Sloane Street, in an elegant parade of menswear shops where the bidding on jackets began above four hundred pounds. The shining storefronts gave the street a glacial quality, as though it was constructed from luminescent sheets of ice. It had turned midnight, and everyone around here kept strict business hours.

'Things have changed since your day,' I pointed out. 'People are less formal. Nobody wears starched collars anymore. There are no valets to iron them.'

'I'm not entirely ignorant of present-day sartorial modes,

Martyn.' Spanky strolled up to one of the elegant Italian shops and pressed his hands against the chromium locks on one side of the door, breathing on the glass and speckling it with spines of frost.

'What are you doing?' I asked.

'Deactivating the alarm system. Security arrangements have become rather more sophisticated lately. Just as well I learned this.' There was a steel click, and a hiss of air. Spanky pressed the door back with the flat of his hand and bade me enter first, but I couldn't. Anyone could get what they wanted by breaking the law, and this was stealing.

'It's not, Martyn. I just want you to look at the clothes. We won't take anything, I promise.'

'You're sure?'

'Not so much as a single hanger. Come on.'

The first thing I noticed upon entry was the smell that always lingered in smart clothing stores, carpet cleaner overpowered by aftershave. Black and white tiles swirled in psychedelic spirals around brushed-chrome torsos. A pair of androgynous mannequins wore matching suits of orange crêpe, as if they had been preserved in amber from a distant century.

'Androgyny is always fashionable,' said Spanky, 'because only the young can be seen as androgynes, and youth remains fashionable for its possibilities.'

I couldn't get used to him reading my thoughts. It was very disconcerting. As we walked through the sparsely arranged racks, Spanky indicated suits and jackets on either side by raising his hands and allowing a sallow light to glow from them on to the clothes.

'Choose what you like. I need to gauge your personal taste.'

Slowly my fear of being discovered here faded. I could see the security beams flashing red in the corners of the ceiling, but they seemed to have been rendered inoperative. I held up a pair of green jeans, a plain white shirt and a floral tie. Spanky was sitting beside the till on top of the counter, cleaning his nails. He looked up at my choice and grimaced horribly.

'Put them back.'

It made sense to take the advice of a man who looked like a million dollars, so I did as I was told.

'Now go to the end rack and put on the grey Versace jacket with a pair of plain black trousers. Take one of those belts over there. Forget about ties, for God's sake. Try this instead.' He threw me a dark roll-neck sweater.

'I'd never wear something like this,' I complained. 'It's too fancy. A leopard can't change his spots.'

'You're not a leopard, and I'll take care of your spots later.'

I've always felt uncomfortable trying on clothes, especially with someone watching. It seems too frivolous an occupation, almost an immoral way of passing the time when there are more important things to be done. Having said that, I was starting to enjoy myself.

'If you have some pressing engagement I don't know about, Martyn, please feel free to attend to it.' Spanky waved magnanimously at the door.

'Will you stop reading my bloody mind?' I whispered angrily, one leg in a pair of tapered Jasper Conran slacks. I couldn't believe I was doing this. 'I'd rather wear jeans than these things.'

'All in good time. Jeans have their place, but it's common to wear them all the time. There doesn't seem to be much class in the present era.'

'We're abandoning the class system,' I said, 'and about time too.'

'So you're happy with these gormless people walking about

in multi-coloured nylon overalls, are you?'

'Shellsuits. No.'

'Perhaps there's hope for you yet.' He hopped down from the counter and appraised my appearance. 'Not bad. At least you're not fat. I hate working with obese people. Melanie was overweight. All in all, I'm glad my offer of help fell through.' He took a boiled sweet from a large glass jar on the counter and unwrapped it. 'The jacket looks good. We need to get you some black boots. Put everything back and let's go next door.'

I began replacing the jacket on its hanger. 'So what happens now?' I asked.

He rolled the boiled sweet to one side of his mouth. 'You tired yet?'

'Not at all.'

'Then we'll go over to Harvey Nichols' menswear department. Might as well get the rest of your wardrobe sorted out tonight.' He sucked on the sweet, studying me oddly.

'What?'

'You don't seem very pleased about this, Martyn.'

I shrugged, embarrassed. 'I'm not very good at shopping for clothes.'

'You will be after I've finished with you. I'm trying to find you an image. A set of visual signals. If you were a woman and I told you we were about to empty out Harvey Nichols you'd be in the throes of a violent multiple orgasm by now. The sexual allure of purchasable fashion is something few females can refuse.'

He raised his hands and the soft blue light faded from them. We were in darkness once more as we quietly let ourselves out of the shop. There was a muted click and a whir as the security system re-armed itself.

In the basement of the department store on the opposite side of the street, my self-appointed style guru tried several jackets on for himself. It was when he slipped off his sweater that I saw the 'horns' Zack had talked about – a row of tiny needle-sharp spines down his back that seemed to have grown out from his vertebrae. They were pink at the base and bone-white at the tips, like the protective spikes of a sea urchin. They didn't look out of place at all. Rather, it made me wonder why nobody else had them, in the same way that it wouldn't really be odd for us to have tails. 'How come they don't stick through your shirt?' I asked, fascinated.

'I make them lie flat,' he said, slipping his arm behind his back and brushing them down with the backs of his fingers. 'See?'

He chose a charcoal grey Armani suit for himself, lifting the arms and studying the lining carefully before returning it to the rack. I found the flashing security cameras disconcerting, and pointed them out.

'Don't worry about those,' he said airily, 'I've blanked the tapes with magnetic interference. Tell me, what do you use on your face?'

'My face? Soap.'

'No astringent, moisturizer, aftershave?'

'I used to have a litre bottle of Brut Splash-On, but we used it to unblock the bathroom sink.'

He drew breath through his teeth. 'Martyn, I find it hard to believe that you're really such a philistine about personal appearance. Grooming is important for acceptance into contemporary society. We live in a time of surfaces.'

I gave in. 'Okay,' I agreed, 'find me a surface.'

An hour later we had finished, and left the store as quietly and easily as we had slipped in. The clothes had all been returned to their racks. We were departing empty-handed.

Spanky told me we were done for the evening, and that I might as well get some sleep while he set about reproducing the clothes accurately.

'One more thing,' he said. 'Hold still.' He extended the fingers of his right hand and ran them lightly over my head. I felt a tickle of static electricity around my ears and over the back of my neck.

'Now shake yourself.'

Scratchy strands of trimmed hair fell down my collar and drifted from my shoulders.

'That's more like it. You look almost as human as I do.'

'Neat trick. What happens now?' I stepped into the road and raised my hand to a passing black cab.

'Meet me outside Sloane Square tube station at eleven tomorrow morning. Don't tell anyone where you're going, or who you're meeting. You mustn't talk about me to others. Did I mention that before?'

'Why?' I asked guiltily. 'What would happen if I did?'

'There are too many people out there looking for a second chance. I don't want to tell them they can't have it.' He smiled and stuck his hands in his pockets. 'You'd better go. If the cabbie thinks you're crazy he won't want to take you.' I looked across at the driver, and he was staring at me oddly.

'He can't see me,' Spanky explained. 'No one else can see me. Only you. So it looks to him like you're talking to yourself.'

'But – the night we met, there were some girls in the club. they turned around when you passed them.'

'They sensed something. Some people can. But it's a very rare person who will actually make me appear to them, like you did, Martyn. Most people can only see me if I choose to let them, and I don't do that very often.'

He waved his hand and sauntered off, whistling something

I half recognized. By the time I had closed the cab door and turned around in my seat, he had vanished among the etiolated mannequins of the deserted stores.

CHAPTER EIGHT

Brunchiology

I AWOKE a little after 9.00 a.m. with a terrible headache.

Sunlight was bouncing in through my bedroom window, searing into shards that reflected from every surface. My limbs ached. My head was pounding. I felt as if I had been partying all night, and I was just starting to think that perhaps I hadn't broken into a department store a few hours ago when I saw the blue boxes neatly stacked at the end of the bed. On the top one was a white square of card reading;

> Wear contents of top box today.
> I want you to make an impression.
> Regards, S.

I shaved and showered, then donned the designer clothes Spanky had duplicated, no doubt with the help of elves, overnight. There were toiletries in the box, Moulton Brown moisturizer, Clinique scruffing lotion, Oxy-10 spot healer, Ralph Lauren aftershave, Australian hair gel, everything labelled with instructions for usage. Obviously, Spanky assumed that I was completely incapable of making myself presentable.

Thirty minutes later I studied the alien figure in the mirror, clad in a red wool Gaultier jacket, black sweater and trousers. My hair was shaped in the kind of smart style I had seen in magazines. I looked good. Better than good. This was a side of me I had never imagined existed, and I had to admit that it felt terrific. My appearance suddenly carried authority. I was closing my bedroom door behind me when Zack emerged from the bathroom, scratching beneath his ratty old robe.

'Holy shit!' He looked me up and down, stupefied. 'It's Giorgio fucking Armani!'

'Jean-Paul Gaultier, actually. Out of my way, pleb.'

'You look like a total breadhead. What happened, did your parents die and leave you money?' He sniffed the air and grimaced. 'Christ, it smells like a tart's parlour in here.'

'It makes a change from the spicy tang of your socks. Is Debbie with you? I want her to see me.'

'Nah, she's still pissed off at me. I assume you're going out.'

'You assume correctly.'

'Does this posh speech come with the outfit or something? I mean, is this a new image? You're trying to impress a girlie, aren't you?'

I left him trying to puzzle it out, standing in the hallway with his mouth hanging open. I wondered if he would make the connection with Spanky. It would probably never occur to him that a spiritual being could behave in such a material fashion. It was a cool, beautiful Saturday morning. Spanky was waiting for me at the top of the Sloane Square escalator. He was dressed in a virtual mirror-image of my clothes, but his jacket was a chill midnight blue. He nodded approvingly at my appearance.

'Be honest, Martyn. Could you tell that jacket from the real thing?'

'Not at all. You even got the labels right.'

'Thank God. I had a team of blinded acolytes slaving over the stitching all night.' I must have looked worried because he patted me on the shoulder and said, 'Just kidding'. We left the tube station and entered the lower end of the King's Road.

'That's got the outer image off to a decent start. Now we're free to concentrate on your behaviour. Later we'll tackle your physical wellbeing, get you off the junk food and into a gym. Workouts three times a week. Today, we'll have brunch together. But first, you need a book.' He gestured to W.H. Smiths. 'Go in there and buy a Penguin Classic. Preferably something Bloomsbury and twenties. Virginia Woolf would be good.'

'But why –'

'Just go and do it.'

I picked up a copy of *Jacob's Room* and paid for it. When I emerged, Spanky unwrapped it and threw away the bag, handing me back the volume. I was aware of containing my movements as people passed us on the pavement. If Spanky was invisible to others, I would have to be careful about reacting to him in public.

'I feel mischievous today,' he exclaimed, breathing deep and patting himself on the chest. 'Glad to be alive. I could spiral through the clouds like a rocket. Anything could happen this morning. I honestly feel that, don't you?'

'I don't know what –'

'*Woah!*' he shouted suddenly, slapping his head and spinning around. 'What's happened here? Everyone's *naked!*'

I looked along the crowded pavement, my mouth hanging open. He was right. No one was wearing any clothes. Two tall, elegant women strode by, denuded of everything but their shopping bags. A beautiful Spanish girl with dark-nippled, pendulous breasts and a virtually rotating backside squeezed past us to enter a Body Shop. Two stern policemen, bare-assed except for their helmets, stood at the kerb. Workmen were sitting outside a pub, their goosepimpled buttocks poking through ironwork benches. Ahead, a sightseeing coach was disgorging a fleet of chubby nude Americans.

Spanky threw his hands over his eyes. 'Enough! Begone!' he cried. 'It's too early in the morning for this sort of foolishness.'

And everyone was dressed again.

We stopped before an open-fronted restaurant. Even at this hour it was full of wealthy young diners. Pony-tailed waiters were negotiating cramped steel tables at dangerous speeds.

'Is this part of my self-improvement?' I asked. I didn't understand the point of sitting down to eat with someone nobody else could see. If I spoke to Spanky, everyone would think I was mad.

'You only have to consciously transmit your thoughts and I'll receive them,' he replied.

Like this?

'Exactly. From now on, if you have a question to ask, just think it. Don't say it aloud. I want to see how you conduct yourself with women.'

What do you mean?

The *maître d'* was looking over at us with a quizzical raised eyebrow. 'Just do what I tell you to do. Go over there and ask to be seated. I'm right behind you.'

I carefully threaded my way through to the reservations desk. The *maître d'* gave his blonde pony-tail a self-conscious flick and looked along the bridge of his nose at me.

''Elp you?'

'Do you have a table for one, please?'

'No, I am sorry.' He rudely turned his back and made himself busy. I was about to leave when Spanky grabbed my arm hard.

'You're not going to take that from him,' he hissed. 'What's the name of the owner?'

I have no idea, I thought.

'Look around. The pictures on the wall over there. The same fat bitch is in virtually every photograph.'

He was right. In one the plump, laughing figure sat at a table with a place-card in view.

'Read the name underneath.'

Anna Tamboure, I thought.

'The place is called Tamboures so it must be her restaurant. But she won't be here now.'

Why not?

'It's Saturday morning. Too early for parties. The type of customer she shines for won't be here yet. She wouldn't receive enough attention from this crowd. Tell the *maître d'* that you're meeting her for brunch, but you're a little early. He'll give you a table, and a good one, even if he has to throw those old women off over there.'

The daemon was right. Taking a deep breath I did as I was told, and I got my table. In the front. By the window. Following Spanky's instructions I told the waiter that I would go ahead and order.

Do you want me to order something for you too?

'I don't need to eat. I only do it for the pleasure of the taste. Ask for the salmon and scrambled eggs, a lemon poppy-seed muffin, English breakfast tea and a Bloody Mary. And leave the book on the table, face up.'

I ordered and looked around the restaurant. Here, my expensive new clothes blended in perfectly. I was dressed in the same manner as everyone else. Chelsea uniform.

'Martyn, pay attention. Look over to the door.'

A tall young woman was standing inside the entrance,

studying the room for a table. The sunlight fell in a crooked stripe across her breasts. Her hair was cropped in a sixties' cut, and coral pink lipstick coated a pair of small but sensual lips.

'Catch her eye. She'll look away at first. When she looks back – and she will – catch it again. Now gesture with the flat of your palm to your empty seat. Smile, but don't look smarmy.'

She looked over at me, glanced off in the direction of the kitchen, then back. I gave a light smile and gestured to the only unoccupied chair. She feigned indifference, but coolly appraised the situation.

Then she caught sight of the novel and seemed to reach a decision.

'Statistics show that women feel safer near a strange man if he's carrying a book,' he said. 'When she comes over, offer her the seat.'

'Would you care to join me?' I asked. She was even taller than I had realized, but beautiful in a highly cosmetic manner. Deep-set violet eyes, wide false lashes. Those lips.

'Thanks, it's always so bloody crowded in here.' She turned over a menu and began to study it.

'Introduce yourself,' said Spanky. I looked around for him, but he had disappeared.

Where are you?

'I don't want you getting distracted. Introduce yourself. Tell her the salmon is very good. Offer her tea. Be natural.'

I did as I was told. Over the next twenty minutes, I heard all about her. Katisha was a model, but it was tough finding work at the moment.

'Not her real name,' commented Spanky.

She'd been offered a job in Japan, but wasn't sure if she should take it. She had gone to a party last night, but it hadn't been much fun. Once I'd started her talking, she didn't let up. Mostly she told me about her career and her recently departed boyfriend, who sounded like a total creep. When I had first looked over at her standing there bathed in sunlight, she had appeared virginal and innocent. Talking to her now, I could tell that innocence was not a recent memory.

'That's because you place women on pedestals. To you, they're all goddesses,' Spanky cut in. 'Men who do that are usually lacking in experience. Stop her from talking about herself for a minute.'

How do I do that?

'Tell her something that has a conversational angle for her. Something that she can see as advantageous. Tell her you work for Gavins.'

What's Gavins?

'It's a very successful model agency.'

That would be lying.

'Don't be a drip. You want to have sex, don't you?'

Sex? I thought you were monitoring my manners. It's still morning! That must be the last thing on her mind.

'Maybe, but it's definitely there on her mind. I assume you caught the nuances in her remarks about the party being so terrible and the boyfriend leaving her. She didn't meet anyone interesting last night. Get it? You are not sitting opposite Miss Goody Two-Shoes here. Really, this wholesome pose of yours is beginning to wear a bit thin.'

I suppose it started there, with the initial lie. The first of very many.

Katisha instantly perked up when I mentioned the model agency. Throughout the conversation that followed I was fed with dialogue lines, Cyrano-like, by my invisible tutor. I found myself explaining the set-up at my agency, and heard myself hinting that they might have work for her. By the time we had finished our respective meals (she had taken my advice and ordered the same dish), she was talking to me with her elbow on the table and her chin resting on her fist, in rapt attention. I felt ashamed of myself. I felt dishonest. But most of all, I felt very, very horny.

'She lives nearby,' said Spanky, cutting across her conversation. 'I just saw the address in her purse. She's out shopping for lip-stick.'

How do you know that?

Spanky reappeared beside me. He had taken a piece of toast from someone's table and was slowly munching it. 'All women are out shopping,' he explained, 'virtually all of the time. They just don't realize it. It is commonly assumed that a woman's main preoccupation in life is the purchase and mass accumulation of shoes. Not true. New shades of lip-stick are, however, another story. Right now she's thinking about the new lip-stick from Paloma Picasso. It's expensive, it's classy, and she has to own at least two of them or she will surely die. Offer to leave with her.'

'So, you're out shopping this morning?' I asked self-consciously.

'Oh, just cosmetic stuff I need.'

'The department store she wants to visit is between here and her flat,' said Spanky, producing an enormous Ordnance Survey map of the area and folding it back. 'Suggest going there with her. I'll plan the route.'

'I love that shop,' she said, agreeing to the suggestion I repeated from Spanky. 'Wouldn't you mind? Men usually hate waiting for me in stores. Because you know, sometimes I can be hours. I lose track of the time.'

'It'll be my pleasure.'

We rose to leave.

'From the random thoughts I'm catching,' said Spanky, following behind us, 'she's going to offer you coffee at her place. But not until you've been hanging around at the shop for a while. It'll be a kind of reward. She already told you she has no plans for the rest of the day.'

As Katisha and I reached the restaurant door, Spanky shifted beside me. 'There's a packet of flavoured condoms in your left pocket,' he said with a smirk. 'Lemon, strawberry and liquorice. You can misbehave yourself as much as you like, but whatever you do, don't offer to pay for the lip-stick.'

Sexography

'THE BODY,' intoned Spanky, 'is a sacred temple. Sex is not just a matter of knowing how to enter that temple, it's finding out where everything is, shifting the furniture about, and remembering to move more slowly and with more respect than you'd really like to.'

We were standing in Katisha's lounge, waiting for her to emerge from the bathroom. Her apartment covered the top floor of a sloping redbrick Victorian block. Large curving windows admitted dusty light over furniture that was expensive but mismatched and lacking in taste. Katisha was Thanet Furniture's dream customer. I liked her. She was ditzy and funny and kind of awful, but seemed to know what she wanted.

Right now, it appeared she wanted me.

I knew that it wasn't just the effect of my changed appearance. Something of Spanky was starting to rub off on me. My confidence was growing. I waited before I moved. Thought before I spoke. Common sense to most people, but a new experience for me.

'Charismatic osmosis,' said Spanky, turning over a fluffy troll with distaste. 'That's what's happening to you, my dear chap. I'm imparting some of my own qualities to you. The more time we spend together, the more your behaviour will change. You'll grow more knowledgeable, more sophisticated. When you reach a point of true emotional independence, the process will be finished. But for now, just relax and have fun.'

I wasn't too sure about that. How much of my personality could change before I stopped being me?

'You'll still be the same person, Martyn. I can't make you accept any changes you don't consciously want. When the muse alighted on Socrates it only imparted those characteristics that the philosopher required. And he was the guy who insisted *know thyself.*'

'I won't be long,' Katisha called. 'Make yourself comfortable.' She sounded as if she was brushing her teeth. She'd drawn one set of blinds, shielding the front half of the room from the brightness of the day. I moved into the shadowed area and seated myself.

I can't believe I'm about to do this. It's two o'clock on a Saturday afternoon, for God's sake. I've only known her two and a half hours.

Spanky gave one of his characteristic shrugs and replaced the troll on the dresser. 'How did you ever get to be so prudish about guilt-free safe sex, Martyn? I suppose I'll find out when I meet your family.'

What do you mean, meet my family? They can't tell you anything about me.

'On the contrary, old bean, they're the key. Look out, she's coming back.'

Behind me, the bathroom light clicked off and Katisha emerged in minuscule black underwear. She stood before me with a faint smile on her lips, then soundlessly reached down and moved her face close to mine. Her strong tongue found its way into my mouth, and I slipped my arms around her waist. In the brief moment that I opened my eyes, I found Spanky standing behind Katisha's right shoulder watching her unclip her lace brassière with unconcealed fascination.

Spanky, can't you fade out for this part? It's embarrassing.

'Don't be so old-fashioned. Anyway, this is a scientific experiment. I'm going to guide you through, help you to make right moves.'

I don't want you here!

'Why not?' He pouted theatrically. 'I thought we were friends.'

It's a matter of privacy. Besides, I won't be able to – you know. Get an erection.

A hand suddenly appeared and grabbed my cock through my trousers. 'I think you already have one. I've put the condoms in your left-hand trouser pocket.'

Katisha leaned forward into the embrace, gently rubbing her groin back and forth across my leg. As I raised my hand and slid it around the top of her thigh, I realized with a shock that my arm was being guided into place.

For Christ's sake, stop that!

'Just trying to help. You know what to do then, do you? What's your next move going to be?'

Take her pants off.

'Charming. Why don't you simply stun her with a house-brick and fuck her through her clothes? Have you never heard of foreplay? Sensitivity? The breasts, man, lightly kiss the breasts.'

Jesus, I don't believe this.

I slid my hand beneath the slipping bra and ran my fingertips lightly over her nipples. She tilted her head back, closing her eyes.

'Listen for the tell-tale sounds that will let you know she's enjoying herself. Keep one hand in the small of her back, the other on her breasts.'

Katisha began to emit a low moaning sound. The more I rubbed and tweaked the nipples, the louder she moaned. She sounded like a mugger's victim coming round.

'What's your other hand doing? You can put it into the back of her panties now and give that lovely rump a good massage. Unbutton your shirt so that her nipples can brush against your chest.'

I can manage this without any more advice!

'I'm sure you know how to enjoy yourself. I was thinking of her.'

I'm sure you were.

Spanky was clearly enjoying the show. I should have been repelled by his presence in the room, egging me on as if he was betting on a racehorse, but oddly it didn't disturb me. His running commentary got on my nerves, though.

By the time we reached the bedroom, Spanky was already sitting cross-legged on one of the pillows, unwrapping a piece of bubblegum.

Christ, Spanky, can't you leave the room for a few minutes?

He thought for a moment, chewing slowly. 'How long exactly? I don't want to miss the big finish.'

I don't know, ten minutes.

'You haven't had sex for a while, have you? Anyone would think you'd been in prison for a year.'

He rose and stood by the bed, cocking his head to one side, admiring Katisha as she removed her panties and flicked them across the room with her big toe. Slowly she opened her legs, smiling at me all the while.

'I say, Martyn. Do you think she might have done this before?'

I glared up at Spanky. *Just go, all right?*

'Can't I at least stay for penetration?'

No!

'Spoilsport.' He crossed his arms, impersonating Arnold Schwarzenegger. 'I'll be back.'

I can honestly say that Katisha showed me things I had never before considered physically possible. At one point she slipped backwards from the bed and actually stood on her head. I tried not to let my amazement show. I was entering her with long, deep strokes, nearing my own climax, when Spanky reappeared beside us.

'She's making an awful lot of noise,' he complained. 'Her neighbours have had to turn their television up. I was very impressed with the acrobatic trick, though.'

You weren't supposed to be watching us!

'I peeked. Forgive me? Tell you what, I'll let you know when she's coming.' He disappeared from sight, then reappeared, smoothing his hair back in place. 'She's almost there.'

How do you know?

'I just popped into her body. Her nerve endings are going absolutely wild.'

Katisha was laying back on the bedspread with her arms thrown over her face, grunting loudly. I was standing at the bed edge with her legs twisted around my thighs, knotted at the ankles. I could feel myself reaching orgasm, and began pumping faster.

'Whoa, slow down there. Remember what I said. Slow and deep. Here.' Spanky raised his leg, placed the heel of his right shoe on my buttocks and pushed down hard. A thrilled cry burst from Katisha as she writhed beneath me.

Thank you.

'You're welcome.'

We reached a mutual climax of cataclysmic proportions, and I collapsed on top of her.

Spanky blew a large pink bubble and burst it. 'And they say romance is dead. Jolly well done the both of you. I for one was very impressed.'

Shut up, Spanky.

'What are you looking at?' Katisha raised herself on one arm and checked the patch of wall where my eyes had been focussed.

'Oh – nothing.' I turned back to her sheepishly, but she was already studying her alarm clock.

'Oh my God.'

'What's the matter?'

'I just remembered. I'm supposed to be at an audition at five, and it'll take me ages to get ready.' She carefully extricated herself, then jumped up and began searching for her underwear.

'That's okay. Do you need any help?'

'No, I'm fine. You'll only be in the way if you stay.'

Her sudden change of attitude confused me. 'I'd really like to see you again, Katisha.'

'She's about to lie to you, Martyn,' said Spanky. 'You asked for it.'

'Sure. I'd really like to see you too. Give me a call sometime.' She didn't volunteer her number, didn't even stop what she was doing to catch my eye.

How do you know that was a lie?

'Oh come on. There are photos of some bearded chap all over the lounge, modelling suits in exotic places. Not the last boyfriend, probably a long-term lover, away on a shoot. Unreliable, treats her like dirt, married perhaps, but she still waits for him. At least you helped her by reducing her STQ –'

78   S P A N K Y

STQ?

'Sexual Tension Quotient. And now she wants you to leave. Let's go.'

And so we left. I looked up at the tall windows from the street and waved, but there was no sign of her.

'I wonder if Katisha –' I began.

'Don't worry about the young lady. You did each other a favour, so you're equal.'

'It's just – it wasn't very *romantic*. More like the Olympics.'

Spanky threw his hands wide in disgust. 'Who said anything about *romance*? There'll be plenty of time for you to settle down later, get a nagging wife, crushing mortgage and screaming kids. You want to play the field for a while, don't you?'

I gave no reply. He looked down at his knees. 'There must have been a cat somewhere in her apartment. My trousers are smothered with white hairs.' He brushed at them, grimacing. 'A few more encounters like that and we'll have sorted out a sexual persona for you. Next time I'll teach you a bedroom trick called "Pearls And Swallows" that you can do with iced water and a shoelace.'

He pulled back his sleeve and checked his Cartier. 'Now, I have to go away for a short while, so you can have the rest of the weekend off. On Monday morning we'll start work on your career. You need to make more money if you're going to run around with a different crowd.'

He gripped my arm warmly. 'I was proud of you today. I honestly think you're going to be one of my best-ever clients. See you later, Sex God.'

I turned to speak, but he had already gone. By now I was becoming used to finding myself alone in the middle of a crowded London street.

Sportsmanship

THE SNOW was several feet thick and carpeted the whole of the city, deadening sound and reflecting brilliant white light. Shocked, I stared down from my bedroom window. Surely it was too early in the year for this kind of weather? It looked as if a fresh linen tablecloth had been thrown over the streets. Below, the people passing on the pavement were dressed for the middle of winter. Clouds of flakes brushed the glass. The geraniums in the flowerbox were completely buried. I turned away to find Spanky sitting on my dressing table, dangling his legs. As always he was immaculately dressed, this time in a black Moschino suit, cream silk shirt and a splendid black waistcoat with gold buttons.

'I thought you'd like a change of weather. Don't worry, it's an illusion I created just for you. I'll get rid of it before we go outside.'

'It's very difficult to get used to you tampering with my sense of reality,' I complained. 'Where have you been?'

'Actually, I went into the countryside to see some old friends.'

'Human or spirit world?' I asked, searching around for my dressing-gown.

'Human, of course. Daemons never mix socially. We exist on tangential planes to one another, so contact is awkward and often dangerous. And for me it's out of the question.'

'Why's that?'

'I'm in a human body. I couldn't cross back even if I wanted to. Each daemon has a choice. He can remain a spiritual entity on a celestial plane, where he will have great power but no physical control, or he can take a human form on earth, where he will have corporeal substance but reduced abilities.'

'And what have your abilities been reduced to?'

'Certain cognitive tricks, like reading the minds of those to whom I am attuned, the production of illusions, simple kinetics, seeing through solid objects, that sort of thing. All rather minor compared to what I can do when I'm freed from the shackles of a mortal form.'

'Then why do you choose to remain down here?'

'I love human company. It interests me. One of the others has spent so little time among real people that he can no longer master an earthly tongue or a solid structure of flesh and bone. Consequently he exists in a rarefied celestial world that has no meaning. How was the rest of your week-end?'

'Boring,' I admitted. 'Yesterday I worked on some sale ideas for the store. Zack got drunk and passed out in the middle of the lounge rug. I wanted to watch TV but he was asleep on the remote and took a swipe at me every time I tried to move him.'

'Well, you won't be having many more week-ends like that, I can assure you. Today we'll begin to sort out your work situation. I must find a way to give you more confidence in yourself.'

I searched around for a towel and headed for the bathroom with Spanky following close behind. 'I've never been very good at that,' I admitted.

'Well, you will be by the time we're through. Notice how you already feel more assured this morning?'

'Not really, no.'

He gripped my bare forearm and held it tight. A tingling sensation, like a thousand tiny ice-needles, goosepimpled over my skin.

'How about now?'

I pulled my arm free in alarm and rubbed at it. 'What the hell was that?'

'I've just given you a little chemical surge that should help do the trick.'

'Wait a minute, I don't want drugs pumped into me.'

'Don't worry, it's naturally pure and organic, nothing that the body isn't used to handling. Now hurry up and shower. I want to visit your place of employment.'

I entered the bathroom still rubbing my arm. The thought of Spanky seeing how I was treated at work embarrassed me. I was becoming increasingly aware of the banality of my daily life. It was as though I existed above my body and was looking down on it, horrified by what I saw. I supposed it was the result of having someone around to monitor me all the time, a kind of spiritual social worker.

But Spanky didn't behave with the self-righteous conscience of a social worker. Showing me how to fit into modern urban society clearly meant learning to conduct my life in a morally dubious manner. I suppose I was naïve to imagine anything otherwise. It was all very well teaching someone to ape late twentieth century behaviour, but what if that behaviour was appalling? While ostensibly improving my life, didn't that make me as bad as those around me? I wasn't sure how much I wanted to change within myself, but I knew that when my limit was reached, I would have to tell Spanky to halt the process.

I shaved, showered and dressed, all the time listening to the daemon's advice. The snow had vanished by the time we reached the street. For once I arrived at work on time. Darryl was in before me, but then he usually was. Darryl was Born To Be In Furnishings. Dokie opened up the store first, but he worked different hours to the sales staff.

'What a depressing building. So much dust everywhere.' Spanky looked around at the gaudy sofas and dining-room suites, then blew his nose and tucked his handkerchief away into the air. 'This is your desk over here, isn't it?' Dokie was standing within hearing distance, so I projected my thoughts in reply.

It's my work station, yes. This is where I happily pass the waking hours of my day.

Suddenly, a sharp tingling jolt passed through my chest, a stinging electric shock. I fell back against a stack of *Tudor Rose* mock-Elizabethan laundry hampers in surprise. Dokie looked over at me, confused. 'You all right, Martyn?' He didn't wait for an answer. He was carrying a sink.

'I'm sorry,' Spanky apologized, lightly shaking out the tips of his fingers, 'but I won't listen to that kind of attitude.'

What attitude?

'That smug happy-with-my-lot chatter civil servants make. I'm amazed you haven't got a little wooden plaque mounted above the desk: *You don't have to be mad to work here, just mentally disenfranchised.* I'm going to knock that manner out of you, Martyn.'

He beckoned me forward, but having been hit with the equivalent of a cattle-prod I was loathe to move any nearer.

'For heaven's sake, I'm not going to hurt you. I couldn't do it even if I wanted to.'

Reluctantly, I stood before him. At close range, the perfection of his face was almost absurd, a physical anomaly.

'Why are you in this terrible job?' he demanded.

It's not that terrible. I get three weeks holiday a year, and there's the prospect of advancement . . .

'Do it again and I'll punish you more severely than before,' he warned. 'Just look at this place! It's a dead-end. It's not even part of a chain, where you could at least move into higher management. Everything stops with Max. You know that. You're not a stupid man, Martyn. You could have entered university. But rotting away in here, it's as if you've abandoned any thought of enjoying your life. When you were at school you must have had dreams, ambitions. What happened to them? Why did you let them all go? Why on earth *are* you here?'

I couldn't answer. I didn't want him to know about Joey. It was an area of my life that I hadn't yet learned to deal with. When the time came I would confront the problem alone, not with the help of some supernatural entity.

Later he came to know everything. But right then, with Darryl hovering in the background and the first customers of the morning entering the showroom, I refused to allow him full access to my mind.

Spanky knew. 'There are some parts of you I have trouble reading, Martyn,' he complained. 'You're subconsciously blocking something from me. All right, I'll drop the subject for now.' He looked about with distaste. 'Well, before you pick a new career for yourself, we might as well see what can be achieved in the old one. Better to leave this place on your own terms, wouldn't you agree?'

I nodded dumbly. Spanky waved his arm in the direction of Darryl's desk. 'How do you feel about your fellow salesman?'

I don't like him much.

'Why is that, do you think?'

He tries to curry favour with Max all the time.

'Well, it's working. He'll get the advancement, not you. There's already a note in his top drawer from Max, congratulating him on those sales ideas and hinting at "increased sales responsibility". Your colleague is out of shape but likes to think of himself as a sportsman, doesn't he?'

I don't know.

'Perhaps you somehow failed to notice the racquet handle sticking out of the sports bag he carried to work. According to his diary, he's playing squash at lunchtime today. I want you to challenge him to a game.'

I don't play squash.

'You do now.'

I haven't got the kit.

'I'll take care of that.'

He must already have a partner to play.

'Look.' He pointed over at Darryl, who was moving around his desk to answer the telephone. 'Oh dear, that's his partner calling to cancel their game. What's that he's saying? He has a terrible cold. Ventriloquism, Martyn, is a most useful talent.'

I watched until Darryl replaced the receiver. *Won't his partner still turn up at the court?* I asked.

'What a worrier you are! No, because I'll get his number from Darryl's phonebook and call him up in Darryl's voice. I'm not in the habit of providing explanations for everything, Martyn. Darryl has been misled. Now's your chance.'

Do I have to do this?

I hated the idea of charging around a sweat-reeking court chasing a little rubber ball. I couldn't see the point of it.

'It's all part of the plan, Martyn.' Spanky smiled and clapped a hand on my back. Don't look so alarmed. You want things to change, don't you?'

Of course I do ...

'Then ask him for a game.'

'I had no idea you played,' said Darryl, pulling his shirt over his head to reveal a sweat-stained undervest.

Neither did I, I thought, removing my racquet and twirling the handle in a less-than-expert fashion. Darryl had stared at me in amazement when I had suggested that he keep his lunchtime booking at the sports centre. The grey concrete locker room smelled of ancient plimsolls, and was filled with overweight red-faced executives who were prepared to risk sudden respiratory failure in the cause of fitness.

As we walked onto the court I realized that I had no idea where to stand. The gym kit Spanky had prepared for me was a perfect fit. Darryl's was far too tight, and stretched over his chubby torso forcing the flesh into banded folds, so that he looked like a joint of beef trussed up with string.

'I hope you like that touch,' said Spanky, sauntering past my opponent and pointing to his exposed midriff and minuscule shorts. 'I shrank his kit down one size.'

'I must have put this shirt on a hot wash,' said Darryl, puzzled. He raised an arm experimentally, and I half expected to see the fabric tear.

Spanky came over to me and showed me how to grip the racquet. He had changed into black gym-instructor sweatpants and a vest that displayed his muscles. There was a golden whistle around his neck.

'Now, this won't be as fast a game as your opponent usually plays, because he won't be able to turn easily in those shorts. It's a matter of wrist and touch, arm and leg strength, eye and hand coordination. That's the service box, just there, and the service line is above – are you following this?'

'I'm trying to.'

'Let me make this easier for you.'

He encircled my wrist with the fingers of his right hand and pressed hard. Once again, the strange tingling feeling passed through the nerves of my arm. Spanky looked pleased with himself.

'There. I've just given you the playing ability of Janet Morgan, the British Women's squash champion from 1950 to 1959. I couldn't remember the names of any male players. You'll automatically adopt her play characteristics. Just be careful how you walk across the court afterwards.'

He pointed up at the gallery to the rear of the court. 'I'll be up there watching. I'll rejoin you at the end of the game.'

Darryl served first, and I was amazed to find myself returning the volley with dazzling speed. I careened across the court, slamming the ball off the back wall with a dizzying right-arm smash that shocked us both.

I span and turned, volleying the ball as it caromed off the front in a blur of rubber. Darryl was dumbfounded. He fought to keep up, puffing from one end of the court to the other, while I hardly needed to stray from one spot. His returns were hampered by the tight shirt, which prevented him from raising his racquet directly above his head. Time and again the ball flashed past his disbelieving eyes as he tried to match my own lightning responses and failed.

By the end of the second game, (9-3, 9-1), he was a crimson sweating mess. Friction had heated the ball until it was barely comfortable to hold. We entered the third and final game of the lunch-hour. My opponent was fading fast, barely able to keep visual track of the ball, let alone follow it up with his body. I caught a brief glimpse of Spanky leaning over the rail, watching with interest as I volleyed back with my most powerful return so far.

The ball shot across the court like a rubber bullet. There was a terrible smack as it smashed into Darryl's left eye, knocking him back off his feet. He landed heavily on the floor, sitting down with a grunt and tipping over backwards. The eye was lost in a welter of blood, and the flesh around it was already swelling, the burst vessels spattering more blood across his cheek.

As he moaned and threw his hands across his face I ran for help, horrified by what I had done.

'It's a dangerous sport,' the doctor said, looking up at me. 'But this is one of the worst injuries I've ever seen on the court. That's a very powerful arm you have there.'

But the power had already deserted me. I had felt the familiar tingling sensation again as I left the sports centre, and every muscle in my body had started to grow sore.

One half of Darryl's face was bandaged, and he had been sedated. He was to be taken directly to the operating theatre, where the surgeons would try to save his eye.

'I feel terrible about this,' I said, watching as they pushed his trolley off along the hospital corridor. 'It's my fault.'

'You can't always keep track of your opponent's movements,' he said consolingly. 'It's too fast a game for that. There's no point in blaming yourself.'

During my time in the hospital, Spanky had been strangely absent. Now he reappeared as I started walking back toward the store. Max would be wondering where his salesmen were.

'I only meant you to beat him, not half kill him,' he said, falling into step with me. 'What did they say about the eye?'

'It looks bad, but they won't know exactly how much damage has been done for several days.'

'I'm sorry to hear that, but at least it leaves you clear for lunch.'

I looked at my watch. It was nearly 4.00 p.m. 'What do you mean?' I asked, suddenly suspicious.

'Lunch on Thursday, with Max. Darryl had invited him out. He figured he was going to be offered a promotion, and decided to beat Max to the punch with a proposition of his own. Now you'll be able to take his place.'

'Has it occurred to you that offering to take his place would be in extremely bad taste?' I asked. 'I don't want to achieve success through other people's misfortunes. I don't particularly like the guy, but it was my fault he was injured. I can't just step over him. It's wrong.'

'That's very noble of you, Martyn, but it doesn't pay to be too squeamish,' replied Spanky. 'You have to seize the opportunity while it's there. That's what Darryl was doing behind your back. Look around. You're living in a tasteless world. The streets are filled with the homeless, men and women down on their luck, scarred by changes in fortune. And walking around them, pretending that they simply don't exist, are people of property; the ten percent who own the ninety percent. Life cheats the poor, and the poorer they are the more it cheats them. Those who improve their circumstances do so through their own actions. There was a time when you were left alone if you did nothing. Now passivity is rewarded by downfall. You must take steps toward your own future, Martyn, even if it sometimes seems to be at the expense of others. You have to reinvent yourself. I won't always be here to help you.'

We had reached the glass wall of the furnishing store. Spanky opened the door for me. 'I have an appointment elsewhere,' he explained. 'Read the note I've left on your desk, and act upon it. Your career is about to undergo a change of fortune.'

CHAPTER ELEVEN

Careerism

IT WAS one of the oldest and grandest dining-rooms in the country. The crystal globes of seven great chandeliers loomed over our heads. Along one wall, before an acreage of hand-etched mirror, ran an inlaid mahogany bar stocked with over a hundred malt whiskies. Tables were circular, vast and separated from each other by a distance of a dozen feet. There were as many waiters as there were tables, and a strict hierarchy was observed among them.

An opaque view of the business district could be discerned between the heavy crimson curtains that draped the far wall. I had the impression that light never penetrated the room very deeply. Presumably the elderly members who dined here preferred not to be reminded of the passing time. I was standing by the reservation desk waiting for Spanky to show up, knowing that if he didn't I was lost.

I had never eaten in such a smart restaurant, and had certainly never set foot inside a place like this. According to Spanky, the Sir Richard Steele Dining Room had once been the recipient of every prestigious restaurant award, although its five-star rating had grown somewhat tarnished in the post-war years. Max had been shocked to the core when I had followed my personal daemon's instructions to invite him here. His lunch with Darryl had of course been cancelled, as my colleague had been forced to take indefinite leave.

'Sorry I'm late.' The familiar low voice at my side. Spanky was wearing a dress-suit of deep maroon wool, a starched wing-collar shirt and a red bow-tie. He looked like a cross between Oscar Wilde and Bertie Wooster.

Why are you dressed up? Are you eating with us?

'How did you guess? Were you surprised when Max accepted your replacement invitation?'

You could have knocked me down with a feather. Where have you been for the last two days?

'Preparing your future, old chap. Nothing too grand at the moment, but I've made a start on it.'

However did you get Max to agree to have lunch with me?

'Your boss is that perfect combination; a foodie and a snob. How could he have resisted the temptation to dine here? You told him your father was a member?'

And his father before him.

'Nice touch. I'll guide you through the social etiquette, but the small talk will be down to you.'

What are we here for?

'You'll see. I had to pull a lot of strings to get this table at such short notice. This isn't one of those flash-in-the-pan fashionable restaurants. It's old money. The reservations list here makes Quaglino's look like McDonalds. Just before you order, a portly gentleman with a grey moustache will approach your table. When he recognizes you, it's important that you recognize him equally. He'll shake your hand and with any luck, join you both for lunch.'

Who is he?

'Look sharp, you're about to be taken to your table.'

The walk across the huge dining-room seemed to last forever. I was the youngest person here by a decade, younger even than most of the waiters. I could feel people staring as I crossed the thick-pile carpet to one of the best-appointed tables. Spanky had already seated himself on the far side, across a hectare of dazzling linen. The waiter pulled out my chair and unctuously solicited my attention.

'Perhaps sir would care for an aperitif while awaiting his guest?'

'Order yourself a dry sherry.' Spanky named a particular bottle, I forget which, and I did as I was told. He heaved open the leather-bound menu and flicked through it, chuckling. 'They've got a cheek charging twenty-seven pounds for Steak Tartare.'

How am I ever going to pay for this?

'Oh, I forgot.' He felt in the pocket of his jacket and tossed over a wad of fifty pound notes. 'Use those. Don't worry, they're not forgeries. It's legal tender. Restaurants like this adore cash. They respect it more than plastic, which they still regard as newfangled and vaguely disreputable. You must remember to tip the *sommelier* separately.'

The who?

'The wine waiter, you clod. Why has so little knowledge of social etiquette survived to this era?'

I looked around at the other diners. Grey men in grey suits, nearly all of them overweight, a few haughty women with terrible teeth. I recognized several; Margaret Thatcher quietly talking in one corner, looking old and tired. Senior cabinet ministers. A legendary cabaret singer whom I'd long assumed was dead. I half expected to see Robert Maxwell tucking into the turbot.

'I know, it's not a very impressive sight, is it? Captains of industry. The men and women who hold the reins of the country. What a pitiful shower. Where are the great leaders now? Instead of the Gladstones, we're left with the Pitts.' Spanky looked blankly at me. 'A little political humour there.'

I'm sorry, I apologized, *I'm nervous. What am I going to say to him? What can I talk about?*

'Here's your chance to find out.'

Max was shuffling across the floor towards us. I hastily rose, knocking my napkin on to the floor. He was obviously more impressed with the restaurant than he was with me, and waved me back down into my seat. Once he had been seated and had ordered a drink, he turned toward me and stroked his jowls, a look of puzzlement settling on his face. I knew he had little respect for me. Perhaps there was something I could do this lunchtime that would begin to change his opinion.

'Well, Martyn, I must be paying you too much if you can afford to eat here.'

'Oh God, I knew he was going to say that,' groaned Spanky, lolling back in his seat.

Shut up!

'I don't do it very often,' I replied, following Spanky's original line. 'Only with my father.'

'I was due to have lunch with your unfortunate colleague, young Darryl.'

'I know –'

'You *didn't* know,' hissed Spanky, kicking me under the table.

'I know – that he must be feeling terrible today,' I covered. 'He may lose his eye.'

I could see Max was more interested in getting his hands on the menu than discussing the welfare of an employee. 'So,' he asked, eyebrows rising toward the red leather volume, 'to what do I owe this pleasure?'

To what does he owe this pleasure, Spanky? Help me!

'Perhaps I should explain the purpose of this lunch,' said Spanky. I could see him leaning forward on his elbows from the corner of my eye. 'Stall him for a moment.'

'Shall we order first?' I asked Max.

'Good idea.' He opened the vast menu and began to peruse the endless pages with great relish.

Spanky turned to me. 'Okay, listen carefully. I went through your boss's private correspondence. Six months ago he was made a generous offer for his horrible furnishing business. The potential buyer was a gentleman named Neville Syms, a wealthy member of the old school who owns a fair amount of office space in the West End. He was on the look-out for a business that was ripe for expansion, one he could disperse into his cash-draining empty properties. As you must know, Thanet's books are looking very solid. Max does very well out of the place, and could easily afford to expand. It seemed like a marriage made in heaven, but Max failed to take up the offer.'

Why? What was wrong with it?

'Syms is a drunk. He holds his booze well and he's still highly respected in the business community, but drinking and horses are his main interests. Max was worried that he'd run the business into the ground without a good manager. Syms offered to bring one in, but Max wouldn't trust his company to a stranger. It was too big a risk. So he left the offer on the table. Syms is still stuck with buildings he can't let, but Max won't play ball. That's the current state of play. You could have found this out yourself, you know, just by keeping your ears open around the office. Here comes Syms, right on time.'

A rotund racing-character of a man was waddling toward us.

His clothes made him look like an eccentric turf-accountant. He was wearing a loud chequered waistcoat, a fob watch, a navy blazer with gold buttons, corduroy trousers and brogues.

'I know he looks like a lunatic, but everyone fawns over him because he has so much property in Westminster, and his daughter's married to a minor royal.'

You've done a lot of research on this, haven't you? However did you get him here?

'That was the easy part, the communication system in the late twentieth century being what it is.'

'Max! You old devil! I didn't know you ate here!'

Syms pumped my boss's hand, shaking his entire body. He already sounded half-cut. Max smiled awkwardly, trapped between two states; irritation at someone he didn't want to see, and elation for being recognized in such a prestigious venue. As soon as the hand-pumping had slowed, he singled me out for presentation.

'I don't think you know my, er –' he began, but Syms cut in.

'Of course I do! Why, his father and I are old, old friends! How the devil are you, young Martyn?'

'I'm very well, thank you,' I replied in amazement. Syms punched Max on the shoulder with unnecessary force. 'I understand this young man is a damned good business manager. Did you know he looks after all his father's financial affairs? Of course, he's far too modest ever to admit it. Makes the chap a fortune, I hear. Wish he worked for me.'

Max stared over as if seeing me for the first time. I looked at Spanky, who was examining his nails in an exaggerated fashion.

'Are you about to have lunch? D'you mind if I join you?' Syms looked first at Max, then at me. And Max held out the chair for him.

After that, it was pretty plain sailing. Within the hour, the idea was firmly planted in Max's head that some sort of merger could be rearranged with Syms, with me elevated to the prime position of area manager. I was amazed at the speed with which he wrote Darryl out of the equation, and me in. So much for business scruples. The lunch took on an air of celebration. The beauty of Spanky's plan lay in its sheer simplicity; Max knew he would be able to keep me under his watchful eye, while Syms had seemingly been brainwashed into having complete faith in me. I just couldn't understand how this had been accomplished.

By 3.45 p.m. we were on cognac and cigars, and Syms was arranging visitations with his lawyers. He went on and on, planning prime West End sites and conjuring images of infinite profit while his prospective partner nodded greedily. I had never seen Max looking like this. As he watched Syms trace his fork across the tablecloth it was clear that he had fully succumbed. In a matter of hours he had been transformed from a sourpuss into a happy man. He kept smiling at me. It was grotesque. He had the wrong kind of mouth for smiling. Too many teeth.

I paid the bill, which stopped my blood circulating for a moment when I unfolded it, and tipped the correct amounts to the right people, thanks to Spanky's continual good advice. In a unique gesture of magnanimity, Max gave me the remainder of the afternoon off.

I walked back across the park with my daemon.

'Come on, then,' I asked as soon as we were alone, 'how did you nobble him?'

'Nobble him? My dear fellow, he's not a racehorse.' He withdrew a cigar he had taken from the restaurant and lit it with great concentration. 'I told you, I'm not going to keep explaining my methods.'

'Just once more.'

'Oh, very well. I simply visited Syms as your father ...'

'You've never met my father.'

'All right then, as someone I imagine to be similar to your father – and proposed a deal. I told him he'd be in with a chance if he championed you.'

'But why would Syms believe him? I mean, you?'

'Because your father had the right credentials.'

'I suppose you forged documents to make him look good.'

'Nothing so complicated or dishonest, I assure you.'

'Aside from the moral issues involved here, how could I ever live up to everyone's expectations? I think I should be allowed to prove my own worth.' It felt as if I was getting deeper into an area of high risk with every passing day.

'Of course you should, but this way you'll actually be offered a chance. Opportunity is nine tenths of the battle. I know you're up to it. Examine yourself and think about your capabilities. Soon you'll be able to show everyone what you can really do.' He blew a stream of blue smoke in my face. 'I mean, you don't have to thank me or anything.'

'I'm very grateful, it's just –'

'What, Martyn, what?' Spanky cried, exasperated. 'You're finally going to get all the things you wanted in life. Why must you feel so guilty all the time? You want to meet another beautiful woman? We'll do it tonight. You want a career with a future? I'm about to hand you the key. I can't give you limitless wealth or movie star looks. I can't change the world around you. I can't halt famine, prevent disease or end political corruption. I can only show you how to change yourself to suit your own ends. Isn't that enough?'

I tried to explain how I felt, but my emotions wouldn't articulate themselves into words. I wanted what he was offering; it just felt wrong to get it this way. Looking back, I suppose it all seemed too easy, like looting a store or jumping a queue. I remembered my father saying that money only had a value if it was earned.

Spanky suddenly removed the cigar from his mouth and watched me, his forehead creasing. 'You're thinking about your family again. As soon as I try to read your thoughts you close them off to me. Why?'

'It's nothing,' I lied. 'My parents are very ordinary and boring. You wouldn't be interested in them.'

'We'll soon see, won't we?' He kicked at a stone on the path, and where it landed a purple orchid grew, forcing its way through the grass as if appearing through time-lapse photography. With each step Spanky took, I noticed that tiny sapphire flowers were springing up in his footprints.

'What do you mean?'

'I think I should meet your parents this week-end. Don't you?'

I certainly did not, but the matter was out of my hands. So, on the Saturday afternoon of the following week-end, I reluctantly took Spanky down to meet them.

Parenting

TWELVETREES IS a suburban estate in Kent, a satellite town of clipped emerald lawns and gleaming cars and neat rows of identical houses with fake lead-light windows. It was built to provide homes for first time buyers and young families who needed a base from which to commute to the city. As the recession hit, it became populated by retired couples who could no longer afford the upkeep of larger houses, and families whose breadwinners had died and whose businesses had failed.

Twelvetrees had few shops and virtually no local amenities; after all, the residents were supposed to be commuters, shopping in the city. The area took its name from the dozen tall elms that rose in a single line across the brow of a hill. According to legend, the trees formed a natural barrier that once hid highwaymen from their victims. In the late nineteen seventies they were torn down, and the hill was levelled so that the hideous conglomeration of banjo crescents and cul-de-sacs that constituted the town could be built over the site. The name was then resurrected to commemorate the site of natural beauty that had been destroyed by the estate.

My parents had moved here over a decade ago, and still

didn't know anyone. My father never noticed the austerity of our surroundings because he spent most of his waking hours at the office.

As we walked along the street leading to my family's house, Spanky peered over the concrete fence separating the pavement from the barren brown fields. A car backfired, and starlings were shocked like cinders into a lowering sky.

'God's green earth,' he fumed. 'See what they've done to it.'

'You should try being stuck here as a teenager, hanging around in bus shelters looking for something to do.' We were both wearing raincoats to counteract the change in the weather. I had asked Spanky why he couldn't stop the rain from touching us with his powers, and he'd explained that he could only make it appear as if we weren't getting wet. His illusions were fun, but it seemed that they didn't have much practical use.

'Tell me about your family, Martyn. I want to be prepared. And don't give me that stuff about how I wouldn't be interested. I need to know everything before I can help. They're the root of your problems. Parents always are.'

I wondered how much I could admit to him, or myself.

'Okay,' I said. 'Their names are Joyce and Gordon. Joyce is very quiet. She used to have a job before we moved here but Gordon made her give it up. She doesn't go out much now. Watches daytime TV and cleans the house all the time. She won't talk to the neighbours, says they're common. She suffers from fits of depression and cries over nothing at least once a day. Gordon disappears to the office whenever there's a crisis, which is most of the time. Mother likes to pretend he's a busy executive and not just a low-paid timeserver in an insurance firm. I don't think he can handle the pressure of being at home. He's more comfortable staying at work. A few years ago they stopped going on holiday together. Gordon says he can't afford the time off, and Joyce wouldn't go without him. My sister Laura is agoraphobic and hardly ever comes out of her room. She makes my mother look like a socialite. My brother Joey, as I think you know, is dead.'

'When did he die?'

'Just over four years ago. This is the house.' I went to open the gate for Spanky but he passed right through it before I had the chance. The paved pathway led to a pebbled glass door decked by ornamental carriage lamps. At first there was no answer when I sounded the doorbell chimes. Then a vacuum cleaner stopped, and I could see the blurred form of my mother approaching. Spanky had asked me not to call them first. He wanted to catch them unprepared, in order to study them under normal circumstances.

'Darling, this is a surprise.'

She held out her cheek to be kissed. My mother was old before her years, with tired blue eyes that must have once been very attractive. Her hair had greyed, but my father would not allow her to tint it, warning her of the dire consequences of looking like a tart. It was blurred about her head, in need of a perm. 'I wish you'd have told me you were coming down. The house is in a dreadful mess.'

As I walked through the spotless, gleaming lounge where a TV game show played without an audience I looked back at Spanky, who shrugged. 'I don't see a mess. Maybe she saw us coming and quickly shovelled it under the couch.'

'Your father is at work,' she continued, heading into the kitchen and filling a kettle with water. 'I've barely seen him at all this week.'

'Where's Laura?' I caught Spanky's eye again. He had removed his wet overcoat and was hanging it on the back of a chair.

'In her room.' The careful matter-of-factness in her voice failed to disguise her concern.

'She still doesn't come downstairs much, then?'

'Well, she has her own television, and she prefers to eat alone.'

She left school in the middle of term when she was diagnosed as suffering from agoraphobia, I explained to Spanky. *Still think you can help us?*

'I've certainly got my work cut out, I agree.' He glanced over at my mother, who was briskly rubbing a spot on the sink with a dishcloth. 'I see a lot of suburban families like this. They paper over the cracks by filling their days with little ceremonies. I think we should start by taking a look at your sister.'

'Can I go up and see Laura?' I asked.

'That's a good idea, darling,' replied Joyce distractedly. 'I have to put the dinner on. Your father will be back soon.'

'These wall ornaments have no dust on them,' said Spanky as we climbed the stairs to my sister's room. 'She must get up in the middle of the night to wipe them down.'

I knocked gently on the bedroom door. 'Laura? It's Martyn.'

'Go away, Martyn.'

'Please open the door.'

'I can't.'

'Why not?'

'I don't want to see you today.'

'What's her problem?' asked Spanky.

You'll soon find out.

'Laura, please let me in. I've come all the way down from London, especially to visit you.'

There was a moment of silence, then the lock snicked off and I was able to open the bedroom door. She'd put on even more weight since I last saw her. Her neck, torso and thighs were insulated with rolls of pallid fat.

'Jesus Christ, she's the size of a fucking house!' Spanky's jaw fell open. 'No wonder she doesn't go out. She can't get through the door. I haven't seen anything this enormous since *Jurassic Park*.'

Don't be so damned rude. She's my sister.

'I can't wait to meet your father. Are you familiar with the term *dysfunctional*?'

'Hello, Martyn,' she said shyly, looking away from the television. She didn't rise to greet me. I wondered if she was capable of standing without help. 'How have you been?'

Her shoulder-length blonde hair fell in greasy ropes on either side of her ears. It was late afternoon, and she was wearing Bugs Bunny pyjamas. Behind her on the floor was a plastic Safeways bag full of what looked like empty chocolate bar wrappers.

'I'm fine. Mum's cooking dinner. Will you come down and have something with us?'

'I don't think so. I already ate.' A TV commercial for breakfast cereal caught her eye and she watched it as she spoke. 'I don't like to go downstairs too often.' The room was decorated with bilious pink and yellow flowered wallpaper. There were teddy bears, magazines and stuffed dolls everywhere. My sister, at the age of almost seventeen, was sitting on the floor with a comic called *Let's Pretend* in one meaty fist.

'Why not? You must get bored being up here all the time.'

'If I go down to eat, Dad always starts picking on me. Then Mum tells him to leave me alone, and they end up arguing. Some things never change.'

'I wish you'd stick up for yourself when Dad starts.'

'Why? You never did.'

'I tried to,' I insisted.

'Come on, Joey fought all your battles for you.' She watched the television steadily. 'I can't blame you for running off after he died.'

'Christ, no wonder you left home, Martyn.' Spanky was walking around the room, picking up each of the dolls in turn, checking to see if they were wearing knickers. 'Is she always this aggressive?'

Most of the time. She hit my mother once and nearly knocked her out.

'All right, leave me alone with her. I need to get inside Laura's mind for a few minutes. This shouldn't be as difficult as it looks.'

You think so?

'Sure. Physical changes start up here.' He tapped the side of his head. 'It's just a matter of knowing what to look for. Go and give your mother a hand. I'll be down shortly.'

Reluctantly, I left the bedroom and closed the door behind me. I stood on the landing for a moment, listening, but heard nothing unusual. Heading downstairs, I watched my mother moving around the kitchen. She took comfort in order, removing a spoon from a neat row of cutlery, arranging the dinner plates with their edges touching. I tried to think back to when Joey was still with us. We were set in our ways even then. Everyone had their own little routines to follow. After his death we stopped sharing anything at all.

I laid the table, then watched some television. We were just getting ready to serve the food when my father came in. He didn't seem too pleased to see me, and nodded a curt hello before heading for his study to dump his raincoat and briefcase. He re-emerged still wearing a jacket and tie, and made straight for the table, seating himself as if in a restaurant.

Nothing had changed here, that was for sure. I had now managed to limit my trips home to around three a year, and every time I saw my father I considered reducing their frequency.

'I suppose you've already spoken to your sister,' said Gordon, unfolding a napkin in his lap and waiting for someone to serve him. He never called her Laura anymore, only *your sister* to me and *your daughter* to his wife.

'Does she ever come out of her room?'

'You'd know if you came here more often, wouldn't you?' He looked toward the kitchen. In the last few years his eyes had grown beady and hard, like a rat's, and it was no longer possible to tell what he was thinking. I decided not to engage him in conversation during the meal. He was capable of finding the negative side of anything we might discuss.

I was wondering if Spanky would manage to get Laura down for dinner when he appeared alone at the top of the stairs.

How did it go? I asked, watching as my father sat back, allowing Joyce to place a pair of dry-looking lamb chops on his plate.

'Fine. Her problem is nothing to do with agoraphobia. She's just terrified of boys, because she knows that they laugh about her size behind her back. She remembers them liking her before she started putting on weight. I assume that was just after her brother died.'

When she started eating heavily we took her to the doctor, but he thought more emotional damage would be caused by forcing her on to a diet. After that, no one told her to stop because she said it made her feel better. Can you do anything to help her?

'I already did.' He seated himself at the end of the table, in a spare chair.

Hey, that's Joey's seat.

'He's long dead, Martyn. You said so yourself. What did he die of?'

A cold, I replied.

'Must have been a pretty bad one. I don't know why you won't let me –'

What did you do to help her?

'I won't tell you just yet. I don't want to alarm you.' He watched as Joyce ladled thick gravy on to my father's plate. 'My God, those chops look disgusting. What did she cook them in, a nuclear reactor?'

What do you mean, you don't want to tell me? Can you help my sister or not? I can't reach her anymore.

'I took care of that. I gave her a time-released medication that will stop her from worrying too much about what I've done. You won't believe the change you'll see in her during the next few weeks. I'm not concerned about Laura now. Her problem will gradually take care of itself. It's your father who bothers me most.'

'You're quiet, Martyn,' said my mother. 'Is that enough for you?' I looked down at the burned chop and the mound of squashy, overcooked vegetables on my plate.

'Fine, thanks.'

He's just a workaholic. All he ever thinks about is his job. What about Joyce? Can you do anything for her?

'That depends. I already had a little poke about in her skull, hope you don't mind. She's not terribly responsive. She feels she doesn't please your dad any more. They stopped having sex quite a while ago. She can't understand what she's doing wrong. If I can put him right, it'll help your mother out. She needs to have her self-esteem restored. You must have noticed how your father hardly even bothers to look at her. I presume you realize he's having an affair.'

Gordon? I stared at him. *My old dad? You have got to be joking.*

'He's seeing a woman in his accounts department. It's been going on for quite a while as far as I can tell. Sometimes they stay late and do it in his office.'

That's disgusting.

'You're telling me. I only probed his psyche for a little background information. I didn't expect to stumble across his smutty fantasies. It was quite a shock. At least now I have some material to work with. I think I can help him out.'

That leaves my mother.

When he had finished, Gordon stared at the ceiling and sucked his teeth noisily. We both turned to watch as Joyce checked my father's plate, watching him for a sign of approval.

'She'll mostly change when he does, but I can probably get rid of this cleaning fetish she's developed. Let me think about it. I'll leave you to enjoy your dessert in peace.'

He rose sharply from the table. 'Thanks for the day out. I'll catch up with you tomorrow.'

'We're having strawberry mousse,' announced my mother, sounding disconcertingly as if she was addressing Spanky.

Wait, where are you going?

'To check out the foundations of the house. There's something I must do before I go. I can set the changes in motion, but it'll be about six weeks before you notice any real difference in your family.'

Spanky leaned against the door jamb, studying the ceiling. He seemed to be looking for something. 'Do you know who they're insured with?'

I can't remember offhand. Why?

'Oh, no matter. I can find out easily enough.'

My father ran his tongue over his teeth and probed his gums with a finger. My mother watched him carefully, her fork poised over her untouched meal. If she was waiting to be complimented on the food, it was going to be a long evening. Neither of them noticed my eyeline constantly straying to the door.

You really think they'll change?

'Oh, I can guarantee it.'

You won't hurt them in any way, will you? I mean, with Laura being the way she is and everything –

'Nothing I do will really harm them physically, I promise you. Sudden changes are bound to cause a certain amount of emotional pain in the process. You can't make an omelette without –'

I love them, Spanky. I know they don't seem much to you. They're all the family I have.

'I know you care. Changing them will help you too. You'll just need to have a little courage. Now, I need one favour from you in order to make it work.'

Tell me. I'll try my best.

'Whatever happens, I don't want you to have any communication with them for six weeks.'

What if they call me and it's urgent?

'I'm sure they'll make it sound urgent, very urgent indeed, but you have to resist the temptation to see them. No matter how often they call you, no matter how many messages they leave, it's imperative that you ignore them. If you don't, your interference will only complicate matters further and adversely affect the outcome of my plans. Will you promise for me? We need a little trust around here, Martyn.'

I watched as his eyes studied mine. He was certainly

changing my world, and it hadn't hurt me so far – but this was different. This was fooling with someone else's life. But I had failed to trust him before, and he had left. I couldn't risk that happening again, not when my life was finally getting back on course.

All right, I finally agreed, *I promise not to interfere.*

'That's a good boy,' grinned Spanky, materializing a long-handled shovel in his hands and raising it to his shoulder. 'Now I can get to work.'

Socialization

I NEEDED to believe that Spanky could do what he'd promised.

I'd awoken one day to find myself sinking in quicksand, and here was someone standing by with a rope, offering to pull me out. I wasn't in a position to question his motives, because he had no known precedent. To whom could I compare him? How could I know if he was real? I could hardly discuss the problem with friends. *I recently met this daemon muse. You know, like the one who appeared to Socrates. Only we went shopping and he gave me a haircut . . .*

Spanky had me at a disadvantage, and I was sure that he knew it.

On Tuesday morning I arrived at work to find a message on my desk from Lottie;

Your mother phoned just after you left last night. Sounded upset. Wants you to call her – urgent!

It took considerable willpower to screw the notepaper into a ball and toss it in the bin. Darryl still wasn't back, so I had to open up the tills and sort through the rest of the week's orders by myself. Max arrived in an absurdly cheerful mood, spreading *bonhomie* through the early morning customers like bubonic plague. At eleven he called me into his office to inform me of his successful meeting with Syms's lawyers.

'Neville is very impressed with you,' he said, beaming creepily at me. 'He's keen on raising you to executive status. But I think it's a little early for that.' Max enjoyed wielding power. He had no other way of getting people to respect him. 'Why don't we see how you get on here for a while, running the showroom by yourself? We don't know when your colleague will be returning to work.'

So my promotion was largely by default. Max had an eager, irksome son, Paul, still in his early twenties. There was no doubt in my mind that he would draft the boy into the new set-up at the first available opportunity. To achieve a position of real power, I would probably have to find some way of bettering – or forming an alliance with – his ambitious offspring.

After lunch I called the hospital to speak with Darryl, but he refused to talk to me. The doctor apologized, and warned me that her patient had been more traumatized by the accident than she had hoped for. The surgeons had been unable to save his eye. At the moment Darryl was refusing to consider long-term plans to return to work, and was being treated for depression. I felt terrible; the doctor warned me not to blame myself. It had been a freak accident, a thousand to one chance. A minute piece of glass had been found embedded in the surface of the squash ball. Part of it had loosened on impact, entering the pupil and making the damage to Darryl's eye more severe. There was the possibility of a court case against the manufacturers of the sports equipment. I begged her to let me speak with him, but she told me her patient was sleeping and rang off.

S o c i a l i z a t i o n   111

Without Darryl my workload had suddenly increased. My colleague's forte had been customer management; his weakness, form-filling. My talents, such as they were, had always lain in the reverse. But now, thanks to Spanky's 'charismatic osmosis', I found it easier to persuade strangers to part with their money, while I proved to have a natural flair of my own for the deskwork.

In addition to selling several complete bathroom and kitchen suites, I followed up a lead Spanky had given me, contacting someone who supplied a number of office buildings in the area, and gave him a hell of a sales pitch. I also off-loaded a number of previously unsaleable items including a *Duchess of Marlborough* pedestal sink and a beige candlewick *Mata Hari* laundry hamper. By the end of the day we had taken record orders.

My feelings of guilt over Darryl's accident were forming a proper perspective. Max was happy. Even Dokie was walking about with an inane smile on his face, humming tunelessly. At the back of my mind, though, was a nagging doubt over the phonecall from my mother. If something was wrong, I wanted to know what it was. But I had made a promise. If I didn't keep it, Spanky would probably disappear forever.

I arrived back at the flat to find Zack crawling around the lounge floor, papering it with pages from dozens of old magazines.

'I'm doing you a favour, man,' he explained. 'Helping you come to terms with your spirit infestation.'

'My what?' I asked, heading for the kitchen and finding there was no milk. 'You were supposed to pick up supplies today, Zack.'

'Sorry, man, I've been busy. You confided in me about your daemon, right? So I've been checking it out for you.'

'Listen, he was just a guy in a bar. I must have imagined the rest.' I had to make light of it. There was no telling when Spanky might next appear, and he had told me not to mention his existence to anyone.

'Come on, I know better than that. I heard you talking to someone in your bedroom the other morning, and there wasn't anyone in there but you. You've been acting strange for a while now.'

I returned to the lounge and helped Zack gather up the loose pages, which he placed in a cardboard file.

'All right,' he nodded, 'I'll wait until you're ready to tell me what's going on. I'll keep the file. You'll find some interesting stuff here on the subject of daemoniality. And it's not all good,' he added darkly.

'I'm sure it isn't.' I headed for my bedroom to change out of my suit. It had been a hard day. For the first time since I had started working at Thanet, I felt as if I had achieved something. It was a good feeling.

I thought Spanky might put in an appearance, but he failed to show. I lay on my bed reading for a while, and fell asleep. When I awoke it was 1.00 a.m., and Zack had left a message for me on the hall telephone pad, something he never normally remembered to do.

Your mother says to call her. Very important!

After a brief flash of guilt I tore up the piece of paper, and went to bed.

The week passed in a blur of hard sell and sales slips. Business was booming, and I often managed the store single-handed while Max arranged his deal with Syms. I empathized with my cash-rich customers as I guided them towards top-of-the-line suites like the *Princess Arthur Of Connaught Lounge Ensemble*, under the watchful eye and beaming smile of my superior, and even managed to flog a set of aubergine-coloured armchairs that had defeated the combined might of the sales staff.

Surely Max would feel uncomfortable about using his son to pull rank on me now. Even Lottie stopped by after a particularly tough sell and mumbled something about me doing a wonderful job. I was touched; praise for my work was a new concept.

By Friday I was beginning to wonder if I'd ever see Spanky again. I'd been too busy to think about him much. I was closing up for the evening when he reappeared on one of the stock cupboards and nearly gave me a heart attack. He was wearing psychedelic swimming trunks and carrying an enormous fluorescent blue surf-board. His hair was still wet.

'Do you have something I can dry myself with?' he asked, looking around.

'Come with me.'

I took him to one of the bathroom displays and threw him a towel. He had left a trail of wet footprints across the store.

'Where on earth have you been?'

'Hawaii. The waves were really fierce today. You surf?'

'There's nowhere to surf around here.' I seated myself on a stack of *Empress* candlewick pedestal covers and watched as he dried his hair. By this time, nothing Spanky did surprised me. He could have ridden into the store driving a coach and four and I wouldn't have batted an eye. But it was good to see him again.

'You've been on vacation?'

'I had to take some time off. Your family are driving me insane.'

'I keep getting messages to call my mother. What are you doing to them, for God's sake?'

'They're undergoing radical catharsis, Martyn. I'm shaking them from the shell of their complacency. Don't worry, it's not as rough as it sounds. You'll see the results soon enough. Contacting them now would only cause complications. So, how have you been?'

'Great, Max has promoted me. I'm getting a salary raise. But I think he's bringing his son in as a replacement for Darryl.'

'Does the son have any prior experience?'

'None at all, to my knowledge.'

'That's unfair. We'll have to do something about that. Your career advancement is occurring too slowly.'

'No more squash games, please.' I told him about the outcome of Darryl's operation.

'I'm sorry, Martyn, but accidents happen. No one else has been hurt, have they?'

'No,' I was forced to agree. I could tell that my daemonic personal trainer had something up his sleeve. There was a glint in his eye I had seen before, and was learning to recognize as a sign of excitement.

'We're going somewhere tonight, aren't we?' I asked, unable to stand the suspense.

'We most certainly are.'

He produced a gilt-edged card covered in scrolled lettering. He opened his eyes wide, playing the *faux-naif*. 'Martyn, would you like to come to a party with me?'

The black Versace evening suit was a perfect fit, the shoes less so. 'I misjudged those by half a size,' admitted Spanky. 'You should have worn thicker socks.'

We arrived at Park Lane's Grosvenor House and made our

way through a cordon of onlookers, through a battery of shouting, strobing photographers to the steps of the grand ballroom. Our table was a gigantic white disc that seated ten guests. The floral centrepiece was so luxuriant that it obscured the people sitting opposite. Spanky was standing at my side, annoyed at not having a place to sit.

Quick, grab that spare chair by the wall. I tried to point surreptitiously. *What on earth are we attending?*

The place was full of theatre celebrities, black ties for the men, sequins for the ladies, much air-kissing and ass-kissing.

'The British Theatre Awards. Congratulations, Martyn, you're a famous playwright.'

I'm a what? Jesus, Spanky, I've only been to the theatre a handful of times in my life.

'I trust they were illuminating experiences.'

Starlight Express and No Sex Please, We're British aren't exactly benchmarks in quality drama. I hate the theatre. It's full of boring pseuds.

'Don't worry. A lot of people feel the same way. Look, there's Andrew Lloyd Webber. Let's kill him.'

Couldn't we have gone to a football match instead? The season's started.

'Certainly not,' said Spanky firmly. 'Whether you like it or not, this is part of your education.'

Anyone who had ever appeared in an acclaimed Shakespearian production was here. Writers, producers and directors of every nationality had filled the room to its corners. The brightest stars in the theatrical firmament were being witheringly nice to one another, presumably on the one occasion of the year when they could be bothered to do so.

Over by the stage, Salman Rushdie was talking to some very nervous-looking young men. To the far right of me Kenneth

Branagh and Emma Thompson were holding court. Beyond them I could see Vanessa Redgrave and Arthur Miller. I was the only person there I'd never heard of. I had never felt so out of place in my life.

'This is a test, Martyn. I know you don't like these people, but I want you to practise the art of socializing tonight. If you're sharp-witted enough, you'll be invited to the winners' private party afterwards.'

How am I going to do that? I can't even string a decent sentence together. I work in a furniture store. I can't hold my own with these people.

'Rubbish. Your vocabulary is excellent. You just need more confidence. Roll up your sleeve and give me your arm. It'll look a little odd to the other guests, but they're so wrapped up in themselves they won't give it a thought.'

I did as I was bade, and he locked his hands around my wrist in a firm grip. Once again, a dizzying cold sensation ran through my bones.

'There, now you have a little of my own chemical structure, enough to give you the confidence you need. Let's see what you can do with it. Don't worry, I'll be around to bail you out if you get stuck.'

I'm stuck already.

'Then I'll jump-start you.' Spanky slapped me hard on the back and promptly vanished.

Something flashed inside my head.

'I think that instead of continuing to rely on texts considered definitive and sacred,' I heard myself saying very loudly, 'it's essential to put an end to the subjugation of the theatre to the text.'

I looked around the table, which had filled with famous faces. Arthur Miller glanced up and scowled.

Socialization   117

Everyone did.

I could feel beads of sweat breaking out on my forehead. I was going to kill Spanky the next time I saw him.

'Isn't that what Artaud said?' asked a very attractive woman with cropped blonde hair. My remark had caught her in the act of ladling smoked salmon into her mouth.

'I, uh –' My muse had placed a single quote in my brain and deserted me. 'That is –'

'It's not a question of supressing the spoken language, but of giving words the importance they have in dreams, isn't that right?'

I peered around the floral arrangement. Emma Thompson was talking to me.

Oh God, she was talking to *me*.

I desperately racked my brain for something remotely intelligent to say. I mean, she had an *Oscar*.

I looked back at her blankly. She was waiting for a reply. She gave me a benign smile, but she was waiting.

'Go on, then, I'll give you one more,' I heard Spanky whisper in my ear.

'We can't go on prostituting the idea of theatre whose only value is in its excruciating magical relation to reality and danger,' I announced.

'Now, I *do* know that's a quote from Artaud,' said Emma, wagging a finger at me. 'Of course, he went mad, so he may have succumbed to that magical relation himself.'

'I greatly admire the Theatre Of Cruelty,' said the glamorous blonde woman, finishing her salmon. 'I assume you share the late Antonin's interests, Mr . . .?'

'Ross, Martyn Ross.'

'And what is your connection with the theatre?'

'I'm – a playwright.'

'Forgive me, I'm not familiar with your work.' She was about to lower her eyes to her plate once more. I knew that Spanky was somewhere watching me, judging my response.

'Nor, unfortunately, am I with yours,' I said plainly.

To my surprise, she raised her head and smiled. 'Do you mean to say that I have finally found someone in this room who is unfamiliar with my Desdemona?'

'Darling, I'm sure everyone here has seen your Desdemona,' said Kenneth. Somebody tittered sycophantically.

'Obviously this young man hasn't,' said the actress, holding out a languid hand for me to shake or kiss, I wasn't sure which. 'Amanda Gielgud. No relation.'

I opted for kissing. 'How gallante,' she sighed, carefully rearranging her *décolletage*.

'Tell me, Mr Ross, is there a part in your new play for me?'

'How do you know I've written a new play?' I asked.

'You wouldn't be here if you hadn't. You'd be at home in a sweat, trying to think of a second act. What do you write about?'

Time to wing it. I looked up at the ceiling, narrowing my eyes in what I hoped was a gesture of intense concentration. 'I try to isolate the sense of betrayed *angst* that inhabits the soul of modern urban man,' I said.

'So no choreography there, then,' said Kenneth.

'Don't be mean, Ken,' chided Emma. 'He's just being playful, Mr Ross. I'm sure your plays are perfectly marvellous.'

She beamed at me charmingly.

'You certainly made a hit with the Branaghs,' Amanda hissed, clearly impressed. 'Would your plays make me feel wretched?'

You don't know how wretched, I thought.

'I suppose it's all modernist stuff, two stools and a stick to represent a fish-gutting shed, that sort of thing.'

'Yes, that sort of thing.'

We downed several bottles of champagne during the interminable awards, following each round of polite applause with sips from fluted glasses. Afterwards, we climbed the great curving staircase arm in arm. We had both been invited to the winners' party. I had done it. I had passed the test. I hoped Spanky was still watching.

Amanda stopped by the gilded balustrade and slid her fingers over the buttons of my shirt. 'I don't want to go to the other bash,' she announced in a slight slur. 'I've a better idea. Come with me.'

She took my hand and led me along an empty corridor toward the private suites, away from the other guests. When she pulled on the handle of a walk-in service cupboard which was clearly familiar to her, I began to suspect that I had made another conquest. I seemed to be attracting a definite type of woman. She had her hand inside my trousers before I had managed to pull the door shut behind me.

There in the warm darkness, surrounded by the clean smells of soap powder and air freshener, we disrobed, and she guided me inside her with a sharp gasp of pleasure.

'Well, well, well,' said Spanky, appearing on one of the broad tablecloth shelves above us. 'So you're managing your conquests without my help now, are you? Quite a little sex-monkey. I thought you wanted romance.'

She started it. Can you come back later? Your timing is terrible.

Amanda was making noisy gasping sounds beneath me, gripping herself around my erection.

'I take it you've decided to skip the foreplay on this occasion.

I thought you ought to know that she loves being tied up.'

No thanks. Sexual perversion isn't my forte.

'Give it a try. You'll be amazed by the change in her, uh, enthusiasm.' He passed me an unfolded napkin.

'Go on – take it.'

Oh well.

I slipped the napkin around her wrists and knotted it to the pipe above her head. This was a lot harder than it sounds, as the cupboard was in semi-darkness and I had to stand on tiptoe. Amanda began squealing, and wrenching me forward into her. Her bared buttocks began hitting the rear wall so hard that towels, toilet rolls and tablecloths began showering down on us.

'There, what did I tell you?' I heard Spanky laughing softly in the dark. The shelves were rattling violently, and my balls were being crushed by the rotating forcefulness of her pelvis. I felt sure that Amanda's prolonged, stentorian orgasm must be attracting attention to the cupboard.

When she finally released me from her, I ejaculated violently across her dress with a force that shocked both of us. For a few moments there was no sound but the ragged catching of our breath as I untied her.

'Darling, you have no idea how hard it is getting semen off a sequin,' she laughed, attempting to rearrange her clothes. I was unable to reply. I felt like I'd been in a car wreck. With trembling hands I attempted to rebutton my shirt. After three tries, she helped me.

When Amanda and I emerged from the cupboard, we caught sight of each other and started laughing helplessly. Her makeup had run and her hair was matted with sweat. My tie was over one half of my collar and my shirt-tail was sticking out of my flies.

'You gave a very professional performance,' she said, kissing me lightly on the ear. 'Do I get the part?'

'I'm not much of a playwright,' I confessed.

'That's okay,' she replied. 'I'm not much of an actress.'

'Well?' asked Spanky as we walked home across the park. 'What are you thinking about?'

'I never realized how easy it was to have sex with beautiful women,' I replied. 'I never thought for a moment that someone like me could have an experience like – that. Christ, I've always been shy before.'

'You didn't know me before.'

'I think I want a cigarette.'

'I thought you didn't like to smoke.'

'I thought I didn't like the theatre.'

Spanky rolled back on the wet grass and laughed. Moments later he jumped up and pointed back towards town. The branches scraped shadows across his eyes, making them glitter like emeralds.

'Look over there, Martyn,' he said, 'the lights of the city. Anything is possible. Everything is within reach. The trouble with these times is, we're all a little shook up, a little too wary of each other, too frightened to swim in dark pools.' He stepped closer, twisting his body into the breeze.

'Our lives are full of small frights, Martyn. Sudden violence, silent infections, secret horrors eat into our closed worlds and swarm around us. Our homes offer no protection from paranoia. Everything is too bunched up. We overdose on images. Wasting brown bodies on the TV news, babies with flies in their eyes, then slimmers baring tanned breasts on white sand. You let things bother you, or you shrug your shoulders and get on with your life. As a child you imagine a peaceful old age spent pruning roses and dandling grandchildren. As an adult you sleep with a knife under your pillow.'

He touched me lightly on the arm. 'Don't worry, you'll make your money and settle down with your love, but first you must taste the night.'

'What does this mean?' I asked

'It means we have to go dancing,' he replied.

'Now?'

'Now.'

Half an hour later I was standing in my usual spot at the edge of a dancefloor in a bar called Club Shame, still dressed in my tux. I hadn't seen Spanky for the last few minutes, and was starting to wonder where he had gone. Two Midwestern American girls who looked like they were visiting the country from another decade kept telling me I had a cute accent and were trying to get me to dance with them.

'I don't like this kind of music,' I bellowed above a reggaefied dancemix just as it ended suddenly, stranding my words without a background. People were starting to move to the front of the club. A spotlight glowed onstage.

'Ladies and gentlemen,' announced the compère, 'please put your hands together for tonight's live PA direct from New York City – MC Spanky!'

And there he was. Live on stage. With no shirt and some kind of complicated bondage waistcoat, hammering white rap into a microphone. Crowd-pleasing funky stuff. For the next twenty minutes he whipped the audience into a frenzy, dancing, hurling himself around, belting out one number after another, encouraging everyone to dance. He ended with a double-speed rap version of the old Philly hit, the O'Jays' 'Backstabbers'.

It's a good job he finally finished when he did, because I was sweating like a hog and ready to drop. The girls went to the toilet together, and Spanky reappeared at my side.

'How'd I do? Not bad for an old man, eh?' He wasn't even out of breath.

'You were amazing,' I agreed. 'But what could the audience see while you were up there?'

'Oh, Martyn, always wanting to know what's in the cabinet when you're watching someone get sawn in half. Don't worry, they didn't see me, they saw someone quite different. *Our secret is safe.* Is that what you wanted to hear? Where did those sexiforous young ladies go? I thought we'd escort them back to their hotel for a nightcap.'

'They won't be able to see you.'

He put his arm around my shoulder and gave a smirk. 'Then you'll have to handle both of them by yourself.'

'Forget it, I'm too tired. Despite what you may think, I wasn't cut out to be a sexual athlete. It's been fun, but I'm ready to go home now.'

'Perhaps you're right. I'll walk with you.'

We left the club and took a slow stroll along the Strand. Above us, the illuminated buildings threw dingy yellow light on to the clouds.

'It's a pity you can't patent yourself,' I said. 'The world would be an easier place if everyone had someone like you to help them.'

'But they already do, in a way – look out.'

Ahead of us a pair of drunk-looking tattooed skinheads were tacking along the pavement, swinging beerbottles and shouting at the buildings. With a sick drop in my stomach, I knew they were going to zero in on me. I was still wearing the tuxedo and had been holding a conversation with the air, which I was sure made me either a 'rich bastard' or a 'poof'.

'Oi, talking to yourself, are you?' shouted one. 'Fucking poof!'

He pushed me in the chest with his bottle. 'D'you hear what I said?'

As the other one joined him in haranguing me, Spanky tapped my shoulder. 'You acquitted yourself admirably in smart society tonight, Martyn. But you also need to be a fighter. Let's see how you deal with this.'

The familiar tingle engulfed me, this time from the back of my neck, where Spanky set his hand.

I knocked the skinhead's arm away with a ferocity that set us all on edge. But when I span around, screamed loudly and unleashed a lethal flying kick that connected with his chin to send him sprawling, even my own jaw fell open. The other one lumbered after me and threw a hopeless punch, only to receive a series of fast shattering blows to the stomach before my powerful ninja kick rocketed him over on to his back. I lowered my leg and looked at the two flattened figures lying half in the gutter.

'Wow.'

'Martyn Ross, part Noel Coward, part Casanova, part Shinobi warrior. There's nothing you can't do if you put your mind to it.'

'What shall we do about those two?' I asked, making an experimental chop at the air. My antagonists were both out cold. Cars were skirting around them.

'Leave them where they are. You can't be Florence Nightingale as well.'

As we walked away, I motormouthed on at Spanky, who had doubtless heard it all before. 'Did you see that punch? Suddenly my hands were lethal! *Fists Of Steel*, wasn't that a Bruce Lee movie? I want to sing like you did, too, can I do that? I mean, I sing in the shower, I have a good voice, but getting up in front of everyone ...'

So easy for him. So damned easy.

CHAPTER FOURTEEN

Accommodation

MY FIRST encounter with Max's son took place a week later. The bank had agreed to finance the fitting of two new branches based in property owned by Neville Syms. Despite my terrific performance on the shop floor, it had been agreed that Paul would help to decide store policy with his father, and would search for an advertising agency to handle the newly enlarged Thanet account. I could hardly be annoyed by the boy's appointment in my place. After all, I had not exactly shown much promise prior to my meeting with Spanky. Max had been looking for someone he could trust; who better than his own son?

Paul had no previous experience of the retail trade. Most recently, he'd been selling time for Westward Television. He was physically imposing, tall and heavy set, with a protruding brow and a rugby player's neck. I'd assumed that I would take an instant dislike to him, but was surprised to find him genial company in a rather booming, hearty way.

My position at the store was greatly improved, but the limits of my new responsibilities were clearly defined. I doubted there could be much advancement beyond a certain point. And arrangements had to be made to accommodate Darryl, should he decide to return to work after his eye had healed.

Ultimately, I was still just selling furniture. Every decision I took had to be approved by Max. It had been foolish to expect that my position would alter overnight, even though everyone was commenting on my personal transformation.

And I *was* changing. I had begun to command a sense of respect from those around me. People who had never noticed me before were starting to strike up conversations. I realized that if this went on, I would actually start to win *friends*.

Sarah Brannigan was never less than friendly, but never more. She came in twice a week to check through the orders with me. She was helpful, pleasant and unselfconsciously sexy. At the end of our meetings she would smile pleasantly and offer me the cool tapered fingers of her hand to shake. It seemed pointless asking her for a date because she was still seeing Roger the opera buff, and gave no indication of being remotely interested in anyone else. But I preferred to wait for someone like her than to survive on a series of no-strings sexual encounters. I knew I could do that now, and like a kid with a new toy, was already tiring of the ability. Spanky had said that there was plenty of time later for romance. He was probably right, but meanwhile I wanted someone to share things with. What was the point of popularity if you were still alone?

One afternoon Spanky offered to change Sarah's attitude toward me and I exploded, warning him that I would never expect a woman to do something against her will. We argued and he took his leave, clearly upset that his protégé had turned on him. He did not reappear for six days.

During that time, I was able to manage without total reliance on Spanky's help. My self-confidence was growing in leaps and bounds.

The pattern of my social life had started to mutate. On the night of the theatre awards I had exchanged addresses with some of the actors on my table, swapping their prestigious embossed cards with my battered furniture store slips. One of the actors had since invited me to a dinner party, and another had called to suggest getting together for lunch. Even Amanda rang for a rematch, although that didn't seem to be such a good idea. Still, I missed my daemonic sparring partner.

When Spanky finally returned, strolling past me in the street as I was heading home toward the railway station, he seemed to have forgotten about our argument and was in high spirits. For reasons that he did not deem worthy of explanation, he was dressed in the crisp white military uniform and peaked cap of a US naval officer.

'I just wondered if you wanted to go and do something tonight,' he suggested casually, keeping pace alongside me.

'I thought you'd want to take things easy after your ocean voyage.'

'Do I detect the bitter zest of sarcasm?' Spanky asked the pale sky. 'Is the boy unhappy with his lot? Is there no pleasing him?'

'I'm pleased. I'm worried about my parents. I want to know what's happening to them. I'm worried about what's happening to me. In case you haven't noticed it, I'm changing so fast I can barely recognize myself.'

'I see.'

Spanky removed his cap and turned it over in his hands, thinking. 'We'd better talk about this. Come through here.'

He held open a small side-door to the railway station, and we climbed a long flight of concrete stairs that eventually led to the roof. Ahead lay a narrow walkway that passed across the platform canopy, fifty feet above the station forecourt.

'Follow me,' Spanky called back. 'You won't fall.'

I took his lead, and soon we were sitting on the edge of the great steel and glass roof, dangling our legs over the curving sepia fan of railway lines that extended beneath us.

'You've reached this point a lot earlier than I had expected,' said Spanky, looking down through his legs at the blue snakes of waiting trains. 'Rapid metamorphosis always has its drawbacks. Self-doubt, discomfort with your new outgoing personality, moral confusion; the side effects are well-documented. Most of the people I help experience difficulty at some point. I just didn't think you'd have an attack until after you'd seen your parents, or moved into your new apartment.'

'What do you mean, my new apartment?'

'Obviously, once you take Paul's place in the company and establish friendships in your changing social circle, you won't want to share a flat with someone like Zack anymore. He's a nice enough guy but he's a loser, and there won't be any room in your new life for losers. You'll never be able to have one of your nice new lady friends over for drinks if you stay there.'

'Do you have an agenda for all of this?'

'I work to a fixed timetable, Martyn. There's a strict schedule of events in operation here. So far you're right on time and on target.'

'What are you going to do with Paul? Arrange a fatal accident?' If I was to succeed, it wouldn't be at someone else's expense.

'Don't be melodramatic. He'll move of his own accord, I promise you.'

'Tell me something,' I demanded. 'Why does my transformation have to be accomplished within a specified time-frame? Have you already got someone else booked in?'

'Martyn, it's already September. I like to spend the winter

somewhere warm. I have less than two months to finish remodelling your psychosocial profile. Then I'll bid you a fond farewell and head off to fabularize another wretched existence.'

We sat in silence for a while. It seemed so strange, watching my old life retreat from me, and yet it felt right somehow, as though I was finally being allowed to come into my own. If I had any doubts then, I certainly didn't stop to analyse them. I watched Spanky from the corner of my eye, happily swinging his legs from the roof. The line of his back, the symmetry of his fingernails, everything about him was so perfect that he looked like he'd been designed on a computer.

The daemon looked across at me with one eye screwed up against the dying sun.

'I've found an apartment I think you'll like. Would you like to see it?'

'Sure, why not?'

Spanky rose and dusted the soot from his white marine trousers. We made our way back across the roof, headed down into the street and hailed a taxi. The apartment building we pulled up in front of had taken its radical design from the Memphis school of architecture, and was located in a newly fashionable part of Bow. It sported curved steel balconies and a rolling wall of blue glass bricks. Inside, there was a split level lounge. The materials were fashioned in cool greys and greens with pale wood floors. Everything else was diamond white.

'It's incredible,' I agreed, my voice echoing in the empty bleached chamber, 'but I couldn't afford something like this. I mean, I'm getting a raise but—'

'It's already paid for,' said Spanky, crossing to the far wall and switching on a pair of curved blue neon tubes. Luminous aqua stripes bisected the sharp planes of his face.

'I did the deal a couple of days ago. I signed the lease in your name, so you're free to move in whenever you like. I knew you'd love it. My taste is your taste, remember? Think of the place as my gift to you for being such a fast learner, and for making my job easier.'

He walked over to a chromium fifties' style refrigerator built beside the wet bar, removed an iced bottle of champagne and produced a pair of crystal goblets. He also opened the bottle without touching it, which I thought was a pretty neat trick.

I had grown up in a small terraced house with bay windows and a nettle-filled garden that hardly ever cleared the shadows. I was unused to so much light and space. As I stood in the centre of the vast semi-cylindrical room I felt a mixture of euphoria and agoraphobia.

'You do like it, don't you?' Spanky asked innocently, sipping his champagne.

'It's beautiful.' I was shaking my head, dumbfounded. 'But I haven't earned the right to live here, no matter what you say.'

'That depends on how much importance you attach to property. I've had clients who would rather live out of a suitcase and spend their lives travelling the world. I help them to do that, if it's what makes them happy. If you don't want to live here—'

'No, no, this is perfect. I've always wanted to be right in the city.'

'Am I to take it that you graciously accept the apartment, then?'

'I certainly do,' I replied, thrilled. I tried to imagine what the rent would be on a place like this. More than I'd ever be able to afford on my monthly cheque, that was for sure. Each room held new delights, things I'd only ever seen in style magazines. A black and white chromium and ceramic bathroom with heated flooring. A faux-marble bedroom with surreal orange uplighters and a gigantic deep green bed. The place was fully furnished and showed exquisite taste.

I returned to the lounge, sat down on the blonde parquet floor and crossed my legs, watching as Spanky paced around following his private thoughts. I had spent the last few weeks in the company of someone who was not, strictly speaking, human, and now I could not imagine a life without him. How was it possible to like someone you didn't remotely understand?

'Men rarely understand women, but they still like them,' Spanky cut in. 'It's harder for them to be friends, of course. Sex tends to get in the way.'

'I don't think that's true.'

'Of course it's true. Why do so many middle-aged women find themselves alone in the city? Because men have stopped talking to them. Males hang on to their pubescent fantasies of child-women unless someone slaps them out of it. But who's going to do that when the media worships nothing else?' He gestured around the apartment. 'You ask me about the morality of accepting these gifts. Against the broader picture of what's going on in the world today, I'd say you were doing just fine. Most of the poor suckers out there will die with their childhood dreams unrealized.'

'That's kind of cruel.'

'People always mistake clarity for cruelty.'

I placed my glass on the floor before me. 'What happened to you, Spanky? Where are the others like you?'

I was puzzled. He'd told me how he had given up his spiritual form in exchange for the corporeality of a human, but he never spoke of his time on earth.

He set the champagne bottle between us and joined me on

the floor. 'There are just four of us to service all mankind. Even with our powers we can't make much of a difference. That must tell you something about the venal stupidity of the human race. The others walk the earth, but have not taken human shape. I wanted tangibility. A body. A linear existence. I chose to be reborn as a human. While my brothers still sought to impose change on the world using external spiritual force, I realized that the only real way to alter the future was by working from inside man. By taking him over and if necessary, bending him to my will.'

Perhaps it was the steadiness of those emerald eyes on mine, but for the first time I felt a spark of madness burning within them. Spanky was holding something back from me. If he wasn't exactly lying, he also wasn't telling me the whole truth.

I dismissed the idea. How could I, a mere mortal, expect to understand the workings of the cosmos? As it was, I always felt that Spanky spoke to me in simplified form, as if dealing with a dim child. His talk of good and evil auras had never rung true; why did he not reflect his biblical image as the acolyte of a vindictive, unforgiving and dangerous god?

Perhaps if I had acted earlier upon my half-formed suspicions, everything might still have been all right.

CHAPTER FIFTEEN

Suspicion

ON SUNDAY, I told Zack about the new apartment.

'What do you mean, you're moving out?' he asked in amazement. 'I thought you liked it here, man. I thought we had a rapport. I thought we'd like, bonded.'

He'd been sitting on the floor all afternoon with his headphones on, smoking dope and trying to get an animated rabbit past a wall of spikes on his videogame console. Spanky had arranged for me to move into the apartment the following week. He had already collected the keys and shown me the paperwork, although he had refused to explain how the deal had been arranged, citing it simply as 'all part of the magic'.

'I've enjoyed sharing with you, Zack, but this offer is too good to turn down. I'll miss the damp patch, though.' Lately, tiny mushrooms had appeared in the corner of the ceiling. Zack's reaction; 'Wow.'

'You know, you're becoming a different guy, Martyn,' he said suddenly, pointing an accusing finger at me. 'You used to be so relaxed and easygoing. Just lately you've been really weird. First with the clothes, then the job. You never ask about Debbie anymore. It's the daemon, isn't it? He's still hanging around, turning you into a breadhead.'

'He's opened my eyes, Zack. He's making me realize what I've been missing, what I should have been doing all this time.'

'Yeah, well that's fine if money's your god. There are other things in life that are more important.'

'Right. I can see you're taking care of the important things.'

'Look, fuck you, man. You don't exist for me any more.'

He pulled his headphones back in place and began guiding the rabbit back through the trap-laden castle. I was pissed off. Zack had been happy to take my spare cash whenever it suited him, and now that he saw his dope money leaving he wanted nothing more to do with me.

I pulled the phones from his ears.

'It's time for us to grow up, Zack,' I said. 'You can't just sit here for the rest of your life. Everything's moving on around us. There's another generation right behind. All these books, these games,' I gestured around the cluttered lounge, 'they're about things which aren't real. Debbie is carrying your child and either she needs an abortion, which you'll have to find the money for pretty damned soon, or you'll have to face the responsibility of looking after both the mother and the baby. You have to get a job and get yourself organized. You're not a kid any more.'

He threw the joystick and headphones away from him and sat hunched over, his head turned to one side.

'Don't talk about me, man. You're the one who needs a fucking spirit guide to get you through the day.'

'It wasn't my doing. It just happened. I don't understand how and I don't know why.'

'Well, it's unfair!' he shouted. 'I'm the one who believes! I've always believed, and where's my help? What's going to get me through?'

I didn't know. I had no answer for him. These days he was

barely equipped to leave the apartment. 'I'll ask him to help you.' I said.

And that's what I did.

I was too busy at the store to move into the new apartment on Tuesday, and anyway the phone couldn't be connected until the following week-end, so I delayed going until then. When Spanky next appeared it was late on Thursday evening, and I was still filling out order forms in the stockroom at the rear of the store. I barely recognized him. He was wearing Levi Silver Tab jeans, a DKNY belt, a plain white T-shirt and cowboy boots, and looked almost normal.

I could tell at once that he wouldn't respond to my request.

'I can't help Zack,' he said apologetically. 'I can't explain why, but he's just not suitable material. Some people aren't, and they're usually the ones who most want to be.' He climbed to the top of a stack of bubble-wrapped sofas and seated himself.

'Well, he's really screwed up and I don't know how to help him,' I said. 'Isn't there anything you can do?'

'Let me think about it.'

'Why are you here? Are we doing something tonight?'

'Nope. I'm a busy little entity. People to see, tangled webs to weave. Did your parents call again?'

'On three separate occasions. I left a message with Lottie saying that I'm away on business and can't be contacted.'

'Good boy. I came by to tell you I won't be around for a few days. Good luck with the apartment.'

'Thanks. Have fun wherever you're going.'

'Forget it,' he replied, reading my mind. 'I'm not going to tell you.' When I looked up again he had gone, his faint spicy odour lingering behind him like a signature.

I had booked the next morning off in order to shift the few boxes of books, tapes and clothes I owned. Spanky had arranged the furniture for the new flat but I still needed stuff like a kettle and crockery. I didn't care. I was prepared to drink out of toothmugs if necessary, I just wanted to be in there. The kitchen was fully fitted, and the few sticks of furniture I owned were too scruffy for such a palatial home. Max offered me a twenty percent discount on the store's merchandise. I hastily declined.

That night, Zack skulked moodily about the kitchen as I packed up my cartons of books. I was careful to leave him everything he wanted, including my toolbox and a couple of saucepans I had recently bought. I would buy fresh.

On Saturday I moved into my incredible pristine apartment. The rooms smelled of paint and fresh wood. The whole place was less than five years old. I had never lived in a modern building, and found it hard to believe that there were no damp patches anywhere. During the course of the day I gradually unpacked, stacking books on thoughtfully provided shelves. I spent my first night in alone, wandering back and forth in front of the vast windows, marvelling at the size and space that had entered my life. Spanky had installed a widescreen TV and multi-system video, which I tuned in and stared at for the rest of the week-end.

On Monday I was supposed to have lunch with Max's son Paul, who had asked if we could meet to discuss the details of the forthcoming expansion. Although summer had started to fade and cool, the front of the Italian restaurant was still open to the street. I took a table and waited for nearly an hour, but Paul didn't show up. I called the office but nobody had seen him. Odd.

Max was out for a legal meeting and an extended luncheon

with Neville Syms, so I worked at the store until eight. Still no sign of Paul.

That night I luxuriated alone in my freshly painted world, wiring up some kitchen appliances and tuning my amp deck. I stocked the refrigerator. All I needed now was someone with whom I could share my good fortune. I decided to introduce myself to the neighbours and knocked on their door, but the apartment beyond remained silent.

On Tuesday morning Max called me in and asked if I had seen his son. Apparently he hadn't come home last night and Beverly, his fiancée, was out of her mind with worry. I explained about our lunch date, but was unable to offer any words of comfort. From the little I knew about Paul it seemed unlikely that he would have just taken off.

That night I went to the actor's dinner party, and ended up staying in Chelsea with an extraordinary girl called Wyoming Charles, who was understudying in the West End production of a new Steven Berkoff play. Her hair was detergent-box red and her breasts defied several natural laws. She was charming and flaky and strange, and we fooled around with each others' bodies all night. A little after 6.30 a.m. I fell asleep and woke up late for work. Feeling distinctly sleazy I let myself out of her flat and headed for the tube, wondering if I should start notching up my conquests on a stick.

On Thursday I rang the hospital to try and speak with Darryl, but the staff nurse told me that he had discharged himself the previous evening. When I tried to call him at home, there was no reply.

Paul hadn't reappeared, either. Max had finally been to the police with Beverly, who admitted that she had had an argument with her fiancé on Sunday evening, the day before he vanished. Hearing this, the cops failed to provide much encouragement. They suggested sitting tight until the week-end before officially declaring him a missing person.

All kinds of crazy thoughts had begun to pass through my mind.

With growing unease I called my old apartment and got a recorded message. Eerily, my voice was still on the tape. If Zack was in, he wasn't bothering to pick up.

Perhaps it was because Spanky had also disappeared, but by the time evening came I was convinced that harm had befallen those around me. The telephone was now connected, so I decided to go against Spanky's wishes and ring my parents' house.

Their line was dead. A single high-pitched note whined through the empty ether. I immediately checked with the operator, who told me that the number had been disconnected.

Now I began to panic.

How could I have been so blind? I had been so wrapped up in my own tawdry pleasures, I couldn't see that something terrible was happening to almost everyone in my life. I took a cab around to the old Vauxhall flat and rang the doorbell long and loud. I had surrendered my keys to Zack when I left. There was no reply, and I could see from the street that the living room lights were switched off.

Don't be alarmed, I told myself.

There's a rational explanation.

But how was I fit to discuss the concept of rationality? *I* was the one taking advice from a daemon.

I decided it was time to visit my family.

I rang Max and informed him that I wouldn't be in for work tomorrow, which pissed him off royally. Thanet was already short-staffed without Darryl, and Max was being forced to work the shop-floor himself.

I didn't have a car, but there was still one more train running that night. I threw some clothes into a bag and called a cab, but the damned thing took fifteen minutes to reach my apartment. We raced down to Charing Cross station through bad traffic, and I slid into the ticket hall about thirty seconds after the train had pulled out. There was nothing for it but to turn around and go home.

The next morning I awoke at dawn, checked the timetable and wearily returned to the station. The first train was cancelled, the second delayed, and the longer I waited the more convinced I became that something terrible had happened.

The journey seemed to take forever. Twelvetrees awaited my arrival beneath rushing dark skies. Just as I alighted it began to rain, and I was forced to walk the last half-mile. By the time I turned into their street I was running.

I quickly saw the problem.

The house was boarded up.

A tall wire fence had been staked around the property, and the doors and windows were covered with sheets of chipboard. The back half of the lawn had been ploughed under, and tractor marks vanished around the side of the house. I ran across to the nearest neighbour's house and rang the bell.

A very elderly woman answered the door. This had to be Old Mrs Sinclair, whom I had never met, but who was categorised by my mother as having 'led a tragic life'.

'Oh, they've gone,' she said. 'You're Martyn, aren't you? They were looking for you.'

'Do you know where they are?'

'They gave me the address, in case you came by. They were very worried. You look soaked. Come in.'

She thumped her cane along a hallway scented with lavender polish, and I followed her, dripping, into a pristine front room that she obviously reserved for visitors.

'Here they are,' she said, passing me a card. 'I can't read it without my glasses.'

It was the address of a villa on the Portuguese coast of the Algarve. There didn't seem to be a telephone number. Although she owned a passport 'for emergencies', my mother had only ever used it once. What the hell were they doing in Portugal?

'You don't know why they would have gone there, do you?'

'Limestone, I think it was. That was it, limestone. They said the insurance people were going to pay.' The old woman was making no sense.

'I'm sorry, I'm not with you.'

'They had to stay somewhere, your mum and dad. I think they wanted to come and stay with you, but they couldn't get hold of you. The house fell down.'

I could see their house from the window. 'What do you mean, it fell down?'

'Broke its back, just like that. They found a big hole underneath, part of a limestone quarry, I think it was. Just opened up beneath them. Good job they were out when it happened. So now the house has to be – I can't remember the word—'

'Underpinned.'

'That's it. The hole has to be filled up before there's any more subsidence. They couldn't live there while the work was being done, and this holiday-thing had come up, so they decided to take it after all.'

An image from my last visit sprang to mind; Spanky armed with a long-handled shovel, asking about insurance policies. His plan was suddenly clear. He'd forced a great change on my parents to break them of their former habits. No wonder he hadn't wanted me to call them. I would have accused him of being cruel.

'What holiday-thing, Mrs Sinclair?' I asked.

'A man from the supermarket came and told your mum that she'd won a holiday. He had the tickets and everything, all first class, but your dad was suspicious and turned them down. I think he was worried about hidden extras.'

That sounded like my father, all right. Spanky could have offered him eternal life and he would have argued the toss.

'Your mum was ever so upset,' the old lady continued, 'because she wanted to go. But then the house cracked and they had to move anyway, so they made use of the tickets after all. It was difficult, what with Laura being so ill and everything.'

'Laura? What's wrong with her?'

Her eyes widened. 'Surely you knew about that. She couldn't hold anything down, poor love. Bringing back everything she ate. Couldn't get a single thing to stay in her stomach. The doctors were worried, but they weren't able to find anything wrong with her.'

'Did Laura go with my parents? How could she travel in such a state?'

'That's the odd thing. Your mum told me her problem cleared up just before they were due to fly out.'

And I bet it resumed the moment they landed, and would stay with Laura until she hit target weight. I needed to see Spanky. If my parents were safe, what of the others?

I returned to my apartment and stalked about the lounge, waiting for something to happen. At five o'clock a couple of guys delivered some furniture I hadn't ordered; a long white linen sofa and two ironwork standard lamps, stylish and presumably very expensive. These continual gifts from

Spanky were starting to feel like bribes.

I took a very hot shower and tried to shake away my doubts about him, but they kept returning. How could I know if my parents were really safe? If Laura was well? And what on earth had happened to Paul?

As I walked back into the living room wrapped in a towel, I gave a start. The daemon was at the kitchen counter, experimenting with half a dozen brightly coloured bottles and a silver cocktail shaker.

'I'm making my own special version of a vodka stinger,' he said casually. 'Want to be my guinea pig?'

'I feel as if I already am. What are my parents doing in Portugal?'

'Ah, *that*.' He gave the shaker a few good thrusts and unclipped the cap, pouring a viscous, lime liquid into a pair of martini glasses. 'Actually, they're rediscovering themselves. It's a beautiful villa, very secluded and romantic. I knew Gordon would pester the insurance people, so I had the phone taken out. There's no TV, just an old stereo, a stack of Frank Sinatra records and a spectacular view of the bay. And they can stay as long as they like. Your father has a lot of holiday time owing, as you can imagine. I think they were quite pleased to get rid of him for a while.'

He ran his finger around the lid of the shaker and gave it a lick. 'You weren't supposed to know about them yet. I wanted it to be a surprise. Present you with a *fait accompli*. I'd like to make sure that their marriage is fully re-established before you start arguing with each other and undoing all my good work. I suppose you know about Laura as well.'

'I know she's ill.'

'She's fine, she just won't be able to absorb more than a few hundred calories a day until she reaches her correct weight. I know it's unpleasant for her, but drastic measures were called for. She's learning to eat less. And, I might say, already becoming a much happier person. She spent the whole of yesterday sunbathing in the garden. In a swimsuit. Taste this and tell me if it needs anything.'

He passed me one of the green glasses. The alcohol content was so high my vocal chords shredded when I tried to speak.

'The interesting thing about your sister, Martyn, is that there's no biological imbalance causing her obesity. Once she returns to her former figure she should be able to keep it fairly easily. The more she gets out, the more people she'll meet, and the more she'll want to keep her weight down. The cause-and-effect circle has been broken. She's worried about you, though. Wants to know where you are. I'll let you speak to each other soon. Tell me something; she started to eat soon after—'

'—Joey died. This drink is awful.'

'Whenever I mention your brother you change the subject. Why is that?'

'Personal reasons.'

'Oh, I see. It still hurts.'

'What have you done with Paul?'

He began to chuckle. 'You think I've done away with everyone, don't you? Just lately your luck has been too good to be true, and you're looking for the catch. Can't enjoy yourself without feeling bad – sounds like our old friend Mr Guilt. I'm sorry to disappoint you, Martyn, but if you'd remembered to play back your messages from this morning you would have found out about Paul.'

He pointed to the Faxfone on the floor in the corner of the room. I would have collected my messages, but I had no idea I even owned a new machine. Now I rewound the cassette and played it back.

'Hi, Martyn.' Paul's booming, genial voice. 'I imagine Beverly and my father are tearing their hair out right now. I'm sorry for all the trouble I'm causing but well, something's happened to me.'

I looked up at Spanky, who was listening with an amused smile.

'I have to tell someone. The fact is, I've met the most incredible, exciting woman. I'm with her right now. I was first at the store on Monday morning, and she just walked in behind me! We weren't even open! She says she had no idea what made her do it, isn't that weird? Her name is Stephane, and we're at her home just outside Avignon. I feel terrible about just leaving like this but I'm not much of a talker, and couldn't think what to say to Bev. I knew I couldn't marry her some while ago, but we just sort of drifted on. Now I'm really in love with someone. It's so different, Martyn, not like being with Bev at all. That's how I know it's real. There's none of that awful *inevitability*, you know, marriage and everything. Listen, I'll give you the number here, but please don't pass it on to Max. I know it's a cowardly thing to ask, but could you tell him what's happened? He'd only hang up on me. Say I'll call him once I've sorted everything out more clearly.'

The number followed, and I jotted it down on a notepad. Spanky watched me with an eyebrow raised, as if to say, 'See? Now do you believe me?'

Another message followed after the beep.

'Hey Mr Breadhead, how are you doing? Just to let you know that *I'm* doing the right thing. I hope you're sitting down because this is, like, a big announcement. I've asked Debbie to move in with me. Actually she needed a place to stay because her landlord keeps hanging around on the landing in his underpants, and your room was free so she's going to have that. I'm collecting all her stuff over the next couple of days. You wouldn't believe how much junk she has like, one of those sixties wickerwork chairs you hang from the ceiling, only I don't think our ceiling will hold it. You forgot a box of books, by the way. I'll put them out in the hall for you. Speak soon?'

It was all very neat. I only needed a call from Darryl to completely allay my fears.

'Oh, I heard that,' said Spanky, reading the thought. 'Give me a break, will you? How much proof do you need, for God's sake?'

'Sorry,' I replied. 'It's just my natural cynicism kicking in.'

'If it'll make you any happier, I'll try to get your mother to call you from the village in the next couple of days. It's difficult, that's all. I don't usually do long distance stuff. It's too draining.'

He gave my shoulder an amicable nudge. 'Come on, deep in your heart you know I'm on your side. You and I are the same, remember?' He raised his glass and tapped the rim. 'Try it now. I've modified the kick a little. Let's drink a toast.'

He was right. My over-reaction was most likely a side effect of my changing life. In any situation I always thought the worst, just like my father. Now I raised my glass, as much in apology as celebration.

'Your health, Spanky.'

'And yours, Martyn.'

We drank deep. 'What's in this?' I asked, already woozy.

'Just a little something to sharpen up your sensory perception.'

I stared at the half-drained glass. There were tiny flecks of crimson in the green residue, like drops of blood. 'Why?'

'Because it's time for something special,' he replied. 'The final part of your education.'

CHAPTER SIXTEEN

Sensitivity

THE HILLSIDE was a tilting field of black emerald. Below us, the city flared up into the night. Pairs of amber jewels snaked from country to town, the lights of the motorway. I sat in the tall damp grass watching Spanky. He was standing before me, half-submerged in the rustling fronds with his arms held out at right-angles, delivering a lecture that sounded as if he'd made it many times before. His pupils glowed faintly green in the dark, like cats' eyes.

'Poetry exists within the most impoverished soul, Martyn. Some manage to rediscover it for themselves, but for most people the muse remains buried and forgotten. Ninety per cent of the world is asleep, and those who are awake exist in a state of perpetual amazement. To cope with the demands of your new life, you need to be one of the woken ones. I have to open your senses a little.'

'To the level of yours?'

'I could never do that. The sensory onslaught would cause irrevocable damage. I can cope with a broader spectrum of perception because I'm not subject to human frailty. With you, I have to be a lot more careful, but it'll be all right for a short period. I want to take you on a trip across the nightland.'

He knelt before me and cupped warm hands over my ears for about a minute. Then he slowly removed them. There was a sharp pain in my eardrums and then a release, as though water had been cleared from them after a swim.

'Listen carefully, then tell me what you hear.'

I listened. At first all I could make out was the continuous dull roar of traffic on the highway behind us, but as I concentrated harder the sounds began to change. It was as if the range of my hearing was ballooning outwards to include other sounds of the night.

First came the millions of minute sounds from the bushes, the meadows and hedgerows of the hillside; branches scraping together, leaves tapping and flicking across each other, insects burrowing into the foliage, the slow, steady munching of caterpillars, the furry fluttering of moth wings beating in darkness.

I listened harder.

Further away I could hear the deep, vibrating hum of electricity pylons, the arcing sparks that crackled across the ceramic and steel generators of the power station. Beyond that, the chopping throb of car engines, the thrumming tyres of vehicles shooting past like angry wasps in aural patterns that formed an undulating skein of noise leading toward the city, the centre of the web.

From above came the low whine of an airplane, wind through the jets, passengers talking softly inside the dimly lit cabin. And beyond all these sounds there stood a massively deep block of discord, impossible to break down into millions of separate voices, the beating heart of a city that lived a collective life as diverse and rich as any single one of its human inhabitants.

But now the cacophony was receding back, not to the level

Sensitivity   149 it had maintained before but to a point somewhere above it.

I became aware of Spanky's hands on my head, the sensation of his fingers tracing whorls across my face, my nostrils and cheeks, inside my mouth.

Fresh senses.

Suddenly I could taste and smell a thousand flavours in the air. The acrid bite of petrol fumes tainted everything, but beneath this inquination there was the bitter chlorophyll of grass and plant stems, the musty soil, the powerful pheremones of plants and bees, the perfumed stench of nectared pistils and stamens, the chlorinated charge of electricity falling from street lights. This overwhelming array of incoming tastes forced the bile to rise in my throat, and I was sick on to the grass.

'Sorry,' said Spanky, clawing a handkerchief from his pocket and wiping my chin with it. 'I forgot about the effect it sometimes has on people. Smell is the most evocative of the human senses, and must not be underestimated. You won't retain that depth of sensation; it would be too much for you. But you'll be a little more attuned than you were before. We'll resume when you're feeling more settled.'

The night was cool, but there was no breeze to chill us. We sat beside each other on the grassy slope, in silent awe of the glittering sky. The augmentation of my perceptions had temporarily removed the need for speech. I was pleased to know that I would not retain such sensory depth. It would be terrifying to know so much of the world.

Spanky gave me a sidelong glance. 'Ready to go again?'

My stomach had stabilized. 'I guess so,' I replied.

This time, he placed his hands over my eyes and pressed the tips of his fingers against the orbs until spinning flashes of colour appeared on my eyelids.

He removed his hands, and I looked out across the fields.

Slowly it seemed that the molecules of the darkened air were clearing to allow the path of my vision. The blurred outlines of the trees sharpened in relief against the sky, their branches and leaves separating to become distinct, the veins appearing in each leaf, the grain on every sepia flake of bark standing out in textural contrast to the blades of waving grass.

Gradually, I raised my head and looked toward the city. The dazzling barrage of light broke down at once into individual pinpoints of sulphur-yellow streetlamps. Larger rectangles of colour were revealed as the creamy exterior floodlights of public buildings. Sharp streaks of cyclamen and sapphire marked the jagged scaffolding of neon that filled the city's theatre district. Soft, buttery squares shone from the interiors of private homes. All were connected with those searing, pulsing ribbons of luminosity, the motorways, arteries streaked with the crimson tail-lights of homebound vehicles, glowing like microfilm of the human bloodstream.

'Concentrate your sight, Martyn. Find the areas you know best.'

Sorting through the visual ephemera was difficult at first, but grew easier as I established my bearings. Soon my vision cleared through each deliquescing obstacle to reveal the street of my old apartment, and then, straining further, I saw the building itself.

'Now use your other senses.'

Suddenly everything Spanky had opened for me returned; taste, smell, sound. There, by the open window, looking out across the city, stood a woman. The apple-shampoo scent of her hair and the warm, milky musk of her breasts enveloped me, and I heard the double heartbeat within her.

'Debbie.'

From somewhere behind her came another heartbeat, and a

male odour of aftershave and cannabis smoke.

'Zack.'

As my vision continued to clarify and deepen I began to blink, swamped by the sensory input that had become available to me. No wonder Spanky had taken me here at night, when the world was at least a little damped down. By day the augmented sights and sounds of the land would have over-loaded my mind, and I would probably have blacked out.

As it was, I made the mistake of raising my head to the heavens, and at once a billion steel-sharp points of starlight filled my sight, shifting across the universe toward me. The sky was clearing, enriching itself by the second to reveal a panoply of galaxies, exploding stars and dying novas, so bright and detailed that when I shut my eyes they were still there, and disoriented I fell back on to the grass bank, pressing the heels of my hands over my eye sockets until my normal sight returned, and my head ceased to spin on the axes of a thousand celestial systems.

'That's what I see all the time,' said Spanky quietly, 'because I am neither living nor dead, neither man nor woman, but something separate, of itself.'

'Can you see on to other planets?' I asked, my eyes remaining firmly closed.

'No. It's enough for us to know that life exists in so many other parts of the universe. I find it a comforting thought, though I suppose others are terrified by the prospect.'

'So do the four of you belong to the greater part, the universe – or are you confined to this planet?' I realized it was an absurd, impossible question, one that could only be answered by providing proof of the existence of God.

'I wish I knew, my friend, I really wish I knew. In some matters my personal darkness is every bit as deep as yours.'

We sat for a while longer, as the temperature fell and the rising breeze chilled our bones. I wasn't cold, though. I felt disoriented and excited by what I had seen and tasted and heard.

'What do you want to do now?' asked Spanky. 'We can go into town and meet some more wild women.'

'I don't know if I want to do that. I feel – unusual.'

I couldn't see his face when he next spoke. 'I've been thinking, Martyn. Perhaps it's time for you to share your life with someone. But first I have to know who you want.'

'What I want,' I repeated dully.

'*Who* you want.'

Spanky placed his palms on my chest, and I felt the warmth of his spreading fingers, only to watch in alarm as his hands sank inside me. It was as though the top half of his body was merging with mine. My natural fear of being touched by another male grew as I seemed to feel him within my body, brushing across the nerve-ends in my immobile form. Now he had completely merged with me, his arms resting into the shape of mine, his legs flexing and filling the space occupied by my own limbs. With the softest of snaps his vertebrae joined with my own, his ribs and liver and heart and lungs invading mine in a rush of blood and sinew so that we were duplex, his skull reaching out into my own head until we were two people holding one place in time.

Although I could not find the power of his thoughts or feel the strength of his will, I sensed that something else was happening in my body. And then I knew.

'Remember, Martyn.' Spanky's voice, whispering inside my brain. 'I am no man, woman or beast, only the very essence of sexual life itself.'

The tingling in my flesh became a scratching, then a burning, and continued to increase until my nervous system tightened into a blistering climax, a long-drawn, racking orgasm that discharged such rushing heat and anger into the outside world that I slipped quickly into a state of unconsciousness.

Before I passed out, I remember saying one thing. One word.

'Sarah.'

'Now we know,' said Spanky, dissolving into darkness.

CHAPTER SEVENTEEN

Compatibility

MY NEXT meeting with Spanky, the following Monday in the office stockroom, was tempered with embarrassment over the bizarre intimacy of our last encounter. I felt uncomfortable about what had happened; he clearly did not. Still, there was a sense that the shared experience had brought us closer toward understanding each other. Not that this provided me with a reason why he was garbed in the gleaming braided gold, red and black uniform of a British Crimean cavalry officer. Finally my daemonic partner finished snapping a chamois cloth across his boots and rose, thumping me hard on the back.

'Have you checked your mail this morning?' He unsnapped an elastic band from the post. 'Your problems are almost over. Take a look.'

A letter had arrived from Portugal. In accordance with his new-found sense of responsibility, Zack had forwarded it to me from the flat.

'The reunification of the Family Ross is a fragile one,' Spanky admitted, pre-empting the contents of the envelope, 'but it does seem to be working.'

Despite having had the whole of the week-end to recover, I was still suffering from the worst hangover of all time; Spanky had warned me about the after-effects of my 'sense-opening'. The usual remedies had failed; it felt like I'd been bashed in the head with a baseball bat.

Spanky picked up the thought and pulled a Mars bar from his pocket. 'Try this. Eating chocolate is supposed to help.'

I bit into it and chewed, then tore open the airmail envelope and checked the tiny sloping script of my mother's handwriting.

She verified Spanky's story; explaining that fast action had been required to save the house from complete collapse. They had tried to reach me; where was I? So thoughtless of me not to call! The enforced vacation at the villa had turned out to be a blessing in disguise. What luck to have been offered it! Even Gordon was enjoying himself!

Enclosed was a Polaroid photograph of an already changing Laura. My sister had lost a considerable amount of weight. Another snap showed a sunbleached wall laced with bougainvillaea, and my parents with their arms around each other. Apparently, they were thinking of staying on for a period beyond their allotted time. Gordon had the holiday owing to him. My mother's account of recent events ended with a wish, that Joey and I could have been there to share their new-found happiness.

Now I knew that their change was real; invocation of the Joey word had long been banned in the family. My mother had declared the subject taboo and yet here she was, casually reviving his memory. Spanky read the letter over my shoulder and periodically nodded his head, making sounds of affirmation, as if to say I told you so.

'What happens when they return?' I asked. 'Won't my father resume his affair?'

'He can try, but he won't have much luck. Mrs Elisabeth

Edgemore has been transferred to an accounts department in Leeds. She moved without even leaving him a goodbye note. She wasn't very happy about it.'

'Your work, I suppose.'

'The company files showed that personnel could be more cost-efficient if certain staff changes were made, that's all. Naturally, my role as a muse requires me to be computer-literate, so it was a simple matter to rewrite a few documents. That was how I arranged your apartment. Did I tell you your sister has a date next Friday?'

'Laura? She stopped dating—'

'Well, she's ready to start again. She's seeing a local boy from the village, Carlo or Pedro, something like that. I have my fingers crossed for a holiday romance. Might go over there myself and give it a helping hand.'

'Maybe you should just let it take its natural course.' I wanted to thank Spanky, and barely knew where to begin. 'I didn't think anything could be done to help my family.'

'It's not over yet. They've been emotionally frozen since your brother died, and thawing them out isn't as simple as it looks. Your parents are going to need a lot of emotional support from you in the coming months, but you'll be busy here taking on all kinds of new responsibilities. You'll have to learn to make more time for them, and I won't be here to help you. You could start by being more patient with your father. He's a good man at heart. And a steady relationship of your own wouldn't be a bad idea. You don't want to screw around for the rest of your life. It's undignified.'

'I thought of that. But the thing with Sarah would never work. It's obvious we're from different backgrounds. She outclasses me.'

'There you go, putting her back on a pedestal. The problem

can be resolved. But it's the last time I'll be able to help you, Martyn. From the end of the week, you're on your own.'

He slid down from his usual perch on top of the filing cabinet and straightened his crimson breeches.

'You mean you're going?' I had known that this time would come. I just hadn't reckoned that it would be so soon.

'Certainly. It's later than I'd realized.'

'Does that mean I'll never see you again?'

He gave a careless shrug. 'I can only spend a short period with each person I help, and I have no idea where I'll be next. My time doesn't run as sequentially as yours. And it's important that I leave you now. People have noticed that you've been acting strange lately. I don't want to undo all the good we've achieved. When is Sarah due for her next visit to the store?'

'She has an appointment here at 4.00 p.m. tomorrow afternoon.' I felt uncomfortable telling Spanky. I didn't want him messing with her mind. If Sarah decided to stop seeing Roger and go out with me, it would have to be because she wanted to, not because she'd been duped into it.

'Relax, I wasn't going to trick her,' said Spanky, interrupting the thought. 'But I read her mind last time she was here. She's an ambitious woman. I think she ought to find out somehow that you've just received the first of several promotions. She might see you in an entirely different light.'

Those were the truest words Spanky ever spoke.

The next morning, I talked to Max about his son, and gave him the telephone number in Avignon. He took the news of Paul's defection with incredibly bad grace. I got the feeling that he was very friendly with Beverly, the jilted fiancée, and had wanted the marriage to happen even if they hadn't. A phonecall to France only left him seething. More calls followed in the course of the morning. I could hear Max angrily voicing his opinions through the frosted glass door of his office. Piqued by the perceived disloyalty, he called me in and raged that he was surrounded by quislings, traitors and cowards. And at the most important moment in Thanet's history, a time of great expansion! Paul had run off with a French whore. Darryl had refused to return to work. Only I had not deserted him. I was a saint, a godsend. I was officially promoted. I would be in charge from now on.

Spanky had forecast the result, right on the nose.

At 4.00 p.m. that afternoon, Sarah came on to me as if the earth's oxygen had just given out and I was an iron lung.

I was finalizing arrangements for the refitting of the shop-front, when I looked up from the diagrams to see a pair of tick-tacking red high heels and long stockinged legs sliding toward me.

Max raised one eyebrow.

I raised both.

Sarah had brought new meaning to the phrase 'dressed to kill'. Her beige silk blouse appeared to have been designed by snipping off half the buttons. Her brassière was too small or maybe her pale breasts were too large, or maybe both. A playful half-smile had settled on her sparkling lips. Loose curls of fiery red hair fell in burning disarray about her shoulders. Her grey eyes caught mine and held them as she spoke. She talked of orders for the new *Arcadia* range of dining chairs, but her surface conversation had nothing to do with what she was really saying. Max hurriedly excused himself and left us alone. My mouth had grown dry, and I found it hard to reply to Sarah's enquiries.

'I understand you're taking over from Max's son,' she said

softly. 'I hope you're planning to celebrate your new position.'

As I attempted to formulate a sentence, she reached over and rested her hand on my thigh, dusting away a smear of chalk.

This was too much. Unable to catch my breath, I jumped to my feet. Spanky had promised me he wouldn't tamper with her mind. He'd told me that she was ambitious. Perhaps she was always like this around men she liked, but her reaction seemed a little overblown.

'We can go to dinner if you'd like,' I said sharply.

'Oh, I'd like that very much.' She drifted towards me, walking her painted nails along the edge of my desk.

'How did you find out about my – promotion?' I asked. I had to know if Spanky had visited her.

'Max just told me about it. I won't let anyone else know, if you still want it to be a secret.'

'It's not that—'

'Good. Then we can have dinner tomorrow night. Can't we?'

I nodded dumbly in agreement. It didn't feel right. Nothing felt right. This was the Sarah I didn't know.

But I had to admit there was a certain symmetry. After all, no one had changed as much as I had in the past two months. If I didn't know her, at least I didn't know myself anymore, either.

We were clearly both ripe for a modern relationship.

Sarah and I ate in a noisy Belgian restaurant in Camden Town. Before the main course had arrived, she'd removed her shoes and was running her toes up my calves. She packed away an incredible amount of food. It didn't seem possible that she could stay so slim. Her ferocious appetite clearly extended beyond nutritional requirements.

For all my newly discovered expertise with women, I suddenly felt awkward and inexperienced. This wasn't what I had expected. But when she asked to come home with me, I readily agreed.

'Are you still seeing Roger?' I asked, searching the street for a cab.

'Sure I'm seeing him. We had dinner together last night.'

'Then how come—?'

'I didn't say I was sleeping with him.'

'I just assumed—'

'Well, you shouldn't. Roger's not interested in girls. I'm his date when he takes out clients. It's a business arrangement.'

We started making love long before we reached the apartment. She had her hand inside my flies during the taxi ride home. After stalling the lift between floors she lowered herself to her knees, tore open my pants and buried her face in my groin. In the corridor outside my apartment she removed her panties and pushed me against the wall, raised her torso and eased herself on to my erection, wrapping her ankles around the backs of my legs. While I was thus inside her, I managed to fumble open the front door lock, de-activate the alarm system and walk her into the lounge with a strength and dexterity that would have qualified me for the Duke Of Edinburgh Award Scheme.

To say that we made love through the night is inaccurate; we fought with each other, using sex as our weapons. Our actions, accompanied by gasps and grunts, were the thrusts and recoveries of military manoeuvres. Ground was gained and lost in equal measure. But when morning came I felt the ravages of war in every vein and muscle of my body. I lay staring at the ceiling like a bayonetted corpse, unable to think or move.

Sarah, on the other hand, had survived the night well and

was rallying her troops for a fresh onslaught.

Depleted but not defeated, my army regrouped.

I was very late for work.

I finally arrived at the showroom, my daemonic accomplice was waiting for me. The first chill winds of winter were coursing between the office blocks, and he was appropriately wrapped in a long black military overcoat with solid silver epaulettes and buckles. The store was filled with carpenters and plasterers and electricians, so I had to watch my behaviour carefully.

'Did you have fun last night?' Spanky asked, casually examining his nails as he walked behind me. 'You look awful.'

I think she's damaged my genitals, I admitted. They were as sore as hell. My dick felt as if it had been pulled out by the roots. *Did you have anything to do with her – athletic – behaviour?*

'Not at all, as it happens. Turns out she's always had a soft spot for you, but you've been too dumb to see it. Sometimes my job is made easier by circumstance. All I did was make you both aware of the attraction.'

How come Max talked to her about me?

'He didn't. I did, but she doesn't know it. She'll be very keen to see you again.'

The feeling's mutual; I just have to relocate my nuts first. She's wonderful, but I don't think there's going to be much romantic involvement between us.

'Why not?'

C'mon, Spanky – like the song says, it's too hot not to cool down. She's never going to settle. She's not the type.

'Did you ever notice how much you complain, Martyn? You're so English in that respect, finding fault with everything. Moan, moan, moan.'

Sorry, I didn't mean to sound ungrateful. On the contrary, I've never been happier.

'Then I can say goodbye.'

Wait, I thought you were leaving at the end of the week?

'I don't need to hang around any longer. Tell me something, Martyn. Be absolutely honest.'

Ask me anything, Spanks. Fire away.

'The night we first met. I asked if you believed in the supernatural, and you said no. Do you feel differently now?'

Of course I do, I replied. *None of this would have happened without your help, and you're not real. I mean, you are real – but you exist somewhere else, in a different way to me. So I have to accept that there are more things on earth than I'll ever be able to understand.*

'Stout fellow. Don't stop learning now; keep going. Change is good for you, the more the better. Well, I must be off.' He stood framed in the broad glass doorway and checked his watch. Leave-taking obviously made him embarrassed.

'It's been fun, Martyn. Remember to use your increased sensory perception carefully, otherwise it'll make you throw up. I hope everything works out for you. No reason why it shouldn't, of course. I have a feeling your boss is about to give you a rather nice car. So, er, good luck for the future.' He sounded like an employer seeing off a fired colleague.

Hey, wait a second.

Spanky walked forward and I reached for his arm, shaking a hand as cold and hard as marble. I didn't care how it looked to the builders working behind me. I felt like I was losing part of myself.

I really don't know how to thank you for what you've done.

'Oh, all in a day's work, you know. Um, I'd better say cheerio now.'

Compatibility

He waved his hand in an awkward gesture of farewell, grinned sheepishly and turned away, walking quickly off down the street.

At the back of my mind, something nagged and worried like a tick in a mattress. Some tiny alarm was trying to make itself heard. But in the bathos of our farewell, the sound was silenced.

CHAPTER EIGHTEEN

Amelioration

AND SO I prepared to settle into my new life.

A few days later I collected my books from Zack and was surprised to find the old apartment freshly decorated, although he had simply thrown some paint across the damp patch, which was already starting to show through again. Over the worst spaghetti bolognese I had ever tasted, I listened to his plans for a future responsibly shared with Debbie.

Zack had uncovered astrological evidence approving fatherhood, and the cosmic okay had given him a new sense of purpose. He'd found signs before, but they didn't usually make sense. This plan had more going for it. He was going to swallow his pride and take a job in his father's company, get some money together, hold Debbie's hand and chant for her throughout the birth, buy the flat, sell it for a profit and put a deposit on a cottage in the Cotswolds where they could keep horses, build stables and raise their child within the natural harmony of the landscape.

I toasted his dreams in warm Chianti.

I finished some decorating of my own and spent an increasing amount of time with Sarah, who occasionally climbed off my lap long enough to eat something. Our relationship wasn't ideal, but at least it was based on the staple human necessities of sex and food, something I figured should sustain us both for a while.

In the hours between eating and going to bed she was happy to sit watching the lights of the city from the tall lounge windows, her forehead pressed against the cold glass, her strange grey eyes lazily surveying the street. At first I thought I'd done something wrong. I soon saw that it was her way of being comfortable with a man. Small talk bored her. She settled for more sensual pleasures. Sometimes she invited Roger over and they cooked complicated vegetarian dishes together. After, we would sit on the floor and play Scrabble.

Max refused to have anything to do with his son, whose new relationship sounded increasingly serious. Presumably Stephane's impromptu arrival at the store had been organized by Spanky to remove Paul from the picture. I wondered whether the daemon provided a sort of after-sales service, or if he just left them to get on with it.

Beverly made a brief, grim appearance in Max's office and together they rang France. The call degenerated into a shouting match, and that was the last we saw of her. Max went ahead and closed the deal with Neville Syms, so that work could begin on the expansion of the company. A healthy pay rise rewarded my company loyalty. I personally supervised the designs and interior fittings for the two new store sites, one in Bayswater and one in Chiswick, and together we planned the grand openings. With me uncomfortably wedged into place as Max's surrogate son, we started interviewing new floor staff.

Darryl sent me a letter, vaguely recriminatory in tone, in which he nevertheless absolved me from any blame in his accident, but announced that he would not be returning to

Thanet. The loss of his eye had adversely affected his balance, and consequently he was planning to take a part-time job near his family in the Midlands.

I began to appreciate just how hardworking and uncomplaining Lottie had remained through the store's various upheavals. Nothing seemed to faze her. I told Max that I hoped he realized what a loyal employee he had, and asked him to consider promoting her in one of the new stores. Typically, he said he'd get back to me at a later date.

It was now October, and for me life was settling itself into entirely new patterns. Sarah introduced me to her circle, and our social life suddenly expanded. Now that I had a girlfriend and could safely be presented at dinner as part of a couple, all kinds of invitations began to appear. Oddly enough, I felt closer to Sarah when we were in public than during the time we spent in each other's company. Our relationship was convenient and our needs coincided, but there was no real depth to it. Friends damned us with faint praise by saying how well we looked together.

Max agreed that it was important for me to reflect the right company image, and allowed me to purchase a smart sea-green Mercedes 350SL from his brother-in-law, who ran a second-hand dealership in South London. I drove through the sunset streets with my arm across the back of the passenger seat, breathing in the scent of old leather. It was the smell of success.

My parents called several times, but had trouble operating the payphone correctly. They mailed me a series of insufferably cute postcards, and Laura sent a picture of her newly slimmed self embracing a leering local boy in gold chains and tight trousers.

As time passed I started to forget the shy, inept person I had once been. With each new day I felt more sure of myself, more confident of my capabilities. And yet it was sometimes impossible to believe what had happened to me. On these occasions I felt unanchored and disturbed, and would stay in bed with the phone off the hook until the sensation had passed.

My time spent with Spanky now seemed dreamlike and unreal. I didn't suppose I would ever be able to come to terms with my 'daemonic' experience. There was nobody I could really discuss it with except Zack, and talking to him was preaching to the converted. I wanted someone to convince me that Spanky had only existed because I'd needed to create him, that I had really made the changes by myself.

But I knew I hadn't.

I would never have been able to do the things he had done.

Spanky had shown me things no one else could see, done things no one else could do. And now, the truth of the matter was, I missed him.

But not for long.

CHAPTER NINETEEN

Reparation

IT HURTS to recall what happened next, just when things were going so well.

It started on a Monday morning in the last week of October. Sarah had stayed at her own apartment the night before, and for once I had enjoyed a good night's sleep. I slapped my alarm off at 7.40 a.m., slipped into a white towelling robe and headed downstairs to collect the milk. There was a letter on the doormat, a plain white envelope addressed to me in script. Fountain pen, violet ink. No stamp, which was odd.

I unsealed the envelope and shook out a single sheet of thick white paper. It looked like a typed, itemized bill. No return address.

It read as follows;

For The Personal Attention of Martyn Ross

INVOICE
To Providing The Following Services:

Improvement Of Subject's Career Prospects
Blinding of Darryl Smart..170.00

Removal of Paul Deakin	220.00
Influencing Neville Syms	105.00
Influencing Max Deakin	144.00

Reconstruction Of Subject's Family Life

Breakup of father's extra-marital relationship	63.00
Weight-loss of sister/improved social life	58.00
Rejuvenation of parents' marriage	218.00
*Sundry expenses, accommodation, travel	274.00

[Itemized receipts available on request]

Personal Growth/Improvement of Subject's life

New wardrobe/dress sense	82.00
Creation of sexual charisma	136.00
Provision of new apartment	292.00
Conversational ability/charm	45.00
Personality enhancement	63.00
Heightening of senses	34.00
Improving general standard of life	70.00
Spending money, sundries	124.00

The following amount is now due:	2,098.00

My first thought was that Spanky had left behind a kind of delayed-reaction joke. Then I wondered if someone was trying to blackmail me. But who would be so jealous of my new-found success? Darryl? Max's son? The paper held no clue to the identity of the sender. It had to be from Spanky. Who else knew so much about the last few weeks?

I examined the sheet again. Yes, that was it. It had to be a practical joke.

'No joke, I'm afraid.'

Spanky was leaning against the doorframe in a red T-shirt,

black lounge suit and zip-boots, cleaning his nails with a toothpick. 'Are you making coffee?'

He picked up the milk bottle on the doormat and passed it to me. I was pleased to see him, but apprehensive. He followed me through to the kitchen and watched as I filled the kettle.

'So what the hell is it?' I asked.

'What does it look like? My bill. For services rendered.'

'Bill? You never mentioned any payment for what you did. What currency is this to be paid in, anyway? Pounds? Dollars? Yen?'

'They're not monetary units. I don't accept cash. Don't worry, you have twenty-four hours to pay in full.'

Hadn't Spanky told me he'd wanted to help just for the pleasure of doing so, or words to that effect? I wished I could remember the specific conversation. A sickness began swirling around in the pit of my stomach.

'I don't understand your attitude, Martyn.'

Spanky was pacing back and forth by the kitchen table, his left eye screwed up in puzzlement. 'Do you really think you can get something for nothing these days? *Nobody* gets something for nothing, surely common sense tells you that.'

'You wanted to help me,' I said lamely.

'That's right, I did want to help you.'

'Then why are you demanding payment now?'

'Martyn, I sold you my services. I gave you my best sales pitch, certainly, but I genuinely wanted to help you. It's possible for someone who rents apartments to want to help the homeless, isn't it?'

'Oh, come on! You're telling me you're a scam artist. You breeze into my life uninvited, give me all this bullshit about being a muse, change everything around and expect me to pay you?'

'Well, you've run up a bit of a debt, but it's nothing that can't be cleared.'

The bad feeling grew worse, a slow intestinal upending of a kind I hadn't felt for years. I had trusted him and this, if it was for real, was going to hurt.

As I stood there in my dressing gown arguing with someone who didn't even exist in the real world, I convinced myself that Spanky had pulled off an even bigger stunt by getting me to believe that he was some kind of supernatural being in the first place. How had he done it? Sure, any decent hypnotist could create the illusions, but the rest . . . okay, so he was a con-artist, plain and simple. He'd picked me out as a susceptible mark and played me like a piano, working on my weaknesses until I was completely under his control. My gullibility was truly shameful.

But if the whole thing was a trick, what did he stand to gain? Did he think I would sign over my bank account to him? He had put most of the money there in the first place. Until now, Spanky had never asked me for anything except trust.

None of it made sense.

'It makes sense, Martyn, so long as you rid yourself of your doubts about me.'

The mind-reading number again. I couldn't believe that this was simply a magic trick.

'It would have been easy enough to lie to you once you believed in me,' he continued, answering my unspoken thoughts, 'but what would that have gained? I offered you my services and you were happy to accept.'

'You never told me there was a price.'

'Can you really be that naïve, Martyn? There's one thing in lifetime upon lifetime of existence that never changes. Nothing is free. No free lunch, no free advice, no free peace of mind, no free happiness. Everything comes with a bill, Martyn. Everything. In your heart, you always knew it. Anyone who says otherwise is a liar.'

He folded the sheet of paper, slipped it into the pocket of my robe and patted it flat.

'Don't worry about the piece of paper. It's really not an invoice; I thought I'd present it in a form you'd recognize, that's all.'

He was reading my mind constantly now; I could sense it. I had no choice but to play along. I needed to find a way of handling the situation without revealing my thoughts.

'If you're not after money, how am I supposed to clear your bill?' I asked. 'What are the terms of payment?'

Spanky scratched the side of his nose, thinking. He seemed to be on the verge of breaking into a grin. 'Ah well, that's the thing. I worked out the amount in units appropriate to your situation. Your currency means nothing to me, just paper and metal. Daemoniality is a matter of balance; charity with harm, kindness with cruelty, equality with subjugation. I have provided you with a considerable amount of good fortune, perhaps more than I should have. My wage should at least equal that debt.'

'Cut the bullshit. Just tell me how I pay.'

'Your payment is something you can afford, but whether you'll want to part with it is another matter. Once an equilibrium is reached between us, the debt is cleared. Do you understand?'

'You're asking me to do something bad.'

'Do you *understand*, Martyn?' A steel chord this time.

'Yes—'

'I'm not asking you to do something bad. On the contrary, it might work out well for both of us. Just give me your life.'

'You mean it's a Faustian thing, like you want my soul—'

'Stop being stupid. I told you, this has nothing to do with your so-called soul. This is real, flesh and blood. Besides, I value your friendship. I would never hurt you. The fact of the matter is, I need your body.' He pulled himself up to the marble kitchen counter and sat, swinging his legs like a pendulum.

'You once asked about my human form, and how I came by it. I'll explain what happened, and then perhaps you'll understand what I require from you.'

He raised his arms and held his legs out straight, like a marionette. 'These limbs, this torso, this face belongs to a man named William Beaumont. He was born in the mid-nineteen twenties, as I believe I told you. His mother Edith was a famous stage actress and his father practised civil law, and they lived harmoniously together in Wigmore Street.

'William was a clerk for a firm of marine insurers. He didn't enjoy the work, but it was considered a solid career for a young man. He was a Protestant and a dreamer and longed to be an artist, to wander the countryside with his easel and water-colours, but his parents wished him to make his own way in the world, and he needed an income. One day, at the age of twenty-five, he suffered a tragic accident while crossing the road just outside his house. One still saw horses on the streets in 1950, of course, trotting among the motor cars. One such creature, attached to a brewers' dray, became frightened by the sound of a car horn and reared, kicking him in the back. He sustained a nasty bruise, but was well enough to rise from the road and walk home. A short while later he felt sick and was put to bed by the housemaid. That night, he nearly died of kidney failure.

'During those feverish hours, William pleaded for an angel to enter his heart and heal his pain-wracked body. At this time, in your year of 1950, I was combing the city looking for a human form that I could take. For three long years I had searched, to no avail. Then I heard the boy's call, inviting me in. You see, I have to be invited. I can't take human possession by force. In the early hours of the morning I visited the gloomy sick-room and saw that William was ideal, so I accepted his offer and entered his body. He had invited me in to ease his suffering, and so we were able to help each other.

'For a while there was just darkness and warmth, like a return to the womb. Then, with the passing of a dozen hours I came to strength, armed with the instinctive knowledge that I had changed. His body healed with my help, and I grew within him. I usurped the youth's fleshly frame, and in its weakened state easily adopted his personality. I became William. That is how a daemon comes to earth, by inhabiting the body of a mortal.'

'So who saw Lawrence dying in hospital?'

'William, of course.'

'My new life quickly grew to seem natural and normal as I learned to exert my spiritual powers in a more discreet form. If the boy's family noticed the change in his behaviour, they never mentioned it.' He flicked up his eyebrows – *stupid humans*. 'The arrangement worked out well for both of us. From the moment I took him, William ceased to age.'

'But you stole his will.'

'As I said, there was something in the arrangement for both of us. In 1962, at the age of thirty-seven, I left London behind and moved to the east coast of America, where no one knew me and I would not have to explain my continuing youthfulness. The life and energy of New York was the perfect antidote to the dreary eons I had passed alone and the dullness of those early years in London. Encased in my human body, time passed quickly. Too quickly. I haven't achieved any of the tasks I once set myself.

'Now, as you quite correctly pointed out, this body is approaching its seventieth birthday. And that's the problem, you see. William's time is almost up. Three score years and ten – that's all your archaic biblical laws allow for a mortal carcass. I have to find another host, and this time spend my years more wisely. Oh, the havoc I could wreak! I tested a few others, but they didn't perform to my satisfaction. That leaves you.'

I could barely absorb what I was hearing. It felt as if I was slipping into some surreal alternate world. Was this what happened to murderers when they were arrested, shouting over their shoulders to the cameras that daemons had made them do it? I backed away from Spanky now, suddenly aware of his powers, alarmed by what he could do if I failed to obey him.

'I'll find some other method of payment,' I said as firmly as I could. 'There must be a way to work this out.'

'There *is* no other way, Mar-tyn.' He drew out my name in a teasing syllable, lightly walking forward on the balls of his feet. The absurdly handsome face took on a darker tone, as his brows lowered to his narrowing eyes. 'My time in this body is running out. I'll never find another host as suitable as you. You're perfect. Healthy. Intelligent. *Weak-willed.*'

'I need time to think about this.'

It was the best I could come up with. He knew my every move.

'Think as fast as you like. You have one working day to come to terms with your payment. Twenty-four hours in which to surrender your life to me. If you haven't agreed to clear your debt by tomorrow night, I'm afraid you're going to see a side of old Spanky that no one's ever stayed sane enough to describe.'

A moment later he was gone. I was alone in my apartment with a bill in my pocket and a price on my head.

I had little time to consider the carefully-laid trap that I had cheerfully wandered into. And no time to find a way out.

Intimidation

'CALM DOWN, calm down. Let's take this more slowly. We'll never get anywhere if we panic.'

This was me talking to Zack, who had pulled out every book on the shelf and was busy strewing them all over the floor. Debbie had gone to the clinic for a scan and Zack should really have gone with her, but instead he was trying to help me find a way out of my obligation.

Zack was the only person I had told about the daemon, and the only one who was likely to believe me. For all I knew my butchered corpse could turn up on the steps of the store one morning, and everyone would simply wonder what the hell had happened. Since I had called Zack and told him about Spanky's threat, he had fallen apart on me.

'I'm sorry,' he kept apologizing, 'I only know the theory. I'm no good at practical application. I've never seen one of these creatures before.'

'Stick around until tonight,' I said, accepting another stack of magazines from him. These ones formed an old partwork entitled *Man, Myth & Magic*. As they mostly comprised charming old woodcuts and fat nude witches, I couldn't imagine that we'd gain much enlightenment from them.

Late last night I had described my recent meetings with Spanky in meticulous detail, hoping that something would spark an idea in Zack's mind. Unfortunately, my former flatmate's thinking was as woolly as his macramé mandala. He was unable to get to grips with the idea of me incurring supernatural vengeance. I had a tough enough time dealing with the concept myself, until I remembered the terrible playful look in Spanky's eyes just before he left. It was the look of a man who would stand over you and watch you die. Whether a man or a myth he was real enough, and I passed the long hours of darkness after his visit pacing my bedroom with all the lights turned on.

If he wanted to frighten me or hurt me, he could easily do so. He knew my hopes and fears. He'd been inside my head. He'd been inside my body.

Surrender was out of the question – who wanted to live without their free will? But failure to do so was unthinkable. One good thing; I felt that I was finally learning to shield my thoughts from him. But I had no idea how to fight back. The trouble was, neither did Zack. Now that his secret hopes had been realized, now that he was being offered proof that the world existed on another plane, he didn't know what to do, and didn't want to be involved. I once saw a newspaper cartoon in which an imprisoned Gandalf summons all his faithful *Lord Of The Rings* fans to come to his aid, only to find himself faced with a terrified group of quaking youths in anoraks. Zack was the same. All he could do was crawl about on the carpet throwing open magazine articles and pointing to carvings. This wasn't going to help me.

'Couldn't you get a body from a morgue and give him that?' he asked in apparent seriousness. 'Or what about digging one up in a cemetery?'

'For Christ's sake, Zack, it's not the nineteenth century. You can't go marching into a graveyard with a shovel and a lantern. Face it, there's nothing in any of these books to cope with a situation like this.'

Spanky wasn't covered by any traditional image. He was a modern man, and his needs matched all the present-day public fixations about youth culture. He liked smart clothes and good times. And he wanted to stay young.

'It's your fault,' Zack moaned. 'If you hadn't been so dissatisfied with your life, if you hadn't accepted his offer in the first place ...'

'I didn't sign anything. He was a good salesman. And he did a good job. It's just that I wasn't ready for the price he'd placed on his services.'

'If you don't find a way to pay him, suppose he summons all the powers of eternal torment? You don't want that coming down on you.'

'No shit.'

I turned to another stack of magazines and began sifting through them. Most of the articles were sensationalist filler-pieces, an excuse to run photographs of naked coven members. Since I wasn't about to risk someone else's life in order to clear my debt, I had to prepare to face my adversary alone. All I knew about him was what he'd elected to tell me. My first task was to understand the way he operated.

'Don't you have any serious works on the subject?' I asked.

'You could try the library,' Zack replied. He didn't volunteer to accompany me. I had to accept his point of view. He was building a new life for himself. His girlfriend was pregnant. He didn't want anything to endanger that.

So I tried the library.

The problem with occult books, I quickly discovered, was

that they all looked the same. I had this image of someone blowing the dust from obscure pigskin-covered tomes. Instead I found myself in the New Age section, thumbing through paperback reprints. Densely set in forgotten typefaces, couched in barely comprehensible English, there were endless transcriptions of possession, vampirism, necromancy, exorcism, superstition, hypnotism, palmistry, Gnosticism, freemasonry, Rosicrucianism and satanic apparitions, all in eye-straining, microscopic print. Despite the dramatic subject matter of these accounts, most were described in deadening, ponderous, unreadable prose.

The book I finally found most helpful was a slim volume published by the Dover Press purporting to delineate the demon world in relation to everyday life. I didn't belong to the library and there was a two-day borrowing delay for new members, so I slipped the little book into my jacket, promising myself that I'd return it later if I was still alive.

It was raining hard when I returned to my apartment. Water sluiced against the tall lounge windows from a blocked gutter, causing a steady stream to crackle on the sill. I poured myself coffee and played back the day's telephone messages. A distant, buzzing call from my sister, having fun, wishing I was with them, why didn't I come out for the week. A message from Max, where the hell was I, there had been an important meeting with the shopfitters first thing this morning, why had I missed it. Sarah calling from Roger's, arranging dinner with me tomorrow night. I would deal with them all later. Right now, I had more important matters on my mind.

I opened the book and began to read.

My hopes grew dimmer with each fresh paragraph. The study of demoniality was initially defined by intellectually curious clergymen, who investigated case histories in their parishes. Victims complained of repeated visitations from the devil's agents. At first, tempting offers were made, riches promised, seductions and sexual enticements displayed. Sometimes the victims succumbed; sometimes they resisted. Either way, the outcome was the same. The daemon – whether succubus, incubus or shape-shifter – would wear the victim down, appearing in many forms, a winged pig, a skeleton, a serpent, a bird. Exhausted, the victim succumbed to unspeakable horrors. But what were the horrors to which they succumbed? The book failed to address the question. With growing apprehension I turned to the next chapter.

Sometimes the daemon appeared in the guise of an angel, androgynous, charming, sincere. I knew that one. The arrival of a daemon could be sensed if concentrated upon; there was a faint smell of snuff, and brandy perfumed with musk. I remembered the slight odour Spanky carried with him. I'd always assumed it was his aftershave.

The daemon had only one agenda; the misery and subjugation of the human host. He possessed the soul of a damned being. Although he bestowed great gifts, he could only introduce others to the torments of hell. There could be no respite in his calling. For this purpose he was allowed to return to earth, and for this purpose only. No mention of there being four of them. I only had his word for that.

He *could* be tricked.

For a moment my hopes flared, only to grow dim again as I read on. In order to avoid being tricked from his purpose, the daemon became intimate with his human host, so that he would comprehend the host's reactions in any situation. Well, I thought, we'll have to see about that.

It was possible to hide objects from the daemon by sealing

them in metal; an old alchemical practice. A quantity of frogspawn, if drunk down fresh, protected the imbiber from possession. The fur of a cat, if carefully skinned from its body and eaten while warm, could also ...

I decided I wouldn't find the answer in a book.

I went to the kitchen, carefully wrapped the volume in aluminium foil and placed it under my mattress. As my sole act of protection against an all-powerful enemy it seemed pitifully inadequate. But it represented my only positive move.

As hard as I tried, I could not think of a single practical act of protection. He needed no key to enter, no invitation to appear. He was as dangerous as he wanted to be, and if he decided that I should suddenly die in terrible agony, there was no doubt in my mind that he could make it happen.

I had to stop my hands from shaking. Wasn't that how witch-doctors worked, by making their intentions known to their victims and setting a time limit? I determined not to be scared, which was easier decided than done.

Several times in the course of that strange afternoon, I thought I heard a noise in the apartment. A continuous tapping sound in the bedroom; water pipes expanding. A faint shuffling noise in the kitchen; mice, perhaps. Every tick and creak of the building was magnifying itself. I imagined Spanky moving silently across the floor behind me. Following my path as I passed from room to room. Waiting in the darkness for the moment when I finally turned out the lights.

And then, sitting there with the incessant sound of rain filling my ears, I considered killing someone, substituting a life for my own. After all, death was with us every second of the day. Around the world, soldiers were doing it without pity or remorse, blinded by their faith. These authors of death and carnage remained unknown to their victims. In my mind's eye

I saw them; the weak, the lost, the innocent, caught between rival factions in wars no one could win. Bullets strayed from their targets. A child stepped on a landmine and was blown to pieces. Warriors still championed savage gods, killing for causes beyond reason, dying without understanding why. For a moment it seemed that the world contained far more pointless savagery than any spirit daemon.

But I knew I couldn't contribute to that cruelty. The dilemma was mine alone to solve.

Just a few hours left.

There was one course of action I hadn't considered taking. I felt sure now that Spanky had been through this before. I wanted to see his handiwork. He had told me about another of his victims, the woman in West London whose 'case' he had felt was a lost cause. He had made a joke about her name, said it described her perfectly.

After a few minutes, it came to me.

Melanie Palmer.

It was a place to start.

CHAPTER TWENTY-ONE

Victimization

FOR THE first and only time in my life, a London telephone directory proved itself useful.

There was only one Melanie Palmer in West London, and she was listed. The address was somewhere in Hammersmith. I called the number, but there was no reply and no machine. I had no time to waste, and no other plan. I made my way over there.

It hadn't stopped raining all day. Hammersmith was a chaotic tangle of roadworks and flooded pavements. My battered A-Z took me to a quiet backstreet of terraced houses, discoloured pillars framing bay windows with taped panes, dead plants in dogshit-covered tubs. Here people made an effort to live decent lives, and were slowly losing the battle.

I found her door, number 75, but there was no light in the hall and no reply. I stepped back in the small concreted front garden and stared up at the lifeless bedroom windows.

'She's gone,' said a young woman who was pulling a bicycle into the hall of the house next door. 'You're looking for Melanie Palmer?'

'That's right, yes.'

'Were you a friend of hers?'

'Not really, no. More a friend of a friend.'

'I'm afraid she had an accident. She's not here anymore.' The woman leaned her bicycle in the narrow hallway and came out to the step. I could tell she was looking for someone to talk to. 'I wasn't here when it happened. I'd gone to my sister's for the week-end. She did something in the kitchen. I think there was a fire.'

'When was this?' I asked. 'Is she all right?'

'It must have been a few weeks ago now. As far as I know she's recuperating, but they couldn't save her eyes. She got some kind of kitchen chemical in them. We'd never been all that friendly with her, to tell the truth. She'd been a bit funny for a while.'

'How do you mean – funny?'

'Acting strangely. Very difficult. Complaining about the noise when we weren't making any, things like that. And she'd started talking to herself.'

'Do you remember anything of what she said?'

The neighbour looked at me to see if I was being serious. 'Not really,' she replied. 'She had conversations, like she was talking to someone. She'd stand outside this window arguing away nineteen to the dozen. I didn't like to let her know I could see. It was embarrassing.'

'You don't know where she is now, do you?'

'I think she was taken to her mother's house on the coast. I have the number, you know, in case of emergencies.'

'Do you think I could have it?'

'I shouldn't really give it out. I understand she's taking things very badly.'

I looked back up at the darkened rooms where Spanky must have appeared to Melanie Palmer night after night, urging her to give up her free will and admit him into her body, whispering poisonous threats in her ears, creeping up on her in the gloom and frightening her out of her wits until she could stand it no longer and had run down into the kitchen ...

He hadn't wanted her after that. He'd pushed her too far. Caused her to become emotionally and physically scarred. So he'd moved on. Back to his other prime candidate. Me. He'd even brazenly told me about it.

The neighbour wrote down the number on a piece of envelope and handed it to me shamefacedly, as if breaking a promise. The streets of falling rain seemed warm compared to the chill seeping into my bones.

I arrived back at my apartment, and was just inserting my key into the lock when I smelled it. Brandy, snuff and musk. Coming from inside.

Although there was no sign of disturbance, I knew he'd been here. The faint perfume of his spoor clung to the furniture and door handles like gossamer. The foil-wrapped book under the bed had not been touched, but other things had been shifted slightly – just enough to inform me of his visit. He'd been checking up on me, trying to work out my next move. Would I simply give in as he hoped, or prepare to face him as an opponent? Surely he knew me well enough to sense which way I would jump. What then, would he expect of me?

I checked my watch. Nearly twenty-four hours had elapsed since his last appearance. I knew that locks couldn't keep him out, but ensuring that all the doors and windows were shut in the apartment made me feel more comfortable.

I thought of Melanie Palmer, conducting desperate public arguments with Spanky while the neighbours assumed she was going mad and quietly closed their doors on her. Was it to be my turn next? As carefully as I considered the situation, there seemed to be nothing I could do to protect myself. I could only continue from moment to moment, knowing that I would have to face up to the problem once Spanky made his intentions known.

The main thing was not to panic.

I pushed the approaching confrontation to the back of my mind, where it crouched in half-darkness, a bill I could not pay and a betrayal I could not accept.

I thought about Sarah. My recent supervision of Thanet's proposed Bayswater office was starting to occupy me late into the evenings. The longer hours were reducing our time together, and left me tired when I spent the night with her. It was hardly surprising that our relationship was a strange one. We shared so little of each other. We ate and slept together, discussed work and movies, but I never knew what she was thinking. Her eyes would break contact with mine, as though she was afraid they would reveal something personal, an act of self-betrayal. Perhaps we had both expected to fall in love, and were surprised when we hadn't. She maintained her independence on every level, no doubt as a matter of future convenience. I doubted she would expect me to rely on her in a crisis.

That was a shame, because right now I needed all the backup I could get.

Less than an hour before the deadline was up, I dug the piece of envelope from my jacket pocket and rang Ann Palmer, Melanie's mother. I had delayed making the call because I had no idea what I could say without upsetting her. When an older woman's guarded voice answered, I knew I had reached Melanie's mother.

'Mrs Palmer,' I began, 'I was sorry to hear about your daughter's accident.'

'Who are you?' she countered. 'If you're a friend of

Melanie's, you'll know she's too ill to speak to anyone on the telephone.'

I hated to lie, but there seemed no other way of getting at the truth. I identified myself as a friend, a neighbour who had just returned from a vacation overseas. I had been worried after calling at the house and receiving no reply. I said I'd heard that Melanie had suffered some kind of accident. She demanded to know my name, so I was forced to make one up. I used the identity of Spanky's host, William Beaumont. I asked if there was anything I could do to help.

'My daughter hasn't been well for some while, Mr Beaumont, and now she is blind, and has undergone a nervous collapse.' She stated the facts without emotion, as if trying to become accustomed to them. I asked what had happened exactly. There was a sigh on the other end of the line.

'She was distraught, and she got something in her eyes, some kind of oven cleaner, and it caught alight. It burned and burned. I don't know how ...' She was close to tears. Ann knew that her daughter had done this to herself. The accusation remained unspoken. *I don't know how she could do such a thing.*

'She was under a lot of strain. She wasn't used to being alone, and didn't enjoy it. Marriages don't seem to last long these days. Perhaps if her husband had been there, none of this would have happened.'

I asked again if there was anything I could do to help.

'I think it's best that she's allowed to recover in her own way, though it's kind of you to offer. They say time heals, but it won't bring back her sight, will it, Mr Beaumont? She's only twenty years old.'

The image of a girl with a bandaged face, staring sightlessly out to sea, stayed in my head. I couldn't wait in the apartment any longer. Spanky would have to come for me. I threw on my raincoat and caught a bus back to the store.

The shopfront spotlights were still blazing behind a curtain of rain. Max had gone home, furious with me for not calling in. For the next hour I worked with Lottie, who sat worrying a nail in her teeth as she logged updated inventory to the computer system, and filled me in on the new workload assignments.

When I next looked up, the display showroom was in darkness, and only the rear offices were illuminated; Max abhorred wasted electricity. Somewhere in the caliginous new-nylon atmosphere of the sitting-room layouts I heard a sound, a whisper of movement that suggested someone shifting position while reading a book. And I knew he was there. Beneath the smell of factory carpet-fibre and armchair leather was the daemon's thickening odour.

Leaving Lottie at the computer, I walked away from the pool of light with my heartbeat rising. Slowly I moved into the gloom, and saw the faint outline of the penumbral figure that sat immobile, glittering like blackened quartz. Before me was the couch where I knew he waited. To my left stood a tall chromium lamp, its switch dangling from a length of coiled flex. I reached out my hand and clicked it on.

The blackness in the centre of the sofa vanished a split-second after light filled the showroom. An indentation showed in the cushions. The smell that usually lingered had mutated into an acrid odour, like perfume tossed on an ageing corpse. The faintest of sounds ruffled the still, dead air, sounding like a word.

. . . *Martyn*.

CHAPTER TWENTY-TWO

Declaration

TWENTY-SEVEN and a half hours after he had made his demand, I was still waiting for Spanky to reappear in my apartment.

Not wanting to confront him in the office while Lottie was working there, I had hurriedly returned home. I cautiously entered the building, then roamed the apartment on tenterhooks, unable to eat or settle to any task that required concentration.

I tried to watch television, but the programmes seemed vacuous and detached from life. I was convinced he would appear, and prayed that he would not. But Spanky had always followed through on his promises. He had spent a considerable period of time preparing me as his next host. I felt certain he would be determined to claim on his investment.

And yet the evening dragged on without a visit from my daemonic entity. By 11.15 p.m. I had half-convinced myself that he wouldn't show.

When he did appear I was totally unprepared, coming out of the kitchen with a glass of milk. As I rounded the counter he was standing in front of me in black leather jeans and a studded chrome belt, bare-chested and tensed. I jumped so badly that the glass slipped from my hand and smashed on the floor.

'Good evening, Martyn. You look like you just saw a ghost.'

'What did you do to Melanie Palmer?' I asked, ignoring the shattered glass and moving away to the tall windows. I wanted to be within sight of the street, where someone might at least catch a glimpse of me if there was trouble.

'I thought you might check into that.' He smiled, pleased to have guessed correctly. 'Melanie's husband had left her. I was trying to help her come to terms with her feelings of rejection, but she was too unstable to take my advice.'

'So she blinded herself.'

'You *have* been doing your homework, haven't you? I hold a mirror up to people, Martyn. I show them their true selves. She didn't like what she saw.'

'She was barely out of her teens. What could she have seen to make her do something like that, for Christ's sake?'

Spanky turned to face me, glaring. 'She was an infatuated little girl who had married too early, and was losing her hold on life. I made my proposal, but she was too headstrong to accept it. There was nothing I could do for her. I told you at the time.'

'So you're telling me she didn't—'

'Martyn, I'm here to talk about you,' he said softly. 'Do we have a deal or not?'

'If you're asking whether I'm willing to surrender the control of my physical self,' I said angrily, 'the answer is no.'

Spanky was shaking his head and pacing the floor as if he could barely believe that someone had questioned the generosity of his offer.

'Well, now we have a problem, Martyn. Obviously, I can't leave the debt unsettled, and I can't extend beyond tonight's deadline. How do you propose to pay me?'

'I don't know.'

'So if you test-drove a car and kept it for a week, and at the end of that week refused to pay for it or give it back, you'd think that was acceptable behaviour?'

'You tricked me.'

'And a car dealer wouldn't enhance the features of the car he was trying to sell you, I suppose.'

'This isn't the same as a fucking car, and you know it. You're screwing around with people's lives. Christ, you *blinded* Darryl to get me a promotion.'

'The thought didn't seem to bother you when the results were in your favour.'

'I didn't realize – I didn't think about the consequences.'

'Of course not. Why do you think I picked you? But now your liberal sense of guilt has kicked in. Excuse my heart if it doesn't bleed for you, Martyn. You've got everything you wanted with a minimum of personal effort, remember? Ever hear the saying, *Be careful what you wish for, you might just get it*? Well, you've got yours, and I've got nothing for it.'

'Then take back what you gave me.'

'I can't take back knowledge. You're not the same man you used to be.'

'You never meant to help me at all,' I replied angrily. 'All the things you did, the improvements you made were to pave the way for when you took possession, weren't they? You wanted everything to be set up in readiness.'

Spanky rolled his eyes to the ceiling. 'Why are humans always so ungrateful?' he asked. 'Martyn, I could have taken you that night on the hill, when I entered your senses. But part of you was still resistant. I wanted you to choose to accept my control unconditionally. I genuinely like you. Now you're turning down the chance for an extraordinary future. Think of the life we could lead as one person.'

'Without my free will, there would be no life.'

He looked away at the windows, his face tightening. 'I won't release you from your debt.'

'And I can't pay it.' I sounded strong, but the nerves in my legs were trembling.

He thought for a moment. 'Remember the first time we met? When I cupped your hands together and asked you to look inside them?'

'Yes.'

'Do it again now.'

I didn't want to. The ceiling lights had suddenly begun to dim, and the corners of the room were already fading into darkness. Reluctantly, I found myself raising my hands and bringing the palms together.

'Now – open them.'

I couldn't tell if he was willing me to do so, or if I really wanted to, but slowly I separated the fingers.

And a fistful of fat, gleaming brown spiders exploded from within, hundreds of them wetly smothering my arms, falling onto my chest and stomach in tangles of mandibles and egg-sacs and long jointed legs.

I shouted and leapt back in horror, frenziedly shaking out my hands as they skittered in every direction across the floor, vanishing under the furniture. But moments later the first ones were already fading. By the time my cries had ceased they were nowhere to be seen, and the lights had risen once more. It was just one of his hallucinations, but I still wanted to check underneath the sofa.

'You know you'll give in eventually,' he said, casually studying the base of a ceramic bowl I had purchased for the coffee table. 'It's all a question of realities. Is this a bowl, for example, or a nest of poisonous cobras?'

'I'd know the snakes weren't real. You told me yourself you're an illusionist.'

'But I'd catch you with your guard down eventually.' He replaced the bowl and walked toward me, pointing at my chest. 'I can make you think that there's a scorpion inside your heart, a transparent, tiny scorpion nestled in your aorta that stings you every time you try to move. You raise your arm, it stings. You try to breathe, it stings. The muscle twitches and it stings, it stings, it stings. You can't always disbelieve the things you can't see.'

'You're wasting your time. I won't give you what you want.'

'You will, Martyn. Don't make the mistake of thinking that you're a worthy adversary for me. Remember, I know you as well as I know myself. But you know nothing at all about me.'

'I want you to leave now.' I moved toward the door, intending to open it, but could not stop myself from searching the floor for spiders.

'It's a pity we're to be enemies.' He seemed resigned to the fact, as though he had long considered it the only possible outcome.

'Unless you can find another way for me to pay,' I said.

'There is only one way to pay me. In blood and in full.' He stood in the door, a seething black outline against the pale hall lights. 'You'll reimburse me for my efforts, Martyn, I promise you that. And your *naïveté* will be your downfall.'

'I wouldn't bet on it. I'm not as gullible as I used to be.'

'Oh, really?' I could see the outline of his too-white teeth as he smiled. 'Then tell me, Martyn. Where do you think your parents are right now?'

I felt as if I had stepped into a falling lift. 'They're in Portugal,' I said dully.

'In Portugal,' he repeated. 'Interesting. Did you ever consider that those postcards and calls might be simple deceptions, created to make you believe that your parents were in good health?'

I tried to speak, but found myself silenced. My throat felt sore and parched, my mouth too dry to form the words.

'Well, you needn't worry on that score,' Spanky continued airily. 'I'm just *teasing*. The postcards were all real and your sister now looks good enough to eat. But you see how easy it is for me to tamper with your sense of wellbeing, don't you? Your family have had a wonderful time, but now they're about to come home. Their house is nearly ready to move back into. It would be a shame if their holiday came to an abrupt and unpleasant end.'

'If you harm them—'

'You'll do what, exactly? Here's another question to challenge your sense of reality; Where do you think Max's son is at this moment?'

'In France, somewhere near Avignon.'

'This time you're wrong. Paul is back in his apartment. He arrived home just an hour ago. The romance I concocted for him doesn't seem to have worked out. The little bitch was already spoken for. I can't be held responsible for unscheduled changes. Tell you what, let's start with poor old lovesick Paul, and put him out of his misery on the stroke of midnight – I'll race you there, shall I?'

I watched as he sauntered off down the hall toward the elevator bank. Then I ran back into my apartment and locked the door from the inside.

Paul's line was engaged. If he had just arrived back in town, he was probably playing back his messages.

I knew where he lived.

I checked my watch. Fourteen minutes to twelve. If I jumped

a cab, I should just be able to make it. There was no point in calling Max. He lived further away from Paul than I did.

I was sure that I could get there in time to save him.

I was so *sure*.

CHAPTER TWENTY-THREE

Bestiality

WHICH BRINGS me back to where I began.

Paul was sprawled out with a poker through his gut, and he died believing that I was his killer. A nice touch from Spanky; he had taken on my appearance while he carried out his work, just in case the boy had lived, or had managed to talk to someone before he died.

I didn't think anyone had seen me arrive or leave, but I couldn't be certain. I should have called the police, but in my agitated state I would have incriminated myself if I had done so. I had caused his death as surely as if I had killed him myself. How long would they take to discover his body? To tell the truth now was unthinkable; no one in their right mind would believe me.

Two hours after I saw Paul die before my eyes I was storming around my apartment, my mind filled with warring, absurd contradictions.

During the last few weeks the only thing that had anchored me to my changed life was my association with Spanky. Now that he was no longer there, I felt lost in my new surroundings; the bright, pristine rooms that felt too large and were always too tidy, the shiny possessions that were hardly used, the new friends who were never at home, the smart car with a permanently clean ashtray, the designer girlfriend who kept her distance, the perfectly groomed figure I no longer recognized when I looked in the mirror.

I badly needed to talk to someone.

I called Sarah, but there was no answer from her apartment. Just the usual cool-casual ansaphone message. Even if she had been in, I knew that I couldn't have asked for her help, and she wouldn't have expected me to. I nearly rang Zack, then thought; isn't that what Spanky wants? If I involve others, they'll be at risk. He'll hurt them to make me capitulate, and have me branded as a murderer. I had to work out the limit of his abilities. Could he read my thoughts at a distance? I thought not, but it was impossible to be sure of anything.

I rang the airport to ask about incoming flights from Portugal, but there were no more arrivals scheduled for tonight. I was told I would have to request a passenger check for each flight as it arrived. What if Spanky decided to intercept my family? I had no idea how to track them down. I didn't even know which airport they were likely to use. I could be sure that my nemesis would take the least expected route.

One part of my dilemma was clear enough. I had made a stand against the daemon, but had no way of backing up my bravado with positive action. As far as I knew, he had no earthly weaknesses. I hung on to the thought that he needed my consent to take control. It was the only defence I had.

For want of something more useful to do I changed back to my old clothes, the jeans and baggy T-shirt I had always worn before I met him. I called Sarah again. Still no reply. I instinctively knew that she was staying out for the night. Fidelity did not register highly on her personal agenda. There was nothing for it but to go to bed.

I threw cold water on my face and tossed my jeans on the floor, crawling under the duvet. But I left the bedside light dimly glowing. The possibility that Spanky might suddenly appear had made me nervous of the dark. I lay there staring at the ceiling, trying to calm my mind and think of nothing at all.

Half an hour later I was still staring, still trying to get to sleep. Every few minutes a distant car would pass, its tyres hissing in the rain. My extended hearing range picked up the mournful lowing of a river tug, the yapping of a dog on the far side of the river.

Then the bulb in the bedside lamp cracked and went out.

I knew at once that there was something in the room with me. I could hear a faint, wheezy breathing in the darkness at the end of the bed. A nose-wrinkling zoo smell was filling the room. I told myself that whatever was there wasn't real. It couldn't hurt me, because it didn't exist. Spanky was playing on my most basic fears. He was an illusionist, nothing more. He had told me so himself. So there was nothing to be frightened of.

Like hell.

No amount of rationalization could make me feel better. I could pull the duvet up over my head and ignore it, refuse to indulge Spanky's taste for the macabre. Convince myself that there was nothing there, breathing and waiting patiently in the dark. That was the best plan. I pulled the duvet in around my ears.

There was nothing out there.

Nothing there.

Nothing.

I was congratulating myself on having made the right decision when whatever it was began to pull at the bottom of the sheet, and the duvet started to slide from me.

I was forced to sit up and try to pull the cover back, but I had no intention of entering into a tug of war without knowing what was on the other end. Instead, I slipped from the bed, ran into the hallway and switched on the light.

It looked like a cross between a chimpanzee and a wolf. That is, it had a flat face, a snout and yellow teeth, but it sat on its haunches and held the edge of the duvet in long, tapering fingers. A row of spines thrust up through its back fur like Spanky's, and it stank of decayed meat. It turned its attention from the bed and looked into the light with red lidless eyes.

That was when I ran for the kitchen.

As I headed along the hallway, I could hear it bounding after me, moving with incredible agility, its palms slapping against the tiles. I reached the kitchen and slammed the door shut behind me as it smashed into the sudden barrier with a spray of spit, nearly jarring me on to the floor. There was no lock, and nothing in reach to jam under the handle.

I tried holding the door shut with my foot, but I still couldn't get to the drawer that held the only weapons in the apartment, a set of carving knives. Suddenly the pressure on the door ceased, and there was silence. I listened carefully, but could hear nothing. No breathing, no movement.

I waited.

Without a clock it was hard to tell how long I stayed like that. The silence thickened. Eventually I knew I couldn't remain in the kitchen forever, so I decided to end the suspense. Placing my foot at its base, I slowly opened the door and peered out.

The flat was still and empty, the lounge faintly illuminated by the hall light.

I opened the door wider. I held my breath and listened.

Nothing there nothing there nothing there.

Bestiality

I walked quickly into the hall, turning on the lounge lights as I did so. Gobbets of flung saliva were roped across the tiles. I sniffed. The acrid zoo-smell lingered in the air. If Spanky had been here, there was no trace of him now. The creature must have returned to the confines of his sick imagination.

I realized that my hands were shaking. Went to the drinks cabinet and poured myself a very large scotch, downing it in one. Forced myself to think rationally. He had slaughtered Paul, and had taken on my appearance to do it, but I hadn't given in to him. Now he would terrorize me into submission. It would only take a single shouted word to admit defeat and grant him admittance. I could end the victimization at any given moment.

But if I agreed to allow him control, it would just be the beginning.

He'd be able to do whatever he liked through me. I was sure if I checked into William Beaumont's past I would find a well-covered trail of carnage.

I looked at the clock. Hours to go before daylight. Suddenly I felt very tired. I cautiously returned to bed, checking the rooms as I went. No sign of the damned thing anywhere. Just silence and stillness. I went to the bathroom, took a piss, wanting to think about Spanky and how I could outwit him, knowing that if I did I would never get to sleep. How could I continue to have a normal life if I spent every waking hour covering my ass? In a few hours time I was supposed to make a major presentation to Syms.

I was still thinking about that when the fucking thing jumped out from beneath the toilet and grabbed my dick, trying to pull me over.

I screamed and fell, cracking my head against the bowl as it crouched across my chest, squealing and yanking at my genitals. Clawed fingers dug into my skin as it chattered and wrenched me from side to side.

As the blow to the head took its toll I felt myself losing consciousness. I remember the red eyes staring into mine as it hissed and squealed like a deranged baboon. My passing out probably preserved my sanity. When I came to a few minutes later, I was still lying on the floor with my T-shirt pulled up around my chest, but at least the damned creature had gone. Had it ever really been here? There were deep scratches all over my groin, and they were real enough. I gingerly touched them, and they hurt like hell.

If Spanky had wanted to make me aware of my own mortality, he had succeeded. By the time I finally crawled back into bed, it was daybreak. I remember thinking that if he planned to pull this kind of thing night after night, I would probably never get to sleep again. So I would buy sleeping tablets. He couldn't harm me if my mind wasn't awake and functioning.

Could he?

CHAPTER TWENTY-FOUR

Subjugation

LOTTIE BROUGHT the news. Her eyes were red and hydrous.

'Paul is dead,' she said simply. 'A neighbour found him in his flat. Max has gone with the police. Two officers came in an hour ago. They talked to him and he started crying. Just sat there and bawled his head off.'

'That's terrible,' I said, sure that I sounded unconvincing. 'Did they say what had happened to him?'

'No, just that he was dead.' She cast around the desk, looking for something to turn in her hands, finally settling for a pencil. 'I've cancelled your presentation to Neville. What an awful thing to happen. All these changes. I suppose we'll just have to wait for things to return to normal.'

She looked lost and sad. I hadn't properly studied her face until recently. A perfect oval half-hidden by glasses, topped with a fringe of sandy fine hair. She fished in the pocket of her skirt and produced a crumpled Post-It note. 'I forgot. There was a phonecall for you just before you arrived. A funny name. Do you know someone called Spanky?'

He had never before allowed the introduction of his name to others. Perhaps my refusal to admit defeat had rattled him.

It was more likely to be the next stage of his campaign.

'He didn't leave a number, said he'd catch you later.'

Spanky's idea of humour. I returned my attention to the lists of figures before me, but my vision started to blur the type. Nothing made sense anymore. If I closed my eyes, all I saw was the chimp-thing clawing at my bed.

No hope. No way out.

Nothing ahead for me but madness or death.

It was then, of all times, that I had an idea.

I needed to find out William Beaumont's date of birth.

I rang Somerset House. They informed me that birth records weren't kept there anymore but at St. Catherine's House, and anyway they weren't allowed to give out information over the telephone. I was given another number to call, and was eventually put through to an extension that was engaged. I wasn't about to give up. I'd go through the national archives of the Public Record Office at Kew if necessary. But I had another idea.

William Beaumont's mother had been a well-known actress. I rang Amanda Gielgud at the London Theatre Society, where she had told me she worked between unsuccessful auditions. She wasn't in today, but an elderly theatrical-sounding woman offered to be of assistance.

I asked if she had any way of looking up the past histories of performing artists.

'I can so long as they were registered with a recognized union. We have brief biographies, and in some cases obituaries, of most of the century's major stage and screen performers on computer. It'll take about a week, and there will probably be a small service charge.'

I told her I needed some details urgently, and would be willing to donate a considerable sum of money to the ACTT or RADA or whoever they liked if I could just get hold of the information at once.

'It still takes a week to be processed, I'm afraid. The computer is in Barnsley.'

I gave her the details anyway. I was looking for biographical facts concerning Edith Beaumont, of Wigmore Street.

'Well of course, I *knew* Edith, so I might be able to tell you myself,' came the reply.

'You did?' I asked, taken aback.

'Of *course*, darling, we *all* did. Marvellous woman, very popular in the late forties. Drawing room comedies mostly. Tragic, the way she died.'

'What happened to her?'

'Why, she and her husband were both *murdered*. They never found out who did it. A dreadful scandal, the papers talked of nothing else for months.'

'When was this?'

'In the late fifties, I think.'

'Do you know when she gave birth to her son?'

'Hang on a minute, I shall have to look that one up.' The receiver went down with a clonk. A few minutes later she came back on the line. 'It was *way* before my time, of course, but we think it was around November, 1925. Such a *beautiful* boy.'

'Can you be more exact? I need the actual date. I'm doing a book.'

'Well, we like a challenge here. Let me ask Mr Marshall, he's our resident historian. He might have something in his personal files. Do you want to call back?'

'I'll hold.'

Twenty-three minutes later she returned to the phone. 'I have the information you requested,' she said casually. 'One son, William Kerwin Beaumont. He'll be nearly seventy now.' She read out the date. 'That means his birthday is one week from today.'

One week, I told myself, if I could survive for just one week his time in Beaumont's body would be up and I would have beaten him. Now I had a goal.

One week could be a hell of a long time.

For a while, everything seemed to return to a state of semi-normality. Customers were coming into the store. Lottie rushed around answering phones and arguing with suppliers while I ordered up stock, attempting to look as if I wasn't going out of my mind.

Lottie guided me through the printout pages, pointing out the areas that needed to be dealt with in Max's absence.

The one thing I didn't need was a formal business meeting with Sarah.

She arrived in a sharp blue suit looking restyled and refreshed, as though she'd dressed for someone special. She seated herself opposite with a pair of underlings and began to outline contract terms for the proposed new branches, and all I could think was; Who the hell were you with last night? Where were you while I was watching a man die?

She peered over her glasses at me, endlessly reciting product features while pushing forward in her seat to splay her thighs beneath the glass-topped table, and I realized she was teasing and urging me to do something if I dared. Right now, sex was the last thing on my mind.

I wanted to tell her the truth, but was sure it would be a bad idea, especially if I told her the part about how we met. So I handled her with as much formality as I could muster, and let her think I was just pissed off about not being able to reach her on the phone.

I thought of Paul lying on the ground, and realized with a stab of sadness that I would not be able to see Sarah anymore. The risk of involving her now was too great. I would have to manage the situation without help from anyone. I watched her saunter across the shop floor, flick back her head and smile as she slipped through the doors, praying that each step away from me would take her to safety.

After she had gone, I rang Heathrow and Gatwick and had the counter staff check through the passenger lists on all incoming flights from Portugal. They weren't happy about doing it, so I told them that I believed my family were unable to travel without medical supervision, and needed to be met. There was no sign of them on any of the airlines. I would have to try again tomorrow.

The rest of the day was a waking nightmare.

Without Max there was too much to do in the store. I hadn't begun to think about the work on the new outlets, and my supervision of the shop fitting was non-existent. Neville wandered in half-cut after a bibulous lunch, and made a fuss about some bank charges Max had incurred until Lottie took him on one side and explained what had happened.

It was impossible to concentrate with carpenters and plumbers hammering and sawing. The crack I had received on the head had left me with a lump that throbbed every time the drilling resumed.

Max returned briefly at the end of the afternoon. He was done in, tired and somehow smaller, shrunk in his clothes. He looked as if he'd been rubbing grit in his eyes, and his face was the same pale yellow as his shirt. Nobody dared to ask about his son, and he volunteered no further information.

As it grew dark, I began to dread the thought of returning home. The tube carriage was packed with soaked, steaming raincoats. I found myself searching the faces of the passengers, looking for the narrow green eyes, the too-perfect features. He was still here somewhere, drifting between the bodies, merging into the crowds. There were traces of him all around. I could feel them. Smell them. Perhaps I was picking up the spoor of other daemons, and was simply attuned to the odour of their blighted race.

The apartment was exactly as I had left it, except for the faintest trace of animal sweat, and one other detail.

Someone had written across the white floor tiles in the kitchen. Two words, capitalized with a thick black felt-tip. More Spanky humour:

SURRENDER DOROTHY

I scrubbed the marks away with firm, obsessive movements, wetting a cloth and grinding in cleanser until there was no trace left. I would not allow the apartment to show signs of invasion.

I cooked a meal and didn't eat it, flicked through the TV channels, unable to settle. Called Sarah to make sure she was okay, but the line was permanently engaged. Outside it was dark once more, the wind was rising, and I was frightened of what the blackness held.

But nothing happened.

The evening passed slowly and uneventfully. I called the airports again. Still nothing. The previous night's sleeplessness began to catch up, and I dozed before the television, finally finding the energy to go to bed. I replaced the bulb in the table lamp, and tried not to think about the thing that had sat at the end of my bed.

But I awoke with a panicky start, knowing that something was wrong.

The lamp was out again.

The room was in darkness but for the dim green flicker of the digital clock beside my bed, which read 2.17 a.m. Still half asleep, I outstretched my hand and turned on the light. There was a man's staring face less than a foot from mine.

It was old, and had no eyes. Strands of grey hair hung from a cracked, skinless skull. The figure wore a filthy suit, rotted and stained with body juices. As I cried out, the face resolved itself into Spanky's smooth features. He stood upright once more and smiled.

'Thought you might like a visit from your old grandfather, Martyn. Hasn't worn well underground, has he? I can bring back all of your dead relatives if you'd like. You'll be able to pay your last respects knowing that they really are the last.'

He flicked a piece of lint from his sleeve. He was wearing black Katherine Hamnett jeans and a green Jasper Conran blazer, but there were splashes of blood, both dried and fresh, over his chest and knees.

'What do you want?' I asked, desperately trying not to sound frightened. I possessed one piece of knowledge that had to be kept hidden from him, one simple fact that I could not dare to think of in his presence.

'You know what I want. Just say the word and we'll be friends again. The perfect team, two working as one. I might even let you have partial mental control.'

All I have to do is hold out for a week. The thought just appeared in my head, too fast to shield. There was nothing I could do about it.

'You'll never last a whole week.'

'I know when William Beaumont's seventieth birthday is, Spanky. Next Wednesday.'

'By then, of course, you'll be begging me to let you die.'

Wednesday. Tomorrow was Thursday. Six days to survive. One hundred and forty four hours. He could only gain entry if I invited him. I repeated the knowledge to myself, running through it like one of Zack's mantras.

'You never wanted to help me in the first place, did you?' I asked, stalling for time. 'All that bullshit about the muses of ancient Greece. This is what you do best, what you really wanted, a chance to cause some suffering.'

'You're probably dying to know what I've been up to,' he said, ignoring my remark. 'I'm getting better at being you. I was quite impressed with my performance tonight.'

I looked at the blood on his jacket, and my heart paced up. 'Who were you with?'

'Sarah Brannigan, of course.'

Oh no, oh God . . .

'Vile apartment, all Habitat wicker and Body Shop bathroom accessories. She wouldn't let me past the entryphone at first. I had trouble getting that awful wheedling tone in your voice exactly right, but she stopped noticing once she saw me in the flesh.' He dabbed his hand against his jacket and smeared blood between his thumb and forefinger, remembering.

'I acted drunk, told her I knew she'd stayed out all night, that I hated her guts, that I'd kill her for sleeping with someone else. Then I tore her clothes off and tried to fuck her. Bony-assed bitch kicked me in the balls, so I kicked her back. I'm glad we didn't do it. She's not my type. Far too *professional*. I prefer a nice uncoordinated, nervous virgin. Which brings us, it seems, to your sister.'

He walked away from the bed and seated himself in the corner, watching me. 'Your family are back, Martyn.'

The room suddenly started to tip. I fought to maintain

control. 'Where are they? What have you done?'

'I'm sorry you missed them at the airport. The stupid computer had them listed under a completely different name. I don't enjoy tinkering with technology, but these days how can one avoid it? Don't worry, they're quite safe. Your mother and father are back at home where they belong, drugged out of their tiny suburban minds, naturally, but I couldn't have them running to the neighbours. No one's expecting them back yet, anyway, and no one is likely to call at the house, so they're fine for the time being.'

His half-smile flickered and faded.

'Your sister, though, she's another story altogether. Since she lost all that weight she's become, well, rather voluptuous. I wanted to welcome her home, but I became more intimate with her than I'd intended. Gave her the same chemical boost I used to give you, although I changed the recipe a little, added some ecstasy and one or two other "relaxers" so that we could get to know each other better. In fact, we had rather a wild session, but I don't think she enjoyed herself toward the end . . .'

I was pulling on my clothes as he talked. Sarah would have to wait. My family's safety took precedence.

There would be no more trains tonight, so I would have to drive down to Twelvetrees.

I ran out of the apartment leaving the front door wide open, with Spanky's deep-throated laughter ringing in my ears.

CHAPTER TWENTY-FIVE

Perversion

I REACHED the darkened street and my waiting Mercedes. Unlocked the door and turned the key in the ignition, only to be met with silence. No sound at all. I didn't know much about cars, but I figured something had become unplugged. I released the bonnet catch from inside the car, then climbed out and carefully raised the hood. As I did so, the hunched little figure sitting astride the engine revealed itself. The damned chimp-thing I had chased from my apartment flung its body forward and wrapped its arms around me, chittering and screaming into my face.

I fell forward against the grille, thumping the side of my head, trying to tell myself that the creature fed from my own fearful imagination, but I could smell its bitter breath, feel its claws digging into my neck and shoulders.

It was pulling at my hair, wrenching me toward the oily metal cavity beneath the hood when the ignition caught and the motor roared into life. Amid the fumes and noise of the racing engine it shoved at my head, forcing me over, determined to obliterate my features against the flashing radiator fan.

The Mercedes began to move away from me. When the

engine started, the brake had been released and the vehicle was now rolling backwards.

I sharply uprighted myself as the creature leapt from me, hopping and loping off to the bushes beyond the pavement. The road curved. The path of the car didn't. It crunched noisily into the front of a new Nissan, crumpling its radiator.

Clutching my burning shoulders, I ran back to the Mercedes and tried to open the driver's door. I could see the keys inside, but they had been jammed into the ignition with such force that they had twisted in the lock. I looked around for the creature, wary of its habit of leaping from dark corners.

I wanted to see if I had been cut, but all I could think of now was reaching my family. I had to find some other form of transport.

The engine of the little Fiat nearly burned itself out on the journey. Debbie had sleepily answered the phone and listened to my frantic jabbering before agreeing to throw down her car keys. I had grabbed a passing taxi and taken it to Vauxhall, where I collected her car. The banana-yellow vehicle was covered in old 'Nuclear Fuel! No Thanks!' stickers, and belonged to the community centre where she worked. It hadn't undergone a service or an oil-change in years.

I drove with my foot stamped hard to the floor, and nearly killed myself overtaking a pair of articulated trucks on the motorway. Perhaps it would have been better if I had, I thought, considering the disastrous effect I was having on those around me. With one eye on the road behind, watching for police, I gunned the protesting vehicle forward, nearly overturning it when I realized that I was about to pass my exit ramp and had to cut across three lanes.

If the rest of the suburbs were asleep, Twelvetrees was in a coma. It was the kind of town where the bedroom lights went on at ten and off at ten fifteen. As I pulled up in front of my parents' house I saw that the mesh fences had been removed, although the garden was still ploughed up.

The place was in complete darkness, which was unusual. My father always left the porch light burning on a timer-switch. The electricity had been disconnected while the workmen were re-laying the floors.

I slewed the Fiat against the kerb and ran up the path, digging for my keys. Inside the front door I groped around for the hall switch and flicked it on.

Nothing.

I returned to the car and searched the boot. Debbie was the kind of girl who kept a torch and a toolkit.

The fluctuating beam crossed bare hall walls. I aimed the torch down, minding my step. The carpets were still missing, and there was a powerful smell of damp. Planks from the floor stood in the lounge doorway, and I was forced to walk between the open boards. In the dining room, the furniture was still under taped-up layers of plastic wrapping. If Joyce and Gordon were back, wouldn't they first have removed the dust sheets? I couldn't help thinking how upset my mother must have been to see this, after all her efforts to keep the place dust-free.

I slowly climbed the bare stairs, fearing the worst.

Spanky told me he had drugged them. Drugged my parents! I wished I had never interfered in their lives. The flashlight beam bounced off a dust-smeared mirror on the landing, more raised boards, and the pitch-black entrance to their bedroom. I could feel my heartbeat shaking my chest as I walked toward the doorway.

The torch picked up a human figure inside. Then another.

When I saw what he had done to them, I froze to the spot.

On the dressing table ahead of me, the radio glowed to life and began to play the theme to an old request show, *House-wives' Choice*. The tune was a familiar one, synonymous with all that was bright and secure about the past.

My mother was standing upright, hoovering beneath the bed. She was dressed as a grotesque parody of a model housewife *circa* 1960, a sitcom character in a frilly gingham apron and blouse. Her make-up had been applied like a clown's, searing red lipstick glossing the lower half of her face, an absurd yellow wig dumped on her head. She was held in position with yards of silver ducting tape which bound her first to a broom, and then anchored her to the floor. More tape clasped the vacuum cleaner handle to her fist.

My father was similarly arranged, an absurd family figure-head seated in an armchair with his legs crossed ankle to knee, a newspaper bound to his hands and a ridiculous briar pipe jutting from his twisted mouth. Both he and my mother had open eyes painted on their closed eyelids. They were alive but unconscious, slowly and faintly breathing.

It took me half an hour to cut them free of the tape, but I couldn't remove the pieces that had adhered to their hair and faces. I managed to lay them beside each other on the bed, massaging the swollen purple patches from their skin where blood had collected. I was unable to tell if their state had been chemically induced, or whether Spanky had simply hypnotized them into a comatose condition.

I recalled something about people in shock being kept warm. I scrambled on the bed and opened the linen cupboards, pulling down a stack of blankets, in which I wrapped them to their necks before running along the landing to my sister's bedroom.

The door was bolted from the inside.

Laura would never allow us easy entrance to her den. For years she had tried to keep out the world. The door was thin and cheaply constructed. Two hard shoves with my shoulder were enough to crack the lintel and tear the bolt out of its mortice.

I shoved the splintered wood back and stepped inside. The room was thick with the smell of burning incense. I shone the torch up through the dense curling smoke, and caught her glittering, twitching eyes within its beam. She was conscious, but could not speak. As I panned the circle of light across her body, I saw the reason why.

Laura was unrecognizably slim. She was suspended from the ceiling by a pair of chains attached to the light fittings on either side of the room. She had been trussed in some kind of complex rubber Betty Page corset, an obscene pin-up, her feet encased in tall laced patent-leather stilettos. Her wrists were roped together and handcuffed, and she was gagged with what appeared to be a black rubber ball, attached to a cat's cradle of bootlaces that were wound around her neck.

Below her were pots of grease, whips and leather flails, half-burned candles and bizarre medical contraptions that appeared to be for use in colonic irrigation. Her arms bore the marks of at least a dozen cigarette burns. She was crying soundlessly, black stripes of kohl running down her cheeks in parallel lines.

I was able to cut her legs free, but could find no way of releasing her from the handcuffs. At first she failed to recognize me and fought me off, screaming into the gag. Then her body became limp, and she allowed me to manoeuvre her into a position from which I could release her from the ceiling.

I managed to untangle the chains, and slide them from her waist. As I cut the gag free and threw it aside she began to wail, her voice high and hard. I told her to be quiet, that if anyone else heard the noise and came to investigate, we'd be in even worse trouble. Luckily, Twelvetrees was a typical commuter-belt town. Nobody gave a fuck about anyone else unless they got their car scratched.

I slipped the black nylon wig from Laura's head and tried to turn her face to mine, but she pulled free, ashamed to be seen and afraid to be touched. Her wrists were still cuffed, but I managed to break the chain connecting them by twisting a piece of metal through one of the links. She turned aside and carefully removed the rubber belts and contraptions around her thighs, heaving and catching with the pain.

After a few minutes she pulled a sheet over her breasts, her misery subsiding to a steady low keening. The sheet was decorated with cartoon ducks. She'd had it since she was nine years old. I asked her if there was anything I could get her, and she said she wanted to wash. I made my way downstairs and boiled a kettle on the still-connected gas stove, then filled a bowl and brought her soap and a flannel. I waited downstairs while she tried to scrub away the memories of the night.

When I returned to the room she had fallen asleep, a child in the dark, retreating into a curled foetal position beneath her favourite sheet. The bowl of soiled water had been shoved beneath the bed. I lay down on the narrow single bed beside her, holding her tight as a dismal dawn flourished behind the shuttered windows.

CHAPTER TWENTY-SIX

Restitution

WHEN WE were children, Laura would finish her boiled egg and turn the empty shell over, trying to fool us into thinking that she hadn't eaten.

I watched now as she delicately pressed the teaspoon into the egg, cutting away a section of yolk. I couldn't force her to speak. I knew her better than that. In times of stress she would simply fold her problems away, refusing to share them with anyone. When our brother died I was the only person she would talk to; but I wasn't prepared to talk to anyone about Joey. So we drifted, Laura and I, and she began her lonely isolation.

I left home, and the changes deepened. As I watched her now, I saw my sister as she had looked when Joey was still alive. The pouches of fat in her cheeks had disappeared. Her jawline had returned. She sat on the other side of the breakfast table with her head down, methodically dipping her spoon and raising it to her lips. Upstairs, our parents were still unconscious, but at least they looked a damned sight healthier than they had during the night. Using my still-augmented powers of perception I could tell that their breathing had changed, grown deeper and more regular, and it seemed that they would awaken as soon as the sedatives they had been fed wore off. At least this way I wouldn't have to explain their comatose state to a local GP.

The kitchen was in semi-darkness. I had kept the curtains drawn for Laura's sake. I had managed to light the boiler, and she had bathed again. She had not spoken a word about what had happened to her. It was nearly noon. With Max away, the office was probably going crazy trying to find me.

Laura finished the egg and softly asked for more tea. I took that to be a good sign. Finally, I took her hands in mine and asked her if she wanted to tell me what had occurred. She spoke so quietly I had to strain to catch her words.

'We were collected from the airport. A big black limousine. I thought it must have been booked by the insurance company. The driver wore a uniform. Everything was paid for. He brought us all the way home. Dad got embarrassed about tipping him, so Mum had to do it. It was dark when we arrived here, and the electricity was still off. It was supposed to have been turned back on. I was carrying one of the suitcases into the lounge when I heard a thumping noise – I think I asked if everything was all right. There was no answer. I went back into the hall and saw Dad lying on the floor. He looked like he had just fallen asleep. I was trying to think how that could be possible when someone grabbed me from behind. He – put something over my face. A chemical smell. I couldn't breathe. Then he carried me upstairs. We went into my bedroom. I'd left the door shut, Martyn. I always keep it shut, you know that. But now it was open. He let me go and I fell on to the floor.'

'Did you see who it was?'

'There were candles, already lit in a circle. I think he was young, your age or a little older, smart clothes, very like you.

I think he was in a blazer. I couldn't see his face, but he told me his name.'

'Spanky.'

'He kept saying it over and over, like a nursery rhyme. He blindfolded me and began to take off my clothes. He was very gentle. I felt something on my arm, a tingling like tiny needles. Everything after that is so – I felt different, sleepy and warm, not really afraid anymore. Then he started touching me, very lightly at first, and he tied me – I stayed blindfolded for the rest, and then I started to get frightened again. I thought the night would never come to an end—'

'It's all right,' I said, 'don't think about it anymore. Take a deep breath and try to stay calm. No one can hurt you now. I'll make sure of that.' Scrubbed clean of the fetishistic make-up, she looked like a child once again.

'How did you know who it was? Why would somebody go to all that trouble, with the limousine and everything?'

I could give no answer that would reassure her.

'And what if he comes back?'

'He won't, Laura. I won't let him. But we have to decide what to do about you.'

'I won't see the police, Martyn, you can't make me.'

'You need to be examined by a doctor. You've been attacked, for Christ's sake. Suppose he's caused an internal injury. Look at the burns on your arms.'

She shook her head violently. 'I'll take care of it myself. I couldn't stand all those people asking questions. The neighbours would find out sooner or later. You know what they're like around here. I can't believe this, just when we were all getting back to normal.'

'All right, but you must see a doctor. Then you can decide about the police.' On the one hand, I wanted her to go and make a report. On the other, I knew that it would do no good. No system of justice was built to deal with a phantom.

I went upstairs and filled a bin-liner with harnesses and sexual restraining equipment, emptying lubricants and nitrates into another bag. By mid-afternoon I had cleared away every trace of Spanky's visit from the house. I knew that I was performing little more than a damage limitation exercise, but could think no further ahead than making sure that Laura stayed on an even keel for the rest of the day.

Just after five, our mother woke up. She raised herself on one elbow and squinted out of the window at the wet lawns of the crescent, disorientated by her memories of Portugal. She couldn't understand why she had gone to bed in her clothes, or why she had failed to take the grips from her hair; Joyce was a creature of habit. The last thing she recalled was coming into the house and falling asleep.

I told her that there had been a small gas leak, and that I had arrived minutes later to find them a little groggy from the fumes. I had put them both to bed and called the emergency services, who had fixed the problem. Laura watched me lie with her eyes wide, surprised by my new-found glibness.

My father awoke and was immediately sick.

Joyce said knowingly, 'that will be from the effects of the gas,' and soon they were arguing about notifying the gas board. It was amazing how quickly they took the whole thing on board. I guess it didn't cross their minds to wonder if their son was lying about such an important matter. Laura and I looked at each other wisely, and knew that we would never share our terrible knowledge. With my sister's agreement, the true events of the previous night could remain buried.

Two hours later, I drove the three of them to a modern hotel, full of salesmen, at the edge of town and checked them in for the night, insisting that they should allow me to put them up until the gas and electricity could be properly restored. The thought of sleeping in clean hotel sheets clearly appealed to Laura and my mother, and only Gordon complained about the arrangement.

At least I knew where they were now. I could keep an eye on them more easily. I gave the hotel clerk a heavy tip and asked him to call me if there were any problems. Then I headed back to town, wondering how long it would take Laura to realize that her attacker knew where her bedroom was, and speculating on what I would find when I visited Sarah.

CHAPTER TWENTY-SEVEN

Contagion

AS I drove, I checked my money. Thirty quid in the wallet, a couple of credit cards. Spanky had regularly boosted my bank account when we were friends. I'd noticed several decent-sized amounts appearing in my statements. I felt sure that he would now attempt to deny me access to this instant finance. He was determining my every move, sending me to Twelvetrees, then back to Sarah, showing me that he could do whatever the hell he liked.

Sarah ... I rang her home number from a telephone box at the end of the motorway, and after three rings got a reply.

'You've got a god-damned fucking nerve calling here again.' Her voice was an octave higher and tense with emotion.

'What are you talking about?' I asked, remembering all too well what Spanky had said he'd done.

'The next time you turn up in the middle of the night to intimidate a woman, I swear I'll stab you first and call the cops later.'

'It wasn't me,' I replied evenly. 'I haven't seen you for days. I called you but there was no answer—'

'Because I spent the night on the floor crying. Listen, shithead, I went to the police this morning. I told them everything. I gave them your address and telephone number. You're a dead man.' She sounded close to tears.

'What did I do?' I persisted.

'What is this, you want me to think someone else tried to rape me? Someone else kicked me in the fucking stomach? Martyn, if you ever *ever* call this number again I'll pay to have someone break your legs, do you understand? Jesus *Christ*. How could you have done it, I thought—' She was sobbing hard now.

The receiver was dropped back into its cradle, and the line went dead.

Mortified, I returned to the battered Fiat and drove back to town, dreading to think of what else I might find. At the very least, Sarah's outburst told me that she was alive and in one piece. I would have to make sure she stayed that way.

For once, the apartment was as I had left it. If the police had come by, they hadn't left a calling card.

No sign of the daemon, either. Maybe even Spanky needed to take a break occasionally.

I sat in the centre of the sofa nursing a tumbler half-filled with J&B, wondering how Laura would recover from her ordeal. Clearly my parents remembered nothing, but the family would never be safe until Spanky was paid in full.

Surely he knew that I would never surrender willingly. Was he simply an agent of corruption, using me as an excuse to create chaos among the living? Once he had likened our meeting to being mugged. I had no idea then how apt the analogy would prove to be. I drained the scotch, sat back and attempted to take stock of the situation.

My parents were confused and frightened, but unhurt and temporarily safe. Laura was internalizing her fears in the face of her attack, but seemed okay. Sarah, in a similar situation, was more outgoing with her feelings. I wanted to see her, to try and explain things face to face, but how could I when she thought I meant to cause her physical harm?

Some form of positive action had to be taken to stop Spanky. I had to find a way to get one step ahead. Okay, I'd found out about the time limit, but there had to be something else. The alcohol was fuzzing my mind, so I deferred the construction of a plan until the morning.

I found the bedroom too disturbing to sleep in after the events of the past nights, and pulled my duvet across the couch instead. My eyelids felt as if they had weights attached to them, and I was barely able to crawl among the cushions before passing out.

I slept for just over an hour.

I awoke to find myself covered in a heavy, stinging sweat. The duvet was soaked through, and so were the cushions beneath it. My hair, plastered to my forehead, was dripping. As I tentatively raised myself the agony began, lightning flashes of pain cracking across my stomach. Gasping with the effort, I stumbled from the sofa across the room.

Beneath my clawed hands, knives of fire were sawing in my gut. I tried to catalogue my symptoms in a rational fashion, but the pain drove all thought from my mind. On the toilet, my bowels opened and searing liquid rushed from me. Once, on a school trip to Athens, I had suffered from dysentery for three days and nights. I felt that miserable, lonely experience returning now, greatly magnified. I had barely eaten anything in the last twenty-four hours, and could not understand how so much liquid could be pouring from me.

I tried to halt the flow now, gripping my stinging sphincter tightly, but it was impossible. The moment I ceased to clench, the torrent began with renewed force. Shifting weakly to one side of the bowl, I looked back.

It was filled with dark blood.

Horrified, I clutched at my stomach as the pain redoubled, and fell sideways on to the floor, pooling the crimson liquid around me. He had put something in the whisky, I was sure. Wasn't there a poison, something they gave to rats, that caused lesions and stopped the blood from coagulating?

Christ, I thought, I'm going to bleed to death before a doctor can get here. I tried to raise myself on to my elbows but the pain was so great I could move no further than two or three feet from the toilet. Behind me the steaming vermilion stream continued its flow, running along the grouting, tessellating over the pattern in the tiles to disappear under the door. I felt my power ebbing, my life-force draining away as surely as a vampire's victim, Talos losing his molten steel, desiccating into death.

Through a mist of pain I remembered Spanky's power. *I am an illusionist*, he had said, *but what I show seems real*. So very real, I thought, that I couldn't tell if he had really poisoned the drink. I could feel the blood leaking from me, could touch my fingertips in the cuprous morass pouring from my body. How could it not be real? But I forced the thought forward.

Whether it was real or imagined made no difference. What was important was to convince myself that it was an illusion.

As the pain punched my breath from me, I began the singsong litany in my mind, *just an illusion, just an illusion. Pretty desperate, Spanky, if that's the best you can come up with*.

But the blood was not staunching.

I tried again, then realized I was aiming at the wrong target. He was here with me, somewhere in the apartment. He had to be. I was sure that his hallucinatory powers could only be worked in close proximity to the victim. That was why he had disguised himself as his familiar when I went to the car.

Feeling the pain recede for a few beats, I pulled myself on to my knees and moved toward the door. I could feel him now, sense his strength growing just a few feet away.

And as I did so, the pain rolled away as quickly as it had appeared. I could not tell if he had allowed it to end, or if I had caused the illusion to collapse. I looked back to find the floor around the toilet dry and clean. I was still covered in sweat, and my heart was kicking beneath my ribs, but the horror of death was receding and I felt absurdly, overwhelmingly grateful for my release from its bony grip.

'The pain never needs to end,' said Spanky, leaning against the door-jamb with his hands in his pockets. He was dressed in black, like an executioner. 'It can go on and on, intensifying all the time, your body filling with contagion. When you think it couldn't get any worse, it doubles. Finally, you take your own life. But it's no fun for me that way. Tell me, what happens when you don't pay your electricity bill?'

I was standing upright now, though still hunched over in fear of the stomach cramps returning.

'Answer me, Martyn. You don't want the sickness to return.'

'Lights – the lights go out.'

'Ah, so you do understand the principles of payment. I suppose that's a start. I just came by to tell you that I've thought of another way you can clear your debt.'

I made no reply.

'Give me Laura. Kill her for me. She was good, but they're even better when they're dead.'

My body responded more slowly than I realized. By the time

I was upon him he had blurred and shifted to the other side of the hall.

'You can't hurt me, Martyn. I'm not real, remember? You said so yourself.'

I snatched a full wine bottle from the kitchen rack and threw it as hard as I could at his head, but somehow it failed to connect and smashed against the wall like an explosion of blood. Suddenly anything that came into my hands was a weapon. I screamed and swung at him with a carving knife, a chair, an iron candlestick, smashing a metal stool into the wall and sending it clattering across the floor. He was moving too fast, challenging me, taunting me to keep his pace.

A lamp hit the coffee table in an explosion of glass. I hurled my PC printer, an absurd weapon composed of light grey plastic, at his darting form, only to watch as it shattered against the room divider, miles short of its target.

'When you've quite finished,' said Spanky, reappearing behind me, 'remember this. The longer you take to surrender, the more painful I'll make my entry into your body.' His fist cracked hard against my head, staggering me.

And he was gone.

Something was burning in the corner of the room, and the telephone was ringing insistently. I remember hearing a violent hammering at the front door as the stomach cramps returned with a vengeance and my conscious mind kicked out.

I fell back on to the sofa, the pain receding into a dark miasmic fog that I was sure would never leave me in peace again.

I awoke in the morning to brightness and silence.

The face of the lounge clock was smashed, but it still seemed to be working: 7.43 a.m. I sat up, gingerly touching my tender head. My stomach felt better than it had the night before, which was something. My chest and arms were smothered in blue-black bruises. And the apartment. It looked as if a herd of buffalo had passed through the place.

There was an acrid stink of burned plastic. One wall was completely blackened, and the charred remains of a lamp lay at the source of the conflagration. The electrics had burned out. There was water everywhere, mainly from the shattered flower vases, but also from the overflowing bathroom sink, which was blocked with smashed toiletries.

I carefully stepped between dying roses and glittering shards of crystal. My bedroom wardrobe stood wide open. All the clothes Spanky had made for me were gone. Other things were missing; my watch and Joey's ring, it was hard to tell what else. I didn't really care. Belongings were no longer important. The only thing on my mind was to find a resolution, a way to rid myself of the daemon forever.

It was Saturday morning. Four more days to get through. I salvaged an old pair of jeans I'd been planning to throw out and dug a rumpled sweatshirt from the laundry basket. It occurred to me that I had managed to upset Spanky badly. I had stood up to him, and for once he had seen the power of my own will. It must have been a galling experience, considering he had helped me to develop it in the first place. I had thrown his chances of claiming my body into jeopardy. Time was running out fast for him, now that the willing victim was proving not so willing after all.

At the same time, I knew that it was dangerous to underestimate my adversary. I was still defining the limit of his powers; he could influence others, plant false memories, mindread, shape-shift, yet in order to have any true strength he was forced to operate from within a human body.

I knew Spanky well enough to guess that he would soon go on another rampage. His growing desperation would force him into greater acts of violence. But who would his next target be? I needed to warn people; Sarah, Zack, Max, anyone who knew me would be considered fair game.

I doubted that the police Sarah had summoned would manage to arrest me. Spanky wouldn't allow the authorities to get involved. He needed to have me available constantly now. Couldn't risk me doing a bunk. What if I persuaded someone to lock me up for a while? Presumably his powers didn't extend to passing himself between prison bars. He had the mind of a daemon, but the form of a man. No, it was too risky; a prison cell could easily become my own death-trap.

Four more days to survive. Ninety-six hours before one of us found himself without a body...

I discovered just how busy Spanky had been when I arrived at Thanet an hour later. Lottie was standing outside the showroom in tears. It was raining heavily, but heavy orange hosepipes still snaked into the building. The front windows were blackened and heat-cracked. Smouldering armchairs, sofas and half-burned beds were being carried out and stacked against a wall. The pavement was covered with slippery black soot.

'You should see the state of the place,' she said, wiping her eyes. 'Everything's ruined.' A considerable crowd of gawpers were watching as firemen unsnapped their breathing apparatus and returned to the engines.

'Does anyone know how it started?' I asked.

'That's the worst thing,' sniffed Lottie. 'They think Max did it himself. I was at the back of the store, so I didn't see what happened. One of the customers says he started shouting, just screaming at the wall. Then she saw him waving a burning rag over his head.'

'Where is he now?'

She began to cry again.

'Inside, Martyn. Max is still somewhere inside.'

CHAPTER TWENTY-EIGHT

Malediction

THE FUNERAL was an absolute bloody nightmare.

In accordance with Jewish tradition, Max was buried quickly. He had been separated from his wife for almost two years, but Lottie told me that they had been planning to try again. I knew he had been with Esther every minute since they had lost their son. I heard there wasn't much left of Max to bury, a fact to which Esther called attention before showing around a retouched 1950s photograph of him. Throughout the service she kept making little lurches, as though she was on medication. Worse was to follow.

They were lowering the casket into the hole when Esther threw herself at the rabbi and began to punch him, screaming and wailing. Some hastily-assembled relatives pulled them apart and took her away to sit somewhere. The service continued, backed with distant howls of anguish. The shiva looked certain to be an emotional affair.

I had not been invited to Paul's interment, which had been kept as a private family function. Presumably that had been equally disastrous because Stephane, the hated French girl-friend, had rung the office one evening and had been given the time and address of the funeral service by Dokie.

I thought about Paul's death. If the police had any leads, they were certainly keeping them quiet. I hadn't even been interviewed. According to Lottie certain substances had been found in the flat, cocaine she thought, and there was talk of Paul 'angering his dealer'. This was patent bullshit. He was the last person on earth to get involved with drugs. It seemed more likely that Spanky had planted them to cover his tracks.

After the service, I offered to take Lottie home. She had not stopped crying since the start of the ceremony. I assumed, like everyone else who worked at Thanet, that she had been having an affair with her boss. It seemed to be common, if unspoken, knowledge. Even stupid Dokie knew about it. But as I awkwardly attempted to console her, she brushed my proffered Kleenex aside and sat upright, wiping away her tears with her own linen handkerchief.

'I suppose you think I was sleeping with him, too,' she said, carefully refolding the handkerchief and pocketing it.

'It never crossed my mind,' I replied unconvincingly.

'I find that hard to believe. It had crossed everyone else's. It was the impression he liked to give. He was old enough to be my grandfather, but men like you are still prepared to think I was sleeping with him. Charming.'

'You didn't discourage the rumour,' I said defensively.

'Christ, I felt sorry for him. His wife treated him dreadfully, changing her mind about the divorce every five minutes. She didn't want Paul following his father into the furniture business. He finally did, and look what happened.'

She brushed her hair back from her face and stared at me. Her attitude had changed. Her shyness had faded in the light of recent events. 'Max used to take me for a drink after work sometimes on a Friday evening, that's all. He wanted people to

234   S P A N K Y

think he was having an affair. Pathetic, really.'

'Then why didn't you deny it?'

'What difference would that have made? Men just think what they want. Max was always decent to me. I've always been Good Old Lottie to everyone else, one of those amiable office people you look right through who vanishes from everyone's thoughts at six o'clock.'

She was right about her transparency. We'd seen each other every day at work for over two years and I knew virtually nothing about her.

'Poor old bugger, all that pressure to expand the store, then Paul dying. No wonder he broke down.' She shuddered and pulled her coat around her. I stared shamefacedly at the ground. If I hadn't invited Spanky to change things, none of this would ever have happened. It was obvious to me that the daemon had appeared to Max. The customer who witnessed his attack had seen him trying to fend the creature off.

'What are we going to do now that Max and the store have both gone?'

I didn't know, but I was soon to find out. As we reached the cemetery gates, Neville Syms sprinted up and tapped me on the shoulder, asking if he could have a word with me at his Bayswater office. His black mohair suit had an unseemly shine that gave him the appearance of a turf accountant rather than a mourner.

I put Lottie in a taxi and headed back into town. I arrived to find that Syms had somehow contrived to be there before me. He was pacing around the bare, echoing showroom clenching and unclenching his hands, and hardly acknowledged my arrival. I stepped across bundles of timber and thick black coils of wiring, looking for somewhere to sit.

'I don't wish to sound callous,' he began, instantly sounding so, 'but I have to think of the financial consequences of Max's death.'

'Have you spoken to the police?'

'They think the fire started in the junction box that was being installed on the ground floor of the shop. Max was probably overcome with fumes. It's a small mercy, but at least he wouldn't have felt anything. There is a problem, however. I haven't been able to contact the insurers yet—'

I should hope not, I thought. It was Sunday. Max had only been dead a day.

'– but I imagine they won't want to pay compensation. If they can prove that Max's mental state was affected by his son's death, they'll try to suggest that he wilfully set fire to the store in order to commit suicide. I believe there was a witness who says Max was ranting and raving just before the fire broke out. That will go badly against us.'

It was easy to see Spanky's hand in this so-called 'accident', but I had no way of explaining or proving his involvement. All I could do was nod dumbly and ask what would happen to the company now.

'There's no point in coming to work,' Syms sighed. 'I'll have to suspend everyone until we know if the insurers will pay up. I'll tell you this, though. You can forget about Thanet's expansion plans. Without Max there is no company.'

He kept staring at the half-laid carpet tiles, finding it too difficult to meet my eye. Something else was bothering him.

'What?' I asked finally, breaking the uncomfortable silence. 'Say what's on your mind.'

'If you had been there when you were supposed to – this terrible thing might never have happened,' he muttered angrily. 'You see, I don't *know* you, Martyn. I'd never set eyes on you before we met that day in the restaurant.'

'But you recommended me—'

'I honestly can't imagine what made me do so. I wish to God I hadn't.'

So that was it. Spanky had rescinded the memory he had implanted in Syms's mind. I was out in the cold. Syms told me he would need to review my terms of employment, and that I would no doubt be paid to the terms of my contract. I walked from his office to join the ranks of the unemployed.

As if the day couldn't get any worse, I returned to my wrecked apartment to find a letter co-signed by two of my neighbours (neither of whom had I ever laid eyes on), members of the tenants' association, warning me that damage had been caused by water seeping through to the floor below me, and that I would be evicted if there was ever a repeat of last night's disturbance. I was tempted to spend the evening hammering on the walls with a saucepan, then remembered that as the extortionate rent was paid up and I had just been deprived of an incoming salary, I could not afford to piss off the neighbours.

But I had to admit that staying there unnerved me. Night had already fallen as I wandered about the lounge, sweeping the broken glass and china into piles. There was only one working bulb left in the entire flat, and I had no spares. I dug out some candles from beneath the sink and set them in saucers, which only made the place creepier. Perhaps it was Spanky's intention to make me doubt my own sanity. In that case, he wasn't doing a bad job.

The situation was absurd, intolerable, and insoluble. I decided to call Sarah again from the only functioning telephone that still remained in the apartment. She answered, but slammed down the receiver as soon as she recognized my voice.

I managed to salvage an unbroken, sealed bottle of Stolichnaya from the mess of splintered wood and glass that had once been a very expensive cocktail cabinet, and poured a generous measure into a tooth-mug. In the last few days I had started talking to myself, muttering under my breath like a lunatic. I stood at the cracked window and looked down into the street, where families walked and cars hooted and life carried on at its usual pace, and suddenly I needed to get out, to be away from the poisoned atmosphere of the room. I left and caught a bus down to the river, where I could sit and think.

I reached Waterloo bridge and descended the stone steps to the promenade. Ahead, the benches passed into darkness and reappeared, as the rising wind threaded through the suspirant branches of the trees, flicking their foliage out of the lamplight. There was not a soul to be seen in either direction. Although it was perfectly safe to do so, hardly anyone walked here at night. I was about to seat myself when the hairs on my neck began to prickle, and I felt a presence, malign, destructive, somewhere ahead of me on the breeze-pocked river.

I realized with a shock that my growing fear of Spanky had followed me from the apartment, and was now infecting the world outside. I had been here hundreds of times, and had always found it a welcoming place. But now a poisonous pall hung over the scene before me.

A thick, sudoriferous smell rose in the river air, but I couldn't tell if it was being produced by the stale waters below, or if Spanky was tampering with my senses. How much of what I saw and heard was real, and how much my imagination? I could not stay beside the bench, and walked on, my sense of unease escalating with every sough of the wind.

I was filled with an overwhelming sensation of death; the

dead were here and all around me, rising from the tide in stinking clumps, crawling from the trees and bushes, waiting ahead in tenebrous alleys. I could smell them. Feel them. I broke into a run, no longer able to screen out my skincrawling panic. I had been a fool to come here. What I needed was light and people; the comfort of a crowded room.

What I found, when I reached the end of the bridge, was an Indian restaurant with steamed-over windows, where the welcoming pungence of curry blotted the stench of the grave from my nostrils.

The place was crowded, but they found me a table for one. I have no proper recollection of what I ordered. Prawns, lamb, familiar spicy dishes. The main thing was that I felt safe. Beside me sat a brace of businessmen, drinking pints and braying at their own jokes. In normal circumstances I would have loathed their enforced company, but tonight I gratefully welcomed them because they made everything ordinary again. Hot bread arrived, and spiced chicken of some kind, on a bed of scented basmati rice. A tipsy girl squeezed on to the table behind me, knocked over her wineglass and started laughing. I found myself smiling in her direction, pleasured by the sheer banality of it all.

'So this is what you've sunk to.'

He was standing on the other side of the table, leaning on it with the tips of his fingers, watching the noisy diners in disapproval. He was wearing a pale blue Paul Smith suit, but the lapels and cuffs had been singed away. The outfit he had worn to torment Max and burn him alive. A Spanky joke. I ignored him and stared down into my plate, praying that he would be gone when I raised my eyes.

'It didn't take you long to return to your old suburban habits, did it? It was obviously a waste of time trying to teach you anything. Have you seen the state of the kitchens here?'

'Just leave me—' I realized I was speaking aloud.

Just leave me alone, all right?

Spanky picked up a fork and examined its tines against the light, scraping away a speck of food with his fingernail. 'I may have to if you keep eating at places like this. You should see what's going on in everyone's stomachs right now. You don't look so good, you know.'

Is it any fucking wonder, after what you've been doing to me? What do you want?

'You know very well what I want, Martyn.'

You can't have my body. It's against my religion.

'You can restructure your personal belief system any way you want to, my dear chap. The fact remains that you have a debt to pay, and it must be paid within the next three days.'

I threw down my fork and shoved my plate back, the food stifling and sour in my mouth.

Why don't you just fucking kill me and get it over with? Do it here, now.

'You must believe me, Martyn, when I say that the last thing in the world I want is to kill you. But the matter is out of my hands now. Submission within three days, or there'll be a public massacre of the most appalling proportions, for which you will solely be blamed in the brief period of awesome guilt you'll suffer prior to your own spectacular death.' He dipped a finger into one of the sauces on the businessmen's table, tasted it and spat the offending liquid on to the floor.

'Witnessing your newly restored passion for downmarket food, perhaps I'll make you walk into McDonalds with a machine gun. During one of their children's parties.'

He glanced at his watch. 'I must leave. I have other matters to attend to. How's your sanity holding up, by the way?

Getting paranoid? Experiencing any difficulties with your sense of reality? It's an overrated concept, reality. I think dreamers have far more rewarding lives than pragmatists. Especially these days. The nineteen nineties bear no comparison with the era of William Beaumont's birth. The poor were much poorer then, of course, and yet they were spiritually richer somehow. Today even the lowliest paupers are well-shod and ill-mannered. What a horrible, bankrupt little era this is. The only advantage is that one can be as tasteless as one likes without anyone noticing. Well, I must be off. Whatever you do, Martyn, keep a tight grip on your mind.'

In a rare moment of restraint, Spanky walked across the restaurant and departed through the front door. Looking down at the tiled floor, I saw that he had left footprints of congealing blood.

Spanky's appearance that night was a departure from his usual form, but preferable to an unannounced arrival in the flat. Perhaps he'd decided to change his tactics.

I should have found these daemonic conversations about my fate odd, but nothing seemed strange anymore. Paul and Max were dead. My life, and the lives of my family and friends were changed irrevocably. And I, most frustratingly of all, could only continue to do nothing, accepting each venomous day as it arrived, until Spanky brought our war to an end.

My meal was cold, the sauce solidifying.

I raised my head, still lost in thought, when the man on the next table began to cough. His excessive bulk stretched his white shirt around the buttons. His grey suit jacket was hung on the back of his chair. There was a mobile phone in the top pocket. I recall these details clearly. He coughed again, and his friends slapped him on the back. One of the women they were with offered him a glass of water.

Suddenly he knocked the tumbler aside and coughed again. A piece of chewed meat flew from his mouth, and I remember thinking that that should have been the end of it. But his next cough brought a spray of blood, and a piece of pink tubing which bounced wetly on to the paper tablecloth. His colleague started hacking, too. Everyone else in the restaurant had turned in their seats, and the conversations were changing, rising in inflection.

A chair scraped back. One of the women tried to stand and was violently, copiously sick down her dress and across the table. The sour reek of bile hit my nostrils as the first businessman collapsed into the serving trays before him, his hands smeared with lime and mango jelly as he retched blood and organic matter over himself.

Within moments, others were coughing and heaving up their undigested meals, streaming blood and gastric juices on to their clothes. Beside me, a yellow geyser of rice and half-chewed meat erupted from the other businessman's mouth. He tried to stem the deluge with his hands, stumbling upright as the torrent turned scarlet with blood.

Horrified, I shoved away from the flooding table and staggered to my feet with a cry. Others shouted in alarm. I fought my way across the heaving, vomiting mass, passing a woman with purple entrails hanging from her gaping mouth, slipping in the food and sputum that was forming a bloody sauce on the floor. I crashed into the main door, yanked it open and looked back again.

And saw a restaurant full of unharmed, interrupted diners staring at me.

Everyone was fine.

No one had been sick.

But I had knocked over my chair and pulled the tablecloth

242   S P A N K Y

from my table, sending the dishes to the floor.

'Where you think you're goin', mate, what the fuck you doin', tryin' not to pay?' called the startled waiter. But I had fought my way free of the ghastly vision, and was now running down the darkened streets as if pursued by all the daemons of hell.

CHAPTER TWENTY-NINE

Culpability

LOTTIE LIVED in King's Cross, on the top floor of a crumbling terraced Edwardian house with a box of sooty geraniums beneath each window. She peered out above one of them half-asleep, then spotted me in the street below. It was late on Sunday evening, or early Monday morning. I couldn't tell the exact time; Spanky had taken my watch.

She raised her finger to her lips. I stepped back and indicated the front door. She hesitated, puzzled, then vanished. Minutes later she appeared in the hall wearing a hastily donned black tracksuit, and allowed me to enter.

'Do you know what time it is?' she whispered. 'My flatmate's a nurse at UCH. She goes on duty in a couple of hours.'

'I'm sorry, Lottie,' I said, following her toward the kitchen. 'I had to talk to someone.'

The kitchen was a chaotic arrangement of dirty plates and empty tins of catfood. She searched around and found a pack of Marlboros on an ancient gas stove, lit up and exhaled the smoke gratefully.

'I didn't know you smoked.'

'There's a lot of things you don't know about me. What's so

important that you have to turn up at half past one in the morning? You never showed much interest while we were sharing an office together.'

I didn't know where to begin, or how to explain what was happening to my sanity. If I only told her part of the story, I would have to lie about the rest, and that would defeat the object of confiding in her at all. Yet there was something about her I instinctively trusted, a clearheadedness that might be able to return some order to my thinking. She made mugs of instant coffee and we sat on kitchen stools around a formica-topped table, sipping it in silence.

'I can't help you if you don't tell me about it,' she prompted, re-knotting the cord of her tracksuit bottoms.

I hesitated. Part of me was scared that if I told her what I knew, I'd be placing another innocent person at risk. But we weren't close friends, and Spanky would have no cause to threaten her. I had to take the chance.

'You won't believe me.'

'You'd better let me be the judge of that.'

So I told her everything.

I began with the night I met Spanky. I told her about his involvement in Darryl's injury, and the deaths of Paul and his father. I described the payment he had demanded of me, and how I was not prepared to provide him with another human conduit. I told her of his visit to Sarah's, and about Laura. I even talked about Joey. When I finally finished, she averted her eyes and concentrated on lighting another cigarette.

I sat in silence, waiting for a response.

'As far as I see it, you have no proof,' she said quietly.

'What do you mean, no proof?' I asked, raising my voice. 'You think I'm staging some kind of elaborate practical joke?'

She brushed her hair from her face as she raised her eyes to mine. 'Listen, Martyn, you don't speak a civil sentence to me in over two years, and then you appear out of nowhere with a lunatic story about being bewitched or something, how the hell am I supposed to react?'

'I'm sorry,' I apologized. 'I didn't mean to shout. I'm under a lot of strain.'

'Well, if this is true, then it's your fault I'm out of a job.'

'You don't know you're out—'

'Come on, Syms told me he wants to speak to all members of staff individually in the morning, and it's not because he's giving us all pay rises.' She waved a jet of smoke from my face. 'I don't know why you came to me. I don't believe in ghosts or spirits. I don't believe in God. I trust my senses, and human nature. Oh, there's good and evil all right, in people. And there's the problem. You have no proof, Martyn. Only you can see this – creature. No one else. You say he took your form to murder Paul? I could be sitting here at my kitchen table with Charles Manson. How do I know it wasn't you? Suppose you're mentally disturbed and just don't know it, have you thought of that?'

I made to speak, but she cut me short. 'Okay, these are the options.' She counted off on three fingers. 'One, you really are possessed by some sort of trouble-making supernatural entity. I'd have a *really* hard time believing that. Two, you did these terrible things yourself, which, from what I know of you, seems unlikely. Three, a series of tragedies have occurred and you've decided to blame yourself for them. That, to me, seems the most reliable explanation. Your life has been dislocated, and you've invented this *being* in your head to burden yourself with some kind of guilt complex.'

'But he smashed up my apartment—'

'How do I know you didn't do it yourself?' Her habit of

studying my eyes was starting to unnerve me. 'How do you know you're not unstable? Listen, once in a while I get depressed and eat bowls of Shredded Wheat in the middle of the night, and I have no idea why I'm doing it. How do *you* know?'

I knew Spanky existed, but she was right; there was no way of proving it. 'Wait, he rented the apartment for me. The agent must have seen him.'

'Oh, Martyn. Don't you get it? Anyone you ask about seeing this Spanky will just say they saw *you*.'

'But he did things, influenced people.'

'You probably just did it yourself.'

'Then how do you know I didn't kill someone as well?'

She shook her head and rose from the table to refill our mugs, talking over her shoulder.

'What, are you telling me you sexually assaulted your own sister? Come on, Martyn. You're not the type, you're imaginative, always filling the order books with little drawings, but you're not one of those obsessives. I've watched you for two years.'

'What do you mean?'

I had always assumed that she had won her employment through Max, and had barely bothered to notice her. I'd always thought of her as weird Lottie because she seemed to hang around me without speaking. I felt ashamed now, knowing that the rumours I'd believed about her weren't true.

'Forget it.' She turned aside, shifting her bare feet nearer to the fire. 'Well, what do you think of my theory?'

'I suppose you may be right.'

She placed a freshly filled mug before me and reseated herself, stifling a yawn. The night air was chilling down the room.

C u l p a b i l i t y   247

'You reckon I'm projecting all this on to myself because I feel guilty about something.'

'It's possible. You said your brother's death upset you. Perhaps Spanky is simply your brother in another guise. You said he's older, more sophisticated, smarter.'

'The same as Joey.'

'But Joey's dead. You relied on him, and he died. Suppose you brought him back as Spanky. Once again you come to rely on him – and once again he lets you down. It's all up here, Martyn.' She tapped my forehead. 'A test you set for yourself, a character you've created from within to explain a series of unfortunate real events. Tomorrow will seem better, wait and see.'

I could see that everything she said made perfect sense. If it was true, then Spanky needed to exist no longer.

'Could I stay here?' I asked. 'I'm sure you're right, but I don't want to go back to my apartment and put your theory to the test tonight. I'll be no trouble. It's not a come-on or anything.'

She threw me another laser-beam stare as she ground out her cigarette. 'No, I don't suppose it is.'

'I can sleep on the floor.'

'The fire's not working in here. You'll freeze to death, and there's cat crap all over the place. You can sleep in with me as long as you keep your pants on and don't try any funny stuff.'

We slept like children, curled into each other in our clothes, the ticking bars of the gas fire filling the bedroom with a dull sunset glow. For the first time since my ordeal began, I fell into a deep, untroubled sleep.

But then, after nothing but a dense warm void, an uncomfortable feeling began to grow. I lay in the bed unable to lift a finger, unable to twitch the smallest muscle. I was covered in a fine membrane that sealed my mouth, my eyes, my nostrils, my ears, and stopped me from moving. There was someone inside me, shifting back and forth. I could feel my nerves tingling as he raged about, hear his muffled shouts and squeals as he ransacked my senses, as if listening to a rowdy downstairs neighbour late at night. He was within me, stealing what he needed, preparing to shut down the remaining vestiges of my will, and I felt my dying thoughts drain off into darkness like glittering drops of water . . .

I awoke with a start.

'Well, this is cute,' said a familiar, sarcastic voice. 'In a grotesque, Hallmark cards kind of way.'

I sat up suddenly, squinting ahead into the darkness, my pulse quickening.

'She has a collection of ceramic turtles in the bathroom, Martyn. I thought you'd outgrown this type of *shop girl*.' I could see him only as a faintly glowing outline in the dark.

'She's attempting to psychoanalyse me out of existence, you *putz*. It's not very flattering being told you only exist inside somebody else's mind. She's hopelessly wrong, of course. She's been crazy about you all this time, and you never even noticed she was alive. If you can't spot something simple like a lovesick floozie, what on earth makes you think you're deep enough to perform some kind of complex transference process on your dead brother?'

You go to hell, motherfucker.

'Temper does nothing to improve your vocabulary, Martyn. Anyway, I just came from there and it was boring. I think we need to teach the little bitch-on-heat a lesson for being so presumptuous, don't you?'

'Martyn? What's the matter?' Lottie had awoken, and pulled herself up beside me.

'He's here in the room with us right now,' I explained.

She became fully alert. 'You have to tell yourself he doesn't exist.'

'Go on, Martyn, do as the little lady says.' He began to glow brighter, lighting the entire room. 'Tell yourself I don't exist. Let's hear you say it. Spanky – doesn't – exist.'

'I can see him, Lottie.' I pointed ahead at the radiant figure. He was naked, bound in a web of leather straps, searing fire flowing from every pore of his body.

'There's no one there, Martyn.'

'There is!'

She reached for the bedside lamp and pulled the switch. Spanky walked around the end of the bed and stood beside her.

'She's nothing much to look at, is she? Pretty eyes, though. I might keep those. Shall we dismember her, take a look at the red stuff, see what makes her tick? Eh?' He patted his jacket pockets. 'I didn't bring a knife with me. What else can we use? Come on, the place could do with redecorating. Let's really cover the walls with blood this time. Go for a Jackson Pollock effect, only with talent.'

'Get the fuck away from her!' I screamed, lunging in his direction as he stepped smartly away from the bed.

'Martyn!' Lottie screamed, falling back. 'For Christ's sake, what's the matter?'

She was looking wildly in my direction, trying to see what I could see so clearly.

Spanky was peering into her eyes, his blinding features mere inches away. 'We could tie her up and do weird, humiliating sex-things to her, I suppose. Use all the kitchen utensils. Teach her not to interfere.'

Suddenly the daemon's hand snaked out and seized her around the throat, physically dragging and lifting her from the bed. She tried to cry out, but his grip was too tight. I snatched at his arm, trying to free it, but the limb was like a steel girder, rigid and immovable. He was looking at me and smiling his wide white smile, barely noticing the girl he held in one hand. There was not a hair out of place on his brilliantined head. His cat-eyes shone a luminous emerald, the colour of excitement.

'But – I'm not going to do anything to her, Martyn. That would be too easy. You're going to do it with a brute strength you never knew you had.'

His free hand grabbed at my hair, but missed as I ducked low. 'You could bite her to death,' he hissed, 'bite and bite until you've chewed a bloody passage through her flesh and your teeth crack on her splintering bones.'

But I was behind him now, and this time when I brought my fists forward I connected with his body, sinking into viscous, semi-solid matter. A painful tingling sensation enveloped my torso as I passed through him to reach her. I tried to remove his hand from her throat, but my fingers passed through his. I didn't dare pull on her body. I could see that she would choke.

Then, as his free hand sought to close her mouth she bit down hard. Unable to hold her in a baggy tracksuit, he released his grip and we both fell back, knocking over the water jug which stood on the bedside table, smashing it against the fire with a sizzling hiss.

'What the bloody hell is going on?'

A plump young woman in a rumpled Nike T-shirt stood in the doorway. Evidently, we had woken the flatmate. Lottie was gasping and clutching her throat, trying to catch her breath.

'It's all right, Susan,' she managed to say. 'It's nothing, just go back to bed.'

One glance around the room told me that Spanky had vanished.

'Are you sure?'

'Really, everything's fine.'

Susan threw me a poisonous look before closing the door behind her. Lottie rolled away from me and sat at the edge of the bed, massaging her throat as I sat helplessly by. 'You have to go,' she said finally. 'I can't do anything. You need to see someone, Martyn, get professional help.'

'He was here in the room,' I insisted. 'He only just left. You must have felt his hands around your throat. You must have been able to tell it wasn't me!'

'No, Martyn,' she said at last. 'I only felt you, heard you, saw you. Ranting to yourself.'

She turned, but found it hard to meet my eyes. 'Perhaps I was wrong. Perhaps you are capable of violence.'

'But it wasn't me who attacked you, Lottie, it was him, don't you see? I tried to grab him but I couldn't. He wants you to think it was me who hurt you.'

'He's doing a convincing job,' she said, coughing. 'Show me your hands.'

I held out my hands and she examined them in turn. Then she raised the side of the right index finger and showed it to me.

'Where I bit you,' she said, pointing to the crescent of teethmarks that were already starting to darken. 'How come you passed right through him, but I managed to connect?' Something else caught her eye. 'What's that?' she asked.

I looked at my left arm just below the wrist. Smothering the main artery at the joint were a number of blue-black specks, like bruised pinpricks. I had felt a slight soreness there for some time. It was where the daemon always grabbed me when he chemically increased my confidence.

'What the hell have you been injecting in yourself?'

'Nothing,' I replied, staring at the sickly track-marks. 'Spanky does it to help me.'

'I think you'd better go right now, Martyn.'

'Wait, wait – please, give me a second – what was the first thing you saw when you awoke?'

I could see her thinking. She was trying hard to let me have the benefit of the doubt.

'Bright light,' she said finally.

'But there was no light on in the room, it was him!'

She looked confused, checked the bedside lamp. Looked back at me.

The odour, maybe it was still lingering, ask her. 'What can you smell?'

She sniffed the air. 'Something spicy.'

'It's his spoor, he leaves it everywhere he goes.' I began to search the spot where he had been standing. 'Take a look at the bed.'

Part of the top sheet was torn.

'You could have done that.'

I held up my bitten nails. 'With these? Think – he was here while you were still sleeping. Insulting you. He woke you up.'

'Wait a minute,' she said indignantly, 'who called me a bitch-on-heat?'

Hallelujah. Touchdown.

'*He* did!'

'I thought it didn't sound like you.'

'Now do you believe me?'

She rubbed a hand over her face, trying to think clearly. 'Yes – no – I'm not sure. I *did* hear something, though. Someone else in the room.'

I was just celebrating the breakthrough when I realized that if she started to believe in Spanky, I would have put her life in

Culpability   253

far greater danger. The daemon had me in a perfect double-bind. I could only make allies knowing that he would take them from me.

'I have to go,' I said suddenly, searching for my jeans.

Ignoring her protests, I dressed and left. I closed the front door quietly and stepped out into the freshly falling rain.

I looked back at Lottie's bedroom window, but she was not there this time. Spanky had confused and frightened her. Hell, he'd frightened both of us. I was alone again. And it was safer for everyone if I stayed that way.

As I walked, I shoved back my sleeve and examined my arm once more. The marks were still there. But which was the illusion, the familiar grip that had not seemed like an injection, or the marks themselves? I couldn't tell, couldn't begin to think through the problem. Logic was starting to give way to panic.

It was Monday morning. In two days' time, Spanky would have to vacate William Beaumont's body and take possession of mine if he was to survive on earth.

And still I had no way of fighting back.

CHAPTER THIRTY

War

I RETURNED home fully prepared for the worst, which was just as well.

He had been back to the apartment and had rampaged through it, inflicting an incredible amount of damage. I'd been burgled before but this was different, far worse than any marauding teenager. He'd thrown red paint up the walls and across the windows, punching holes through both, ripped the guts out of the sofa and armchairs, which lay on their backs exuding Kapok like dying mammals, and poured a black sticky substance, either treacle or oil, all over the parquet flooring.

He'd used my iron to smash a hole in the fishtank, and the delicately tinted creatures lay dead and faded in pockets of glass-filled water. The television and stereo system were strewn in shards of plastic and twisted sheets of solid-state circuitry from one end of the lounge to the other. Bare live wires hung from the wall, blackening the carpet.

I should have been shocked, but after the events of the last few days I merely felt numb as I stepped through the wreckage. Besides, the apartment had hardly been a home to me.

But my chequebook was missing from the bedroom, and so was the cash reserve I kept at the back of one of the kitchen drawers. My credit cards were in my wallet, and that remained where it always was, in the rear pocket of my jeans. I hadn't yet had a chance to withdraw my money from the bank. I had meant to do it before he managed to seal off the account, but now it was probably too late. I knew the way his mind worked. It's what I would have done first.

Oddly, I felt no compunction to leave the flat. Wherever I went I would take the chaos with me, so it made more sense to remain in a place that had already been demolished. If I had become a danger to others, it was best to hide myself away.

The bed was still in one piece, although the frame was slightly twisted. I would still be able to sleep in it if I had to. The telephone had been torn from the wall, so I had to go back into the street to make calls. First I rang Neville Syms and apologized for not being able to attend the staff meeting. I needed to do something that would make me feel normal again.

'Well, it's no secret,' said Syms. 'You'll be receiving notification any day now.' The cadence was measured, the attitude guarded. 'I've consulted with Max's lawyer, and he agrees with me. Without your boss, Thanet has no way of continuing. And that means we no longer have an agreement. If I were you I'd start looking for another job, son. Given the amount of petty cash you owe the company, there'll be no outstanding money owed to you.'

It sounded to me as if the old bastard had struck some kind of deal with the lawyers. A man like Syms had spent too many years in gentlemen's clubs to ever be a gentleman. He'd found a way to get his hands on the business or Max's money, or both, and wasn't about to share it with the staff. One thought pleased me. Wait until he saw what had happened to my company car.

The last remaining ties had now been severed. I was free to

come and go as I pleased. Free to face a daemon. Next, I called the hotel where my parents were staying, but the receptionist informed me that they had checked out an hour or so earlier. I tried the house and Laura answered.

'The place isn't ready to move back into,' she explained, 'but the hotel wouldn't accept your credit anymore. The management were very nice about it. Mum offered to put the bill on their joint card, but you know what Dad's like, he doesn't understand hotels. I tried to call you earlier, but your phone was out of order.'

I asked how she was doing.

Laura insisted that she was coping well, but hadn't been sleeping much. She still wasn't prepared to go to the police, or see a therapist. There was a resolution in her voice that I had never heard before. She said she would make an appointment with her doctor, but only because he wanted her to have a medical after experiencing such dramatic weight loss.

I told Laura that whatever happened, I would find her attacker and take care of him.

'Let it *go*, Martyn. That's what I'm going to do. There's been enough pain in this family.'

'I can't,' I replied. 'If I don't do something, he's never going to go away. Do you need anything?'

'No, I think we're okay for now. The electricity's back on. Mum's been moaning about the amount of cleaning she's got to do, but I can see she's secretly thrilled at the prospect. Dad's gone to have an argument with the gas board. I guess some things never change. Martyn—'

'Yes?'

'He's not going to come back here, is he?'

'No, he's not.'

'Promise me that. I don't know how you're involved with

him and I don't want to know. But promise me he won't hurt us.'

'I promise, Laura.'

My duel with Spanky was escalating into a war. As long as I stayed away from the family, it was safe. The daemon could not afford to stray far from me over the next few days.

I promised to keep in touch until I could get my telephone repaired, and agreed to call again tomorrow. Then I went to visit Zack. I didn't want to involve him, but I still had to return Debbie's Fiat. Besides, I still felt sure that something Zack had read or heard could help me survive until Wednesday.

Debbie answered the door.

She looked tired – she always looked tired – but healthy. Her figure had blossomed with the burden of the child she held within her. 'I'm glad to see you,' she said, hugging me. 'He's been impossible lately, up at all hours with his books, leaving bits of paper all over the place – and he shouts at me if I move any of it. What have you two been up to?'

'Nothing,' I assured her. 'Let me speak to him, will you?'

'He's in his bedroom.' She gestured along the passageway. 'Go on through.'

Zack looked even crazier than usual. It was impossible to imagine when he'd last washed his hair, and his old green sweater was matted with balls of dust, as though he'd been crawling about under the bed.

'Martyn, I've been trying to call you,' he said, pulling me into the room and closing the door. 'What's wrong with your phone?'

'Spanky tore it out.'

I proceeded to explain what had happened since we last met. He listened with barely contained impatience, occasionally nodding or shaking his head sharply. As soon as I had finished, he pulled open the drawer of his desk and removed a file of pages torn from books and magazines.

'I've been doing a lot of reading, Martyn. You're not the only one. Several other cases like yours have been reported around the world in the last three years, but the mainstream press dismisses them. And there'll be more and more, wait and see. We're approaching the Apocalypse, 1999, the fulfilment of the Nostradamus prophecy. And when that happens, daemons will take the place of man. They're proliferating all around us, making themselves known to the human race, preparing for power.'

I let him speak, unable to decide how much of his cosmic theorising I could handle tonight. Zack could talk the most liberal thinker out of believing. He spoke with the energy and passion of a true zealot, but came over as a nutcase.

'They operate from within, Martyn. Do you see? That's why we never have proof of their existence.'

'I'm not sure I understand you.'

'They exist through human imagination, and the power of suggestion. We, us, humans—' he thumped his chest, 'are subconsciously getting in touch with our Old Selves, our former Pagan lives. Lovecraft was right. We're bringing back the old gods, man, drawing them out from our own bodies.'

'You're saying Spanky has always been a part of me?'

'Of course he has! He's your other self, your Mr Hyde, your Dorian Gray.'

'Where's yours, then?'

'I don't know, man. Buried too deep, I guess. Spanky can't hurt you, because if he does he'll hurt himself. Man and daemon are one and the same.'

'If that's true, the only way to get rid of him would be to commit suicide.'

'Isn't that why people kill themselves? To be rid of their personal daemons? The voices in their heads that whisper to them, encouraging them to go out and do harm?'

'Thanks, Zack. I really needed to come around here and be told to bump myself off. I tried to kill someone this morning. I'm going mad trying to figure out what's real and what's an illusion, and all you can suggest is a handful of fucking sleeping tablets.'

'You're shouting, man. Debbie's in the next room.'

'I'm sorry. I'm very shaken up. Something very – *confusing* – is happening to my sanity, and I have to find a way to stop him before it disappears completely, you understand? I mean, how can I prove that it's not just me, that I'm not simply going round the fucking twist?'

'I'm trying to help you,' Zack's tone grew sullen. 'I've never done anything practical in this field.'

I apologized. And I heard him out. I had nothing else to do.

'Listen to me, a daemon can't exist without its host. That's what all the books say. He's an extension of your own id, and whether you meant to or not, you conjured him up yourself.'

'How?' I asked, trying to stay calm. 'Why the hell would I do that?'

'Maybe your subconscious is more fully developed. Why can some people see better than others? We all have differing abilities.'

'That means I'm a murderer. I killed Paul and Max and set the store on fire.'

'No, you only brought Spanky into being, like others before you. This woman who blinded herself, she called to him, and so did a thousand other people before her. Daemons appear to humans and lie to them, telling them whatever they want to hear.'

'To find new hosts?'

'I suppose so.' He rummaged around in the cuttings. 'These things only tell you so much.'

'What if I contact the people who write this stuff. They'd know, wouldn't they?'

'It's possible.'

'I mean, there must be a way of returning him to wherever the hell he came from.'

I picked up an issue of *Fortean Times* and began searching through the bylines. Soon I had a couple of names but no telephone numbers. I rang the magazine's offices, but they were understandably reluctant to give out the addresses of their contributors to someone who must have sounded like a raving madman.

'Wait,' said Zack, 'I've got a contact number for you somewhere. Hang on.' He dug through the stacks of newsprint on his desk and found a slip of paper. 'A lot of these articles quote the same reference sources, and one name rang a bell. Do you remember Simone, the astrologer who used to come around here in the afternoons?' I had a vague recollection of the drunk new age hippychick I used to find passed out on the couch with her blouse over her head. By the way he was always smeared with patchouli oil after her visits, I suspected she did more than just read his charts.

'Well, Simone goes drinking with this guy. She says he knows all kinds of esoteric stuff. She gave me his number, but said to call in the morning, before he goes up the pub.' He handed me the paper. 'It's Notting Hill, if he still lives there. Why don't you check him out?'

Some recommendation. As clutchable straws went, this one felt pretty desperate. But it was clear to me that Zack wanted no further involvement beyond reading in his beloved reference books. I knew he was frightened. He'd finally made a commitment to his girlfriend. He owed it to her to stay out of trouble.

I called the number and asked to talk to Mick. A soft, well-spoken voice replied that I was already speaking to him. I tried not to explain too much about my situation on the phone. I didn't want to put him off.

'I've been reading your articles on daemoniality,' I explained, 'but they don't tell me what I need to know. I just want some advice.'

'I was on my way out.'

I looked at Zack's mantelpiece clock. The pubs were open.

'Look, you're supposed to be an authority. What good is that if you're not prepared to back up your position with practical help?'

'You may well have a point there, but I'm really just a hack. You want a proper scholastic source.'

'I don't have time. This is urgent. I can be there in half an hour.'

'I *was* going out,' he persisted.

'What's your favourite beer?'

He answered without missing a beat. 'Theakston's Old Peculiar.'

'I'll pick some up on my way.'

That did the trick. He threw in the towel and gave me his address. After all, I wondered how often he got the chance to meet a live subject. Seizing the moment I thanked Zack and left, then caught a train to Notting Hill.

'Be careful, man,' Zack called from his window. 'Let me know how it goes.'

CHAPTER THIRTY-ONE

Consultation

AT FIRST I figured that whatever Mick Chantery did for a living, aside from writing occult articles, obviously paid well, because he lived in a large neo-Georgian house set back from the road in what looked like the most fashionable part of Notting Hill. Sealed behind a veil of rain, it was the kind of intimidating place you found in St John's Wood or Hampstead Garden Suburb, and suggested that the owner was either a millionaire, a crook or both. Then he opened the door, and I revised my opinion.

The inside of the building was a pigsty. Chantery was a slightly built man in his late forties, a time-frozen hippy of the Woodstock generation. He looked as if he'd experimented with too many chemicals for too many years, and walked with a stoop, as though permanently ducking through a low doorway. He examined me carefully before opening the door wide, presumably checking to see that he wasn't admitting a lunatic.

He appeared to be living alone in the house, which stank of damp and was filled with cats. They ran about on the mantelpieces and across sideboards covered in old magazines and newspapers, and appeared suddenly from behind sofas. I didn't need a heightened sense of perception to get the full picture. Chantery was an upper-middle class version of Zack with a few years added. The house was all he had left, and he would probably have sold that if the family had let him.

From somewhere above came the steady drip of rainwater leaking in. No doubt Chantery was happier contacting the astral plane than a roofing merchant.

'I hope you're not allergic—'

'Martyn Ross. No, I like them.' I stepped over a pair of tortoiseshell kittens that were attacking each other.

'They're very sensitive to psychic presence, you know. Sometimes they'll stare at a spot on the wall behind you, and you'll swear they can see something you can't.'

I had always assumed cats did that because they were incredibly stupid. Chantery showed me to an uncomfortable-looking armchair and bade me sit. I shifted a pile of books and a McDonalds carton containing an ancient half-eaten burger to the floor, and found another tiny, whining kitten beside my foot.

'That's the only trouble. They get everywhere. Toss him over there somewhere and his mother will come to fetch him. Then pass me one of those—' he indicated the cans I had brought, '—and tell me about your daemon.' He used the pronunciation I had found in the book.

Once again I found myself impatiently explaining everything that had happened. Telling other people about Spanky had so far failed to change anything at all. Chantery (who as far as I could tell had no aspirations to fame beyond writing the odd magazine article) listened intently, resting nicotine-stained fingers at his lips. I finished my story, and for a few moments neither of us spoke. Then he rose and searched through the vertical stacks of books that lay beneath the dining-room table.

'I suppose you'd like some magic formula, some spell that would make this creature vanish,' he said, returning with a single sheet of newspaper. 'I'm afraid there isn't one. You can't exorcise something that doesn't have corporeal form. I've heard of cases like yours before, but I've never managed to actually speak to a victim.'

'Why not?'

'They've always been dead before I could get to them.' He peered closely at the cutting, searching for a particular paragraph. 'Your friend was right to suggest that the daemon has become a part of you. You can't exist without each other. Kill him and you kill yourself. There are four main entities, all male, corresponding roughly to the Four Horsemen of the Apocalypse. If you do manage to get rid of this one, you'll probably get the other three coming after you. They're a bit like the Inland Revenue. Once they've made you a target, they'll stay on your case forever.'

Just what I wanted to hear.

Chantery hit me with a ton of convoluted new age psychology that I didn't really grasp. I remember one thing he said, though.

'The human form is a yin-yang balance of positive and negative attitude. The war between the two sides is a powerful one. Some people feel too much, and give up on life. That's good for daemons. They're attracted to a certain – blankness.'

I asked him about himself.

'I read,' he said simply, tossing back his head and draining the can. 'I've read every known book on daemoniality, but when I was finally ready to publish something of my own, the only imprint that would accept my book was the *Weird And Wild Worlds* series. Crackpot Corner.'

There was something I had to ask. 'Do you think I had a

hand in killing Paul and setting fire to the store?'

'No, that was the daemon. He wants you to blame yourself.'

'There must be something you can do to help me,' I asked, my desperation growing. Chantery was my last hope.

'Why? We can't cure madness. We can't even find remedies for bodily ills. We haven't begun to touch the mysteries of the psyche. The four spirit daemons search the world for receptive minds. When Spanky "taught" you to open up your senses, he was simply unlocking the gates to your inner self. You have to find a way of shutting him out. Trouble is, I don't think there are any. The daemon can't enter while your own identity is still intact. You can't have one body with two wills, two minds. He needs you alive, undamaged – but without your self-control. So he'll either send you mad, destroy your mind completely. Or drive you into such a state of desperation that you willingly invite him in. The latter is preferable, because he can keep you in a comatose state of compliance, feeding you pleasurable stimuli while he uses your physical form for his own purposes.'

'What would those be?'

'Any number of things. I suppose he could turn you into an assassin, a rapist, a child molester. Have you looked into this William Beaumont's past?'

'Enough to suspect that he murdered his own parents.'

'There you are. Who knows what other acts he made his host perform? I don't know what advice I can give you. It's a tricky problem, because any psychologist will be delighted to tell you that possession is purely a mental state. But you've seen and felt the physical effects. You know it's real, and can harm others. You can't even try an auto-suggestive ceremony; hypnosis would erase your memory of the daemon, but that would only aid him in the battle for your mind. He grows stronger the more you doubt yourself. The harder you try to get rid of him, the more tenacious and powerful he'll become. Daemons dig in.'

'Look at all these books, Mr Chantery.' I indicated the uneven rows of leather-bound dissertations, paperback novels, newspapers, encyclopediae, dictionaries and document-holders that lined the far walls. 'Surely there must be *something* in one of them that will help?'

Chantery shrugged and opened another can of beer. 'We can look,' he said.

So we looked.

By six o'clock we were no better off, and Chantery was drunk.

We had covered just two and a half shelves. I worked out that it would take over a week to go through every relevant volume.

'Not like this in the movies, is it?' said Chantery, shaking the beercans until he found a full one. 'There's no cure for cancer. Why should there be a magic formula for anything else?' He seated himself back in his chair and continued to drink. It was all right for him. He wasn't about to die.

'What the fuck should I do, then, kill myself?' I cried, my panic heightened by my growing awareness of the changing atmosphere in the room.

'You're just talking to anyone who'll listen about this, aren't you?' said a familiar voice.

Spanky was standing beside Chantery with a small black kitten in his fist. He was wearing a T-shirt and shorts, and could have been mistaken for an ordinary jogger. Except that his back-spines were erect and sticking through his shirt.

'First a shop-girl, then an airhead, and now a hippy witch-doctor. Why don't you see if you can get it on the seven o'clock news? After the break, Martyn Ross possessed by devil.' He squeezed his fingers tighter and the kitten started to yowl and twist about. Then it began to scream.

Chantery looked up and shrank back in alarm.

He could see something.

'What is it?' I shouted at him. 'What can you see?'

Spanky dropped the crushed, lifeless ball of fur and bone on to the floor and picked up another.

'He can't see or hear me, all that's visible to him is this little thing.' He shook the kitten between his thumb and forefinger, then sharply twisted its head around. Its thin squeals were pitiful to hear. 'I hate cats. They leave hairs on your clothes. I think this game has gone far enough, Martyn.' He raised his voice over Chantery's, who was crying out in alarm. 'It's about time you invited me in to stay. I can make it a very pleasurable experience for you.'

'Get away from me.'

I rose from the chair and backed to the far wall. I didn't want him standing so close to Chantery, who was studying the empty air like one of his cats.

'I'm not going to hurt the old hippy,' he said, scanning my mind. 'There's no point. He means nothing to you.' He thought for a moment, studying Chantery. 'Oh, I don't know, though. Let's give him a heart attack as a punishment for being annoying.'

'No! Leave him alone!'

But Spanky had reached his right hand down into Chantery's chest and was squeezing his heart, clawing his fingers over the pumping muscle, expelling the blood and forcing the valves to shut. Chantery released a sharp little sob of fright, as if he knew exactly what was happening, and fell on to his knees as Spanky yanked his hand free from the poor man's ribcage. He flicked his dripping fingers at the floor, leaving a spray of crimson drops, then directed his attention away from the convulsing body.

'No point in you rushing to the phone, Martyn, he'll be dead before you dial. Actually, the organ was riddled with disease. It virtually came apart in my hand.'

I tried to push my way toward the writhing figure, but Spanky threw me back.

'I said *forget* about him. Tonight I'm after different quarry. Let's play something nastier, you and I. Just to remind you that I mean business. Let's play Murder In The Dark.'

He was searching the floor, looking for another kitten to crush. Behind him, Chantery was suddenly still. Blood was gushing from his nose.

Spanky's voice took on a playful tone. 'I've got it, the perfect victim. It's someone you know. Someone who doesn't wash their hair very often. Someone of no use at all to society. Guessed it yet?'

He thrust out a petulant lip with an impatient sigh. 'One last clue, then. His first name begins with an unusual letter.'

There was a telephone on the sideboard. I ran to it and dialled Zack's number.

'Ssshh,' Spanky was hissing into his hand, 'storm's coming and the lines are down!'

I skidded across the waxed wooden floor, and was out of the room before Spanky had a chance to move. This time I had a head start.

But as I reached the front door and yanked it open, I knew that the daemon would find a way to be there first. To give Zack final, terrible proof of his existence.

CHAPTER THIRTY-TWO

Immolation

AS I had on the night Paul died, I found myself running through the darkened streets in an attempt to save a life.

The wind had risen, bringing with it squalls of freezing rain, and my sneakers slipped on the freshly doused pavements. There was nothing I could do but head for Zack's apartment. With a sinking sense of horror I imagined Debbie, heavy with her unborn child, fighting to protect her lover's life.

As I rounded the corner I was amazed to see a black taxi with its light on, coming toward me through the rain. I hailed it and jumped in, gave the driver Zack's address and asked him to get there as quickly as he could. He made no reply, and pulled away from the kerb at a slow, deliberate pace.

We turned up toward Kensington. I sat forward in the seat and watched the empty streets crawl past beyond the condensation-smeared window. I tried not to think of the odds stacked against my arriving in time.

The taxi missed one set of lights, then another. It had moved to the inside lane, and seemed to be creeping along more slowly than any of the surrounding traffic. I knocked on the connecting glass, but the driver ignored me and remained hunched over the wheel.

I tried to slide open the window, but oddly, it was bolted shut. The door handles were immovable. The locking lights glowed red; they were controlled from the driver's cabin. I hammered on the glass, shouting as we suddenly accelerated, running a red light and narrowly missing a cold-storage truck.

Suddenly, the driver turned around to stare at me.

'Blimey, guv, I don't think I'm going your way at all.' Spanky laughed, white teeth flashing as his mouth opened wide, then wider and wider until his head split apart into a polished black morass of insects, beetles, scorpions, flies and ants fountaining everywhere as his body dissolved into teeming, spidery life. Moments later there was no one driving the cab at all, which was picking up speed as it moved from its course across the central reservation and into the opposing traffic lane.

An oncoming Honda Accord broadsided the cab with a shattering metallic slam and span off toward the pavement, sliding over the wet tarmac. There was another crunch as the side of the cab connected with a steel lamppost and we rocked to a standstill. The side window had smashed with the impact.

With an effort born of panic, I was able to pull myself through it. I ran forward on wobbling legs as a woman began to scream and pedestrians appeared from nowhere. I prayed someone would see to the injured Honda driver. Only I knew that Zack was about to lose his life.

At the next corner I stopped, winded. Just a few streets now. I hadn't realized it but I was crying, tears mingling with the rain that streaked my face. Zack had done nothing wrong. I should never have involved him. I couldn't – wouldn't – let him die.

As I ran into the familiar turning I was assailed with remembrances of my former life, sharing with Zack, leaving him in the apartment while I went to the store, drinking cheap wine while his friends tried to convince me there were supernatural forces on earth. Where was my superior, sceptical attitude now?

I reached the front door and rang the bell, gasping for breath. The first floor lights were on, good sign, but the door was unlocked, bad.

Harder to breathe now.

Ran through the hall and took the stairs two at a time. Reached his front door and hammered on it with both fists. Stepped back and waited, fighting to draw breath.

I could hear someone inside.

Footsteps coming. Latch coming off.

'Hey, man, you can use the bell, it would be less aggressive, you know?' He was fine, same old Zack, scratching himself, hair all over the place. Behind him, Debbie was walking stiffly into the hall.

'Zack, you have to get out right now, he's coming. Right now.' I couldn't catch my breath, words strangling in my throat.

'Who's coming? How'd you get in? Did somebody leave the front door open?'

'Spanky,' I managed to gasp. 'Coming for you.'

His old look of fear returned. He knew better than to disbelieve me. 'Why me, man? I've done nothing.'

'Wants to hurt me.' I was pulling him toward the door.

'Then let him hurt you. Christ – Debbie, come here.'

She was standing in her dressing-gown with her arms pulled in around her, confused. 'I don't understand, Zack. What's going on?'

'Martyn here has got this like, really pissed-off daemon after him, and he's coming for a visit. Get some clothes on.'

Stupidly, they began walking further back into the flat. I needed them out, but couldn't manage the words. As I tried to speak the air was torn from my throat, and I felt myself starting to black out.

The front door slammed, making us both jump, and I realized my mistake.

Spanky had been waiting in the main hall, and had entered the apartment when Zack opened the door. I turned and pulled at the lock, but it couldn't have moved less if it had been welded shut.

'The window,' I shouted hoarsely. 'Is there a way to climb down?'

'I don't know! I've never tried to jump out of a fucking window before, I'm not Batman!'

Zack ran back along the corridor as the lights overhead buzzed and cracked into blackness.

'Is there anyone else in the house?' I asked Debbie, pushing her through to the lounge.

'Only the Wallaces,' she replied. They were the old couple who lived on the ground floor, both in their eighties and as deaf as the dead.

The lights had burned out right through the apartment.

'Where are you?' Zack called.

I could see him outlined by the street light coming in from the far windows of the lounge. Outside, the rain fell in a blind reflective sheet. The three of us stood waiting, catching our breath; something terrible was about to happen.

There was an electric charge rising in the room. I could smell the ozone, and felt the static building in my clothes, prickling my skin.

'What's happening?' called Debbie. 'Zack, what's going on?'

'I don't—'

'He's here.'

Through a sparkling haze I remembered the network of drainpipes that extended beneath the kitchen window. Grabbing Debbie's hand, I pulled her in their direction.

'I want to stay with Zack!' she screamed, as if she already knew that he would not move from his spot in the middle of the room. As we watched, a garish blue glow snaked around him, dragging him to the tips of his toes, gently forcing him up to his fullest height.

'I can feel it, Debbie!' he called out, tipping back his head and watching excitedly as the accelerating static lifted his hair around his face, waving it back and forth before his eyes like the fronds of an underwater plant. 'It's wonderful!'

The storm continued to bristle around him as though his body was a generator, and then the rope of electricity snapped, cracking itself around his face and neck, piercing his throat, forcing open his jaws, illuminating his tongue and the cavity of his nose like a living X-ray. Spears of lightning were playing everywhere on him, running across his teeth to make his fillings glow red-hot, punching at his eyes, drilling into his ears.

For a split second I saw Spanky's figure etched in flame. Then there was a massive, silent flash, and the storm was gone.

Zack fell heavily forward to the floor, and we saw that his hair, his shoulders and back were glowing like the carbonized embers of a dying fire.

I grabbed at the Mexican blanket covering one of the armchairs and threw it across him, smothering the flames. Even in the dark, we both knew he was dead. The room was filled with the sweet stench of charring skin. Debbie began to scream, so I hugged her tight, and stayed there hugging her until her sobs subsided to a level wail.

I still couldn't get the front door open, and finally had to prise out the lock with a knife-sharpener. The fuses had blown, and the telephone line was dead.

Spanky had gone. He had taken Zack's life but left his girlfriend and their unborn child unharmed. As if I should be thankful to him.

I had been such a witless bloody fool. I'd returned to Zack bringing evil right to his door, acting once more as a conduit for the daemon's murderous malice.

CHAPTER THIRTY-THREE

Pugilism

WE CALLED an ambulance from the phonebox at the end of the road. When the men arrived they were horrified by the state of Zack's body, and immediately notified the police.

It was a gruelling night.

Unsurprisingly, everyone wanted to know what had happened. They could see that Zack had received a huge electric shock, but could find no dangerous or exposed wiring near the site where he had fallen. Debbie and I described what we had seen to a pair of officers, a man and a woman who behaved as if they didn't believe a single word of our story.

I was questioned in a separate room, and questioned again until they could see that we were telling the truth. How could we not be? The police shut down the mains supply to the flat and suggested that we make alternative accommodation arrangements for the night, as the place could still be unsafe.

They gave Debbie a lift to her sister's house. Before she left, she looked back at me with blazing hatred in her eyes. I knew she thought that if Zack had not opened the door to me, he would still be alive tonight.

I refused a lift and stumbled off in the direction of my wrecked apartment, more disoriented and frightened than ever.

Realizing that I couldn't walk all the way, I stopped a minicab and had him take me to Bow.

When I got there I found that my wallet was missing. Either Spanky had taken it, or it had dropped out in Zack's flat. The cab driver threatened to duff me up, but I was bigger than him and a lot more desperate. He drove off, streaking out in a squeal of tyres.

The lock had been changed on the door, and there was a letter addressed to me taped across the bell.

The lease had been cancelled due to 'the non-fulfilment of the rental agreement', which I took to mean that the standing order had been rescinded; Spanky tampering with computer records again. No reply had been received to their previous enquiry, etc., etc. Worse, the flat and its contents had been impounded by the landlord because of the damage I had allegedly caused, and because of constant complaints from the other tenants about noise. Prosecution would probably result. My belongings were stored with the caretaker. Should I attempt to gain entry to the apartment, I would find that the alarm code had been changed, and the police would be instantly notified.

Big fucking deal.

It was 4.32 a.m.

Zack was dead.

Debbie was terrified.

I had £4.72 in my pocket.

No wallet.

No watch.

No clothes but the ones I stood in.

And nowhere to go.

I couldn't head for Sarah's, even if she would have me. I could no longer trust myself with her – or anyone else, for that matter. He was with me wherever I went, dogging my footsteps, turning me into a plague-carrier.

I screamed 'What do you want from me!' and kicked at the wall, over and over until the lights went on in the corridor and doors began to open. Then I had to make a run for it, before the neighbours called the police.

Out on the street it was raining harder than ever, filling one of my sneakers with icy water. I set off in no particular direction, without a destination, glad to be moving away from the apartment.

Oddly enough, it was an image of Joey that filled my mind as I walked. Thinking about him still made me angry. In the last weeks of his life the thing I remembered most was his evasiveness, always leaving a room when I asked him a difficult question, always acting like he had something more important to do than talk to me.

As I walked toward the railway bridge, its brick arches built to hold in shadows, a hazy figure divorced itself from the blackness and strolled to the light. I recognized the gaunt yellow face immediately. He was in his old striped pyjamas, and the jacket collar was way too big, a sure sign that he was dying. His feet were bare, and he didn't seem to notice that he was standing in a puddle of dirty water. He seemed very real. The water was absorbing into the cuffs of his trouser bottoms.

'Hello, Martie.'

'Hello, Joey.'

'You look like shit, little brother.'

'At least I'm not dead, like you. Spanky send you here?'

'I don't know. You tell me. The last thing I remember is being back in my old bedroom at Twelvetrees.'

'Listen, this isn't going to work.'

'What isn't going to work?'

'You're not my brother. You look like him and sound like him, but Joey's dead.'

'Spanky can bring memories to life, Martie. You'll be able to as well, once he's inside you.'

'So you know who he is, then. I suppose he's made a convert out of you, wants you to persuade me that it's better on the other side.'

'He doesn't want to hurt you, Martie. He likes you, and he wants what's best for you, believe me.'

'Why would I believe you?'

I knew that Joey's effigy was just another weapon in Spanky's armoury, but still found myself responding to him as if he were my dead brother. 'You lied to me when you were alive, why shouldn't you now? I'm not letting him in, Joey. He can find himself another host.'

Joey leaned back against the wet, black bricks of the arch and released a long sigh, like gases being released from a corpse. 'You don't know how difficult you're making this, Martie. He'll hurt me. You don't want to see me hurt, do you?'

'I don't give a flying fuck, actually,' I said, looking into the brambles at the trampled fence that hedged one side of the arch. Reaching into the undergrowth on the embankment, I pulled one of the wooden staves free from its torn wire mooring and hefted it in my hand.

'But Martie, think of the things you'll be able to do once he inhabits you, the places you'll visit, the sights you'll see.'

'In the last few weeks I've seen enough sights to last a lifetime,' I replied, breaking into a run and ramming the pointed end of the stave hard into Joey's chest.

There was a pop of foul air and the figure collapsed like a rubber balloon, liquefying into the shadows until the stave became unanchored and fell to the ground.

P u g i l i s m   279

I walked out of the archway and didn't look back at the putrefying mass on the pavement. That thing had not been my brother. Joey – the real Joey – had never called me Martie in his life. If Spanky wanted to trick me, he had to learn not to trust what he read in my mind. I was pleased with myself. For once, I'd been one step ahead of him.

I stayed in the backstreets, moving from one empty road to another, lost in a maze of neat terraced houses, getting wetter, growing angrier. Spanky had taken back a lot more than he had given me, that was for damned sure.

I hadn't eaten for ages, but at least my nervous empty stomach had energized me. Now, though, the effect was starting to wear off, and exhaustion was setting in. My legs felt as though lead weights had been attached to them. I just needed shelter, a dry place to sleep. So this was what it felt like to be homeless.

I wondered what Spanky would attempt next. I had been thinking about it distantly, as if these things were happening to someone else, a person with whom I was barely acquainted. That was when I knew something bad was happening to my mind. When a man stops caring about his existence, it's time to take stock of the situation.

I passed back through another dripping railway arch. Either the overhead line curved through the streets, or I had doubled around on myself. I sat down under the arch and rested my head against the wet bricks.

I wanted so badly to sleep, but it seemed to me that if I shut my eyes right then, I would never wake again. I kept seeing Zack with his skinny arms outstretched, engulfed by tongues of blue flame, like some lurid biblical illustration.

I concentrated on building a mental wall around myself to keep Spanky at bay. I was determined to make sure that he could not enter while I slept in such a weakened state, so I tried to weave a net of subconscious commands across my real thoughts. Visualization was the key, and I visualized Spanky shut out from the sealed steel fortress of my mind. I was shivering and hungry, but still in control. How that must have infuriated him. Nothing could frighten me while I knew he was being frustrated, not even—'

And right then, I made a dumb mistake.

For the most fleeting of moments, I thought of what scared me.

And a few seconds later imagination became reality, and I heard the fast pounding of boots in the alleyway ahead.

It was a common fear, nothing exotic, just a simple terror of being beaten up, hurt by mindless hooligans, something I often thought about walking alone through the city streets at night – but I knew that Spanky had seized upon it.

Here they came all right, half a dozen of them rounding the corner, five men and one girl, with razor-cut faces and cropped bullet heads. They were all dressed identically – Spanky was no longer bothering to maintain the deception of reality – in spotless white T-shirts, too-short jeans, heavy black lace-up DM boots and ringing steel toecaps.

They had spread out across the pavement and were running hard, issuing guttural commands. Two of them were swinging iron bars in their fists. I shoved myself away from the wall and broke into a run, but the muscles in my legs were seizing up fast. There was no way of informing my mind that these people were apparitions, no way of overriding my soaring panic. I had seen their type too many times before in the streets.

There was no chance that I could possibly outrun them. They were built for speed, truncated creatures of muscle and venom, born to hate and hurt. As I passed beneath the next railway arch I heard more of them jumping down from the embankment, swearing and shouting to me, daring me to stop and face them, the unfair odds never entering their minds.

My lungs were scorching and felt as though they would split if I didn't slow down, but the fear of pain drove me on. I could hear the boot-stamps of more than a dozen people now as the hysteria of the mob infected others. No, I tried to tell myself, not true, Spanky's doubling up the numbers because he knows it'll make me more scared. Ahead was a brightly lit main road. Even if there was anyone around at this time, I knew they wouldn't dare to interfere.

Spanky's power was growing as my sanity disintegrated; there was no knowing how far his illusions had become realized in human form. I could no longer tell if the gang of thugs bearing down on me was composed of air and magic or flesh and blood. One of them had rushed ahead and was right behind me, grabbing at the wet sleeve of my jacket, shouting filth into my ear. I was a Jew, a Paki, a nigger, a queer, a hate figure that stood for anyone he couldn't understand.

He swung his iron bar and it glanced against my shoulder, real enough to hurt, punching me sideways into the road. Another of them seized on the back of my coat and pulled, so that I skidded around and slipped over. Swinging with the momentum, I rolled and landed in the middle of the road. I looked up into the ink-clouded sky and saw their dark forms appear around me, blotting out the little light that remained.

The first boot landed in the centre of my back, and felt as if it had broken my spine. A fist smacked hard against my chin. As they all began to swing their boots at my face and chest and genitals I screamed, and the sound merged with the blast of a truck horn. I was in the middle of the road. There were shouts of confusion about me as the vehicle hit the first of my attackers. I remember the wall of chrome atop vast tyres, the stink of burning fuel, and a series of ear-splitting shrieks – then nothing but the welcoming sable cloak of night.

CHAPTER THIRTY-FOUR

Hospitalization

OVERWASHED FRESH linen lay beneath my body. A hard, brilliant light in my face. The sharp smell of disinfectant. A distant clatter of trolleys. I awoke in the public ward of a hospital, but had trouble opening my eyes to the bright day dawning through the windows. The left eyelid seemed to be gummed shut. I turned my head to one side, and the muscles in my neck flickered with burning intensity, warning me not to move.

My back was the worst. When I tried to sit up it felt as if someone was throwing knives into my spine. I lay there staring at the ceiling for what seemed like an age, listening to the sounds of the rising ward.

'So you're awake and taking notice then,' said a young Irish staff nurse. I could see her from the corner of my eye, but could not move my head to follow her as she passed around the bed to check my chart. 'You've had a nice little sleep.'

My first attempt at speech failed, but the nurse passed me a plastic water bottle with a clear flexible pipe attached, and I found myself able to sip from it.

'How long?' I managed to ask.

'You were brought in early this morning.'

'Tuesday?'

'That's right.'

'Where am I?'

'University College Hospital.'

'Can't see.'

'No, you won't see from the left eye for a little while yet. You have some stitches in there.'

'—hurts, move.'

'Well, you're not going to be dancing the tango for a while, that's certain. Open your mouth.' She slipped a thermometer between my teeth. 'You have a fracture in your right knee, three cracked ribs, some damage to your left wrist. And the little finger of your right hand is broken. That was quite a fight you got yourself into. However did you manage it?'

'Gang—'

'You lads can surely find better ways to spend your time than making work for us. You're going to be in here for a day or so yet, then out as soon as you can walk because we need the bed for more deserving souls. The police would like to talk to you, and will be by in the afternoon.'

She tapped me on the chin, withdrew the thermometer and checked it. 'That's normal enough. You'll recover quickly. The bruises look worse than they are.' She gave a brisk smile and was gone.

I lay in bed thinking of Spanky, knowing that Laura must be worried by my lack of communication. The only way I could protect them all was by staying away.

By carefully twisting my head back, I had been able to see the patient ID board beside my bed. There was no name written on it. Hadn't they been able to discover my identity? I was no longer carrying a wallet. Perhaps it was for the best. They might start asking more questions about Zack's death, or worse still, try to connect it with Paul's murder and the fire at the furniture store.

At 5.30 p.m. the boys in blue arrived, a uniformed duo, one thin, one fat. A comedy team, Laurel and Hardy without the laughs. The larger of the two had dandruff-covered shoulders and sat beside me asking stupid fucking questions while his partner laboriously wrote up my replies. I was finding it easier to speak now, which was just as well because the first thing they requested was a list of names.

'You think I *knew* these people?' I asked, incredulous.

'Didn't you?'

'Of course not.'

'Then why did they attack you?'

'They just appeared from nowhere.' That was certainly the truth.

'What's your name, son?'

So they had no clue to my identity. I couldn't afford to tell them the truth. I tried to think of another name, but nothing would come. I looked over at the man in the next bed. There was a bunch of mottled bananas in the bowl on his table. 'Fyfe,' I told them, 'James Fyfe.'

'And you'd never seen these others before?'

'No. A truck hit us. What happened?'

'The driver says he saw you, surrounded by some kind of a mob. It was dark and very wet, and he caught you in his lights too late to safely apply his brakes. To be honest, he was travelling too fast for a built-up area. He says he hit two or three people hard, but they'd all gone by the time he'd climbed down from the cab, so they couldn't have been too badly hurt. He reckons he really ploughed into them, though, and there are tyre marks on the road.'

'There must have been blood.'

'No blood, and no marks on the vehicle, either. The rain may have helped to remove them, but I would have expected some sign of the collision to be left behind. It's a bit of a mystery.'

The driver had seen them.

Spanky's manifestations were becoming real. The news was both good and bad. Good for my mental state, as it meant I was no longer imagining everything. Bad for my health, because his illusions could now kill.

According to Zack's magazine article, Spanky needed to be near his designated host to create full-scale manifestations. His powers were increasing, and I was helping to make it happen. He was feeding from me, and I still had no way of stopping him.

There was nothing more I could tell the police that would help them in any way. They left, disgusted with my lack of cooperation, and warned me that next time an innocent person could be left for dead. I just hoped it wouldn't be me. But then, I no longer considered myself innocent.

Later I lay on my back, listening to the sounds of quiet suffering that surrounded me. There in the darkness bodies were battling infection. Cell walls were being broken down by invading viral hordes, bloodstreams polluted, tissue corrupted, bone and viscera riddled with the alien venom of disease. The world didn't need a creature like Spanky. It had already found a million other ways to destroy itself.

But there he was at the end of the bed, tinged with his familiar blue glow, dressed in a leather Harley jacket and faded black jeans, whispering not because anyone else could hear him, but because it was expected in a hospital ward.

'Good evening, Martyn. I'll come right to the point. I think the time for pleasantries between us has passed, don't you? You clearly have no intention of letting me in.'

Why does it have to be me? I asked weakly. *Why not someone else?*

'Because I don't fail. I will not fail. I have never, ever failed. And I cannot do so now.'

There must be someone else. What happened to Melanie Palmer, the woman you blinded?

'She'd only ever been prepared as a back-up, in case my preliminaries with you fell through. As I told you at the time, she was too unstable to be ideal. When you asked me to help you, I had no further need of her.'

I had never seen him like this before. He paced around the bed, passing a coin back and forth in his hands, tense and short-tempered. I wondered what would happen if he did fail. It made me want to hold out against him even more. I wanted to be there, to see for myself.

'I'm aware that your own life doesn't matter to you,' he said, sensing my thoughts. 'The taking of other lives hasn't convinced you, either.'

If you hurt my family in any way, I will kill myself and you will never have me. You know that.

'I'll be honest with you, Martyn.' He was wagging his finger angrily at me. 'I haven't come across this – attitude – in a mortal before, and it's making me very upset. So upset, in fact, that I feel a growing need to cause pain. I'm going out into the city without you, Martyn. If you've seen this evening's newspaper, you'll know that I've already started. I am no respecter of human life, and I'm going to start taking it in great quantities. Now, you can stop me. You have that power. Say the word and the killing will end. Injure yourself in any way, and I will bring violence of such terrible proportions, this city will have seen nothing like it since the Blitz, do you understand?'

He stopped striding about and checked his watch. 'Time to go and kill. Find me, Martyn. Find me and surrender. And you'd better do it quickly.'

He marched from the ward with his usual speed, and didn't even bother to leave behind one of his unpleasant hallucinations. The bedside clock read 9.55 p.m. He had a whole night of destruction ahead. I tried to raise myself out of the bed, but the muscles in my leg released spasms of pain in protest.

I had a pretty good idea where I could find him. Spanky was fond of reminding me how easily he could read my mind. Now it was time for me to read his.

My intention was to leave at once. On a nearby locker I found a late edition of the *Evening Standard*. The front page carried news of a death; refuse collectors had discovered the body of a teenage girl stuffed in a dustbin in an alleyway off Leicester Square. Mutilation was hinted at. Police were not yet prepared to release the identity of the corpse, nor details of its condition. There was a photograph of the alley, eerier in monochrome, and an arrow marked the site of the bin in order to render the scene more vividly in the reader's imagination.

I knew this was Spanky's doing. I studied the picture and stretched my senses taut, searching for him in the back alleys of the city. He was out there now, preparing to haunt the kind of clubs where victims went unnoticed and unmourned.

I planned to leave as the evening shift changed to night. I needed clothes and cash. More than that, I needed someone I could trust. Asking Debbie for help was out of the question, and Laura was too far away. My best bet was Lottie, but I didn't want to put her at risk. Then I remembered Susan, her flatmate. She was a student here at UCH . . .

My blood-soaked shirt had been thrown out, and the nurse had taken my trousers and shoes away. My locker contained the contents of the pockets; the princely sum of 35p. I hobbled to the payphone outside the patient's day room and made the call.

'I could get you some professional help,' Lottie suggested unhelpfully, 'someone who could explain what these – hallucinations – mean.'

'I don't need to see a doctor,' I whispered, realizing how absurd that sounded from someone stuck in hospital. 'You saw what happened when we were together. You sensed someone else in the room.'

'You're right, I did.'

'So you believe me.'

'Yes, but – your behaviour isn't normal, Martyn, you must admit that.'

'Of course it's not normal! I explained to you exactly what had happened.'

A sigh on the other end of the line. 'So you don't think there's anything wrong with you?'

'Lottie, you can think of me as Jack the Ripper if you want but right now I need your help. I'll do a deal with you. If I haven't been able to rid myself of Spanky by midnight tomorrow, I'll come in, have counselling, get thrown in jail, whatever.'

'You promise?'

'Sure. You can personally walk me to the police station or if you prefer, the nuthouse.'

'I wouldn't do that, Martyn. I believe you. Or at least, I believe that you believe. What do you want me to do?'

'Come to the hospital right now. I don't have any clothes.'

'It's late. Why don't you get a decent night's rest first?'

'We're both running out of time. It has to be now.'

'I'm not sure I can—'

'Lottie, if I fail now I'm dead. Please, help me this once. You don't even have to see me.'

She thought for a moment. 'All right. Getting in won't be a problem if Susan's on call tonight. But what shall I tell the duty nurse?'

'Say you're my girlfriend and you just found out where I was. I've got to get out of here. I need some stuff, jeans, a sweater, shoes and socks. And some money. Is that possible?'

'Susan's boyfriend is always leaving his clothes lying around. He'll be pretty pissed off. You'll have to take whatever I can find.'

Lottie arrived in the ward just as one of the shift nurses was leaving, and although they spoke in a friendly enough fashion she was only allowed to look in on me from the door. She gave a little wave from the fingers of her left hand, and a small, uncertain smile, but I could tell she was shocked by my appearance.

Like a bowler going for a strike, she slid a plastic M&S shopping bag across the tiled floor and beneath my bed.

I waved her away, telling her to leave in case the incoming sister saw her and started asking questions. I was frightened that Spanky might sense her presence near me. She glanced briefly back at the ward's swing doors, then placed two fingers over her heart and pointed them at me. I pushed down beneath the covers and waited for the night desk to settle.

When the ward had once more subsided into total silence, I walked to the toilet with the bag inside my hospital-issue gown and changed into the clothes Lottie had found for me.

Susan's boyfriend presumably belonged to the World Wrestling Foundation, because the baggy black sweatshirt, jeans and black sneakers were all several sizes too large. They would get me out, though, and wouldn't constrict the dressing on my ribs or my knee. There was a fair amount of money taped inside the back pocket of the jeans. She'd obviously been to a cashpoint on the way. In the other pocket was one of those red Swiss army penknives.

Lottie was the last person I had expected to come through for me, but now she was my only lifeline to sanity.

There was one more thing I had to do. Turning to the washroom mirror, I dug beneath the dressing on my face and binned the bloodstained tape. Then I carefully tugged the stitches from my left eye until I could open the lid. The ball beneath was bruised and bloodshot and stung like a son-of-a-bitch, but I needed full sight if I was to face Spanky again.

I waited until the coast was clear and walked out of the hospital, squeaking along the empty corridor in the slippery sneakers, resisting the temptation to break into a run. Half an hour later I had made it back to the West End, and was ready to begin my search.

CHAPTER THIRTY-FIVE

Clubability

DIS-ESTABLISHMENT. BLUETOPIA. Sanitarium. Mr Whippy. Pierced. SubStation. Fuck City. After a while, one club started to look just like the next. Black walls, black light, high tech, low tack. I soon perfected the technique of the search. I only had to stand above the pulsing dance floor and scan the room to know if he was there. I didn't even have to enter half of the bars. I could walk up to the entrance and tell if he'd ventured inside.

I was learning to play his game.

In one deafening sweatbox, The Pain Bar, I sensed his cooling spoor, less than an hour old. He was leaving visible traces now, tiny blue specks that shone like dandruff under ultraviolet neon. Clubs were second homes to him, perhaps his only homes. He thrived on the barely veiled aggression and sexual electricity that these places generated. Here victims and predators shone forth as clearly as if they were labelled cuts of meat. It was ironic that these dance-bars derived their names from fashionable masochistic rites, while their patrons retained no genuine concept of intolerable pain or cruelty.

Leaving the club I walked south toward the river, following the fading trail of my nemesis. My right leg hurt badly and slowed me down, but I pushed the discomfort from my mind and made Spanky's imprint my only frame of reference. I had earmarked another club on my list, a small streamer-covered bar/dancefloor behind Charing Cross Road called Raw Deal.

There were too many people gathered around the entrance. Too many mixed-up signals. I had to enter the club to tell if he'd been there. Inside, there was barely room to move. I noticed that people were drinking beer here, a change from the Evian and Ecstasy crowd. The place was having some kind of party night, which involved most of the customers wearing *mardi gras* masks.

His spoor was strongest near the edge of the balloon-filled dance area, in the same kind of corner where I had first met him. He had gone, but his tracks were so fresh that I knew myself to be right behind him.

I wondered if he, in turn, could sense his hunter.

I had attempted to keep my mind shielded at all times, but it was difficult to maintain such a high level of concentration. I returned to the club's main entrance, but the trail had already grown cold. Backtracked to the fire exit, and it was so strong that I could smell his distinctive odour above the sweat and amyl nitrate of the club. I pushed on the bar of the door and found myself in a long, litter-strewn alley running between a pair of Victorian brick office buildings. My heart was stabbing against my ribs now, for the blue pinpricks of light were becoming amber with body heat, so recently had they been shed from their host.

As I turned the corner, I braced myself for what I would see.

He was standing with his shoulders hunched over the girl, and his glistening scarlet hands buried deep within her chest. She was dead or dying, her shaven head thrown back so far that her face was pressed against the wall. Her plastic skirt, glistening darkly with his seed, had ridden above her thighs, which were awkwardly splayed around his bare hips.

The spines on Spanky's back had sheared through his leather jacket to stand erect up to the nape of his neck. He turned his head slowly and looked at me with red unseeing eyes, caught in the middle of his death-lust. His mouth was bared in a rictus of a grin, saliva pattering on the paper-strewn ground at his feet. Although he took the form of a man he no longer appeared mortal, no longer possessed a recognizable human spirit.

'Martyn.'

His voice had deepened to a guttural drawl between man and pig, like a tape running slow. He pulled his hands free and dropped the body into the litter without a downward glance.

'You seem to have caught me red-handed. I've just eaten her soul. I was surprised to find she had one at all. There wasn't much to it. If I'd have known you were coming I'd have saved you a sliver.'

'But you knew I was coming.'

He turned to face me, wiping his dripping hands across his still-engorged penis. With a vague sense of disappointment, I noted that it was slightly smaller than my own.

'To tell the truth, Martyn, I had a vague inkling that you might show up.'

'You'd have been fucked if I hadn't, wouldn't you?' I checked the alley for exits as I spoke. 'You made it obvious that my presence was requested tonight. Why was that, do you think?'

'I don't understand this new tone in your voice, Martyn.'

He had never been more dangerous than he was now. He raised his trousers and buckled his belt, then stepped over the body and walked slowly toward me, still wiping his hands.

'Remember how I wouldn't tell you about my brother, Spanky? I didn't want you to know how I felt. I carried his memory inside me. Joey was never far away. I kept him where he would burn. Who's inside you? Who's the young man who invited a daemon to come and live inside him?'

'My former identity is no longer of interest, Martyn. It was wiped out long ago. William Beaumont's body dies at midnight tomorrow.'

'You think you gave him a decent life? You killed his parents.'

'They wondered why he didn't age. They found out who he had become. But look at the good things. Before William met me, he knew the route of every desperate day. Who wouldn't seize a second chance? I gave him life and youth. As I will to you.'

'I don't want it.'

'You don't have a choice.'

He was standing less than three feet from me now. I could smell the hot taint of his barely controlled breath.

'Beaumont allowed you to destroy his personality.'

'He put up a fight, but it didn't amount to much. Others have before. It's human nature.'

'I think you're frightened. You're shitting yourself every time you look at your watch. If you don't get me, and you can't find another human host, you'll be trapped in a carcass that's collapsing and decaying with every passing second. The unthinkable will happen. Your living soul will be trapped inside a corpse.'

The roar grew in his throat and he stepped forward, barely able to stop himself from harming me. He did not dare. I was his only remaining hope of survival.

'What happens a few seconds after midnight tomorrow,

Spanky? You can't just take off into the ether, can you? You chose mortality, and you must continue that way or die.'

Silence. He was always silent when I was right.

'Many innocents will be slaughtered before then, unless you're willing to trade your life for theirs.'

I didn't doubt it, but for the moment I had to call his bluff. I needed time to think.

'I always feel that large-scale atrocities are a cry for help, don't you? They're beneath you, Spanky. You'll be the one going into McDonalds with a shotgun, another newspaper statistic, not me. It's a lot of effort just to prick my conscience. You could try the old hallucination routine again, but it wouldn't work. You see, you made a fundamental error with me. Don't worry, it's not your fault. It wasn't foreseeable.'

His face clouded, an almost human response. 'What are you talking about?'

'You thought you were giving me freedom by giving me what I wanted. Nice clothes, a fashionable apartment, sexy women. All the lifestyle things you see on TV. Accessories. I just swapped one trap for a better-furnished one. But take everything away and you give me real freedom. Now I have power.'

I turned my back on him and walked out of the alley. I was sure he wouldn't hurt me, but I still had to force myself to control each measured step.

I had no way of preventing him from causing harm. The supernatural had failed me. There were no charms, no spells, no antidotes that worked on something spawned from within the human psyche. The main thing was to keep him in my sights. And I was pretty damned sure that he wouldn't stray far from me, either. It was after midnight. Spanky's last twenty four hours of earthly existence had begun. There would be no more sleep until it was over.

'I'll win, Martyn,' he shouted after me. 'You have nowhere to go. No one to help you. And if I die, you'll die with me.'

As I walked into the street, the fear returned. I had almost allowed him to possess me once before.

I wondered what he could do to make me consider it again.

CHAPTER THIRTY-SIX

Duality

WEDNESDAY MORNING. Dawn was still far off. In spite of the rain, the streets remained stale from the night before. Fried onions, perfume and sweat. The scent of an overcrowded city.

We watched each other from a distance, Spanky and I. Nowhere else to go, nothing else to do but walk the streets of London and keep each other in our sights.

Sometimes he caught my eye from across the street and gave a wry smile, trying to make light of our situation. I was thinking furiously, getting nowhere. There was no way of second-guessing him without revealing my own thoughts.

I'd borrowed a cheap watch which had been lying on the hospital locker next to mine. Its owner was in a coma; he wouldn't be needing it for a while. I tilted it to the streetlight: 3.15 a.m. The hours had never passed so slowly as they did now.

We had moved away from the main thoroughfares of the city, into the gloomier avenues that backed them. The daemon walked on the opposite pavement, always keeping pace with me, bouncing lightly on the balls of his feet, biding his time.

As the deadline approached I could sense that his strength was growing, feeding on his cruelties, and yet he continued to keep his distance. Perhaps any increased proximity would allow me to figure his intentions. I didn't know what to expect next, and I was starting not to care. I was dog-tired, soaking wet and desperate for sleep. But I was afraid that if I dropped my guard for a moment he might now be strong enough to take control.

The splint on my little finger kept sliding loose, but my right knee was really killing me. I tried not to let him see how badly I was limping. I looked over at Spanky and instinctively knew that he had picked up the thought.

By 5.15 a.m., it felt like we had covered half of North London. The streets were still empty except for the red mail vans heading for the King's Cross depot. We were somewhere near the Angel, but were now heading West. The bastard never tired. If we kept walking like this, he would eventually wear me down. I had to make him stop.

'Hey, Martyn.'

Maybe he'd caught the thought, because he was beckoning me from the other side of the road. I hesitated, carefully watching him.

'This is getting us nowhere. Come over here for a minute. I'm not going to bite you.' To break the impasse, I crossed over to him.

'We need to talk this through, you and I.' He began to walk again, and I was forced to fall in step beside my enemy. 'Much hangs on the outcome. Suppose I left you now. What would you do? You have nothing to live for. I could leave, you know. Despite what you think, there might still be time for me to find another host.'

'You think someone would consciously, willingly invite you in?'

'I can appear to others in any form I please. I can make the offer very attractive.'

'Then go and do it. You're almost out of time. Why risk everything waiting for me?'

'You are the one I chose, the most suitable host.'

'No, we couldn't be more opposite, you and I. All I have to do is hold you at bay until midnight tonight, and you'll be gone forever.'

He laughed softly. 'Martyn, I've already thought of a way around that. If you continue to resist me I'll simply enter the body of a derelict with no time left to live, a homeless drunk, a lonely old woman. You think they wouldn't accept my offer in an instant? Then I'll come back to you again. How will you recognize me? A face in the crowd, a beggar in an alley. Who will I be? How will you ever know?'

'If you come back I'll sense it. You brought out certain abilities in me, Spanky. I'll always know when it's you.'

He was silent for a minute. We walked on past the overgrown front gardens of large Victorian houses, proud homes hacked into flats, each porch eerily lit by rows of plastic illuminated bell-pushes. Spanky lit a cheroot and drew on it pensively, as if he had all the time in the world.

'It was easy to tempt you, Martyn,' he said. 'You begged me to do so. I heard your call and answered it. A thin, high sound, borne on the breezes above the city. The invocation was made. It always is. You'll never be able to resist me totally, because you summoned me in the first place.'

He held out his arm and brought me to a stop. Ahead, traffic lights pulsed to an empty road. When he turned, he appeared more human than he ever had before. His eyes had softened somehow. His features were less severely defined. As he pressed his hand against my heart, my stinging ribs creaked in protest.

'I am you, Martyn. The dark side of every man contains a hiding daemon, and I am yours brought forth. I showed you how to effortlessly take advantage of people and you loved it. Think of the nineteen eighties, when the nation was suddenly told that it was fine to be greedy, to be rich and callous, to be blind to poverty and suffering. How did we react? We *partied*, Martyn. We partied for an entire decade. Everyone has the capacity for cruelty.'

'Hit me with every cliché in the book,' I said dully. 'I've only got to listen to it for a few more hours.'

He hadn't heard me. His voice grew harder, his words reverberating and overlapping in my head. 'I'll always come back to dog your steps,' he promised, 'to whisper in your ear, to tamper with your senses, to wear you down. I exist in every malicious thought, every angry moment, every minor cruelty you inflict. It's your fault that I live. And with you I'll create a cruel new life on earth. The old gods, Martyn. They were the ones who brought me here.'

I knew he spoke the truth. He had never really lied to me. How could he? I wondered about everyone who had been hurt since I met Spanky. How much of me had wished each one harm?

'You know, what shocked me was the ease of it,' he was the lighter Spanky now, suddenly airy and expansive, 'finding someone like you. The times have grown callous. I could have inhabited a thousand others – virtually anyone I spoke to would have allowed me in. When I first met William Beaumont, in 1950, I had been searching for three years. Now it's like shooting fish in a barrel; everyone's an opportunist. Suggest something wicked and you'll find a dozen takers. Have you noticed, there are no separate compartments on the railways any more because people can't be trusted not to rape or kill each other? These are the signs of the times, Martyn, and I must move with them. You have to let me join with you. It's like Frankenstein and his bride. We belong together.'

As I listened to his steady, even speech, something within me was worn away. I could see his point all too clearly. Instead of spending the rest of my life as confused as everyone else, at war with feelings I barely understood, why not give way to a bolder, ruthless nature? Surely it was a more honest way to live, to acknowledge temptation and exist with it . . .

I felt him swarming into me then, attempting to storm into possession while my resistance was at its lowest. The sensation was a sickening jolt, a drop into an abyss of the darkest misery, and my instant reaction was to force it away like a cell rejecting a hostile infection.

I fell to my knees and vomited violently, retching until my lungs and stomach burned. Spanky had seized his chance too early, and his precipitate action had cured me of any remaining doubt. I rose unsteadily to my feet and lurched away from him, determined that he would never obtain the human host he needed, even knowing that I could never win. Listening to Spanky was like having anaesthetic needles slipped into your veins. As the state of euphoria wore off you looked down to find yourself bristling with syringes.

'You can't run away from me, Martyn. I'm going to break into houses and do terrible, disgusting things to people if you don't stay.'

'I've seen all your parlour tricks,' I called back. 'They've rather lost their edge.' But I knew he could kill. The question was, how many would I allow to die before I surrendered? He was behind me, moving across the bloated gutters like a wraith, and he had snatched up the thought.

'Want to find out? Here comes someone now.'

About a hundred yards away, a young labourer was rounding the corner. He had a Dodgers baseball cap pulled low over his eyes and was carrying a canvas bag of tools. He walked without looking up, whistling and swaggering, familiar with his route. Spanky crouched forward and broke into a loping run. I watched him moving faster and faster along the pavement, rushing toward the oblivious workman with such speed that I had no time to react.

An ominous rumbling scaled the air, distant lightning called to earth in a thunderous vacuum. The daemon was barely yards from his victim and closing fast. I remember bellowing something so that the man looked up in surprise just as Spanky smashed into him, his ethereal frame now carrying corporeal weight.

The startled workman was punched from his feet and lifted backwards into the air like a window-dummy rammed by a quarterback. His body overturned itself and dived headfirst, grotesquely hitting the pavement with his face. I was near enough to hear the sinuous snap of his neck breaking. As I approached I saw that his eyes were open and fixed upon me, even though his head was twisted in the wrong direction.

For a few moments he remained alive, long enough, I thought, to identify me as his assailant and to carry my image to his death. I fell back against a low garden wall, breathless with shock, watching as the workman's face grew pale and watery blood began to leak from the corner of his mouth into the gutter. I wanted to turn his body over, but Spanky would not allow me to approach.

'He'll remember you for eternity,' he said slyly. 'They all will.'

'And how many more would you kill with me as your host?' I shouted.

'Oh, I won't commit murder once we're united. Nothing so crude, I promise you. I see you more in the role of ambassador.

A future in politics, perhaps. The progress of civilization is a waking dream. Let's fill the world with scorpions.'

I watched the young labourer fade into a leaking, twisted corpse, its head in the gutter, its arms bent back like a sprinter breaking the tape. A bread van drove past without even slowing down. The driver must have seen the body. Nothing seemed real anymore.

'A future in politics,' I repeated.

Dawn was a gradient of grey, dim and pointless. The dull soaking streets began to fill as I walked on with folded arms and chattering teeth, doggedly accompanied by the daemon. I felt sure it was only the soaked iciness of the sweatshirt Lottie had brought for me that was keeping me alert.

I talked to him openly now, no longer caring what people thought. It had crossed my mind that I could arrange for myself to be arrested, but as Spanky pointed out, the ruse would not protect me from invasion.

When pedestrians approached I quickly crossed the road, fearful of Spanky's murderous whims. I sat inside a green wooden shelter in a bedraggled little park, bought a ham baguette and a coffee from a breakfast bar, walked on in the renewed rainfall to force myself awake.

I was walking in broad circles now, tracking across the endless wet streets with Spanky talking constantly every step of the way, wheedling, persuading, threatening, cajoling, even telling jokes, and his voice formed a barrier of sound that precluded any clear thought. I knew he was doing it to wear me down, to catch me out, to keep battering at the wall and weaken my defences. He knew how to bide his time.

We descended a stone staircase to the canal which crossed the upper half of the city. As rain frosted the still green water we passed through tunnel after tunnel, moving ever forward.

By midday, my leg was hurting so badly that I knew that I could not stay on my feet for more than a few more minutes. My soaking jeans had rubbed raw strips on my thighs. All I could think about now was rest and silence. I needed a chance to gather my strength.

And I knew that was the one thing he would never give me.

CHAPTER THIRTY-SEVEN

Schadenfreude

ANOTHER DAMNED speech from him, as if words mattered anymore.

'Judge yourself, Martyn. Knowing that only one of us can live, who would you choose? There's hardly anything to debate. You've consistently squandered every opportunity you've been given. Before we met, you failed to take advantage of anything life had to offer. Humans are like furred-up engines operating at one sixtieth of their capacity, but my mind is open to the possibilities of the world. I can single-handedly redress the balance.'

'Then why didn't you when you first invaded William Beaumont?' I asked doggedly. He would start like this every few minutes, expecting me to listen in silence, and I would always argue the point, refusing to let him think I was retreating.

'There were complications. During the war it appeared as if the world would be given to the night. Had that happened, we would have seen such sights! When I became William, Britain was busy rebuilding itself. It was hard for me to operate in such a grim atmosphere of hope and determination. What could one do, faced with all that appalling optimism?'

He was studying me all the time now, watching from the corners of his eyes. His shape seemed to have changed. His legs were slightly bent, his back arched so that a shadow had room to fall between chin and knee. As he breathed, his fingers opened and closed slightly, like anemones. The daemon within the human was coming to the fore.

I had no idea where we were, or where we had been. We were walking – always walking – but my pace was starting to falter badly. When I stumbled over a broken paving stone, he could see I was in trouble.

'Having a problem with your leg?' he asked, suddenly concerned. 'Here, I can fix it.' He reached out and grabbed my thigh, pinching the flesh hard. Hot pinpricks of energy ran over my skin, and the agony of my injuries slowly withdrew, burning away to nothing.

'Once we're united,' he promised, 'I'll make sure that you never feel any pain again.'

Finally, we had reached a recognizable landmark. The gates of Regent's Park, where Spanky had first shown me his illusions. His threats to carry out random acts of murder had ceased, perhaps because he knew that I would not be swayed by them. He couldn't reach my family either, because he needed me with him and couldn't get me to Twelvetrees. I couldn't see how he would proceed now, what he could do to make me surrender.

My resolve was holding, but my body was giving out. Spanky had fixed my knee, but now my right foot was bloodily blossoming with each painful step. Earlier, after another argument, he had made me think I was crossing hot coals and I had jumped back, scraping the lower part of my ankle against some broken brickwork.

By now the hours had crawled nightmarishly to lunchtime,

and a few hardy office workers had braved the inclement weather to sit in shelters unwrapping sandwiches and opening bags of crisps. I had decided that if Spanky didn't kill me within the next few hours, pneumonia would.

I was no longer concerned for my own safety. All I cared about was seeing him hit midnight trapped outside my body. I had to make him believe that he would eventually win. It was the only way to stop him from searching for a temporary host. I would watch him shrivel and rot without achieving his aim to continue on in my corrupted flesh.

'You're thinking aloud,' he said, turning aside and looking off along the misted green avenue of trees. 'I taught you to guard your thoughts more carefully than that.' As I followed his gaze, a figure emerged through the drizzle, walking uncertainly toward me.

As I saw who it was, I realized that Spanky had found a way into my soul. He could read things inside me that even I failed to understand.

Lottie was holding her handbag over her stomach like a shield. Her hair was plastered to her head, and the fur trim of her cheap winter coat was matted with rain. Her heels made it difficult to walk on the soft wet grass. She looked lost and in need of reassurance. Unable to tell if she should approach me, she remained at a distance and gave a faltering smile.

'I'm sorry, Martyn. After you called, I didn't know what to do,' she said. 'I had to come.'

'I didn't call you, Lottie.'

'Yes you did, you rang me an hour ago.'

'No.' I suddenly realized, and pointed to where Spanky stood. 'He did.'

'Martyn, it was you. Remember what you said? You warned me that you'd be like this. You were calling from the telephone boxes in the underground at Piccadilly Circus.'

A dim memory of being in the underground assailed me. Could I have called her?

'You were cold and asked me to take you to a doctor, but you said you might become unpleasant when I reminded you. You said you were going out of your mind, that you hardly knew what you were doing anymore. You were frightened for your sanity, Martyn. You asked me to meet you here, near the park gate.'

'He tricked you, Lottie. You shouldn't have come. You're not safe near me.'

I knew that Spanky had recognized something, an emotion he had never seen in me before. He could tell I had some kind of bond with her, even before I was fully aware of the fact.

'No, Martyn. I wanted to see you, to make sure you were all right.'

'Listen to her,' said Spanky. 'In everyone's life there is one person for whom any sacrifice could be made. Guess who it is for you, Martyn? This wet little thing here.'

He was standing too close to her, looming over her right shoulder. I moved toward them but Lottie stepped back, glancing around to see if there was anyone in the park who might rescue her if I should become violent.

'Funny how someone can suddenly care for a complete stranger, a plump-thighed young woman hanging washing in a courtyard, a golden boy glimpsed at the edge of a lake. Who knows where the heart leads? It's an ugly truth, Martyn, but if you could save the life of just one person, you wouldn't choose your mother. She wouldn't appreciate the deed, and she'd fail to make use of the sacrifice. You wouldn't choose your sister, either. You were never close, because there was always Joey between you. Your father? He barely exists for you. No, it's this skinny little bundle of bones, the girl you barely bothered to notice for two years.' He prodded at her breasts and pulled her around by the arm.

'What is that?' Panicked, she turned and stared back at me, touching her face. 'I felt—'

'That's him, Lottie. He wants me to save you.'

'Oh my God, he's really here isn't he?'

'You must try to see him.'

She turned in panic. 'I can't, there's nothing—'

'*You have to see him!*' I screamed.

'Martyn, you must let me become mortal through you now,' said the daemon. 'If you don't, I will kill your little lady.'

'Martyn, come with me and we'll see someone, talk to someone, try to sort this thing out. I don't know, I wish—' She stepped forward and back, alarmed by her indecision.

The daemon's eyes filmed over as his thoughts drifted to anticipated pleasures. 'I'm going to start eating her now, Martyn, and it will appear to her and the world that you are doing it. She will die with your image fixed upon her eyes. It's time for you to choose.' He grabbed her arms and pulled them behind her back. Lottie gave a fearful moan, her eyes catching mine.

'Martyn, what are you doing? Stop it!'

I was three feet away from her.

What had Spanky done, clouded her senses or mine? Had he rendered me invisible and adopted my form? When I tried to pull him away from her, my hands passed through his arms as if he had been projected on to the air. Lottie was trying to scream, but the sound was stifling in her throat.

'No – Martyn—'

She shook as he ripped her coat down around her shoulders, the buttons popping on to the wet gravel. With a flourish, he raised the back of his hand and studied his fingertips as the nails lengthened and silvered over. He ran the nail of his left index finger across her neck. The pale skin parted in a razor-thin line that welled thickly with blood.

'Come on, Martyn, no more delays. Issue the invitation while you can. There's still time.'

I wanted to save her, but I couldn't allow him to win. I remained frozen to the spot, staring as she silently screamed, locked in his embrace, and he ran the index finger of his other hand across her white throat.

'What kind of pathetic gutspawn are you?' His face was contorted with fury, yellow spittle flecking his chin. 'You'd let her die to save yourself!'

Not to save myself, I thought, *but to damn you*. I knew that if admitted, he would first destroy the remaining part of me, then kill her for the sport of it. She was in terrible agony, haemorrhaging badly now, straining to clutch at the spreading wound in her gullet. Her pain became my own and I cried out, gasping for breath as she fell to her knees on the flooded path.

I tried to touch her, to reach out to her but he kept me away, in the same way that he was keeping the others in the park from seeing the truth.

Instead, I turned to Spanky and pushed my perceptive senses outward, as he had shown me, to see inside his mind. The nightmarish cacophony that resounded in my head sent me reeling. She was dying, and he was close to orgasm. I focused my concentration, and saw clearly.

'Her life is fading, Martyn. It's not too late to submit yourself.' He watched me excitedly, then realized that I was not going to speak and thrust his fingertips back and forth across her face, opening a dozen wounds. The figure before me was losing consciousness.

'She is bleeding to death and you do nothing. You really are more spineless than I imagined.'

'She's not bleeding.'

I had seen into his mind.

'Lottie's not even here. You called her and she didn't answer. It's a good likeness, though.'

He threw her bloodied body to one side, and it sank down into the sodden grass to disappear completely in the earth. 'But you do love her, Martyn. At least I've made you see that.'

'I don't know.' My knee-joints protested as I rose to my feet, gravel stuck to my sodden jeans.

'And you would do anything for her. Even allow me a new lease of life.'

'I told you, I don't know.'

'Then it's time to find out.'

He gave a friendly smile as he brushed the creases from his jacket sleeves and straightened the collar of his black roll-neck. 'You know, Martyn, with each compounding moment of your misery, my heart grows a little lighter. A final race, I think. You know the form by now. Let's see who gets there first.'

'I won't do it. I won't lead you to her.'

'Then I will go alone.'

'If you do, I'll get away from here and you'll never find me in this city before midnight.'

He shrugged and started to walk away. 'I'll take the chance.'

He had called my bluff.

I started to run.

CHAPTER THIRTY-EIGHT

Phantasmagoria

MY LIMBS had seized in the incessant rain, and my stomach was gripped with a constant nagging ache that spiked whenever I tried to move quickly. I couldn't tell if Spanky was deliberately hindering my movement, twisting my intestines, or if it was the result of being in constant motion for twenty-four hours with a set of cracked ribs.

Pushing my way on to a crowded bus was easier than I had expected, as most passengers shied away when they caught sight of me. By now I was smeared with grass and mud, and probably smelled pretty bad. The gash over my eye had opened, and was wet with blood. I alighted back at King's Cross, two roads from Lottie's flat. I knew he would be there first. He always was.

There was no doubt in my mind that if I gave in, he would kill her for sport. But I could not stand by and watch her die.

I arrived to find the front door of the house ajar. A slat of yellow light printed on the bare front garden from the hall. There were wet footprints on the stairs leading up to the landing. Her apartment door was open, too. The lock was still intact, nothing was displaced, but a familiar fear grew in my stomach as I walked toward her bedroom at the end of the central corridor.

The curtains were still shut, but I could discern her form in the bed, the pale blue sheet across her chest rising lightly as she slept. I sensed him behind me and turned to find Spanky sitting in an armchair at the end of the bed. He placed his finger to his lips and inclined his head.

'Funny time to be sleeping,' he whispered. 'You used to call her weird Lottie, but she seems downright ordinary to me. Still, she looks peaceful, doesn't she?' Lottie shifted slightly in her sleep, fingertips flicking at her hair, the movement uncomfortably reminiscent of her imagined torture in the park.

'Would you like to see her look even more peaceful?'

He raised his eyes to a space above her head. I looked too, but at first could see nothing in the gloom. Then it appeared, breaking camouflage with the wallpaper behind. It was a small black spider, spinning a silvery line down from the ceiling. The creature had long tapering legs and a bulbous abdomen. I recognized it as a Black Widow.

As I made to swat the thing away, Spanky grabbed my arm and pulled me back to his chair.

'This time it's real, Martyn. You have seconds left.' The spider had already lowered itself to her face and was tentatively feeling its way across her eyelid, on to her cheek, exploring the rim of her nostril, prying its legs between her lips.

This time my movement was so sudden that Spanky was caught unprepared as I dived for the figure on the bed, my hands raised to slap the tiny creature from her face. But it had scuttled away and I fell heavily on to her sleeping form—

—only to have the skin burst ripely beneath me, dissolving into a hundred thousand sticky webs that caught across my face and chest, gumming my eyes and filling my screaming mouth with the wet warmth of a million tiny crimson eggs that spilled from the incubating carcass on to the floor.

My eyes opened.

I was naked.

Hanging in darkness. Turning slowly on a thick nylon rope that had been knotted around my throat. My neck was burning and broken. I could tell that much from the choking, disjointed sensation that consumed me. I floated in the filthy excremental air, suspended by the throttling strands.

I looked down. Hairless animals shifted over each other in brine and vomit, braying expectantly. Feeding time. Broad yellow snouts caught my scent. Bull-heads raised themselves. Jaws parted in slavering anticipation.

Above my skull, the rope was suddenly released and I fell sickeningly—

—to the moonlit alleyway with the running gang and the screams of violence, their crowbars banging and booming against the iron railings as they closed the gap behind me, spitting and screaming for blood as I turned the corner and found myself against the reeking concrete stairwell that led nowhere.

I turned back to face them as they attacked, and my head was punched and my heart split within the cage of my ribs and I grimaced in the agony of cardiac arrest, crunching up my eyes until I could open them again and find—

—that Spanky was leading me by the hand, guiding me over stars and coals and serpents to the only place of safety, the warming hearth of my shared soul. His pale, naked torso fluctuated beneath my caressing hands, randomly changing sex so that at first he had breasts and a pouting vagina, then a satyr's protuberant erection. He was the fairest way, the surest path, the purest light. I welcomed him into me, enclosing his freezing form within my overheated body, longing for the icy cleansing fire of consumption, but as I did so something in my mind cried out in anger and refusal, and horrified I propelled him away to be free again—

—and to find myself strapped to a wooden table, naked, in an empty metal room, rusted iron plates rivetted to the floor and walls. Outside, the universe was roaring by in a trail of stars, like the wake of a ship.

I was spreadeagled, my hands and feet bound to the wet red butcher's block with ropes. If I strained I could lift my head from the overhang of the table. Above me I saw, fixed in the ceiling, densely packed darts of tapered steel, like an acoustic pattern in a concert hall roof.

Directly over my bare stomach, one of the darts was working its way loose.

Sniggering laughter echoed behind me. I twisted my head as far as I could to see Spanky, resplendent in a shining emerald green suit, sliding his hand beneath Sarah Brannigan's skirt, rubbing his leg between her thighs. She was naked to the waist, her breasts opaque in the glare of the steel room.

'Sarah's here to help me punish you, Martyn. This is my torture box, where a minute can be stretched to last for an eternity.'

Sarah slipped her arm around Spanky's waist and pulled him close. 'This'll teach you to treat women like dirt, Martyn, you sad little shit.'

She stamped her foot hard on the floor and the steel dart broke free and fell, cleaving through the heavy air to pierce the skin of my abdomen, pinning me firmly to the table. Three feet of shining grey metal cut through my burning intestines and protruded from my stomach as the next dart plunged down into the skin of my left thigh, tearing it and pinning me—

None of this is real he's trying to make you lose control he'll slip in when you cry out in agony slip inside your mind and

promise to take away the pain you'll let him, too, anything to
make it stop just make it stop but it's not real not real not real
not real not—

—I was standing soaking wet in the middle of the traffic-packed road at Hyde Park Corner.

A bus horn was blaring at me. I ran for the safety of the far pavement, slipping on wet tarmac, nearly falling beneath the tyres of a delivery truck. Even in the rain, exhaust fumes saturated the air. I landed beside a concrete litter bin, cracking my forehead, and sat there, trying to regain my breath.

What the hell was happening to me? The face of my stolen watch had cracked, sticking the hands together. I looked up at the waves of cloud driving across the dark sky. It had to be mid-evening. I was missing some hours. I'd been in Lottie's room. Spiders in my mouth. The taste of daemon flesh. The ecstasy of becoming lost—

Where was Spanky?

My hands stretched out across the cold spattering pavement at my side. This was real. This rain, the concrete gutter filled with dogshit and discarded chips and empty packets of crisps, these homegoing commuters in their steamed-up cars, the neon of the fried chicken takeaway on the corner of Oxford Street. They were all real.

Where the hell had I been for the last few hours?

I figured he'd been trying to disorient me, barraging me with hallucinations – and what had I been doing, wandering the streets like a strung-out junkie, lost in some hallucinatory internal flight. My jeans were torn out at the kneecaps and smeared with blood. I had grazed the palms of both hands and gashed my right arm. There were bits of gravel stuck all over me. My head was hammering. My back was sore and felt massively bruised.

Where the *hell* was he?

He couldn't be far away, I knew that. I tried to rise to my feet, but the pain in my legs was too great. I felt as if I had run a marathon with broken knees, but I didn't care. I searched the corners of my body and knew that I had not given in. Only a short time to go and I would be free – if there was anything still left of me by midnight.

By gripping the lip of the litter bin I was able to slowly raise myself into a standing position. Thank God he had no desire to engage me in physical combat; right now I couldn't take on a five year old. I needed to get to a call box and find out what had really happened to Lottie. I'd spent the day fighting apparitions, and felt like a drunk coming down from the bender of all time. My head stung and throbbed harder than ever, and I could feel a fresh crust of blood around my damaged eye.

I limped into the subway. I wasn't about to try crossing the road again. I entered the public toilet and washed the scarlet-black streaks from my face and hands, but my reflection in the mirror was still unnerving.

It took me half an hour to make it to a callbox, only to find that I had no money in my pockets. I was able to beg/threaten ten pence out of a wide-eyed Japanese woman armed with Harrods shopping bags, and dialled Lottie's number. Susan answered. She told me that she'd only just come off duty, and hadn't seen her flatmate. She sounded as puzzled as I was.

'Do you have any idea where she might be?' I asked, trying to sound as normal as possible.

'No, but she can't have gone far. Her purse is still here.'

Had I managed to surface from Spanky's psychedelic onslaught long enough to warn her to escape? My immediate past was a morass of half-seen visions and muffled cries, fading fast from my bludgeoned mind like overloaded circuits burning out. I hung up the receiver and limped toward the lights of Oxford Street. According to the clock above Selfridge's it was almost 9.30 p.m.

Two and a half hours.

One hundred and fifty minutes.

William Beaumont's mortal flesh, descending into collapse and corruption with each passing moment, making Spanky stronger with desperation, less mortal, ready to make the leap across.

Why wasn't he here to hound me? His time on earth was fast coming to a close. I breathed deep, forcing the cold fume-laden air into my lungs, shaking my head free from the remnants of Spanky's aphrodisial embrace. Then I looked along the street.

He was waiting for me, of course.

Changed into his tuxedo for the big finish.

The suit he was wearing when we first met. Very smart.

Nonchalantly leaning against the doorframe of the newest Oxford Street entertainment complex, still open for business. Inside, warm bodies and sheer glass walls. Bad combination.

'You're late,' he said, smiling warmly. 'You mustn't be late for your own rebirth.'

CHAPTER THIRTY-NINE

Transmutation

THE OXFORD Street entertainment complex.

Five landings of glass and chrome suspended by angled steel cables for that user-friendly industrial look I associate with the arse-end of the eighties. The place was busy because there was a special promotion going on at one of the stores. Lines had formed to see an ancient American TV star sign autographs for anyone who'd bought her perfume.

Spanky marched swiftly ahead of me through the shoppers, who veered from my unsteady path when they caught sight of me. I was still suffering from the after-effects of my hallucinatory trip, and was trying not to walk into things.

Nothing seemed real any more, especially in here. The shops were bursting with bright photographic displays of crotch-thrusting teenagers stroking tanned thighs. Around them milled fat young mums with desperate eyes and beer-gutted dads in garish tracksuits.

Spanky seemed perfectly at home in the EuroDisney fakery of the mall. Perhaps its tatty car-ferry chic fulfilled his criteria for hell on earth. A condensation of human misery, Spanky-world. It was an odd place for him to choose, though. Too bright, too crowded – and then I realized that it was exactly what he wanted.

'Quite,' Spanky agreed.

We had arrived on the second floor of the building. Spanky stood at the top of the escalator, backlit by the vast ficus-filled atrium. My foot was hurting so badly that I could barely manage to stand. From behind us came a sickly aroma of popcorn, as one of the multiplex screens voided its chattering audience.

'What a palace of modern culture,' declared Spanky. 'A shrine to the new obsessions. So warm and friendly and *human*. Those people down there.' He pointed at the crowd surrounding the wizened celebrity at the perfume stand, which had been decked with garish gold balloons at the entrance of the store. 'How many would you say are in that group? Thirty-five? Forty?'

'What are you going to—'

'—offer you a trade, of course. No time to waste now. Their lives for yours. A straight swap, no blinkum, flim-flam or jiggery-pokery. What a deal, forty for one. Doesn't that make you feel special? What do you say?'

'You can't hurt them,' I said loudly, causing a woman to pull her child from my path. 'Your illusions can't possibly affect so many people.'

'Who said anything about illusions? This will be real. First, let's stir up some panic.'

He drew a deep breath, rubbed his hands together hard and then opened them. A roar of stinging white flame scorched the air between us as I stumbled back. He blew on the plume of fire, spreading it evenly across the floor, buckling and blackening the tiles. Overhead, the sudden localized change in temperature caused electronic alarms to sound.

The open design of the building had prohibited the installation of a complete sprinkler system, but part of the damaged area was sprayed from overhead pipes. Within moments shoppers began pointing and glancing up at the ceiling, as if expecting to find instructions displayed there.

'I've closed all the deadbolts on the entrance doors. No hallucination, just good, hard kinetic chemistry. There are escape routes through to the next building on this floor.' Spanky pointed out across the confused, milling crowd. 'So now they get on the escalators.'

Spanky was flicking gobbets of fire from his fingers as he walked, tossing one burning spear into a stationery shop, another into an orange-juice stand. Did it appear that I was the cause of the fire? Whether it did or not, people were staying the hell away from us.

All around our feet, the rubberized floor tiles were starting to leak tarry black smoke. Looking from the balcony I could see that already, dozens of people were pouring on to the lowest of the moving staircases.

Spanky had always operated with a fluid grace that made his miracles appear effortless. Now he concentrated, closing his eyes, a thin blue vein pulsing at his temple.

'What are you doing?' I shouted at him. 'Tell me what you're doing!'

And as I stared at him I knew for the briefest of moments what was happening in his head. I saw what he could see. Inside some kind of machinery, oil-covered parts were slowly revolving around each other, then one sheared with a crack like a gunshot. I ran to the balcony and looked over as the steep escalator carriage jammed dead, cascading its screaming passengers over each other. Elderly women, mothers and children pitched forward, heavy husbands and folding prams and pregnant girls tumbling on to each other. Anguished shrieks could be heard over the piercing alarm.

Despite the sprinklers, the fire was spreading across the floor in a luminous orange sheet, setting light to the dry tubbed trees.

Spanky still had his eyes shut and his teeth gritted tightly together. He hadn't finished.

One of the nearby shopfronts cracked across its largest pane, glass diagonals tottering lethally in their frame. One section lazily divorced itself and fell forward, shearing down on to a running child.

I darted forward, too late to do anything in the ensuing explosion of glass. I tried to reach the screaming sprawled infant but Spanky's hand dug into my shoulder and he dragged me back, away from the bloody carnage.

He raised his hands to the ceiling and slowly clenched his fists, drawing down his arms. The floor above bowed and gave way, groaning and cracking apart in a spray of plaster, concrete and steel pinions. A woman fell through, still clutching her shopping bags against her breasts, as though they were more precious than her children. One of the ceiling service pipes stretched and fractured, spraying shit across the screaming crowd as another began to pour gallons of effluvia on to the burning floor.

I looked back at the tuxedoed figure, half-obscured by smoke, backlit by flame.

Spanky was laughing. Really enjoying himself.

I had no way of fighting him. My hand brushed against the penknife Lottie had left in my pocket. What could I do, try to plunge it into his heart? He sensed my every move. He was invulnerable, all-powerful, and he was prepared to kill as many people as it took to let him win.

I knew at that moment it was over.

'Spanky, stop. I'll do it.'

His eyes snapped open, and for a moment only the whites showed. Then the emerald pupils rolled disconcertingly into place. When he spoke, his voice was little more than a guttural croak. Psychokinetic activity clearly debilitated him.

'Good', he grunted, panting slightly, 'I always knew you'd see it my way.'

'You must end this. Don't hurt anyone else.'

He stared up at the ceiling. The electronic wailing above the screams suddenly ceased. He looked back at me and smiled.

I shifted uncomfortably on the crackling, hot floor. I wanted him out of here as quickly as possible.

'What happens now?'

I had committed myself. Thinking back, I suppose I'd always known that I would have to admit him. After all, as he liked to remind me, we were one person with two radically opposed sides. Isn't everyone?

'Not here. Can't do it here.'

He took stock of the unfolding chaos, flicking his head from side to side. 'Has to be somewhere quiet. Follow.'

He unlocked the safety doors at the back of the second floor, and we left behind the wailing tangle of arms and legs at the foot of the jammed escalator.

The rain had died to a spattering, carried by the rising wind. We avoided Oxford Street, where police cars and fire engines were now arriving, and moved into one of the squares behind the main thoroughfare.

We passed beneath a blue neon clock, and I saw that it was still only 11.00 p.m. I had hoped it would be later. My plan, if such a thing existed in the buzzing remnants of my brain, was to hold out until just before midnight. I had this idea that I would give in with just minutes to go. Then I'd find a way to hold him at bay until the appointed time had passed.

But it was too early, and he knew it.

This was no vampire locked from his coffin at sunrise, but a fast-thinking wraith, a quicksilver spirit-human. I had no way of stalling him at close quarters, not when he could read my mind. Worse than that, I was having trouble just remaining on my feet. My vision kept blurring, and there was something wrong with my sense of balance. I felt as if I was suffering from dysentery. My stomach and bowels seemed to be filled with warm churning water.

My daemon-kin strode on ahead, ever ahead, hale and hearty, a grotesque British rambler, all fresh air and cold baths, dragging behind his wasted human incubus like a man rescuing a mongrel from the gas chamber.

I could not keep up. My eyes wanted to close, my mind to descend in the comforting murk of sleep. I just wanted it to be over. He would occupy my body and crowd out my mind and I would simply cease to exist. Let him wreak the havoc he so dearly desired. I no longer cared. I was abdicating my responsibility toward the rest of the world; I hadn't asked for it in the first place. Let someone else save them. I was too fucking tired.

I wanted to die.

We were there, at the gates of the park once more, back where it had all begun, back in my old life, as distant to me as an earlier incarnation. The wind was pulling at my torn wet sweatshirt as I crossed on to the grass, following his lead.

'Here,' he said, turning and pointing down at a spot three feet from where he stood. 'Stand here.'

My watch was broken, but I knew no more than fifteen minutes could have passed since we left the chaos of the shopping mall. There was no stalling now, and no turning back. What could I do to distract him for three quarters of an hour, perform a few musical numbers? I knew that my bluff had been called, and that I would have to go through with it.

Hearing the sound of a footfall on leaves, I looked behind myself and fancied I saw a figure between the blustering bushes, but there was no one. This was the eleventh hour, all right, but nobody was going to rescue me at it.

'Take off your clothes.'

'Jesus, it's freezing. I'll die in this rain. I'll be of no use to you.'

'Take off your clothes.'

The sweatshirt was stuck to my chest with blood and mud. I laboriously removed my jeans and made a display of folding them, careful to concentrate my mind elsewhere.

'Stop wasting time. Throw them over there.' He glanced carelessly at his watch, and waited. 'Empty your mind. Think of nothing.'

And then I was newborn naked, standing beneath the roaring trees in the middle of Regent's Park, in more elemental contact than I had ever experienced, waiting to be taken like some parody-sacrificial virgin, host to something beyond my powers of comprehension.

Around us the wind hissed and soughed in the flapping branches, as turbulent as whitewater. I looked back at Spanky, who removed his jacket and shirt, pulled off his shoes and socks, stepped out of his underpants and tossed the whole bundle back at the trees, knowing that he would no longer have need of them.

'Ask me to enter you. Invite me in. Say the words.'

'Enter me,' I said quietly.

'Louder.'

'Enter me.'

He released a low sigh of anticipation.

There was something different about Spanky's body now. He raised his shoulders and hunched forward, the skin of his chest darkening.

It wasn't darkening.

It was drying out, starting to slough off like a snake's.

As the translucent epidermis, all that remained of William Beaumont, gradually flaked away, torn into tatters by the wind, I saw my *Spancialosophus Lacrimosa* for the first time. I saw what was about to inhabit me.

And I cried out at the sky.

Scarlet eyes, searing and sore, narrow slits, barely visible at all.

A raw, cracked texture to the skin, painful blotches of pink and brown, like severe sunburn.

No lips.

No teeth.

Mouth like an unhealed wound.

Flickering crimson triangle of a tongue.

Bony starved body, angular and cramped, suffering under too-tight musculature, a figure aching to be sheathed in the plump soft flesh of humanity.

I had wondered about his – its – true appearance, but I had expected nothing like this. Here was no brave, broad-backed daemon but a painracked, twisted thing, a peeled starving concentration-camp corpse of a creature that could not bear to be exposed, and had to hide itself away.

It opened its mouth to speak but it had blood for saliva, and the redness leaked from the sore opening, so it quickly sealed shut once more and contented itself with flexing the scabrous little stumps of its fingers.

I thought I was going to be sick as it started to stump its way toward me, wincing with each step. My revulsion exceeded anything that had gone before.

I had failed everyone for whom I had an ounce of respect. Failed my family, my friends, myself. Pissed away my life, got suckered into greed and paid the price. When it came to sins, the fact that I warranted eternal damnation told me all I needed to know about the sheer scope of my deficiency.

As the Spanky-creature grimaced and wheezed a foot from my face, fighting to stay upright in the gale, I wondered if this was how it had been for others. A more ignominious end was impossible to imagine.

It reached out its arm-sticks, more naked than I could ever be, and I flinched back, but the bony digital stumps dug into my skin. My body started to heat and burn, and I looked down to see that it was already sliding into me.

The elbow of one arm was pressing into my corresponding limb, then its left leg was pricking and coruscating its way into mine. Although the merging process was excruciatingly sharp, the creature's bones were soft and wet, like a salt-stung slug or an unprotected mollusc. The sensation was the most revolting I had ever felt.

Both of its legs were now inside my acicular limbs, sliding over my bones as if donning a pair of trousers. Its groin locked into place with mine, ribs cracking into position in pairs, starting with the lowest.

I could sense the thing's spine and nervous system joining with mine, and for a moment I felt the wind buffeting my body with dual receptors, like out-of-phase stereo. One arm joined fully, the left.

I pulled the other back, moving it out of the way, fighting to keep it free.

The creature's bony head, balanced on a skinny, too-flexible neck, was looming closer to mine, its sore lidless eyes staring covetously at my face. Within seconds our flesh would touch, my teeth joining with that bloodied bare mouth, eyes and sinuses and crania connecting as one. I was dreading the sensation of our brains joining.

I opened the fingers of my right hand and released the sprung blade of the penknife. I had taken it from the pocket of my jeans as I was folding them.

Without thought, and as fast as I could, as fast as our duality would allow, I raised my hand and stuck the knife hard into my own throat. For a second or two it didn't hurt, then it began to sting and sear as I pulled it across my tensed larynx, opening the skin to release a broad, flattened spray of blood.

And the terrible pain punched in.

I began to cry out.

He was inside my dying body now.

His old carcass lay shed in rags on the grass. He would be left encased in a corpse. There was no one else in sight, and without a human host there was no way out. As the realization hit him and the screaming, writhing mass began to shift within me, I knew I hadn't failed after all.

I fell as softly as I could.

I wanted to feel my life leaving, and his staying on behind.

I landed on my side in the long wet grass, to await my final disconnection from a world I had never really seen.

CHAPTER FORTY

Revenance

WHAT IS real, and what is not.

Differentiating between the states had been my problem before. Now it was impossible, and I remained in a smothering fugue of sounds and images, most of them unreal, all exaggerated. Lottie figured frequently, talking and joking with – of all people – my sister Laura.

Lottie and Laura. Gordon and Joyce.

Alternating brightness and dark.

Puzzling snatches of conversation.

The phrase 'nothing to lose' running around in my head, spoken by an elderly man.

Chemical smells, overpowering and sour. A high-pitched whine, first electronic, then mechanical. Extreme discomfort. Something lodged in my throat. I hawked and coughed, trying to clear the obstruction, but it would not budge. Horrific flashes of the peeled face beneath the trees, the bony, twisted limbs melting into mine.

Distant music, an off-key pianist practising scales. A gentle surfacing, rising slowly to the top through the warm viscous liquid of sleep, and finally a view; a cream-painted wall and a reproduction painting, swans feeding on a dull green river.

'Martyn.'

Lottie was sitting on an orange plastic chair with her hands folded in her lap, quietly watching. Her sandy hair was down, the fringe over her eyes, and she was wearing a black sweatshirt and jeans. She looked different, older and somehow more relaxed.

'Don't try to speak. There's a tube in your throat.'

I couldn't move my head, but it was possible to raise my right hand. The bones in my wrist ached. Everything did. I brought my fingers to my throat.

'Don't touch anything, Martyn. Just rest. I know what you want to ask. You've been here over a week.'

That wasn't what I wanted to know.

What I wanted to know was, was it me?

Had I retained my own identity?

Was I *alone*?

I couldn't think, and so I slept.

Later, the doctors confirmed the duration of my unconsciousness. They couldn't risk having me awake and tearing up the delicate work that had been performed on my oesophagus.

Pushing my battered senses through my body, I found no sign of Spanky.

Nothing but me.

Another occasion, Lottie still in the chair.

'I was there at the park, Martyn, watching you. I bet you're surprised about that, but when you called me that morning—'

—*I really did call her*—

'– and told me where you were, I knew what you were near. The park. You'd mentioned Regent's Park before. Your favourite place. You used to go there with your parents. And it was where you'd first met him. The way you spoke on the phone, I knew where you were heading—'

—*I hadn't even known it myself*—

I faded into sleep, realizing that she had listened to me, to the intention beneath my words, properly listened. The first person to do that in a very long time.

Daylight. Laura by the bed, guess who's with her, my parents. Toothy smiles. 'On the mend.' 'Doing well.' 'Looking good.' Grapes. I'm on an IV diet and they bring grapes.

Then Lottie again, to continue her story.

'When I found you in the park I wanted to run to you, but I had to understand what was going on. I couldn't see him, but I knew he was there by your side, tormenting you. So I waited. You dashed off into the street and I couldn't keep up. I lost you. I was sure you'd come to harm, get killed in the traffic. I was frightened I'd never find you again. I searched everywhere, went to your old flat, even returned to the burned-out store. I didn't know where else to look, so finally I retraced my steps and ended up back at the park. I was worried out of my life.'

She reached forward and took my hand, stroking the backs of my fingers.

'Martyn, you were quite alone, talking to the air everywhere you went, acting as if you could see someone next to you. At one point you had a kind of fight with yourself. I wanted to call an ambulance, but I had no idea where the nearest callbox was. Then – well.' She looked down at her hands, thinking.

'I knew you believed in what you saw. I wanted to believe it, too. And as I stood in the park watching, you undressed, and something crazy began to happen. Another figure appeared beside you. I couldn't make it out clearly. It was like a little old man, covered in sores, all bent up and skinny, and it started to turn into you. I saw Spanky, Martyn. I saw him with my own eyes.'

I knew I was crying, but couldn't help myself. I hung on to her fingers and let her image waver and dissolve before me.

'I didn't see you take out the knife, everything happened so quickly. I ran forward, calling to you. I tried to staunch the wound with my scarf. There was so much blood. Luckily, you didn't do a very good job. I used to help Susan with her practicals, when she was training. I couldn't remember much, but I managed to keep the cut closed. You were making strange sounds, angry grunts. I didn't know if it was you, or him. I shouted to someone, got help.'

I slept then, but whenever I awoke she was there.

Two days later the tube was removed, and I was allowed to sit up. I still couldn't speak, and no one seemed to know if I ever would again.

Then I found out something extraordinary.

While I was riding in the ambulance with Lottie, my traumatized heart stopped beating. For nearly two minutes it ceased to pump and lay silent in my body before the medics managed to return it to life. I died and lived again, just as Spanky wished. But I had been reborn alone. His presence was nowhere to be felt. Two minutes had been long enough to kill the daemon, but not me. Perhaps the human body was stronger after all. The spirit supported and strengthened the flesh.

Lottie and Laura really had become friends. They met at my bedside and remained to describe the events of the day in great detail, knowing that my throat was still too damaged for me to reply.

When I was deemed well enough to vacate my hospital bed, I received another shock. I was not allowed to go home. Instead, I was to be released into the care of a psychiatric clinic, for a period of not less than two months.

I scoured the papers for details of Spanky's attack at the shopping centre, but found nothing. Lottie had no idea what I was talking about. She went there for me, only to find the glass and marble halls undamaged.

Three weeks later I regained my voice, although now it sounded different, softer and deeper. The scar had been too severe to fully heal. I passed the time at the clinic denying Spanky's existence and rationalizing my aberrant behaviour to my disappointed doctor, while writing up my actual experiences in a private journal. I hadn't been able to find details of a modern daemonic case in any of Zack's magazines. Now I was going to make damned sure that there was one on record. I was interviewed by the police, who were bothered by my appearance in a psychiatric ward, and longed to draw some positive conclusions. I made sure they left my room more confused than ever.

Lottie visited whenever she could. She found herself a job in a department store. The pay was lousy, but there wasn't much else around. When my time was up I was released with the advice that I should live with my family, a prospect that appealed to none of us. Instead, I accepted Lottie's invitation to stay with her for a few days, while I worked out my next move.

It was seven thirty in the morning, and I was walking through the misty drizzle in Regent's Park. The mournful calls of the zoo animals could be heard behind the rain. I no longer slept very well, and had lain awake beside Lottie since four, so a walk seemed the best solution. The circumstances of my visit were very different this time. For a start, I was wearing some clothes.

I had been thinking. If Spanky was created from my bad side, surely I could draw on an equal amount of good within myself. I turned the idea over, wondering how much of the daemon's residual power remained.

As I walked beneath the dripping plane trees, I thought back to those final days with Joey. He had lied to me, pretended that everything was fine when he knew he was dying. Sometimes you lie to kids to stop them from getting hurt. He'd thought he was making a quick exit, but he screwed up. Didn't think I'd flip out and blow my exams.

His mistake, not mine.

I couldn't keep conjuring up his memory anymore.

And I couldn't stay with Lottie.

The police had started making connections. It was only a matter of time before they came for me again.

But something else was worrying me. There were two attendants in the ambulance. What if – *somehow* – the daemon had managed to enter one of them? So far I hadn't been able to trace their identities.

I remembered Chantery describing Spanky as being like the Inland Revenue. On your case forever. Assuming that he had been obliterated, could I now await the arrival of his vengeful brethren?

Late that night I quietly left the flat in King's Cross. I wrote a letter and placed it on the table beside her bed. In it I explained my reasons for leaving, and instructed her to tell my family nothing. I knew Laura would be hurt, but it was safer this way. Before I left the bedroom I watched her sleeping, breathing lightly, shifting her limbs across the pillows, lost in the farthest reaches of her dreams. It seemed amazing to me that within this placid form was an extraordinary power of conviction, enough to save my life and return my soul. I watched and thought; who knows how much strength we really possess? We're more concerned with weaknesses.

It hurt to leave Lottie behind, but she was too important to me now. It was my turn to do some good. She needed to be protected.

Now I travel alone, stopping here and there, doing odd jobs for cash. I change my name, and sometimes my appearance. At the present time I am in the North. I have long hair and a scruffy beard. I recently spent my twenty-fifth birthday alone in a riggers' bar ten miles beyond Aberdeen.

When I visit a new town, I look for people with whom I can share my experience. No one ever believes me.

I am ever vigilant for those other souls who walk alone, possessed by devils. I recognize them easily, and when I do, I am able to tell them what they must do to save themselves.

I tell them to act while they still have their own free will.

I explain what will happen if they don't.

I am known to the police. I've been picked up a couple of times for harassment. I have a psychiatric record. I refuse to be branded a lunatic, a charlatan. But Spanky has left me with a bad habit – I talk to myself.

I spend my time alone. I read a lot. I study the Greeks. Homer describes a daemon as the active aspect of a god, a manifestation of divine power. Lottie mailed me the book I once stole from the library and wrapped in foil. In it the author suggests that daemons keep watch over all mankind, and perform the will of the gods through us. To the Romans they were signs of genius, and proof of the soul. To the Christians they were evil spirits, to be debased and banished to Pandemonium, the capital of hell.

But I believe the Greeks. To me a daemon is a guardian spirit, a *djinn*, a distillation of the self, the essence of one's character.

And without it, I am something less than a man.

Sometimes, late at night, I walk to a public callbox at the end of a quiet country lane and ring Lottie. I listen to her waking in confusion, then relaxing as she recognizes my voice. She shifts upright in bed, gathers her thoughts and asks me if I'm keeping well.

I tell her yes, I'm fine. She doesn't ask where I am, or where I am going. Often, I don't know myself.

Then there's a gap, a silence between us, and only the wind can be heard in the lines. In that silence, she tells me she knows of the hole left within me, the vast echoing dark emptiness that I must find a way to fill.

And if I do, and if I live – I'll return to her, and no power on earth will ever make me let her go again.

I keep the memories of my past alive.

Remembering is easy.

There, at least, Spanky is always with me.

RED BRIDE

Christopher Fowler

John Chapel is a statistician's dream: he's twenty-nine,
has a loving wife and son, a comfortable home, and a
promising career. And then he meets the stunningly
beautiful, mysterious Ixora . . .

He first sees her running across the rainswept steps of
Waterloo Station. When they meet again, Ixora denies
having been there. Odder still, John discovers her in a
film containing exactly the same sequence. So begins a
dreamlike relationship that escalates into a nightmare.

Despite his good intentions, John finds himself embarking
on a passionate affair. But violence and death track the
ill-fated couple as John risks his home, his career and his
life to save Ixora from a horrific destiny. Now the subject
of a police investigation, he finds himself trapped in a
vortex of spreading evil which may claim his very soul . . .

'Smarter-than-usual media-wise London setting from the
author of *ROOFWORLD*' *Daily Telegraph*

'Clever-clever English pop gothic' *i-D*

GENERAL FICTION/HORROR
0 7515 0159 X

DARKEST DAY

Christopher Fowler

Jerry Gates is a receptionist at the Savoy Hotel. When one of her guests expires in the lobby, Jerry is drawn into a dark underside of London she never knew existed – a world of secret paintings, rising corpses, exploding commuters, mysterious guilds and mechanical murder devices.

Aiding decrepit detectives Bryant and May, Jerry meets an appalling London family steeped in generations of blackmail and finds herself up against an ingenious, unstoppable evil that threatens the entire city. As the lights start going out all over London, Jerry remembers how scared she is of the dark . . .

Darkest Day is a fast-paced frightener of the first order. You'll never trust the dark again.

'Christopher Fowler is a great guide to the dark side'
Time Out

WARNER BOOKS
0 7515 0765 2

<u>CITY</u> <u>JITTERS</u>

Christopher Fowler

There are no eyeless, crawling things in this town, no vampire slumbers unseen behind the rustling rails of the city necropolis.

Here are only car parks, and nightclubs, and taxi cabs. The pavements are bright and thronging, people laugh and telephones ring.

But there is another world within the city, where reality may suddenly skip a heartbeat, where for a moment there is no recognition of the face in the mirror.

For in the very ordinariness of the city, there lurks its greatest terror.

'A unique voice' *The Dark Side*

WARNER BOOKS
0 7088 5377 3

<u>SHARPER KNIVES</u>

Christopher Fowler

Take a trip to the cutting edge of terror and discover:

Why an obsession with sixties British comedy stars can make you a murderer . . .

The mother who dreads the sound of hymns – with good reason

How schooldays can be the weirdest days of your life

A couple who regularly visit the supermarket from Hell . . .

And why people who collect table-mats are dangerous – only when they're dead . . .

'One of the hippest and sharpest horror writers around'
iD

'An Alan Bennett-like enjoyment of domestic trivia in Fowler's work . . . provides a foil for the horror and an unexpected seam of humour' *ST*

WARNER BOOKS
0 7515 0766 0

☐	Red Bride	Christopher Fowler	£4.99
☐	Darkest Day	Christopher Fowler	£5.99
☐	City Jitters	Christopher Fowler	£4.99
☐	Sharper Knives	Christopher Fowler	£4.99

Warner Books now offers an exciting range of quality titles by both established and new authors. All of the books in this series are available from:

Little, Brown and Company (UK),
P.O. Box 11,
Falmouth,
Cornwall TR10 9EN.

Alternatively you may fax your order to the above address. Fax No. 0326 376423.

Payments can be made as follows: cheque, postal order (payable to Little, Brown and Company) or by credit cards, Visa/Access. Do not send cash or currency. UK customers and B.F.P.O. please allow £1.00 for postage and packing for the first book, plus 50p for the second book, plus 30p for each additional book up to a maximum charge of £3.00 (7 books plus).

Overseas customers including Ireland, please allow £2.00 for the first book plus £1.00 for the second book, plus 50p for each additional book.

NAME (Block Letters) ....

....

ADDRESS ....

....

....

☐ I enclose my remittance for _____

☐ I wish to pay by Access/Visa Card

Number ☐☐☐☐☐☐☐☐☐☐☐☐☐☐☐☐☐☐

Card Expiry Date ☐☐☐☐